Bonefire of the Vanities

ALSO BY CAROLYN HAINES

Bonefire of the Vanities

CAROLYN HAINES

MINOTAUR BOOKS

NEW YORK

Hai

BONEFIRE OF THE VANITIES. Copyright © 2012 by Carolyn Haines. All rights reserved. Printed in the United States of America. For information, address St. Martin's Press, 175 Fifth Avenue, New York, N.Y. 10010.

www.minotaurbooks.com

Library of Congress Cataloging-in-Publication Data

Haines, Carolyn.
    Bonefire of the vanities: a Sarah Booth Delaney mystery. — 1st ed.
        p. cm.
    ISBN 978-0-312-64187-0 (hardcover)
    ISBN 978-1-250-01485-6 (e-book)
    1. Delaney, Sarah Booth (Fictitious character)—Fiction. 2. Women private investigators—Mississippi—Fiction. I. Title.
    PS3558.A329 B654 2012
    813'.54—dc23

                                                                    2012005491

First Edition: June 2012

10 9 8 7 6 5 4 3 2 1

For An'gel Molpus and Kathy Bergold—

sassy ladies who love books

Acknowledgments

A book takes such a long time to write that many people have a helpful finger in the pie before it's baked. I want to thank the usual suspects: my wonderful agent, Marian Young; my editors, Kelley Ragland and Matt Martz, and the entire editing team at St. Martin's Minotaur; and Hiro Kimura, whose covers capture the fun element of the books.

Suzann Ledbetter kept a sharp pencil when she read the manuscript, along with Kathy Bergold and others. The people who read my books are an amazing resource. They often provide near-instantaneous answers to any questions I have about my own work. Amazing.

Each book is a different journey. Some are easier than others, and all of the stories surprise me. This is the joy of writing. With each book, the characters reveal more of themselves to me. Tinkie has grown and changed in ways I didn't imagine when penning *Them Bones*. And Jitty—that ghost truly has a mind of her own.

For those of you on Facebook, please join the sassy ladies (and gentlemen) on the Carolyn Haines fan page. There is always mischief afoot.

You can sign up for my newsletter on my Web site: www.carolynhaines.com. We're planning another Daddy's Girl Weekend. Since no one was arrested at the last one, we feel confident to do it again. The newsletter is the best place to keep up with our plans.

And finally, I want to thank the booksellers who have hand-sold my books. Booksellers and readers who personally recommend my books to patrons, friends, and family have my total gratitude.

Bonefire of the Vanities

1

There are times when every woman needs to sit on the porch and listen to Emmylou Harris. One of those times is when she realizes she's overplayed her hand. I now find myself in such an awful moment. I haven't spoken with my fiancé, Graf Milieu, for seven days. And not from lack of trying.

Graf warned me that my work as a private investigator troubles him. Not the work, but the fact that I often find myself in danger. My partner, Tinkie Bellcase Richmond, and I have had more than our fair share of close calls and injuries. I gave Graf my word I wouldn't court danger—and I have kept it. Or tried to. Who would have thought an insurance claim would turn deadly?

But Graf won't even give me a chance to explain. He's

in Hollywood, filming, and I'm in Mississippi, stewing in my own juices. My offer to fly to Los Angeles and explain how I'd nearly drowned in secret tunnels in Natchez with Tinkie has been rebuffed. He hung up on me when I phoned, and now he won't take my calls. He's furious.

The worst part is that I don't blame him.

There are no simple decisions in life. When I took the Leverts' insurance case, I made a choice I thought was reasonable and sound. Delaney Detective Agency would examine the evidence for a missing necklace and write a report. Simple enough. Each action that followed seemed based on a reasonable expectation of safety. In the end, though, both Tinkie and I placed ourselves in danger—the one thing Graf had asked me not to do.

I betrayed him. And now I'm here at Dahlia House, my ancestral home, surrounded by cotton fields and reflecting on the dozens of missed opportunities I had to avoid bodily harm. Why hadn't I listened to my gut and walked away? No, I'd ignored each throb of my instincts and stayed on the case.

Hindsight has the clarity of perfect focus. No matter how I try to stop the wheels of my brain from retreading the past, I can't. The sun heats my bare legs as I mope on the steps in cut-off jeans and a T-shirt advertising my Tennessee friend, Jack Daniel's. Though I'm too depressed even to fix a drink. Emmylou sings the story of my life in the words of "Making Believe." The CD shifts and Rosanne Cash takes over with "Blue Moon with Heartache."

What would I give to be a diamond in Graf's eyes again?

A lot.

The land of Dahlia House, lush with waist-high green

cotton that's forming into bolls, stretches as far as my eyes can see. The marvel of Mississippi in September is not lost on me. No matter how tragic my life, the land exists far beyond my momentary troubles. While the loam holds the hopes of the future, it is also saturated with the past. In my despair, I drift through scenes: Graf and I riding through the fields at sunset, my mother's laughter, my father walking down the drive toward me, Aunt Loulane holding my hand in the backseat of a funeral car. So many images crowd the fertile soil. There were many happy times, too, and that is what I should focus on. Despair breeds depression. I force myself to see the present.

The weather has held all summer, and the cotton crop will be bumper. My valiant steeds, Reveler, Miss Scrapiron, and Lucifer, the black Andalusian that once belonged to Monica Levert, are grazing peacefully in the side pasture. My hope is to find a new home for Lucifer, but that will take some time. There was an initial period of tension between the two males—hot weather isn't the best time to geld, but Lucifer is healing nicely. On this sunny Friday morning, peace reigns at Dahlia House. At least in the pasture, if not in my heart.

Not even Jitty, the resident family haint, has come around to disturb my pity party. She's pissed off at me, too.

Only Sweetie Pie, my noble redtick hound, keeps me company. Rosanne Cash is working on her, too. Sweetie, with her long ears and wide eyes, looks sadder than the last first grader in a bathroom line.

We both exhale, a sound forlorn and weary. "Sweetie, I didn't mean to get in danger. I tried hard not to. Graf won't even let me explain." I could rationalize to my hound, if not my future husband.

Sweetie gives a grumble and slumps over on her side.

Even her ears look defeated. She's not going to be a bit of help in getting me over the doldrums.

After rising, I walk across the porch. "Jitty!" She never appears when I summon her, but I'm desperate enough for a distraction from my self-flagellation that I'll try. "Jitty! I need you."

Jitty is the ghost of my great-great-grandmother's nanny from the 1860s. Like my ancestor, Alice, Jitty was a young woman during the War Between the States. Working together, Alice and Jitty managed to keep Dahlia House and the surrounding land intact after the war, during a time of great hardship and deprivation. They were strong, determined women who didn't let the worst circumstances break them down. They were not quitters, and I need to remember that.

It wasn't until I returned to my hometown of Zinnia and Dahlia House, battered and bruised by my failed attempts to act on Broadway, that I knew Jitty haunted my family home. During my childhood, I'd never seen her. I think she came back from the Great Beyond just to keep an eye on me. But now, when I need her, she is playing coy.

"Jitty!"

Perhaps it was the fact that I was about to weep, or maybe it was Sweetie Pie's soft slumbering howls, a sound as desolate as a train whistle at a Delta crossroads on a winter's night. Whatever the reason, I finally heard Jitty. She'd responded to my call. She came around the corner of the house, arms akimbo, and I was stunned at her A-line skirt, twin sweater set, pearls, and Toni-permed hair. She appeared to be in her late teens or early twenties, though she was dressed like a spinster.

"Where is that Ned?" she demanded. "He was supposed to bring the convertible around to the front of the house. I've got a hot lead. I think I know the resolution for the case of *The Hidden Staircase*. I need the car and I need George and I need to strike while the iron is hot."

"That's three 'I needs' in a row. Who are we today, Nellie Narcissistic? Fashion tip, Jitty, you *need* to update. Your wardrobe is about sixty years behind the times."

"Your problem, Sarah Booth, aside from the fact that you're like a heat-seeking missile aimed at destroying any chance at love, is that you have no concept of history. You call yourself a private investigator, but you don't know squat about the women who came before you."

Somehow I knew she wasn't talking about the Delaney women. She referred not to my ancestors, but to a literary heritage. Women sleuths. And I had her pegged. "Miss Nancy Drew!" I pointed my finger at her.

"At last," Jitty said in a proper voice. "Now, stay out of the way. I'm on a case."

I narrowed my eyes. "Are you deliberately mocking me?" Jitty was stern, but she wasn't mean. "You know I'm sitting out here watching my life crumble because of my last case and you—"

"You're out here moping and wallowing in guilt, listening to music about heartbreak and hopelessness. Nothing is quite as delicious as self-pity. And as an aside, you might want to turn the music down. You've got it cranked up so loud, folks at neighboring plantations can hear it. Let me just say if anyone with testicles wanted to come around Dahlia House, that music would shrivel up his vas deferens and send the little swimmers back upstream."

"I'm guilty as charged with moping. Just let me remind

you I wouldn't *be* moping if it weren't for a man. These songwriters know a thing or two about heartbreak. It's nice to have company in a trip down Depression Drive. I can't count on you, and my friends are busy. Tinkie is doing all she can to patch up things with Oscar. Cece is working on some big story for the Black and Orange Ball in New Orleans, and Millie is breaking in a new chef. I'm left with the brutal facts of bad romance and the songbirds."

"They got a call-in line for bad romance stories? You could give them some grist for their song mill. You're about the most accomplished gal I know for screwing up relationships." Jitty's tone was dismissive and sassy. Taking on the persona of a privileged, ahead-of-her-time girl detective had given her a bad case of attitude.

"What do you deduce from that?" My heart was only half in the debate. Normally I could give as good as I got from Jitty, but today, I was blue.

"That Graf is mad and he's punishin' you, and you're curled up like you don't have a backbone in your body. You need to put on your boots and go to Hollywood and kick his butt. He ought to at least give you a chance to explain. What he's doin' is just downright wrong."

I straightened my shoulders. "Say what?" Jitty never took my side over a man's. Especially not Graf's. She adored him and had populated her imagination with the images of the gorgeous children he would "get" on me. Jitty was all about propagating the Delaney line.

"Look, he's angry. Any fool could see why. This private investigation issue is somethin' you two got to lay to rest. Once and for all. I hope he knows you as well as I do, or he's gonna lose you. No matter how much you love him, you're not gonna let him dictate your life. And he can't go sulkin' off each time you take a case and get in trouble. He needs to buck up or back off."

I liked Jitty in her Nancy Drew mode. She was sassy, independent, and she wasn't won over by viable sperm.

"Well, thanks." I leaned against a porch column. "He is being unfair. In fact, he's being uncharacteristically childish. He's not willing to even listen to what I have to say."

"So what are you going to do about it?" Jitty pulled out a notebook from the handbag hanging on her arm. She also whipped out a scarf and tied it around her curls— which had not moved an inch, even when the wind blew. She did look good as a blonde, but I wondered how she'd gotten her hair to coil like that.

"What do you recommend?" I asked.

"Call him again," Jitty said. "Make it hurt."

I had an idea. "This time I'm going to leave a message and tell him if he won't talk to me, I'm not calling again. I'll send the ring back FedEx."

Jitty nodded. "Nice. That should get his attention."

I gazed at the beautiful yellow diamond on my ring finger. The thought of taking it off, of shipping it back, of ending things with Graf made me sadder than I could say. But Jitty was right. I couldn't wander around Dahlia House feeling guilty and sad because I worked a case. That was what I did for a living, and I still owed a mortgage and taxes on my ancestral home, plus the grand old place needed a lot of repairs. Delaney Detective Agency was how I made my way in the world.

It was something of a sore point with Graf that I wouldn't take his money to fix my home or even to live on, but I had my reasons. Dahlia House was the Delaney home. I was the last Delaney. While I might live here—in the future—with my husband and children, it was my responsibility to keep the house in good order and to pass it down to future generations. My responsibility and no one else's.

Tinkie didn't understand why I couldn't take money from Graf to renovate Dahlia House, but Cece, a working journalist, understood, and so did Millie, a businesswoman, and Tammy Odom, aka Madam Tomeeka, my childhood friend and Zinnia's resident psychic. They got the concept that Dahlia House was a trust of blood and heritage. My heritage, my responsibility.

Tinkie came from a privileged life where men were *always* expected to pay the bills. I'd been raised differently. My folks had taught me to *always* assume responsibility for myself. No matter how much I loved Graf or how much he loved me, I needed a job. My self-respect was bound up in my ability to support myself and take care of the things I loved. To do otherwise would be a slap in the face to generations of Delaney women, and even Jitty understood that.

"Hey!" Jitty snapped her fingers in my face and I noticed the charm bracelet on her wrist. A *charm* bracelet. With little miniature items in silver—a tennis racket, an ice skate, a forty-five record, a Scottie dog, a cat, a horse, a bird, a magnifying glass. Holy cow! That should be in a museum. Next she'd be attending a sock hop in a poodle skirt.

"Hey!" She snapped her fingers again.

"What?"

"You drifted off. I thought you were gonna call Graf."

"I thought you were going for a ride in the convertible with Ned and George. You know, hidden staircase mystery and all."

"Call that man and get it straight. Then get off your duff and do something constructive. Those horses need ridin', and your hound needs a run."

She was right, dammit. It was time for action. I pulled my cell phone from my pocket and hit Graf's Hollywood number. He would be on the set of the movie he was filming, but I could leave my message. When I got the signal to record, I cut loose.

"Graf, you have to give me a chance to tell you what happened. You're judging me without all the facts. I honored your heart. You'll never understand unless you allow me to tell you everything. But if you don't want to hear it, I have no choice but to accept your unwillingness to listen. If I haven't heard from you by this time tomorrow, I'll send you back the ring. I love you, but I can't be punished any longer without even a chance to talk to you."

I turned to see if Jitty approved, but she was gone. She'd slipped away, perhaps in her classic convertible, to chase down clues. Sweetie Pie and I were alone on the porch.

But not for long. A teal blue sedan headed down the drive of Dahlia House and my spirits lifted instantly. Tammy Odom was coming to pay a visit. I frowned as I realized she was flying down the drive. Tammy was normally a cautious driver. She definitely had a bee in her bonnet about something. I hoped she hadn't had a bad dream about me. Tammy's ability to gaze into the future was a good thing—except when she saw danger or disaster.

She parked at the front steps and got out, her orange silk pantsuit billowing in the breeze off the cotton fields. "Sarah Booth, call Tinkie. I need the professional skills of Delaney Detective Agency."

"What's up?" I asked.

"Take a look at this!" She pulled a letter from her pocket and thrust it into my hands.

"Would you like to go inside and have a cup of coffee?"

"Just sit right here and read it, please." She sank onto the top step and I joined her.

The envelope was addressed to Marjorie Littlefield. While I was a professional snoop, I hesitated to read another's personal mail. At least someone who wasn't a client or a suspect. "Is this *the* Marjorie Littlefield? The woman who was married to four of the men on *Forbes*'s 'top ten wealthiest people in the world' list?"

I'd heard that Mrs. Littlefield had retired to a palatial—and reclusive—home not too far from Zinnia in Sunflower County. When she'd been younger, a beautiful belle who blossomed in the gossip columns of national media, she'd walked down the aisle in turn with a rock star turned record producer, a physicist who invented some super-duper recycling system, an importer of exotic antiquities in New Orleans, and the head of the largest arms dealership in the world. During those halcyon days, she'd sought the limelight and the cameras. Now, though, she was in her sixties and tired of public attention. So she'd come home to the Delta, where she was just one of a number of incredibly wealthy eccentrics who sought courteous neighbors and a bit of anonymity.

"Yes, it's that Mrs. Littlefield. She's my newest client."

"Well, hush my mouth!" I tapped the letter against my palm. "Is Marjorie Littlefield on the lookout for another husband or trying to communicate with someone from her past?"

"I can't discuss my clients, and you know it, Sarah Booth."

"Then why are you here? So I can pry into her private mail?"

"I told her I would show this letter to you and Tinkie. I've tried to talk her out of getting involved in this mess, but she won't listen to me. She's agreed to hire you to investigate this organization she's involved in. Sarah Booth, you have to check into these people and prove they're frauds."

"What people?"

"Read the letter. Now."

Tammy was never bossy, unless she was really upset. I opened the envelope and drew out the heavy stationery. The letter was typed.

"Dear Marjorie," it began. I scanned through the paragraphs, growing more horrified by each sentence. When I got to the end, I noted the signature. "Sherry." Just the one name and nothing more.

"What is this Heart's Desire secret society?" I asked Tammy.

"It's a scam," she said. "Look at what they promise—that she's included in a global group of the ultra-wealthy. She's been chosen because of her 'unique abilities.' Hell, Sarah Booth, Marjorie's talent is marrying well, but that's about it. She's a likable woman, but she's not a rocket scientist or a healer."

I considered for a moment. "So why do you care if she joins this group and they bilk her out of ten or twenty grand? She has money to burn."

Tammy stood up and mimicked the pose Jitty had struck earlier. She put her hands on her hips in a no-nonsense gesture. "Because they are liars. The things they're promising—it's just a play on an older woman's vanity. Even worse, this Sherry woman is claiming to have medium abilities."

"And you don't believe in such things?" I wasn't clear what Tammy was objecting to. She knew people had special gifts. She was one of those people.

"This is obviously a play on Marjorie's self-image. Look at the letter. They claim she's 'one of a special, select group' chosen to be part of a 'secret society that will shape the policies and practices of the world through investment opportunities.' Come on, Sarah Booth. This is aimed directly at the recipient's conceit, and they could take her for a lot more than twenty grand."

"If pandering to the ego of a wealthy person were illegal, thousands of young women would be in jail."

"You are missing the point, Sarah Booth."

Obviously I was. "I'm sorry, Tammy. I don't feel the need to intervene. Mrs. Littlefield is rich, ego-driven, and ripe for the plucking. Why should I interfere?"

"She was told she'd be able to communicate with her daughter." Tammy paced the length of the steps.

"I wasn't aware she has a daughter."

"She had two children by her first husband, Paul la Kink, the rock star."

"The guy the religious right went after because he claimed he deflowered a virgin in every city he played?"

Tammy gave a rueful smile. "Bingo. He was hot. I had a huge crush on him. God! He wore those tight pants and moved across the stage like a panther. He dated a black girl before he married Marjorie. He broke down some barriers."

No wonder he'd figured so prominently into Tammy's fantasy life. He'd taken a stand that most folks, at the time, were afraid to take.

She laughed. "Oh, he had that bad-boy appeal down to an art."

"What happened to him?" The musician inhabited only the fringes of my childhood world.

"La Kink died very young in a wreck. His car didn't make a curve on Highway 1 in California. Went straight over a cliff into the Pacific. It made news for days." She frowned as if I were deficient because I'd forgotten the death of a rock singer known more for his sexual prowess than for his music.

"Marjorie Littlefield was married to him?"

"She was. A stunning widow with her two kids. Tragedy stalked Marjorie. The daughter, Mariam, drowned when she was about ten. The drowning was ruled an accident, but Marjorie believes her son, Chasley, killed his sister. Marjorie and Chasley's relationship is worse than strained. They hate each other, I think. Marjorie wants to communicate with the spirit of her dead daughter and ask if Chasley killed her. This could get really ugly, Sarah Booth, especially if my suspicions are correct and this Sherry is manipulating Marjorie for her money. Marjorie is seriously depressed. I'm worried she'll harm herself."

"You think she'll take her own life?"

"I'm worried. The Heart's Desire organization may not be illegal, but it's immoral. Using grief to manipulate is just wrong. In Marjorie's case, it could have deadly consequences."

I had to agree. "You're sure Marjorie is hooked by this scam?"

"I know for a fact. She's already gone, and she left her cat, Pluto, for me to keep while she's at Heart's Desire. Sarah Booth, I don't think she ever intends to leave. At least not alive."

"You're being a little melodramatic, Tammy."

She hesitated for a split second. "Marjorie left her will with me, too. Pluto inherits everything."

"The cat?"

She nodded. "Her son, Chasley, will be very, very angry."

"I gather Chasley and the cat are not . . . friendly?"

"An understatement. And when he finds out the cat is the sole heir, he'll do everything in his power to kill it."

I wondered if Tammy was exaggerating, but one look at her face told me no. She was genuinely upset. "This is a rich woman's troubles, and yet you're honestly scared for her."

"Marjorie is pampered and vain and all the rest, but there's more to her. She has a good heart, and she's been hurt. When her daughter died—" Tammy shook her head. "I can't imagine, Sarah Booth. My daughter and grandchild are everything to me."

Tammy had certainly made sacrifices for Claire and little Dahlia. And god knew, Tammy had risked her life more than once to help me. "Okay, what do you want me to do?"

"Find out about this organization. What are they really up to? They hint at a link to the 'other side.' It's just plain crazy. I've tried to reach Marjorie on her cell phone, but there's a new message on there saying she's in deep mediation and is no longer taking calls from *this plane.* Like she's gone to another dimension or something."

"You're asking me to walk into a den of whackadoodles who think they'll gain control of the world. You realize that, don't you?"

Tammy's tension eased and a smile lit her face. "Lord, Sarah Booth, you'll blend right in."

I had to laugh. "Where is this Heart's Desire located?"

"I'm not certain. Within driving distance. Marjorie dropped the cat off with me on her way there."

"She could have taken a private jet if it was a long distance." I spoke aloud more to clarify my thoughts than anything else. Marjorie had the money to charter Air Force One if she really wanted it. She was worth billions.

"She always travels by limo with a driver. She told the cat she wouldn't be far away."

I flipped the letter and envelope around. "It says here to send a response to a post office box in New Orleans. I guess that's where I'll start."

"We don't have a lot of time, Sarah Booth."

So now we were getting down to the gristle. "What's so urgent, Madam Tomeeka?"

"I had a dream last night. Mrs. Littlefield was being held in a white tower. Like a prisoner. Pluto, her cat, kept jumping in and out of windows and popping out of bushes. Except for the cat, everything was pure white, until a streak of bright red blood leaked out of Marjorie's window. It scared me. I think someone means to hurt her."

"Sounds like if she is at that nutcase compound, she might be out of the reach of her son, Chasley."

Tammy wasn't placated. "I have a bad feeling. Try to find her, and fast, Sarah Booth. Marjorie left a lot of money for me to care for Pluto. I can pay the retainer with some of that. Marjorie has agreed to hire you, and she'll be glad to see you when you find her."

I waved her away. While Tammy was psychic, I wasn't certain she had a great reading of Marjorie's desires. "Don't be silly. Graf won't speak to me, and I'm at loose ends. I'll look into this. It'll keep me from moping around and feeling sorry for myself."

"You and Tinkie have to figure a way to handle these cases and keep yourselves safe."

"That's easier said than done."

Tammy's brow furrowed. "Do you think what I'm asking you to do is dangerous?"

I caught her hand and patted it. "Absolutely not. This looks like a little bit of legwork. I'll find Heart's Desire and speak to Mrs. Littlefield and make sure she's not being rooked by con artists."

Tammy nodded. "That doesn't sound dangerous, but somehow I suspect all of your past cases started out simple enough."

"Therein lies the rub," I agreed. "I would never deliberately put Graf's heart in danger. Nor would Tinkie risk her husband, Oscar's, feelings. But things happen. Beyond our control. Graf has to accept this is who I am." I bit my lip.

Tammy grasped my hand and pulled me to my feet. "Help me find Marjorie and make sure she isn't being held hostage by con artists, I'll work on Graf and Oscar."

It was a solution I hadn't considered, but I knew it was a winner when I heard it. "You've got a deal."

"I should be going. You have company coming."

I was so used to Jitty's wild predictions that I didn't bat an eye. "How do you know?"

"Because I can hear the car coming down the drive." She pointed toward a curve in the driveway, and just then Harold Erkwell's black Lexus came into view. Harold worked at the bank Tinkie's father owned and her husband managed.

I checked my watch. It was nine thirty in the morning. Harold should be at the bank. So what was he doing cruising down my driveway with ... an evil, goateed little face in the front seat with him?

"He's brought Roscoe!" I had actually missed the dog that once belonged to Millicent Gentry—before she embarked on a prison sentence as her reward for a life of crime. He'd been in my care only a few weeks, but the pooch had a way of stealing one's heart, not to mention underwear, food, shoes, garbage, and secrets.

The car stopped, the driver's door opened, and Roscoe leaped to the ground. He ran in frenzied circles for about thirty seconds and then dashed around the house to the doggy door. He was intent on finding Sweetie Pie for a romp.

"Ladies," Harold said as he joined us.

"Taking Roscoe out for a playdate?" I couldn't help but tease Harold. The dog was vile. In the first night he was at Harold's house, he ate the stuffing from a leather sofa, knocked over the garbage cans all up and down Harold's street, snatched barbecue off the grill at a neighbor's party, and chased another neighbor's cat up a tree. Harold had done nothing but bail Roscoe out of trouble ever since the dog arrived in his life. Yet Harold adored the creature.

"Indeed, Sarah Booth. The furniture store is delivering a new sofa, and I was hoping you could keep Roscoe for a few hours. At this point, I'm afraid he'll bite the delivery man and the weight of his misdeeds will put him on doggy death row."

I had to laugh, and after days of self-pity, it felt good. "I'll keep him."

"You can bring him home this evening, or I'll stop by and get him. He adores riding in the car."

"And ice cream from the Sweetheart drive-through."

Harold wasn't even ashamed. "Yes, he loves those soft cones of vanilla. We go every evening."

"Harold, if you ever have children, you'll be a pushover."

"Right now, Roscoe is all I need. But I have to say, Sarah Booth, he's brought great adventure into my life. I never thought I'd enjoy a dog, but he is so . . . awful! He thinks things through, and then he does the worst he can come up with."

"And that's good?" Tammy was laughing with me, but she was slightly horrified.

"It is. He's like my alter ego. He does all the stuff I want to but can't. Why, the other day, he peed on Mrs. Hedgepeth's foot. It was just the best. That old bat has made life hell for everyone in town for the past forty years. Roscoe went up to her and cut loose. It was the funniest thing I've ever seen."

Mrs. Hedgepeth was the neighborhood fun police, and once she'd tried to get Sweetie Pie sent to the pound for no reason. She wasn't a friend to dog or child, and I'd seen Roscoe pull that same stunt on another old witch. The dog did seem to have the ability to plan out his outrageous actions. "I'm surprised she didn't file some kind of assault charge against you and Roscoe."

Harold couldn't stop laughing. "She didn't know I owned him or she probably would have. Now I have to make certain he doesn't run around the neighborhood loose. I'm having one of those underground fences installed tomorrow."

I thought to say good luck, but I didn't. Somehow, I didn't think Roscoe would be confined by a mere shock, but who was I to dampen Harold's newfound love of doggyhood?

"Well, ladies, I must be off to work. Take good care of my boy."

"I'm gone, too," Tammy said.

"And I'll get after this post office business in New Orleans, Tammy."

I stood on the porch and watched as my friends drove away. I had to call Tinkie, though I didn't want to make more trouble for her with Oscar. Still, I was curious about this mysterious New Orleans post office box and the disappearing Mrs. Littlefield. It was time to move on with my life, whether Graf spoke to me or not, and a trip to Sin City was just the ticket to get me out of the dumps.

2

"Drive faster, dammit!" Tinkie gripped the leather seat of my classic Mercedes Roadster. She looked back over her shoulder as if she thought the hounds of hell were on her heels. "Get out of Sunflower County before Oscar changes his mind and sends the state troopers after me. That man has been on me like white on rice for the past two weeks. I'm about to go stir-crazy. He's even gone shoe shopping with me!"

The sun was just coming over the horizon, and the day was dawning bright and clear. Perfect travel weather.

"I'm surprised Oscar let you leave Hilltop with me." I turned away from Tinkie and Oscar's beautiful estate and onto the road leading southwest toward New Orleans.

"When you called yesterday, I thought he would have a conniption," Tinkie admitted. "He doesn't blame you, Sarah Booth, but he associates you with danger." She frowned. "Well, maybe he blames you some. He thinks you talk me into doing things, and no matter how many times I tell him that nobody talks me into anything, he wants to blame someone other than me."

I understood. Every time Tinkie and I got involved in a case, one or both of us ended up in a bad situation. I honestly didn't blame Oscar for wanting to keep us apart. I also knew Tinkie well enough to know that Oscar, despite his best intentions, wouldn't come between us. He couldn't. In the months since I'd returned to Zinnia, Tinkie and I had grown closer than sisters. It wasn't that she loved Oscar less, but she'd developed a new dimension of her personality. She'd become her own woman, and that woman was a bang-up private investigator and stalwart friend.

"We'll check on this mailbox in New Orleans, have lunch in the French Quarter, and head home." This was the scenario I'd thought through a dozen times. Except for traffic or an unforeseen accident, there wasn't a sign of danger.

"Maybe we could hit a few of the little boutiques in the Quarter. There's this fabulous lingerie store. If I find just the right thing, maybe I can jolly that frown off Oscar's face." Tinkie tied her scarf tighter under her chin in a very Marilyn Monroe gesture. I had no doubt she'd have Oscar eating out of the palm of her hand in the near future.

"Sure. Lingerie would be a nice touch."

"We could find you something sexy, take a photo with your phone, and send it to Graf. That should knock him off his high horse."

I sighed. With Tinkie, I could be honest. "I don't think it'll be that simple, Tink. Yesterday I left him a message pretty much saying if he wouldn't even give me a chance to explain, I'd return his ring. I can't do this. If we can't even talk, we don't stand a chance."

I expected Tinkie to argue, but she didn't. The miles rolled past as the wind whipped at my hair and her scarf. We were driving topless—in convertible mode—and the heat beat down on us.

At last she broke the silence. "Graf feels out of control. He's across the continent, and he's working fourteen-hour days finishing his film. Don't do anything rash, Sarah Booth. Don't break the engagement until he has time to think this through."

Her advice was sound. I nodded. "Okay. It's just so hurtful that he won't even hear me out."

"Oscar behaves like that, but he's right here in Zinnia. He can hardly avoid me. Once Graf finishes the film, you can go out there and talk to him. This has to be done face-to-face."

"He mailed me the engagement ring," I reminded her.

"It's one thing to receive a ring by mail, and quite another to return it. Daddy's Girl Rule number sixty-three: Never break up by letter or phone. The severing of an engagement demands a personal meeting. To do less is to dishonor what you shared. Both parties deserve a chance to fully express their feelings. Good Lord, do you realize people are breaking up by text message these days? What is the world coming to?"

I couldn't help but laugh. The Daddy's Girl handbook had a rule for everything. The older I grew, the more I appreciated that fact. Good manners often made bad situations more tolerable.

I turned on the radio, and we listened to the blues as we flew along the near-empty highways of the Mississippi Delta, the triangle of rich soil that stretched from Memphis down to Vicksburg, bordered by the Mississippi River on the west and rolling hills on the east. The smell of earth, baking in the sun, gave me a sense of deep connection. A million different shades of green rippled out from the wild roadside grass to the darker green of the horizon. A yellow crop duster buzzed low over the fields. This was September in the South, the last of the blistering heat, the time when bolls burst with cotton.

Tinkie and I chatted and laughed. It was good to be out of Zinnia and on an adventure, even a tiny one. Instead of the more scenic route along the river, we went south to Jackson and then crooked southwest, aiming for the City that Care Forgot. The hours passed pleasantly and we made it to the outskirts of New Orleans by lunch.

"Shall we eat or shop first?" Tinkie asked.

"Let's head to the post office and see what we can find before we become ladies of leisure," I suggested. We'd hatched a plan, and the outcome would depend on how well both Tinkie and I could act.

"If you insist." Tinkie pulled the letter Madam Tomeeka gave me from her pocket. "It was mailed from the French Quarter post office. Just leave the postal clerks to me," Tinkie said with a wink. "I didn't wear this minidress for nothing." It was a rather eye-catching outfit.

I pulled into the parking lot, glad the post office wasn't too busy. "Give it your all."

In the lobby, we each took a different line. When I got to the counter, I asked to pick up the mail from the P.O. box number listed on the letter sent to Marjorie Littlefield.

The clerk assessed me. "I don't have any instructions to turn mail over to anyone." She waved me away. "Next!"

I didn't budge. "My employer asked me to retrieve the mail. She said it would be a large bundle. She's in town for the weekend and wants to go through it. She was supposed to make the arrangements."

"I'm very sorry, but unless you have something in writing . . ." She crossed her arms over her chest. "Now, there are people waiting. Move along."

National security issues had changed a lot of things. Back in the good old days, I'd often picked up the mail for various neighbors. Of course, it was Zinnia and I had been known as "the Delaney child."

"If I don't bring the mail back to her, she'll fire me." I put on my most worried expression.

From the far end of the counter, Tinkie's yelp of pain drilled my ears, right on time. When I looked, she was on the floor, wriggling and screaming as if she'd broken her spine.

"Help! I slipped on a slick spot. Help!"

Postal workers poured out of the back and rushed around the counter to help Tinkie. The other postal patrons backed away. Tinkie was putting on quite a performance, and showing about two miles of shapely leg as she did it.

"I really need to pick up the mail." I pressed the point, hoping Tinkie's distraction would gain me information, at the least.

"Excuse me. I have to call a supervisor," the clerk, whose name tag read MABLE, said.

"Mable, all I know is Sherry asked me to bring the mail. I don't have a choice here. If I go back to her empty-handed, she'll be furious." Though the clerk clearly wanted to do something to help Tinkie, I kept talking. "Call her and ask. Can you do that?"

Tinkie let out a screech that made my ears ring. In the echo chamber of the post office, it was like an ice pick in my head. Several people waiting in line covered their ears and ran out of the building.

"The mail is sent to her each week. I've received no instructions to change anything." Mable was done with me. "Could you step aside, ma'am? There are others waiting."

"No, I cannot step aside. Sherry sent me for the mail, and I don't want to get fired. Call her and ask. Can you do that? Just call and ask."

The clerk's face reddened. "Not my job," she said. "If you want to get Sherry Westin's mail, you're going to have to bring a notarized letter telling me that. Otherwise we'll mail it to her Friday, like we always do. Now, *please* step aside and let others be served."

I pulled out a notepad. "There's a problem here, Mable. Are you mailing everything to 113 Brady Lane? Sherry said she didn't receive any mail last week. That's one reason she wants me to get it now."

She rolled her eyes. "We sent it to Layland. Like always. Now, I don't know what you're trying to pull, Miss—"

"Layland, Mississippi?" I couldn't believe it. Layland was a crossroads community in Sunflower County. It wasn't half an hour from Zinnia. As far as I knew, there were five farmhouses and miles of cotton. Certainly not an organization like Heart's Desire. Perhaps that was the appeal of the location—anything could be tucked away in the vast woods, brakes, and fields.

"Who are you?" the clerk demanded. "I'm calling the postmaster right now."

Tinkie let out another heartrending scream as two employees helped her to her feet. Her knees buckled and she almost went down again. She would have had they not supported her. "I need an ambulance," Tinkie cried out. "I need medical attention. My lawyer will sue this place out of existence. I slipped on a slick spot on the floor. This is a dangerous, dangerous place. I think my spine is damaged."

She didn't slow down to draw a breath.

"Thanks for your help, Mable." Before she could answer, I skedaddled out of the post office and waited outside for Tinkie. In a few moments, she appeared, supported by two strong clerks. Both male. Tinkie did have a way with the menfolk, and her tight red jersey skirt and matching five-inch heels were a siren call.

"You are so big and strong. I thought for a minute I'd be crippled for life, but I'm feeling much better now." Tinkie looked up at first one, then the other.

The people inside the post office pressed against the window, watching Tinkie. I eased down beside the car. Out of sight, out of mind.

She profusely thanked the men and let them know she was perfectly fine before she finally got in the car. When the coast was clear, I followed suit.

"What did you find out?" Tinkie asked.

"Her name is Sherry Westin, and she's in Layland, Mississippi."

Tinkie's eyes widened. "That's just around the corner from Zinnia."

I nodded as I pulled out of the parking lot.

"Is it time for lunch and shopping?" Tinkie's brain had jumped ahead to the next thing on her to-do list.

"First call Cece and ask if she can dig up some dirt on

Sherry Westin in New Orleans and Layland, Mississippi."
Cece Dee Falcon was a fine journalist, but more important, a loyal friend. Her skills had come in handy more
than once. While Cece's family had disowned her over
her sex change operation, her friends supported her in
her quest to be the best she could be. Gender wasn't part
of the equation.

Tinkie made the call, and when Cece was on the line,
she revealed what we'd discovered. As I drove down the
crowded one-way streets of the French Quarter, Tinkie
waited. At last she spoke. "Bert Steele, a photographer
for the *Times-Picayune*. Perfect. Thanks, Cece. We'll give
him a call."

There was another moment of silence as Tinkie listened. "Okay, keep looking if you have any free time."

She closed her phone and turned to me. "Nothing on
the Westins in Mississippi. There's plenty about New
Orleans. Cece would only say they were an interesting
mother–daughter team and she gave me Bert Steele's
number to ask him to meet us for lunch today. He knows
more about the Westins than anyone else, she said. It's
serendipitous because he just called her this morning
about some photos for the Black and Orange Ball she
organizes each year. Bert always photographs the mod-
els."

I drove slowly along Canal Street, taking in the sounds
and smells of the South's most cosmopolitan city. New
Orleans was a mixture of dozens of cultures. Hurri-
cane Katrina had wrecked her, but she was rising from
the ashes. I made a turn and stayed within the region
of the Vieux Carré while Tinkie dialed Bert Steele.

When he answered, she explained our friendship with
Cece and our quest. In no time at all, Bert agreed to meet

us for lunch at one o'clock at Napoleon House, a New Orleans landmark on Chartres Street.

By the time I found a parking spot and we walked to the restaurant, Bert was waiting for us. Apparently he'd talked with Cece, because he recognized us. His dark glasses and spiked hair had a certain distinctive air, as did his rolled-up shirtsleeves. I might have pegged him for a jazz musician, but the camera case beside his chair and a Nikon with a telephoto lens on the table were dead giveaways.

Tinkie ordered a round of Pimm's cups and po'boy sandwiches. Our table was beside an open window, and I caught the unique clatter of New Orleans—the laughter of pedestrians racing along the sidewalks, the honking horns of traffic, the clip-clop of a carriage horse, and the cry of the hot dog vendors.

Bert got right to the point. "What's your interest in Sherry Westin?"

"I'm not sure I'm really interested in her," I said. "A friend is worried about someone she knows. She thinks this Sherry might be pulling a scam."

He nodded, but his expression was noncommittal. "What kind of scam?"

I told him about the letter, signed by Sherry.

"You don't look surprised," Tinkie pointed out.

"Brandy Westin is synonymous with the word *scam*, but that's not true of her daughter, Sherry. I always figured Sherry for a pretty good gal." A finger traced the condensation on his glass.

"What do you know about Brandy?" I asked.

"She'd fleece the pope if she had a chance, and do it with a smile."

"But not the daughter?" Tinkie pressed the point.

"She's been under her mama's tutelage for a long time now. Everyone can be corrupted, given enough time and the right incentive."

Bert sipped his drink. "Been a long time since I had a Pimm's cup."

"Me, too. Perfect for a hot September day." Bert had drawn a line separating mother and daughter. For whatever reason, he didn't mind showing his negative feelings for Brandy Westin, but Sherry was a different matter. "So what do you know about the elder Westin?"

Bert frowned. "Brandy ran a high-class brothel in New Orleans for a number of years."

That was unexpected news, and I didn't bother to try hiding my shock. "I thought she was a medium. Talked to the spirits."

"That's Sherry. She had nothing to do with the whorehouse. It's impossible to tell, but she seems to have a real gift, a connection to the other side. Brandy is the *business*woman. Her business was pleasuring men, and she had a stable full of beautiful young ladies who knew exactly how to do it. When Brandy evacuated New Orleans, she probably had a stash of at least three million."

"Wait a minute!" I held up a hand. The names just struck me. "Her name is Sherry and her mother's name is Brandy?"

Bert dropped his gaze to the table. "Brandy Alexander and Sherry la Crème. Some people should be hanged for the monikers they stick on their kids."

"Totally uncouth," Tinkie said. "If she had a child, it would be called what, Merlot Bordeaux or Gin Sapphire?"

Bert's grin was slightly crooked, giving him a rakish air. "Don't think just because Brandy and Sherry play on the desires of their clients, they're stupid. They're clever women. Sherry is shy and on the innocent side. Brandy is accomplished with solid connections to the New Orleans political and financial world. She's like a shark, silent but always swimming looking for her next meal."

"Why would the Westins leave a profitable business in New Orleans and move to the rural stretches of Mississippi?" I asked.

"One word: Katrina. That bitch sent half the city packing. It's hard to sell pleasure when people are worried about day-to-day survival. If you ask me, they left at the right time. The economy's gone to shit now. Discretionary income, even for CEOs and lobbyists, is being watched more closely. Tabloid journalism." He arched an eyebrow. "I wouldn't object to selling a photo of a holier-than-thou lawmaker coming out of a whorehouse. The fat cats used to frequent the Pleasure Zone openly. Now they're more discreet, and afraid of being caught indulging their appetites. They stirred the religious fanatics up to fever pitch and now they've lost control of them."

"Maybe Sherry looked into the future and saw the handwriting on the wall," I posed.

"Whatever happened, they left at the right time. I'd wondered where they went. The Mississippi Delta. Not surprising. There's money in the Delta. Sherry can smell big money like a bloodhound on a scent."

"Did you ever hear rumors of séances, spirit sessions?" I didn't care how much money Brandy had taken from men who had to pay to get laid.

Bert didn't answer immediately. "Yeah. There was talk. The mayor used to go to the Pleasure Zone and he always claimed it was for a séance." He grinned. "Séance, blow job, whatever."

"You're pretty blasé about a mayor participating in either."

"It's the Big Sleazy. Sex and ghosts have always been the stock-in-trade of this city. Throw in a little voodoo, Catholicism, swamp creatures, music, and corrupt politicians and you have a heady brew. The Westins ran a clean house. No complaints. Brandy might be a con, but she only conned people who wanted it. She epitomizes the word *greedy*, but there was never a single complaint filed against her or the Pleasure Zone."

His gaze lost its sharp focus for a few seconds. "Sherry, though. She was different. Something spiritual about her. I saw her a couple of times in Jackson Square, coming out of the cathedral. We chatted, and she seemed . . . haunted. And sad." He shrugged it off. "I must be getting soft. So what are you investigating?"

"The Westins have moved up around Sunflower County. They may be up to their old tricks—" I grinned at my wit. "—but we have only rumors and gossip so far." If we had a big story about whorehouse madams setting up a séance business in Sunflower County, it was Cece's to break.

He pulled a card from his pocket. "Give me a ring if Cece needs photos. I'd love to work with her on a story, and this sounds like it could be big headlines. And if you run across Sherry, give her my numbers. I always felt if she could escape her mother, she could have a good life with someone who cared about her."

I put his card in my billfold and we settled down for a pleasant lunch. Bert had worked the French Quarter for over twenty years, and he was a wealth of great stories and fun facts. When Tinkie mentioned lingerie shopping, he knew exactly the place to send her.

"Fran's Loft." He winked at Tinkie. "And it's not a block from the building where Brandy ran the Pleasure Zone. Real nice couple bought the place. They're renovating. You should drive by and check it out."

"Thanks." A shopping trip would appease Tinkie's need for something frilly and give me a chance to poke around. New Orleans was a hard place to keep secrets. I wondered what Sherry's neighbors remembered about her establishment.

He gave us the address in an upscale district, and when we finished lunch, we left the Quarter and entered an area where original New Orleans settlers had built their homes. At the lingerie shop, while Tinkie wallowed in the joy of silk and lace and titillation, I walked the block to find what had once been the Pleasure Zone.

The building was a surprise. I'd expected a seedy, rambling old place with a dreary front and sad windows. Instead I discovered a triple-tiered Renaissance palazzo. Each floor had balconies all around, and the three-acre lot, which included a cluster of old oaks, exuded graciousness. A high privacy fence kept the backyard from prying eyes, but the front was planted with azaleas, oleanders, and marching rows of delicate spider lilies. Those were heritage stock plants, and they complemented the structure perfectly.

The house was getting a face-lift. Workers on ladders repaired and painted the stucco. An electric drill whined as new shutters went up. Another crew was installing a front porch swing. The old pleasure palace would soon be a home.

A woman in her sixties came out of the house carrying two giant black trash bags. She wiped the sweat from her forehead with the sleeve of her shirt and gave me a smile. "May I help you?" She dropped the rattling bags onto the sidewalk. A seam split and several DVD cases, a hairbrush, some plastic dishes, and old disposable food containers slithered onto the walk.

It was a delicate moment. She was obviously hot and annoyed. "I'm curious about your home," I said.

Her laughter was unexpected. "The sordid history, you mean. That's exactly why we bought it. My husband's a writer. I'm shocked people still remember the Pleasure Zone. These old buildings have seen a lot of incarnations."

"I don't want to inconvenience you, but would it be possible to ask one or two questions?"

"Is it the old history or the more contemporary history that interests you?" A furrow appeared between her eyebrows. "I know only a few anecdotal tales. My husband has researched the property. You should speak to him. I doubt I'd be any help at all."

"Did you ever meet the Westins?" I asked, hoping to engage her in conversation before she decided not to speak with me at all.

"No, they were long gone when we bought the house, but rumors die hard in New Orleans. I find the history mildly curious, but most people don't know how to react when I tell them I live in a former whorehouse. Rather startling to my friends and relatives. I don't want to be rude, but I have crews waiting for me to instruct them."

"I understand." I pulled a business card from my purse. "Sarah Booth Delaney. Would you mind if I telephoned you? If I have more questions."

She hesitated. "I really can't help you, I'm afraid." She

turned toward the house and tripped on one of the trash bags. A half-dozen DVD cases skittered along the cement. "Dammit," she said.

"I'll pick those up for you," I volunteered.

"I wouldn't touch them without gloves. We bought the property as is, and we've been hauling out trash bags full of junk each week. There are all kinds of interesting nooks and crannies in the house, and every single one was filled with crap I have to cart away." She kicked them back into a pile, stepped over the bags, and walked briskly across the lawn to the house.

I bent to the task of gathering the DVDs. I couldn't stop myself from checking out the labels as I returned them to the trash bag. There were dates, and then a sequence of symbols and male names written in a clear, feminine hand. Code for something? I couldn't say what, but the possibilities danced in my head like sugarplums.

Once the DVDs were restacked, I stood up. A curtain fluttered in the second floor, as though the owner of the house was watching me. I turned down the sidewalk in the direction I'd parked the car.

I was almost at the lingerie store when Tinkie, buried in boxes and bags, saw me. "Sarah Booth! I just found the cutest stuff! Oscar will go nuts. I'll have him chasing me like a . . . well, like a man." She threw her purchases in the backseat and I did a U-turn in the road and drove back toward the old whorehouse.

"I'm going to stop at the curb. Jump out and snag those garbage bags on the sidewalk," I said to Tinkie.

"We're picking up trash now?" Tinkie's face said *distasteful*.

"They're old videos. Homemade stuff. From the Westins."

Her attitude changed. "Sex tapes? Can we have them?"

"I didn't ask, but they're trash. Snatch them and let's head home." I stopped at the curb.

In a flash, Tinkie was out of the car. With some effort, she hefted the big black bags into the backseat. "How many recordings are there?" she asked as she climbed into the seat and slammed her door.

"A lot. Let's hope there's something useful on them."

3

Tinkie and I drove straight to Madam Tomeeka's clapboard cottage on the outskirts of Zinnia. I was happy to see the roads in this section of town, known as the Grove, were paved. Two years ago they were dirt. Historically, the Grove's residents had been neglected, but recently, road improvements, sidewalks, and city plumbing had been put in. And not a single one of the beautiful oaks that gave the section its name had been sacrificed. The citizens of the neighborhood had held vigil to protect the trees. Progress was great, but shade trees were more important.

"Now that we sort of know the location of Heart's Desire, maybe Tammy can stop worrying about Mrs.

Littlefield," Tinkie said as I pulled into the grassless front yard and parked beside a line of old, gnarled cedars.

Tinkie got out of the car, hitching down her skirt as we walked to the front door.

Tammy met us on a cloud of mouthwatering smells wafting from her kitchen.

"Fried chicken?" I swallowed and managed not to drool on myself.

"Yes, indeed. With okra and tomatoes, corn bread, and mashed potatoes with gravy. I thought you might be hungry."

Millie Roberts, our friend and frequent source of gossip and rumor who ran a café in town, was the best cook I knew, but Tammy could give her a run for her money when it came to down-home Southern fare. "Lead me to it," I said.

"Sarah Booth, you ate your po'boy and half of mine at lunch. Are you truly hungry?" Tinkie was shocked at my appetite.

"I wasn't, until I caught the scent of fried chicken. Don't get between me and Tammy's cooking, Tinkie."

Tammy led the way to her kitchen, where the table was set and the food was steaming hot on it. Sighing, Tinkie settled onto a chair. "It does smell good. Can I take a plate to Oscar?"

"Already dished one up for you." Tammy pointed to the counter, where a plate piled high with food sat covered by plastic wrap.

As I wolfed down a pan-fried breast and big helpings of everything else, I told Tammy about our adventures in New Orleans.

I pushed back my plate. My pants were so tight, I

almost couldn't breathe, but if I didn't stand up, I'd eat more. "Let's check those recordings before I explode."

"If these are sex tapes the Westins made . . ." Tammy didn't finish the thought. "These people are very smart, Sarah Booth. This could be more dangerous than I thought. We need to rethink your involvement in this. It could be blackmail or porn. I don't like the turn this has taken."

Tinkie and I exchanged a look. Here was the moment where we either honored our deepest desire to keep our men happy, or we helped our friend Tammy.

"So far it doesn't seem too dangerous," Tinkie said. "Let's see what's on the DVDs before we rush to make any kind of decision. If it's something juicy, maybe you can use it to convince Marjorie to leave Heart's Desire. She wouldn't want to be associated with a scandal."

The three of us went into the living room, where Tammy inserted the first DVD in her player and turned on the TV. The quality of the video was awful. It crossed my mind that the recording could have been deliberately degraded.

The image of a middle-aged white man with too much belly and back hair jumped onto the screen. He sat down on the bed with an attractive young brunette. In less than thirty seconds, they were engaged in grainy, perfunctory sex. The film, thank god without sound, played for the next four minutes. The man finished, stood up, and turned to face the camera.

"Is that—?" Tinkie was aghast.

"The well-respected federal judge," I supplied. "Indeed. I only have to say he screws with the same creativity with which he interprets the law."

Tammy cackled, and even Tinkie joined in, but my

partner was disturbed. "This is potential dynamite. Why would the Westins leave this stuff behind?"

I stopped the player. "The owner of the house said she found a lot of stuff tucked in hidey-holes and crannies. Maybe the Westins overlooked these. This is damaging footage. Judge Praytor is sitting on the bench. He's wide open to blackmail."

"And to think the tapes were left at the curb for the trashman." Tammy picked up the empty disc case and examined it. "Almost like a trail of bread crumbs leading to the Westins."

Tinkie signaled me to start again.

We rolled through four of the recordings, learning that the judge was a regular at the house, along with two governors we recognized, powerful senators obviously partying in New Orleans on a junket, local politicos and law officers, and two famous Hollywood celebrities who shouldn't have to pay for sex. What they had in common was a lack of originality, a lack of foreplay, and the endurance of a gnat.

One client we didn't recognize was a tall, slender Caucasian man, a regular, who wore a mask, as if he knew the sessions were being recorded. Or perhaps his fetish was more sinister, since the mask was modeled after the one worn by the notorious Dr. Lecter in *The Silence of the Lambs*.

"Creepy!" Tammy made the sign of the cross, the classic parody to ward off vampires, with both index fingers. "Ugh!"

"This is awful." Tinkie's palms covered her eyes. "I can't watch any more. I had my heart all set on going home, putting on the divine little pink fluff nightie I bought at Fran's Loft, and bringing out the tiger in Oscar. Now I just want to shower! Depressing as hell."

"Empty sex." Tammy held up her hands as if to ward off a blow. "That's why the woman has to be paid. For most women, sex has to mean something. Wham, bam, thank you, ma'am calls for a cash exchange. I hope these girls were handsomely paid. They don't even look twenty years old."

"Turn it off." Tinkie waved a hand at the television.

"Let's finish this recording. It's the last one," I said. Like it or not, I felt compelled to view all the DVDs, even if I did it on fast-forward. We were investigating the Westins, and this was part of the gig, as distasteful as it was.

As the television screen fritzed and jumped, I heard a dog barking outside and shifted to look out a front window. Night had fallen and a gibbous moon reflected off the roof of a large, dark car parked across the street from Tammy's house. A solitary figure sat behind the wheel. My gut instinct jumped to red alert. I was about to suggest a little reconnaissance when I heard Tinkie gasp.

"Shit!" Tammy said.

I turned back to the television, suddenly riveted by the flash of a grainy image, the ghostly face of a young girl. It was there, superimposed on top of a sex scene, and then gone. The faint image appeared on the screen again.

In the recording, a couple in a bedroom had sex by rote, but another layer of images showed an interior hallway. There was no sound, just the fuzzy image of a staircase that curved up and up and up. It was there, then gone.

The tape went black, filled with static. When it cleared, a young girl stood on the stairs. Water dripped from her hair and clothes. The image flashed over the mechanical sex and disappeared as on-screen snow filled the screen. It cleared once more—the girl had advanced a dozen paces toward the camera.

"What the hell!" Tinkie stood up.

I slid onto the sofa, my body rigid. Tammy, too, was transfixed by the girl in the film.

Her face was a grayish blue, lifeless, her eyes haunted. She looked directly into the camera for a split second. "It's your fault, Mommy." Her voice was as cold and dead as her bluish face. The screen went blank.

We were all so intently focused on the TV that when a large black pillow leaped from the sofa and landed in my lap, we all screamed, even Tammy.

"Jesus turning cartwheels!" I yelled, reaching for the pillow. Two sharp teeth sank into the tender flesh of my girdle of Venus. "It's a devil!" I tried to disengage from the creature.

"Hold still, Sarah Booth." Tammy grabbed the writhing black thing. "Stop struggling."

"It's biting me." I tried to shake loose, but now the creature's claws dug into my wrist and wrapped around my lower arm. It weighed at least twenty pounds, but I wasn't sure what it was. All I knew was that the videotape had somehow generated an evil black thing with sharp fangs—and it was after my ass.

Tammy pushed me back onto the sofa. She sat beside me and clenched the creature's scruff. In a moment, the demonic animal was sitting in her lap. Purring. The cat, for cat it was, raised golden-green eyes at me and meowed.

"When in the hell did you adopt a cat?" I asked her.

"Sarah Booth, this is Pluto, Mrs. Littlefield's most precious companion."

The cat who would inherit everything—it all came back to me. "Suddenly I have more sympathy for Chasley." Pluto didn't blink as he gave me the once-over. What is it about felines that make them feel so superior? I glanced down at my hand, oozing blood, and knew the answer: They were very smart.

"Oh, don't be a crybaby. You scared Pluto. He's normally docile as a lamb."

"Right. And Chucky is just a cute little doll."

Tammy shifted so the cat could stretch across her lap. He was enormous. And he seemed to have fallen into a stupor.

"If you'll quit whining, Sarah Booth, we need to discuss the recording." Tinkie tapped a stiletto heel.

"Was the girl a ghost?" I asked Tammy. She was the authority in the room on noncorporeal beings. I had Jitty in my life, but Jitty was a special kind of haint. She was family.

"Dripping water! And she was bluish, like someone who'd drowned." Tinkie made the obvious connection. "What did she mean, 'It's your fault, Mommy'?" She hugged her arms around herself. "I hate to admit it, but I'm terrified."

"It doesn't make any sense," I pointed out. "Those tapes were recorded at least six years ago. Mariam Littlefield has been dead for two decades or better."

"Do you think the girl was Mrs. Littlefield's daughter?" Tinkie asked Tammy.

"I can't say. It looked . . . real, but video is so easily manipulated."

"Why would Marjorie Littlefield's dead daughter show up in New Orleans?" I asked. "At a shut-down whorehouse? Don't you think that's just a tad convenient? *If* the ghost girl is supposed to be Mariam Little-field. It could be anyone, you know." The whole thing had my sixth sense grumbling like I'd been on a bean binge.

"But how would—? Internet." Tinkie nodded know-ingly. "Let's see if we can find some photos of Mariam Littlefield."

Tammy deposited Pluto on the sofa without disrupt-ing a single snore. The cat was out cold. We went to her computer and Googled *Mariam Littlefield*. As the daugh-ter of a member of the privileged class, Mariam would have been photographed at various parties and events. When Tammy clicked on the first image, I felt a chill run through me. The little girl in the recording definitely resembled the portrait of Mariam that popped up. The painting, by John Howard Sanden, depicted a preteen girl, blue eyes dancing with mischief, and the hint of a secretive smile.

"Look at her dress." Tinkie spoke on a whisper. "The lace is exquisite. You know lace can be traced back to the place it was created. There are whole stories woven into the patterns."

"Fascinating history of lace, but is it the same child?" I asked.

"It's impossible to tell," Tammy said. "The . . . ghost was bedraggled. Mariam Littlefield is beautiful. The por-trait makes her alive." She pushed her hair back from her face. "If this is real, I can understand why Marjorie is determined to speak with her dead daughter. The ac-cusation the child is making . . . imagine the guilt."

I had a bigger problem. "How would Sherry and her mother know that Tink and I would end up at the old Pleasure Zone or that its new owner would find the DVDs and put them at the curb just at the moment I showed up? That's a lot of luck, all lining up in the right direction. I get a sense we're being manipulated." Too many opportunities for a different outcome for my taste. But who knew we'd even be in New Orleans?

"Has Marjorie viewed a similar recording?" Tinkie asked Tammy.

"She never mentioned it, but that might account for her abrupt decision to join the loonies at the compound and her total depression. I mean, the child in the recording is blaming her mother. Something like that is serious; I fear it might push her into suicide." Tammy punched the remote so we could watch it again.

"Don't even say that, Tammy," Tinkie admonished. "Marjorie Littlefield has managed four stupendous marriages. She isn't a fool. She's not the kind to buy into a suicide pact."

"Except where her dead daughter is concerned," Tammy said. "Guilt and shame can drive a person to desperate measures."

"How did Mariam Littlefield drown?"

"Marjorie was married to an importer of artifacts and antiques." Tammy paused the replay. "Ramón Salazar was popular in society circles. They entertained lavishly. Marjorie's job was to throw parties that brought the wealthy into the fold. She enjoyed the lifestyle and New Orleans."

Tinkie patted Tammy's shoulder. "Mariam didn't drown to punish Marjorie for enjoying life. That's a crazy and very egocentric thought."

I waved her to silence. "Tell us what you know, Tammy."

"Marjorie said Ramón took an interest in Chasley.

Paul la Kink died in a car accident when Chasley was young. Up until Marjorie married Ramón, the boy had no real man in his life. Ramón took Chasley to the docks to help unload and appraise the artifacts and antiques. Under Ramón's guidance, Chasley thrived. He was just a kid, but he worked with his stepfather every day after school and even on weekends. Marjorie said Ramón's attention changed Chasley, brought him out."

"What went wrong?" I asked.

"At first, it was really good. As the weeks passed, though, Chasley became mean-spirited and secretive. It troubled Marjorie, but she and Mariam were busy fulfilling the female roles as hostesses for the gala parties, the society ladies. She said the press photographed them and remarked they were like sisters. She attributed Chasley's dark moods to growing pains."

"Does Marjorie think Ramón influenced Chasley in a negative way?" I asked. Guilt was a monster that, once it began feasting, could consume a person.

Tammy shrugged. "She's convinced herself the seed of Chasley's darkness crept into him at this time. Bad associations at the docks, or something worse. That's what she said."

"Like he's possessed?" Tinkie inched closer to me.

"Whatever you want to call it, she believes that summer Chasley changed into a boy capable of killing his sister."

"But surely she doesn't believe . . . I mean, the drowning had to be an accident."

Tammy aimed the remote and clicked the player on. The image of the little girl blurred across the screen. She stood on the stairs, water dripping. "That summer, Mariam came into her own. Ramón began to take an interest

in her. She was a child with a lot of social graces. Marjorie thinks Chasley got jealous. He felt Mariam was taking something away from him. Late one afternoon after
the stevedores were gone, Chasley convinced Mariam
to go down to the docks with him. She fell in the river
and drowned. There were no witnesses to the event, and
Chasley was not in the habit of spending time with his
sister."

The image of the little girl shifted on the screen. She
seemed to glide forward toward the camera. Her mouth
didn't move, but I heard the words, "I await." I couldn't
be certain anyone else had heard them, but my heart was
pounding.

Lights from a car shifted across the wall. Walking
over to the front window, I looked out. I'd forgotten all
about the car parked across the street. Whoever it was
had packed up and left. The street was empty but for
pale moonlight dancing through the oak leaves.

It had been a long day. I dropped Tinkie at Hilltop and
fled for Dahlia House. I hoped the heaping plate of food
from Tammy would be a peace offering to Oscar, but I
didn't wait around to find out. Besides, I had horses to
feed and a hound to coddle.

The barn on the grounds of Dahlia House was built
back in the 1950s with six stalls and room for hay and
equipment storage. With the exception of my pastures,
the acreage around the house was leased to a local man,
Billy Watson, who knew cotton inside and out. The lease
money paid the taxes, and Billy also bush-hogged my
pastures and maintained the fences.

Reveler, Miss Scrapiron, and Lucifer were glad to see me. They whinnied softly as I scooped up their grain and dumped it into their feed buckets. The sound of their contented chewing did a lot to settle my frazzled nerves. The video of the little girl had upset me.

After the horses finished eating, I opened the stall doors and let them return to the pasture. Sweetie and I headed into the house. I fed my hound and found myself pacing the kitchen. After I made a drink, I went outside to sit on the porch, but the humidity was awful. As were the mosquitoes.

Sweetie and I went back in. After fifteen minutes, it became clear that if I didn't find something to do, I would worry myself sick. There were no messages from Graf. I'd thrown down the gauntlet, and he'd failed even to acknowledge it. While I might rue my ultimatum, there was no way to take it back. If he wouldn't talk to me, I'd have to box up the engagement ring and return it. But I wasn't going to rush. Tinkie had shown me the wisdom of waiting until Graf finished filming.

"Jitty!" At least my haint would be some company. "Jitty!"

There was no answer. She did have her own business to conduct, and from what I could tell, she stayed active in the social whirl of the Great Beyond. She also had an unwritten rule against answering me unless it was a dire emergency—or she wanted something from me.

"Jitty!"

On the third try, I called it quits. Instead, I whistled up my hound for a drive to the Sweetheart Café. Sweetie adored the soft vanilla ice cream cones.

Once we were headed to town, I called Harold to

invite him and Roscoe to join us. Harold would have some doggy misadventure to relate, and perhaps he could lift the feeling of doom hanging heavy over my head.

"Why, Sarah Booth, Roscoe and I are charmed at your invitation. We'll wait for you on the front porch."

True to his word, he and the devilish canine were ready and waiting when I pulled up in his front yard. With Harold riding shotgun and the dogs in the backseat, we headed to the burger joint. We were picking up the cones at the drive-through when Harold put a hand on my shoulder.

"What's wrong?" he asked.

"That obvious?"

"Even a blind man could see you're upset. Oscar told me he and Graf are very unhappy with the detective agency. I assume your funk extends from that matter."

I sighed. Yesterday I would have bridled at Oscar and Graf teaming up to discuss their displeasure. Now, though, I couldn't even muster a good defense. "Tink and I do keep getting hurt."

"True," he said, "but in the last case, no one could have foreseen how far south things would go. I mean, really, the Levert sisters! Preposterous."

"I know, but still, Tinkie or I could have been killed."

"But you weren't. And you took every precaution. Sarah Booth, I don't know how I would feel if you were my fiancée and persisted in solving crimes, but I do know you aren't the kind of woman who can be happy staying at home."

"I could be an actress. That's safer than a detective."

"Is it?" Harold's smile was devilish.

The server handed us our treats and I pulled over, licking my chocolate cone while holding Sweetie's vanilla. Harold did the same for Roscoe. In less than five minutes, the dogs were finished and I put the car in gear.

"How is acting dangerous?" I asked.

"There's a whole world of pitfalls out there. Sexy men, powerful producers, stunts that seem safe. Danger is everywhere in the world. I mean, a schoolteacher these days runs the risk of exposure to flu viruses or even a bullet. Nothing is safe."

I liked it that Harold argued for me. "I wish I could make Graf see that."

"I wish I could give him a word to the wise. If he tries to control you, he'll lose you. That's the bottom line. James Franklin understood your mother's nature. Those two . . ." He smiled and wiped a speck of ice cream from my cheek. "My parents were very fond of them. According to my mother, they had the best marriage in the South. They somehow managed to grow together as well as individually. I think James Franklin knew your mother inside and out, and he trusted her to do the right thing. Graf has to find that place with you."

"He doesn't want to be hurt."

"Nobody wants to be hurt, Sarah Booth. Now let's drive. It's hot as blazes even with the sun down. Drive fast and stir up a breeze."

The best advice ever. I turned onto a county road and headed north. Inspiration struck. "Let's drive to Layland."

"Layland, Mississippi?" Harold was incredulous. "What on earth for? It's a crossroads. There's nothing there but cotton fields and jackrabbits."

"And Heart's Desire."

Harold leaned against the door so he could watch me. "Heart's Desire. Is this a place, a person, a jewel? Do fill me in."

For the first time all day, I grinned. "It's a cult."

"Lord have mercy, Sarah Booth. You do have a nose for trouble. Cult as in religious or—?"

"They claim they're drawing in the world's most talented people to create a sort of think tank to control the world through business investments. They get insight from the dead."

"What I wouldn't give for a bit of financial advice from some dead folk with a historical perspective."

The cotton fields flew past as I drove down the straight Delta road into the night. In the backseat, Sweetie Pie and Roscoe let the wind flap their ears. They were in doggy bliss, and Roscoe was even behaving himself. The dog had a penchant for trouble, but riding in a car outweighed his desire for mischief.

I filled Harold in on Tammy's predicament. Harold frequently helped Tink and me with financial expertise on our cases, so it was just as well to clue him in from the start.

"I can't believe Marjorie Littlefield has fallen for these scam artists," he said. "To be manipulated like a pathetic . . . It isn't her style."

"Tammy said Marjorie's giving up on life. She's made out her will and left everything to her huge black cat, Pluto. The cat is hiding out at Tammy's right now. Marjorie fears Chasley will kill him."

"Chasley Littlefield. I've had a dealing or two with him. Smart businessman. Very smart. Ruthless. About five years ago he offered me a partnership in an agribusiness he was building."

"And?" I shot a glance at Harold. He was thoughtful.

"I didn't take it. I believe in making money, Sarah

Booth. But this agribusiness is not something I want to participate in. They're in cahoots with big industry to create nonfertile crops, not to mention all of the genetically engineered corn and trees and salmon. These companies don't really know what they're unleashing. The real problem is they don't seem to care."

Harold wasn't an alarmist, and if he walked away from a profitable deal, I knew he had grave concerns about the consequences. We'd been through one plague scenario in Sunflower County, which luckily turned out to be less devastating than first anticipated, but the potential for real disaster loomed over the land.

"So Chasley would do anything for a buck." It wasn't what I wanted to hear.

"Absolutely anything."

"Do you think he'd harm his mother?"

Dozens of white center road lines disappeared beneath the car as I waited for his response.

"One reason Chasley is like he is stems from his mother. He didn't bother to hide his contempt for her. He said she was nothing more than a high-priced whore who got the ring on her finger and then stopped putting out."

"Wow." Pretty harsh words from a son.

"I heard the gossip—she blames him for his sister's death. I remember how ugly the talk was. Chasley hadn't watched Mariam. He'd let her drown."

"I think it's more than blaming him for negligence. I think Marjorie believes Chasley murdered his sister. She's despondent. Tammy fears she'll take a rash action unless something is done."

The lights of Layland, a dozen at best, blinked half a mile ahead.

"Such an accusation would explain Chasley's deep anger. Think how awful it must be."

"Only if he *didn't* kill Mariam," I said.

"As I recall the story, he was fifteen and she was ten. She drowned off the docks by Marjorie's husband's import business in New Orleans."

"Right." I slowed as we entered the outskirts of the town, passing deserted buildings, a closed tire store, an abandoned cotton gin, and two service stations with hot food offerings. Layland had gone downhill in the two years since I'd driven through. It was in a corner of the county not connected to any major roads or business centers. Few people had a reason to visit the community, which was composed of cotton fields and stretches of woods mostly leased by out-of-state private hunting concerns.

"This is depressing." Harold spoke my thoughts.

In the backseat, Roscoe gave a deep growlish grumble. Sweetie's yodel was soft and feminine.

"The dogs are intrigued."

"Roscoe smells fresh opportunity for trouble, I'm sure." Harold was droll, but also strangely proud of his new canine. "Where is Heart's Desire?"

"I was hoping a service station would be open so we could ask. The organization is rather secretive and I'm afraid I don't have a real address." I sighed. "Everything around here is closed, though."

"There's a person closing up that Texaco mart."

I had to wait on a sedan to speed past; then I whipped the car into the parking lot and pulled up beside the young man who was locking the door. He gave the Mercedes an appreciative once-over before his gaze settled on the dogs in the backseat.

"We're looking for Heart's Desire," Harold said.

"Who isn't?" The young man tucked his thumbs in his back jeans' pockets. "Why should I tell you?"

Harold opened his billfold and pulled out a hundred-dollar bill. "Because we don't have time to waste and because you want this money."

The man reached for it, but Harold jerked it away. "Information first."

"Go six miles down Truman Lane, take a left on Bishop, then a right on Drury. That's a narrow road and you'll miss it if you aren't careful. And if you aren't *real* careful, you'll end up hurt. Make a wrong turn, mister, and you'll find yourself sinking in Compton Slough. Only the gators would be able to find you." He snatched the money. "Won't do you any good, though. Heart's Desire is surrounded by an eight-foot wall and armed guards on the gate."

"How many people live there?" I asked.

His narrow lips pursed. "Once they go in, they never come out." He laughed. "Our very own Hotel California. Gossip is, they party with the dead. Some kind of coven, you know."

The skin along my arms danced. Aspects of this case gave me the creeps.

"Food delivery?" Harold asked.

"They buy some local stuff from old man Hayes. He's into all that organic shit. The folks in the compound don't eat anything worth having, as far as I can tell." His grin revealed a missing tooth. "Just goes to show having a lot of money doesn't give people good sense."

"You can say that again," Harold said.

"Have you met the women who run Heart's Desire?" I asked.

"Nobody in Layland has *met* them, but I've seen them a few times. The young one is hot. Red hair down to her ass. Creamy skin. A figure—" He whistled. "The old one is like Red Devil Lye in your shoes. You just want to keep hoofin' it out of her vicinity before your feet catch fire."

"Do you see them around town?" I asked.

"Yeah, right. They come shopping for slushies and potato chips." He was a cocky young man.

"Can the sarcasm. Have you seen them passing through town?" I clarified.

"About once a month. They drive out and come back the next day."

"Do any locals work for the compound?"

"Are you kidding? They wouldn't let us in there to rake leaves. Far as I know, nobody from Layland has gone on the property since the ladies bought it. They don't take lightly to trespassers. The Butler boys went back there last January to do some deer hunting. Those guards likta scared them to death."

"Not many people appreciate poachers," I pointed out.

"Folks around here don't appreciate witches who talk to the dead." He brought a can of Skoal out of his back pocket, but he didn't use it.

"Is that a fact?" Harold said.

"Fact or no, I can't say." The young man straightened up. "My name's Wilbur. If you want more information, bring more money. I'm at the mart seven days a week." He tipped a nonexistent hat. "Now, don't nose around that place and get yourself in trouble. We got the word for nobody to go messin' with those women. Huey Hampton, the local justice of the peace, says we're to leave them be."

"Thanks," Harold and I said together as I pulled away and headed for the twisting road to Heart's Desire.

4

At the end of Drury Road was a metal gate that looked like something from *The Haunting of Hill House*. At least fourteen feet high, it was heavy wrought iron. Pointed spikes decorated the top, centered by a huge ornate heart. A chain and padlock signaled that visitors were unwelcome. Did it also mean those inside were prisoners?

Beyond the gate a rambling Spanish-style structure sprawled across a landscaped lawn bright with bougainvillea and shrubs shaped into fantasy creatures, putting me in mind of a Hollywood movie star's mansion.

"Paradise or prison?" Harold asked.

"No chance of drop-in visitors."

Two armed guards materialized. They walked in lockstep toward the car.

"Creepy!" I said.

Before Harold could respond, Roscoe's insanely penetrating bark reverberated in my skull. I wiped at my ears to see if they were bleeding.

"Roscoe!" Harold made a grab for the dog, but he wasn't quick enough. Even though Roscoe weighed only about thirty pounds, he hurled himself out of the car and went after the guards.

"Saint Paul in a pinafore!" I'd lately been trying to upgrade my swearing, but so far I had only come up with ridiculous phrases. I started to chase the dog, but Harold snagged my arm.

"Don't you dare get out of the car."

A guard took slow, deliberate aim at Roscoe. In the backseat, Sweetie's mournful howl created the sound track for a surreal scene.

I laid on the horn, much to Harold's dismay. "Hey! Hey!"

"Stop it, Sarah Booth. They could shoot *us*." He slowly opened his door and stood beside the car. "Roscoe, come back." He spoke softly, reasonably—in other words, as if he were totally insane. Roscoe was in a maniac's crosshairs, and Harold was pleasantly requesting he return to the car.

To my utter amazement, Roscoe hunched his butt at the guards and dumped a pile of poop. In the car's headlights, I watched in awe at the mountain of shit Roscoe produced, as if he'd been saving it for days. Maybe for weeks.

"Uh-oh," Harold said under his breath. "The dog has no common sense."

When he was done, Roscoe sprinted to the car like his ass was on fire. He flew past Harold and into the backseat.

"Hey, Cisco, let's beat it out of here." Harold's terrible Spanish accent quoted a long-ago television show, *The Cisco Kid*. He jumped back in the car.

"*Sí, Pancho.*" I put it in reverse and stepped on the gas. Gravel and dust churned under the tires as the guards ran toward us. There was nothing to gain by talking to them, and I didn't want them to get a good look at me.

The security guards yelled at us. Roscoe put his paws on the back of my seat and barked a challenge. I had no doubt he was taunting the men. Sweetie was too dignified to participate in baiting sentries.

"So that was Heart's Desire," Harold said after we were safely able to turn around and speed away. "How will you get inside? Not even I can fake a Dun and Bradstreet to open that gate for you."

"Tinkie could convince them she's a wealthy heiress, but it would never work for me." Tinkie had the clothes, the graces, and the mannerisms of the upper class. I was an accomplished tomboy.

Harold laughed. "You're an actress, Sarah Booth. Of course you could do it."

"Thanks for the vote of confidence, but I'd rather go in with access to the whole house." I had an idea. "I require a license to snoop in every nook and cranny, but there's one type of employee who moves freely through every wealthy person's home."

"What are you thinking about?" He knew me well enough to be concerned.

"I think Tinkie and I will be maids."

"Oh, Tinkie will love that!"

"She'll balk at wearing housekeeping garb, but she'll come around." My partner was a fashion statement even in her sleep, but she would dress down to solve a case.

"The truth is, she'll do anything for you, Sarah Booth."

"And me for her."

"That's why you're such excellent partners. Now, let's plan this out."

As we raced toward home, Harold and I laid the groundwork for a sneak attack on Heart's Desire. If Tinkie and I could get inside, the first order of business would be to communicate with Marjorie Littlefield and convince her to come out of the compound and return to her life.

"I keep asking myself why she'd do this," Harold said. "She isn't a quitter. She's a savvy lady with a flair for life. My family knew her socially in New Orleans. I grew up occasionally playing with Chasley on summer weekends when our families visited. Marjorie is smart, well educated, well read. . . . Going into a place with a bunch of phonies, that isn't Marjorie."

I hadn't told Harold about the DVD, but now I did.

"That's cruel!" He was furious. "Even worse, it's like an invitation to death."

I hadn't really thought of it that way, but he was right. When the child said she was waiting, was it an invitation to leave this life behind and join the dead child in another place? It had to have been crafted for Marjorie. But why leave it behind in New Orleans? I still had no answer.

"The video doesn't make complete sense. The other footage on the tapes dates back to when the Westins ran the Pleasure Zone in New Orleans. Pre-Katrina, so before 2005. It could date back as far as 1995, when the Westins started their . . . business. Mariam's been dead a lot longer than that."

"It's pure luck you stole the trash bags." Harold clearly

saw my skepticism. "And that you looked at them is a miracle. Anything else interesting?"

I dodged the question, uncertain how to handle the content of the videos I'd seen. "I've had several people tell me that Sherry Westin can speak with the dead. What's your take on that?"

"I've never met Sherry."

"That's not an answer."

"I do believe some people have a gift, Sarah Booth. Madam Tommeka, for instance. I believe we all have a sixth sense or whatever you want to call it, but most of us blunt our sensitivities. So it stands to reason others have developed theirs."

"You think a ghost can be captured on film?" I'd never tried to photograph Jitty. It was somehow a violation.

"I don't know."

I hadn't expected Harold to be so open to the idea of communicating with spirits. If he believed it . . . others might.

"Haven't you ever wanted to talk to someone who's passed on?" he asked.

I thought of my parents. "Every day." Now was the time I could tell him about Jitty, but I hesitated. I'd never shared the truth about my heirloom haint with anyone. I was a little afraid if I said anything, she'd simply disappear, as if I'd betrayed her somehow. So I kept silent, wondering if I'd ever have the nerve to tell Graf.

"Me, too," Harold said. "I'd love to tell my mother about my life. Maybe get her advice, and thank her and say how much I appreciate the many things she taught me and the time she took with me."

"Yeah." If he didn't stop, I would get emotional. "But

if someone does have a special gift like this, doesn't it stand to reason they should use it only for good?"

"One would think, if one were a naïve fool." Harold patted my hand. "The strongest human drive is greed, Sarah Booth. A few people might be altruistic, but others wouldn't be able to resist the impulse to use their talent to make money. Obviously, if Sherry is the real deal, she's yielded to the compulsion to use her abilities as a medium for money, not to help people."

"That's creepy and wrong."

"Doctors do it. Lawyers do it. Policemen, teachers, musicians, artists, and don't forget the politicians. Why should someone who can speak with the dead be any different? There's an old saying: Everyone has a price. For most, it's money. Others sell out for companionship."

He made a good argument. Still, it depressed me. Communicating with the dead was a truly special gift. To use it to manipulate people to give up money seemed more wrong than robbing them at gunpoint.

"You're right." We crossed the city limits into Zinnia. "Harold, I need a favor."

"Ask away."

"Can you call Mrs. Littlefield and tell her to demand her personal maids?"

"Presuming I can find a number for this reclusive place, of course I will."

"First thing tomorrow?"

"What's the rush?"

"I'm worried about Mrs. Littlefield, and also I need to stay busy. If I don't, I'll make myself sick about Graf."

"I'll take care of it as soon as the bank opens. Do you want access tomorrow around noon?"

"Yes." If Tinkie and I planned to continue with Delaney

Detective Agency, we needed to act. If Oscar intended to make Tinkie quit, I had to know. As for Graf, if he didn't contact me by tomorrow morning, I would be out of touch. Physically and emotionally.

"Consider it done," Harold said as I pulled into his driveway.

I slowed beneath the arching limbs of the old trees that created a tunnel down his winding driveway. Once, he'd wrapped the branches of the live oaks with twinkle lights just for me. At the memory, my thumb gave a tiny little pulse.

"Thank you, Harold."

"Sarah Booth, I wish you and Graf the utmost happiness, but a part of me still would like a chance to court you."

I leaned over and kissed his cheek. "The future is a scary place, Harold."

His hand grazed my chin. "Keep it in mind. I may be the only man you know who can give you the freedom you need and the support you deserve."

His words almost broke my heart. "Now isn't the time, Harold. I'm wearing Graf's ring."

"Life moves swiftly. If things don't work out with Graf, I want you to know my feelings. I've played the field my entire life. I know what I want. And I know you, warts and all." He picked up my hand and kissed the base of my palm. "But whatever happens, we will always be friends. That you can count on."

He opened the door and got out. "Come along, Roscoe," he said as he mounted the steps to his porch.

Sweetie gave a low groan of good-bye to Roscoe and then hopped into the front seat, where she curled up for a nap as we drove home, my thumb tingling in a way that made me feel as if I'd betrayed my fiancé.

"Sarah Booth, I'll risk my life for you any day, but I will *not* wear that!" Tinkie walked around her desk in Delaney Detective Agency and dropped the white housekeeper smock on the floor beside the white rubber-soled shoes. "I just can't do it."

"You'd leave Marjorie Littlefield to the tender mercies of the Westin women?" I fought hard to keep my giggle in check. The maid's outfit was a tiny bit of meanness on my part. It was the ugliest uniform I could find at the local Goodwill store.

"I'll wear something plain. And practical. But I will not wear that . . . monstrosity."

"What about the shoes?" The devil had me by the ear.

"No. I can't. It would break my spirit. They're just so . . . ugly!"

"Harold went to a lot of trouble to get us access to Heart's Desire." I picked up the clothes from the parquet floor and put them in a plastic bag. From behind the desk I brought out another bag with khaki slacks and polo shirts, along with some beige lace-up shoes claiming to firm one's tush as one walked.

"I'll speak with Harold and—" She caught sight of the other bag. "What's that?"

I tossed it to her. "What we really have to wear."

"Sarah Booth! You are pure-dee mean!"

I laughed out loud. "No, it was just a little fun—at your expense. We need to head out to Heart's Desire ASAP. I've wrangled a compact car for us. We can't take your Caddy and we sure can't show up in an antique Roadster."

I'd been a busy girl all morning, acting on the belief Harold would get through to Marjorie and make her understand the importance of demanding her "personal maids." I'd been right to place my faith in the man who worked so strangely on my thumb.

"I meant to ask you about the car parked at the side of the house." Tinkie rifled through her clothes suspiciously, but they obviously met with her approval as she began to step out of her stylish Capri set.

I went to the desk for a photo I'd printed from Google Earth. Using satellites and photography, the aerial surveillance showed Heart's Desire, complete with the eight-foot-high solid wall around ten acres surrounded by woods. Barrack-type structures were barely visible through the dense trees, and there was an apple orchard, and what looked like an old stable and pastures a half mile from the house.

The main house of Heart's Desire was a U-shaped three-story mansion with a single-story outbuilding at the back and a large parking garage.

"Holy cow." Tinkie studied the map. "That's a serious compound." She tapped the page. "It's great to know the layout of the buildings, though. There are two levels of security. The wall, which is guarded, and perimeter roads around the entire tract, which must be close to two sections of land."

"Exactly two sections. The property is a rectangle with two sides running two miles and the short sides only a mile."

She whistled. "None of it is in cotton. It's all wooded."

Fertile soil that wasn't planted might be considered a waste by some.

"Oscar told me the Westins bought the property in foreclosure."

"The sad thing is that someone always profits from the misfortune of others."

It was a touchy point with me. I'd almost lost Dahlia House for the mortgage and back taxes. "What did Oscar say about this job?"

"He's pissed right now. Then he'll be worried. But honestly, we're going to be maids for a day, two at most. That doesn't sound too dangerous to me."

Nor me, but this was how it always began—with some innocent-sounding case that should take only a day or so and involve nothing more than a report or a bit of snooping.

"And Graf?" she asked.

I was working hard to avoid the fact that Graf still hadn't called. The doorbell rang, and I opened the front door to the UPS man. I signed for the flat package he gave me and then hurried back to Tinkie. She was dressed for maid work when I got back to the office.

"A present?"

"From Graf." My heart sank to my shoes. He hadn't called, but he'd sent a package clearly containing paperwork. Not a good sign in a distressed relationship.

I tore it open, and a heavy, bound document fell out. DELTA BLUES was stamped on the cover of a movie script. I looked at Tinkie. "Graf won't return my phone calls but he sent me a movie script."

"What's it about?" Tinkie asked the logical question.

I thumbed through it. "It's a crime drama centered

around the Mississippi Delta blues music and two private investigators, a male and female, who are tracking down the bad guy."

Tinkie's teeth gleamed. "So, he won't talk to you but he sent you a script with a role perfect for the two of you. It's a wonderful answer. And it could be filmed right here in Mississippi, so you wouldn't have to travel! It's ingenious! Don't you see, Sarah Booth, he's trying to patch things up."

The relief was intense. Almost enough to make me overlook his wrongheaded approach to our relationship. "You know, it would have been so much simpler for him to pick up the phone and dial it."

"Simpler from the female perspective. You're dealing with a man. They don't have logical thought processes."

"And they don't know how to say they were wrong."

"That, too. But for heaven's sake, missy, this is great news! What are you going to tell him?"

I thought about it for a moment. "I'll call a Los Angeles bakery and order a dozen homemade biscuits delivered to his trailer on the set." Two could play this game.

Tinkie patted the script. "What a strange engagement you two have. Movies and biscuits. Hurry up and place the order. We need to get to Heart's Desire so we can talk to Mrs. Littlefield and get back to our men."

We arrived at the compound a little after eleven. At the gate, armed guards surrounded us. Even though I'd prepared Tinkie for the security, she protested loudly as the vehicle was thoroughly searched. The security team confiscated our cell phones and her camera.

"No electronic devices allowed," a guard said. "Pick them up on your way out."

"Do they interfere with the communications with the dead?" Tinkie asked sweetly.

I tried a few wisecracks, but the boys in black had no sense of humor. They went about their task as if Tinkie and I might be smuggling in C4 explosives. They even took the floor mats out of the car and pulled out the backseat. Thorough. To Tinkie's dismay, they found the second cell phone she'd secreted in the spare tire of the car.

Before they let us back in the car, they called the main house to check our credentials. Harold had done a good job, because a female voice gave permission for us to enter. The lead guard produced an electronic gizmo, which opened the gate. Feeling as if we might be shot if I sped, I let the compact roll down the drive at five miles an hour.

"This place is beautifully landscaped," Tinkie said. "Harold is researching the history of the property for us. The house has been empty for years."

"Someone did a lot of work." Near the pool, which had a waterfall and a miniature volcano, palm trees swayed in a gentle breeze. I planted the layout firmly in my mind. It would come in handy.

When we got to the front door, I stopped and started to exit the car.

"Do not park that ugly car there." A butler in full tails strode out the door. He shooed us as if we were naughty children. "The help parks in the back, where you will be accommodated. None of your personal things are allowed in the main house. You will enter the main house empty-handed each morning and you will leave the same way in the evening. Is that clear?"

Tinkie did a slow boil. "I don't know who the hell you think you are, but—"

"Yes, sir," I answered as I pushed her away. "I'll move the car."

"Back talk is a mistake. The next incident will be your last. And I am Mr. Palk."

"Yes, sir, Mr. Palk," I said with more enthusiasm.

Easing the car around the drive, I found the servants' parking lot and pulled into a slot. Tinkie had finally cooled off.

"How dare that man speak to us in that tone."

"We're maids," I reminded her.

"What does it matter? I don't treat Melinda like she's dirt. She's family, and I want her to know it."

"Mr. Palk may be upset because Mrs. Littlefield is demanding her own servants. It may reflect poorly on him and his management of the staff. If that's the case, he'll ride our asses day and night." An unpleasant thought.

"Well, he'd better be careful. I'll make him wish he was back in butler school in Merry Old England."

I popped the trunk so we could grab our bags. "Remember, Tink. You're Tinkie Jones, not Mrs. Richmond. We can't back-talk the butler."

"Not right this minute, but if he treats me ugly, payback will be hell, I assure you."

I didn't doubt it for a minute. Tinkie treated all people fairly. The one thing she couldn't tolerate was using position or status to suppress a subordinate.

We found our quarters. We'd be sleeping in a bunkhouse behind the main house. Our room was comfortably appointed, but Tinkie and I needed access to the big house. Marjorie would have to ask for us to stay in her suite.

When we were unpacked, we followed Mr. Palk through the house. It was an impressive place with a dining table that seated at least eighteen.

"You're not to speak with any of the guests, unless they speak to you first," Mr. Palk said as he showed us around the library and meeting rooms where a handful of people listened to a speaker talk about global debt and the role of government.

"Do not touch any of the glassware or artwork," Palk continued his rant.

"As if I would want to touch such tacky stuff," Tinkie said under her breath.

"Were you speaking to me?" Mr. Palk rounded on her. "Do not mumble. It's intolerable."

I was standing behind Tinkie, and I pinched her as hard as I could on the back of her arm. She jerked forward, but she bit back the reply meant for Mr. Palk.

"Mrs. Littlefield is our employer." Tinkie was all bristle and no common sense.

"She pays you. I direct you. Is that clearly understood?"

"Yes, sir, Mr. Palk." I'd once played a maid on off-off-Broadway, and while I'd gotten no stellar reviews, I also hadn't been fired. Tinkie was about to get us both kicked off the property. "May we see Mrs. Littlefield? It's close to lunch, and normally Mrs. Jones and I read to her while she dines. It's one of the services we provide."

"She dines with the other guests."

I only arched my eyebrows.

"Her room is this way," he said.

I deduced from his actions that Mrs. Littlefield hadn't yet signed documents turning her fortune over to Heart's Desire. If she was still getting her way, she hadn't caved.

We followed him up a lovely staircase that split at the second level and then continued on to the third. The house was solid, well built.

"Mrs. Littlefield has the Periwinkle Suite." He pointed to a door painted a pale lilac. "The bedclothes and bath towels are periwinkle blue. All of her personal spa materials are also periwinkle. It is required that guests wear the spa robes and toiletries provided for them. They are not allowed in the spa unless they are appropriately attired in the color-coordinated robes." He leaned down, his nose inches from Tinkie's. "Since you'll be doing her laundry, understand that each item is counted and will be recounted once you leave for the day."

"You think I'd steal a towel?" Tinkie's face slowly flooded with red.

"Thank you, Mr. Palk." I grabbed her shoulder and tapped lightly on the door. "If Mrs. Littlefield needs anything, I'm sure she'll call on you." I didn't wait for the heiress to open the door but dragged Tinkie in behind me. She shot a death ray at the butler as I closed the door.

"Don't let him get under your skin," I whispered. "Remember, we're here for the greater good."

"The greater good is telling me to kick his pompous ass."

Tinkie seldom cursed, but I felt her pain. "When this is over."

I nudged her away from the door and through a foyer to a sitting area. *Suite of rooms* didn't begin to describe it—*elegant apartment* was more accurate. The pale lilac walls were calming, and white sheers shaded the bright September sunlight but allowed plenty of illumination.

Mrs. Littlefield reclined on a chaise longue, a lavender throw tucked around her legs and a Miranda James Cat in the Stacks mystery on her lap. Figured, since she owned the redoubtable Pluto, demon-possessed kitty.

"Ladies," she said, putting the book on the table beside her. She looked us up and down. "Mrs. Richmond, your haircut gives you away. Miss Delaney, you're perfect."

I didn't know whether to feel complimented or offended. Tinkie preened. "The butler is vile. What an officious oaf."

"Mr. Palk takes his duties seriously. If he finds out you're pretenders, he'll be very upset. I don't like lying to the Westins, but Madam Tomeeka and Mr. Erkwell convinced me it was vitally important for you to be here. I understand Madam Tomeeka had a dream of some sort." She swung her legs to the floor and stepped into child-sized slippers. "At any rate, I'm glad you're here. You'll help to pass the time."

When she stood, she was no taller than Tinkie. A munchkin. A munchkin dripping in rubies and diamonds. She must have had fifty grand around her neck. And she was in a robe. I wondered what jewelry she wore out. Did women contemplating suicide bother with jewelry?

"Would you ladies care for tea?" She faltered and nearly lost her balance.

I gripped her elbow. "We can't have any," I spoke before Tinkie could accept. "You can't ask the kitchen for a pot and three cups. We're your maids."

"Of course, how thoughtless of me." She went to the window. "A lovely day. Once upon a time, I would have gloried in the sun. I was quite the accomplished tennis player." Her words were casual enough, but there seemed to be sadness beneath them.

"They have a court here," I said. "I'm sure there are other players visiting."

"I'm not up to the game any longer. I'm preparing for my final transition."

I took in her petite figure. She was only in her mid-sixties, far too young to play the geriatric. "Mrs. Littlefield, Madam Tomeeka is very worried about you. She's afraid you're—" Tinkie's shoe, even though it was canvas, caught me right on the shin. The warning made me clamp my lips shut.

Tinkie took over. "We met your cat at Madam Tomeeka's. Tammy wanted you to know Chasley is asking too many questions about Pluto. We think you should leave this compound and see to the cat."

"Chasley is asking about Pluto?" She faced us, concern displacing the nostalgia. "What does he want?"

"He wants Tammy to give up the cat," I said. Tinkie had been correct to play this card. The cat was our ace in the hole. "Tammy fears he may want to harm Pluto. Because of the inheritance. We should help you pack so you can retrieve Pluto and keep him safe. If anything happens to the cat, wouldn't your son inherit?"

"Well, I'm not dead yet!" she snapped.

"Of course not." I felt a sudden unease. The rooms could be bugged. Sherry or her mother—or anyone—could be listening to this conversation. Tinkie and I had been extremely reckless. I waved them to silence.

"Let's step out on the balcony." I moved toward the French doors.

Outside with the doors closed, I continued. "We're concerned for your safety, and for the cat."

"I'm here of my own free will, Miss Delaney."

"Miss Booth," I reminded her. "Miss Sarah Booth." I pointed at Tinkie. "And Mrs. Jones."

She held my gaze. "I appreciate your concern, but I'm here because I want to be. Heart's Desire offers a chance I can't find anywhere else."

This was tricky. I glanced at Tinkie for help.

"Sarah Booth and I have reason to believe Heart's Desire might not be on the up-and-up."

Mrs. Littlefield stiffened. "I'm not a dotty old woman. I'm in my right mind. And I'm not a fool. I've agreed to the ruse necessary to get you here so you can look out for me. Mr. Erkwell, at Madam Tomeeka's insistence, convinced me it was in my best interest to hire you and bring you here, but I have no intention of leaving. I'm well cared for, and we're making progress in contacting Mariam. Sherry believes we'll get a breakthrough any day. Sherry has caught glimpses of my daughter, but Mariam's confused. And timid." She brushed past me and went back inside.

"Did the Westins show you a video?" I asked.

Marjorie walked to a liquor decanter on a table behind the sofa. She tried to hide it, but a sob broke from her. She poured a good measure of Scotch into a glass and added two ice cubes. It might be five o'clock somewhere else, but it wasn't even lunch in Mississippi. She was getting a head start on the day.

"My daughter drowned and it was my fault. I didn't watch her closely enough. I want to speak with her before I transition. I have to know if her death was an accident or a deliberate act. Once I speak with Mariam, this will all be settled. Had I not been busy with a social engagement, had I known the true character of my son—" She broke off on a gasp of pain. "It's all my fault."

Guilt consumed her, and I knew that nothing Tinkie or I said would change it. She was here to make amends with her dead daughter, and perhaps to join the child. And whatever the Westin women's goal, I felt certain they were manipulating everything.

5

Mr. Palk reluctantly brought up a lunch tray to Marjorie, but he made it clear she was expected to dine with the other guests for dinner. Tinkie and I preferred for her to join the communal meal, because we needed to know who else was on the premises. Unfortunately, Marjorie was too upset to leave her rooms.

So we tidied up around her—or I did, Tinkie was about as useless as tits on a boar hog—as we tried to talk sense into Marjorie and convince her to pack her things. To no avail. She wouldn't consider leaving Heart's Desire until she made contact with her dead daughter. She wasn't even the least bit embarrassed to admit it. She totally believed that Sherry Westin could channel spirits.

Tinkie handed me the lunch tray, and I returned it to

the kitchen, hoping food was available for the hired help. I wouldn't be surprised if Mr. Palk took a page from the Dickens School of Butlers and fed us crusty bread and water.

On the way to the kitchen, I passed several other employees who kept their gazes on the ground. Well trained by Palk the Bully. Laughter tinkled from the dining room, where a half-dozen people gathered. A pretty woman laughed at something. They looked hale and hearty. At least the guests weren't being starved.

"Miss Booth!" Palk's voice reverberated in the cavernous room.

"Sir?" I had about had it with him.

"Are you lost?"

"Indeed, I am." I smiled sweetly. "I'm trying to find the kitchen, but the house is so big. I was confused."

He pointed and gave my shoulder a push. Had I not held the tray, I would have belted him.

"Mr. Palk, I think you should know if you touch me again, I'll hurt you." I spoke in a calm voice. "I'm Mrs. Littlefield's maid. If I tell her you've manhandled me in any way, I'm sure she'll pack her things and leave."

Color climbed his neck and into his cheeks until his forehead almost glowed. Even his balding scalp looked hot. "I beg your pardon," he said stiffly.

I clutched the tray and went the way he pointed. I could feel daggers in my back. While I had risked making him an enemy, I had to make him lay off. Tinkie and I couldn't snoop if Palk lurked around spying on us. I hoped I had scared him sufficiently to make him avoid us. I had no doubt if Mrs. Littlefield threatened to leave Heart's Desire because of his conduct, he'd be a gone goose.

I pushed through a swinging door into the kitchen and put the dirty dishes on a counter. Several young women were busy chopping, stirring, and washing up. Standing with her arms akimbo was a slender and quite beautiful Asian woman, obviously the mistress of the kitchen.

"I'm Sarah Booth," I said, holding out my hand. "I work for Mrs. Littlefield."

She clasped my hand in a firm grip. "Yumi Kato, master chef." She took my measure as she held my hand.

"Would it be possible to get some lunch for my co-worker and myself?" Mrs. Littlefield had eaten, but Tinkie and I had not.

"The maids eat in the staff dining hall. Mr. Palk does not allow special preparation of food for anyone." Yumi glanced around. "But I shall make an exception this time. Robert! Prepare sandwiches for two."

"Thank you." I leaned against a counter, but her frown made me push away. Yumi ran a tight ship, but I couldn't imagine how difficult it would be trying to please a roomful of wealthy people.

"Please do not reveal to Mr. Palk that I gave you sandwiches," she said. "He is not pleased when the help requires special privileges. In the future, please come to the staff dining room."

The hierarchy of the hired help at Heart's Desire was more rigid than the caste system of India. I understood efficiency and attention to detail, but Heart's Desire pushed it to the extreme. I was highly *agitato*, as my hero Kinky Friedman would say. "I'm sorry, I didn't mean to create a problem."

"Not a problem for me. For you, if you are caught taking food upstairs for your personal consumption." She watched me with an opaque gaze. "I tell you this to help you. Come back in ten minutes. Your sandwiches will be ready."

I left the kitchen and stopped outside in a hallway to get a lay of the land. Footsteps tapped behind me.

"Hi, Sarah, I'm Amanda." The young woman held up a high five. "Good one on Yumi. I can't believe you wangled sandwiches out of her. She's such a bitch to work for. She sucks up to Palk and treats us like we're insects."

"What's her story?"

"She just came two weeks ago. She's impossible to please." Tears started in her eyes but she blinked them back. "I can't take it anymore. Everyone here is awful."

"I work for Mrs. Littlefield, not Heart's Desire."

Her eyes widened. "She's nice. It must be wonderful to work for a pleasant person. I never thought working here would be like this."

"Why don't you leave?" I asked.

"All of my life I wanted to work in a kitchen with a real chef, someone I could learn from. I can cook. No problem. I had a job at a great restaurant, but it closed last year. Bad economy. I thought Heart's Desire might be an opportunity. I keep hoping one of the guests will see my potential."

"The kitchen has expensive equipment. A chef's dream."

"It does, but this isn't the job I thought I hired on to do. I only chop up vegetables or spices or wash salad greens. Once in a blue moon I get to make a dish. Yumi doesn't like me. She says my accent makes me sound like I'm a hick."

Her voice was soft and held the lilt of the Vicksburg area. I found her tone soothing, and she was well spoken. Yumi obviously had a regional bias, not so unusual.

"That's too bad. How are the other guests?"

Amanda looked down the hallway. "Let's go outside so I can smoke a cigarette and we can have some privacy. Sometimes I think the rooms here are bugged."

Strange she would have the same reaction I did. Big Brother was obviously busy around Heart's Desire.

Once we were outside, she pulled a crumpled pack of Marlboros from her hip pocket and lit up. In an instant, the craving was on me. Instead of bumming a cigarette, I stuffed my hands in my pockets and leaned against the wall. We were on the east side of the house in an alcove beside the kitchen entrance. Out of the breeze and out of sight. Amanda took a seat on top of a garbage can and inhaled. "Man, I hate this job." She wiped sweat off her forehead. Hades could not be hotter than the Delta in September.

"Surely this isn't the only job you could find?"

"Layland isn't the capital of industry and opportunity, and I don't want to leave the Delta. I hoped this job would give me a chance to meet people, folks who might hire a private chef."

She'd approached her dream thoughtfully. Working in an establishment patronized by rich people was a good plan. "Not panning out the way you hoped?"

"Since Yumi arrived, the rest of us are kept in the kitchen like slaves. We do all the tedious stuff—and Yumi takes the credit. Between her and Palk, we're never allowed to speak with a guest. I'll never get a chance to meet anyone if I follow the rules."

"You said Mrs. Littlefield was nice. What about the others?"

"Mr. Addleson is okay. His wife is a little . . . Let's just say she's really pretty but not so bright." She inhaled,

clearly daydreaming about a different life. I hadn't realized until that moment how young she was—maybe
twenty-five.

"What does Addleson do?"

"Coal mining. He has this country estate in West Virginia near the Greenbrier. Shimmer, his wife, showed me
a photo of it. Before Yumi clamped down on us. Anyway, the Addlesons' place is incredible, Sarah. There's
this long drive with trees, and the foothills seem to rise
up out of the backyard. And in the winter there's snow.
Like I said, I want to stay close to home, but I would like
living in West Virginia."

"Maybe that'll work out for you. Have you let them
know you're interested?"

She shook her head. "They'd think I was mad. If I ever
had a chance to show off some of my dishes, maybe they'd
notice me and ask about me."

The pesky protocol of working for the rich and famous. "Shimmer is an interesting name."

"I think she made it up, to go along with the perfume
she's designed. Shimmer talks about it all the time. Even
to the help. Or she did before Yumi ostracized us in the
kitchen."

"Shimmer has created a perfume?"

"It's a cosmetic line, really, called Ribbons. She's
brought samples of the packaging to the dining table,
which really annoyed Mr. Palk. He says dinnertime is
not for show-and-tell. Anyway, the package is beautiful.
Each one is tied with a pale blue shimmery ribbon. And
what she showed me smells great."

"QVC will be beating down her door."

Amanda looked hard to see if I was making fun of

her. I kept my face solemn. Just what the world needed, though, another fragrance by a wannabe celebrity.

"Anyone else interesting here?"

"A woman named Amaryllis." At my look of confusion, she added, "It's a flower."

Shimmer. Amaryllis. Next would be Fairy or Rainbow. The names sounded made up. "What's her story?"

"I overheard her talking with the elder Ms. Westin, Brandy. Someone close to Amaryllis died in a freak accident and she's interested in connecting with the ghost of the dead person." Even though no one else was about, she leaned closer. "Amaryllis thinks her friend may have been murdered. She's twitchy as a rabbit."

Amanda had stepped into a puddle of interesting. "So do people ever hook up with the dead?"

She tossed her butt to the ground, stepped on it, picked it up, and put it in the trash, all in one smooth motion. "They make us stay out at the servants' quarters. We aren't allowed to participate in the evening sessions. In fact, they force us out of the house at eight o'clock sharp. There are strange things here. You'll see."

"What do they do at a 'session'?"

She shrugged and glanced anxiously at her watch. "I never saw one. Hey, I gotta get back. Yumi times our breaks."

"I'll put in a word with Mrs. Littlefield. Maybe she knows someone who needs a chef."

Her face brightened. "You would do that? You don't even know if I can cook."

I patted her shoulder. She was just a kid trying hard to build a dream. "I think you can cook. Intuition."

"Eat the asparagus tonight. I'm preparing it." She

stepped out of the alcove, checked both ways, then disappeared.

I sniffed longingly at the lingering smell of cigarette smoke and headed back to the house. I tracked down Palk. "Security took my cell phone and car keys. I want to run and get a pack of smokes." Smoking was likely taboo for Heart's Desire employees, even those contracted to someone else.

"If you wish to leave the premises, you must speak with Ms. Brandy Westin." His mouth gleamed with teeth. "Though I doubt that will be allowed. You're here until you're released from duty or you leave with Mrs. Littlefield."

"Where might Ms. Westin be?"

"She might be anywhere." He waved a hand, enjoying himself. "But she isn't available to the likes of you."

Good thing I'd quit smoking, but at least now I knew the score on getting in and out of Heart's Desire. It was, indeed, Hotel California. We could check in but weren't checking out any time soon.

Tinkie was playing gin rummy with Marjorie when I returned to the room with two ham sandwiches. My partner ignored me, which led me to believe she had plenty to reveal once we were alone. I had information for her, too. But first we needed to do some housekeeping or else Mr. Palk would be on to us.

When the card game was over and the sandwiches consumed, Tinkie and I stripped the bed. Dusting was a snap, and it allowed me to check for hidden microphones or spyware. Nada. The room was clean.

Marjorie chatted about her travels as we tidied up.

When the room was shipshape, Tinkie and I sought a break under the shade of a beautiful mimosa tree in the side garden. We settled onto a wooden bench and I told her all I'd learned, and she filled me in on Marjorie's loneliness.

"She's pitiful. I think she really has come here to die. The weight of the guilt and grief is simply too much for her now. She puts up a front when you're around, but she's on the edge, Sarah Booth." Tinkie pushed her glitzed blond hair back from her face. The day was hot, and even in the shade of the tree, we wouldn't be able to endure the temperature much longer. "She wants Tammy to bring the cat here. She won't leave Heart's Desire, but she wants Pluto with her."

"I'm sure the Westin women won't tolerate a cat on the premises." The future looked bleak for Pluto. Being a billionaire kitty was not all it was cracked up to be.

"I tried to make Marjorie understand the smart thing to do would be to leave here, but she simply doesn't comprehend it. She's desperate to connect with Mariam. She'll give up anything."

Tinkie's pensive tone told me the heiress had gotten under her skin. Money couldn't buy happiness. Marjorie was far from happy.

"We need to get in touch with Cece. And Harold." I had a special assignment for Cece. The whole matter of the video was strange. Cece, better than anyone I knew, might be able to make sense of it. Harold was already poking into the history of the Heart's Desire property, and I needed some facts. How did the Westins even find out the property was available? Who sold it?

"And Oscar." Tinkie pushed my shoulder. "And Graf. You know you want to talk to him."

"The guards have our cell phones." I wanted my communication device for more than a conversation. Since I'd become enslaved to a smartphone, I used it for photos, video, recording conversations, and much, much more. "Palk won't let us leave. I tried to go buy a pack of cigarettes."

"Sarah Booth! You've quit!" Tinkie was no supporter of the demon tobacco.

"I have. I just used it as an excuse to test how hard it would be to come and go. Apparently it's impossible. They have the car keys."

"So what are we going to do? Marjorie told me when Harold called her, they brought a phone to her room."

"Find a phone. I checked as much of the house as I could, and I didn't see a single telephone. Surely someone here has a cell phone." Palk, Yumi—someone—had to place orders to vendors. A computer would do as well, but I hadn't noticed one of those, either.

"We'll keep our eyes open for a way to communicate with the outside world," Tinkie said. "Tonight, Sherry is conducting a séance to connect with Mariam."

"Marjorie has to demand that we be there to help her."

Tinkie's chin lifted. Her smile was slow, but it chased away her gloominess. "That's why I let her win at the card game. She's eating out of my hand now. She'll finagle us a pass into the big house tonight."

For the first time I worried Marjorie's health was at risk as we descended the staircase to the foyer. Tinkie and I flanked Marjorie, who stumbled once on the stairs and seemed to almost faint.

When we grabbed her, she drew away from us and insisted that we continue to the "spirit room."

This was a part of the house I hadn't been able to explore, because of Palk's vigilance. The butler popped out from behind doors and shadows whenever I set a foot outside Marjorie's suite.

We passed the library and turned down a long hall. Palk opened a heavy door and we descended stairs to a subterranean level lit by flickering torches. Electronic torches, I noted, but the effect made me feel I'd walked backwards in time.

At last we entered a room lit by at least six dozen candles. The flames, unwavering, blazed along every surface. Mirrors created the illusion of a room extending far into the distance. I could make out hulking pieces of furniture, what I'd seen described as spirit cabinets in my research, but the room was so dark, any number of tricks could have been hidden. This area would require a thorough search with a good flashlight.

If there were windows, they were covered. I focused on the large round table in the center of the room where five people sat. One empty chair remained.

Sherry Westin held the midnight position, and her mother claimed six. Sherry was a tall woman, her pale skin flawless in the candlelight. Red curls framed her face and she wore heavy eye shadow and bright red lipstick. As the young Texaco mart employee had said, she was beautiful. And sad.

Her mother, Brandy, was average build with brown hair and light eyes, but what caught my attention was the hard intelligence shining in the pale depths. She was smart. Very smart. And I suspected she could be ruthless, if required.

To Sherry's right was Roger Addleson, the CEO of a mining company, and, based on Amanda's description, his wife, Shimmer. The delicate blond woman across the table had to be Amaryllis. Every guest wore expensive clothes and jewelry.

Marjorie took the empty seat at the table and Palk pointed to a far wall where Tinkie and I were to stand. No chairs for the hired help. I expected the butler to join us, but instead he whispered to Brandy and left the room. The door shut with a solid thud.

"Thank you all for participating," Sherry began immediately. Her voice was low, husky, almost as if she'd been crying. "We've come to join our energetic forces to pierce the veil between this world and the next. Let me assure you, spirits do exist. They're constantly around us. Some are sad; some are happy. Others are angry. My work allows me to communicate with the dead. My intention is to help them resolve the issues that hold them here, bound to this dimension, so they can be free to transcend into their next life."

Sherry's voice settled into a smooth, almost hypnotic cadence. I found myself relaxing, trusting. Tinkie, on the other hand, was jumpy as a cat at a dog show. She kept flexing and contracting her body.

Sherry continued, "Marjorie Littlefield has asked me to help her communicate with the spirit of her departed daughter, Mariam. Shimmer Addleson wishes to communicate with Empress Joséphine, and Amaryllis Dill wishes to speak with a recently departed friend. I've explained I can't call up spirits as a certainty. I can only invite them to appear. Some are willing, others are not, but I have agreed to try. To do so, I will require the help of everyone here." She paused dramatically and cast her gaze on Tinkie. "I sense a nonbeliever."

Now I saw how she meant to get us out of the room. Not even Marjorie would defend us if Sherry said Mariam wouldn't appear as long as we were present.

Sherry rose and came toward us. "You are Mrs. Littlefield's personal maids, yet you stand between her and her desire to speak with her daughter."

"No," Tinkie said softly. "We want only the best for Mrs. Littlefield. She's been very good to us."

Sherry seemed to sniff the air around Tinkie. She turned to me. "You doubt my abilities?"

"I want Mrs. Littlefield to find peace." I could say that without lying. I feared Sherry could smell a lie. "Mrs. Littlefield has been feeling weak. We're only here to assist her. We have no interest in impeding her wishes."

"If I detect that you're disrupting the evening, you'll be dismissed from the room."

We both nodded, and Sherry returned to the table. I wondered how much of that was drama and how much was truly her psychic abilities that showed we were there with ulterior motives.

Sherry's hands skimmed the contours of her body—but not touching—several times, and then she shook them as if casting off ants. She smiled at everyone around the table. "My energy is clear and we can begin."

The air in the room shifted. I couldn't put my finger on it, and I was used to the sudden appearance of my own personal apparition, but this was different. Tinkie edged closer to me, and I knew she felt it, too.

"Lay your hands flat on the table," Sherry directed. "Mine are visible to you all, as are Mother's. I want you to relax. Let go of all your thoughts and desires. Can you do that?"

Marjorie inhaled sharply through her mouth, but she agreed.

"Watch Sherry," I whispered to Tinkie. I would keep my eye on Brandy. If something strange happened, I wanted to be able to detect how the Westins were manipulating it. Of course, Palk could be anywhere in the house or even this room. It was likely there was another door.

"Allow your thoughts to calm," Sherry said. "I'm taking you on a journey. You may not all arrive at the same destination. Some of you won't leave this room. But those who do travel into the land beyond the veil will meet with a number of spirits. Just remember, these entities are merely energy. Some of them can be very treacherous, though. They don't always tell the truth. As with any person, they have their own motivations and agendas, so beware."

All around the table, eyes glittered in the flickering firelight.

"I call upon the spirits to assist us. We come in peace and love. We merely wish for communication with our departed loved ones or guidance from behind the veil. I am seeking a child, a beautiful child of ten. Her name is Mariam. Mariam Littlefield. Mariam, your mother wishes to speak with you. There are things that must be settled before she can rest."

"Ask her about Chasley," Marjorie said.

"Please!" Brandy's voice was sharp. "Do not interrupt. Let Sherry communicate if she can. Don't break her concentration."

For a long moment, the room was quiet. When Sherry

spoke, her voice was different, lower. "You seek a child named Mariam. I know her. She is afraid to come forward."

"What is she afraid of?" Brandy asked.

"Paper!" Sherry said in that strange, raspy voice. "Give me paper."

Brandy went to a sideboard and opened a drawer. She brought out plain white typing paper and a fistful of pencils. She put them on the table in front of Sherry, who'd gone into a trance with her eyes rolled up in her head.

Brandy forced a pencil into Sherry's hand and put it on the paper. The hand began to move in circles. Spiraling lines filled the page, and Brandy removed it and replaced it with a clean sheet.

"Mariam?" Brandy said. "Is that you?"

The erratic motion of Sherry's hand slowed. A very crooked Y E S was written.

"Your mother is here, Mariam. She misses you. She loves you and wants to talk to you. Will you show yourself?" Brandy kept the paper shifting under Sherry's rotating hand.

"Your mother is ill. She needs to speak with you."

Sherry's hand went nuts. Tinkie and I leaned closer to watch what she was writing. *Mommy!* she wrote. *Mommy! I'm afraid. It's cold.*

Marjorie let out a cry of animal pain. "Mariam! Oh, Mariam! It's my fault. It is. I'm so sorry. Did Chasley harm you?" she asked. "Did he?" She leaped to her feet. "Tell me what happened that day!"

Sherry slumped sideways. She would have fallen from her chair had Brandy not caught her.

"We're done for the evening," Brandy said as she supported her daughter. "Palk! Palk! Hurry. I need help."

"I have to talk with Mariam." Marjorie remained frozen beside her chair. "I'm sorry I stood up."

Brandy rounded on her. "You've endangered my daughter. She was in a deep trance, and you broke the circle. Do you realize you could have seriously injured her?"

"I'm so sorry," Marjorie said. Tears dripped down her cheeks. "My baby is scared and cold. And it's my fault!" She pushed past Tinkie and me and ran out of the room.

Tinkie and I hurried upstairs after her.

"Sherry is a very accomplished hypnotist," I said. "She's dangerously talented. We have to be careful."

6

Tinkie and I soaked washcloths in ice water to make cold compresses for Marjorie's forehead. She was in a state, and misery held her in a firm grip. If she hadn't been near suicide when she arrived, she was now.

I buttonholed Tinkie and whispered, "We need Doc Sawyer."

"He doesn't do house calls." Tinkie barely pulled her attention away from Marjorie to answer me. She indicated she needed a fresh cloth and I went to the bathroom to fetch it. I'd dumped ice in the bathroom sink and had several hand towels chilling.

Marjorie reclined on the chaise and Tinkie sat beside her. I handed Tinkie the compress and continued pacing. Nursing wasn't one of my talents.

Tinkie smoothed Marjorie's hair back from her forehead. The poor woman trembled, and her skin flushed and then went pale in repeating cycles. A pulse throbbed in her throat. I feared for her health.

"Call Doc. This is serious. He hasn't left the ER in years, but beg him." Tinkie was really worried.

"He left Sunflower County to take care of you."

"You're right." She returned to the stricken woman and picked up her limp hand. "We're calling a doctor, Marjorie. He's a friend. He'll be able to help you."

Marjorie moaned and shook her head. "No, no doctor. I just want to die."

There it was, the thing we'd come here to prevent. While Tinkie tried to comfort her, I went in search of Palk. I meant to have a phone. He was lurking at the bottom of the stairs like a hungry rat with cheese in his sights.

"Mrs. Westin wishes to speak with Mrs. Littlefield. Rising from the table during a session is *not* permitted. She's highly upset—"

"That's not my concern," I interrupted. "Mrs. Littlefield is ill. She needs a doctor. I'm calling Doc Sawyer at the Sunflower County Hospital and asking him to come here or send an ambulance. I'm afraid if Mrs. Littlefield doesn't calm down, she'll have a stroke."

Palk scurried away like a cockroach. I followed behind him on my rubber-soled shoes. He went into the library and pulled a phone from the drawer of a library table. He took it to a wall jack behind a curtain and plugged it in. At least I knew where the phone was now.

"Just remember, this is an emergency. Phones are off-limits to the staff."

I made the call to Doc, who was strangely willing to

come to Heart's Desire. "I've had a yen to visit that place," he said.

"You knew about it?" I couldn't ask many questions; Palk was watching me.

"I've heard rumors about a think tank in the Delta," Doc said. "Mrs. Littlefield is the first person I've known who actually bought into the concept, but there's been talk. To be honest, I thought it was a bunch of hooey. You'd be surprised at the things a doctor hears in confidence."

"Mrs. Littlefield is very ill. Tinkie's with her. Please hurry."

"Is Tinkie involved with Heart's Desire?" Doc was surprised.

"No, we're maids for Mrs. Littlefield."

There was a pause and I could imagine Doc's startled expression. "This will require a face-to-face explanation. I'm on my way."

"Thank you." I replaced the receiver and Palk put away the phone.

"Is he coming?" Palk asked.

"He said he didn't make house calls, but when I told him it was Marjorie Littlefield, he agreed. They're old friends, I gather." I started upstairs. "Send him up as soon as he arrives." It felt good to order the butler around for a change.

Without waiting for an answer, I ran up the stairs and back to Marjorie's suite. Tinkie had calmed her a little, but when she saw me, she became agitated again.

"You should go outside for a while," Tinkie said to me. She wasn't being mean, but she was worried. We'd come to help Marjorie and now she was more upset than ever. My anxiousness wasn't helping.

I eased from the room and stood for a while outside the door. Then I decided to snoop. Palk had taken a powder and for the first time since arriving at Heart's Desire, I had some leeway to poke around.

Taking care not to make any noise, I slipped around the upstairs hallway, pausing outside doors and listening. Roger and Shimmer bickered in the suite next to Marjorie's. The Ginger Suite, signified by a cinnamon color. The heated conversation and raised voices were audible, but even when I put my ear against the door, I couldn't make out what they were fighting about. Whatever it was, Shimmer was greatly upset.

The adjacent suite was occupied by Amaryllis Dill. Her room was still as a tomb, but her name was beneath the yellow insignia on her door. I was about to investigate further when I heard someone on the stairs. Moving quickly, I returned to my post outside Marjorie's door, and just in time. Brandy Westin barreled toward me like a bulldozer.

"I want a word with your employer." Her voice carried authority. "I've been waiting, and I don't like to wait. What are you doing out in the hall?"

"Doc Sawyer is on the way here. Mrs. Littlefield is very ill."

"A doctor wouldn't be necessary if she hadn't acted like a fool."

I didn't like Brandy. Her features were pretty, a classic Joan Crawford look, but her expression was hard. I guessed her age to be early fifties, which meant she'd been twenty or younger when Sherry was born. I wondered where Mr. Westin went—or if there had ever been a Mr. Westin.

She walked around me like I was meat in a shop window. "It was a mistake to allow you and Mrs. Jones in here. You've encouraged an old woman in her eccentricities."

I didn't want this fight now, but I wasn't backing down. "I'm sure Mrs. Littlefield will agree it was a mistake for all of us to come to Heart's Desire. She should go home. Tinkie and I will be happy to pack her things after the doctor leaves. I believe he'll take her to the hospital. Her blood pressure is off the charts."

Something shifted in Brandy's expression. "I don't believe she's ill enough to require hospitalization. We can keep her quiet here."

My aim had been true. "As I said, my only concern is her welfare and comfort. If she wants us to leave, or if she wants to return home, which is my recommendation, I'll make it happen. She was very upset."

"She's here to speak with her daughter. She won't invest anything until she settles the matter. Sherry can't help her if she's going to disrupt—"

The doorbell stopped her. She rushed downstairs. Moments later, black bag in hand, Doc hurried up the steps. I drew my finger across my lips in the grade-school signal for silence, and he brushed past me as though we were strangers.

Tinkie joined me in the hallway while he examined Mrs. Littlefield. Brandy waited with us, casting killing glares as the minutes stretched into half an hour.

At last the door opened, and Doc Sawyer beckoned us inside. When Brandy tried to follow, he closed the door in her face. Doc drew us to a far corner of the room where he could speak—emphatically—and not upset his patient.

"What in tarnation are you two involved in now?" Doc's white hair was even more unkempt than usual.

A deep line between his eyebrows told me how worried he was. Doc had been the family physician for both the Delaneys and the Bellcases. He'd known me and Tinkie since we were born, and he'd tended both of us through some difficult and dangerous cases.

"We're trying to take care of Mrs. Littlefield. We're afraid for her life," I said, which wasn't much of an exaggeration.

"So you're here, in this very strange establishment, pretending to be her personal maids?"

"Correct." Tinkie put her hand on Doc's arm. "We think the Westins are after her money."

Doc waved the idea away. "It's not her money I'm concerned about, it's her life. Her blood pressure was 210 over 180. That's far too high. I gave her something to calm her. She was babbling about the ghost of her daughter appearing during a séance." He glared at me. "The child has been dead for years. What are you involved in, Sarah Booth? Marjorie is in no condition to be tortured, and frankly, I'm surprised you would play on the emotions of a desperate woman."

"I agree with you. She needs to go home."

"You all three need to clear out of here."

I didn't argue. "We're trying to convince her to go home. That's why we came, as her maids, to protect her. But she won't budge. She's convinced Sherry Westin can reconnect her with the spirit of her dead child."

"Hogwash!" Doc's hand chopped the air. "No wonder she's in a state. And you two! In it up to your ears again. Honestly." Doc was a little overprotective.

"I know you're aggravated with us, but we need a favor. Can you deliver a message to Cece?"

"I'm not certain I should help you. If you get hurt—"

"We're maids, not CIA operatives. No one will be hurt, but I need Cece to look up Roger Addleson and his wife, Shimmer, from West Virginia, and a woman named Amaryllis Dill. I don't have any way to snap a photo, because they took our cell phones. Just ask Cece to do the best she can. I need their backgrounds."

Doc went back to the chaise where Marjorie reclined and checked her blood pressure again. When he returned, he was relieved. "She's relaxing, thank goodness. This situation smacks of trouble, Sarah Booth. They took your cell phones? You're virtual prisoners in a house where the owners claim to speak with dead spirits."

"We're only keeping an eye on Marjorie." Tinkie had a belligerent tone in her voice. "Doc, Oscar and Graf are already riding us. Please don't. If we leave Marjorie here alone, I'm not sure what will happen to her. She's depressed already and says she wants to die. The Westins may oblige, if they figure out how to get her money signed over to them."

"Okay." He rubbed his forehead. "Her health is fragile. She told me she didn't want to live. This is a delicate predicament."

"She feels guilty about Mariam's death. Do you know anything about the circumstances?" I asked.

"I knew Marjorie when she was a very young woman. Vibrant, sensual—I hardly recognize her tonight. I'm sure you know the story of her marriage to Ramón Salazar. From all indications, it was a happy union. Marjorie embraced the city's society, and her husband's business boomed. Marjorie was always a woman people gravitated to. She loved parties and fun and entertainment. It hurts me to see her like this, an old woman broken by her losses."

"She thinks Chasley deliberately killed his sister."

Doc stopped, his eyebrows arching. "I see. That explains a lot. No wonder she's lost the will to live. But why now? Mariam has been dead for years." His eyebrows drew together. "When the little girl drowned, I sent her several notes and flowers, but I didn't visit her. I should have. I wasn't a very good friend. So this is the hold the Westins have on her. She believes they'll tell her if Chasley is a murderer."

"She's being manipulated, Doc." I told him about the video. "Will you help us?"

He sighed. "Against my better judgment. I'll send word to Cece. And Coleman. I'm sure our sheriff can find a reason to pay a visit to Heart's Desire."

"Ask him to bring me a cell phone," I said. I figured not even Palk would have the balls to try to take a sheriff's cell phone.

"And how will she relay the information she gathers to you?" Doc asked.

"She needs to interview the Westin women. If she can get inside, she can find a way to leave us a packet with the information. Also, I think Madam Tomeeka needs to bring Marjorie her cat. She misses Pluto. I think the feline would help her attitude a lot." The cat would give Marjorie a reason to live.

"Okay." Doc wasn't 100 percent convinced, but he was going to help us.

He checked his patient one more time and spent ten minutes lecturing her on the importance of remaining calm. "A stroke could leave you paralyzed. At the mercy of those two." He gestured at us. "I urge you to go home and leave this place, but if you won't, then you're to mind Mrs. Richmond."

What about me? I wanted to ask, but I knew better. Tinkie was more practical, and she had a way of making Marjorie behave without coming across as bossy.

When Marjorie had given her word, he motioned me to the door. "Watch yourselves. Something's not right here. I don't know what the Westins are up to, but it doesn't bode well for Marjorie. She's completely vulnerable to whatever foolishness they show her at one of those séances."

"As soon as we convince Marjorie to vacate, we'll blow this popsicle stand," I promised him.

He left and I heard him speaking with someone, presumably Brandy, outside the door. In a few moments, Brandy knocked. Marjorie was dozing on the chaise.

"I need a word with Marjorie. Now." Brandy tried to brush past me, but I blocked her.

"No can do," I said. "She's resting. Doctor's orders."

"I believe you and Mrs. Jones have upset Mrs. Littlefield. I'll speak with her tomorrow about dismissing you both." Brandy studied the suite as if she thought I might be harboring illegal drugs, aliens, or Chippendales dancers.

"Good luck with that," I said. "And just so you know, her cat, Pluto, will be arriving. Let the guards know that Tammy Odom will drive the cat here."

"We don't allow pets."

"Fine by me." I motioned to Tinkie. "Get the bags. We're going home. Mrs. Littlefield won't stay without her cat. I've researched other mediums who can bring Mrs. Littlefield the closure she seeks. You and Sherry aren't the only game in town."

Tinkie shot me a look of concern, but I ignored her. I'd decided to play hardball with Brandy. It was time for some pushback.

Brandy's lip curled in distaste. "Keep the creature in her suite of rooms, and I will have the area professionally cleaned and billed to Marjorie's account when she departs." She walked to the door and pivoted. "I don't know who you two are, but I intend to find out. You aren't maids."

"I'm not a maid, I'm a paid companion," Tinkie said.

I couldn't believe it. She'd elevated herself from maid to Mistress of Manderley in one sentence.

Brandy was unimpressed. "Chasley has expressed concerns about you two. He believes you intend to worm your way into his mother's confidence and then rob her blind."

"Chasley would know all about such scams, wouldn't he?" I smiled slow and wide. "I'm glad to know he's been talking with you, Ms. Westin." It was a dangerous game I played. Behind me, I could feel Tinkie tense.

"Have a good evening." Brandy stepped into the hall. "Make sure to lock the door behind you, Miss Booth. I wouldn't want anything bad to happen to any of my guests." Her tone made it clear she wished us the exact opposite.

7

Marjorie was comatose by the time Tinkie and I shut the door—and locked it. We found pillows and blankets and made a bed on the foldout sofa in the sitting room. Before I could say Jack Sprat, Tinkie was stretched out, her eyelids fluttering, a victim of total exhaustion.

I, unfortunately, was wide awake. For at least an hour I sat at the window staring into the star-studded night. Heart's Desire was isolated. There was no question.

My imagination worked overtime, populating my brain with questions. Were the Westin women luring in the rich and doing away with them? Gruesome images of corpses walled into the house or buried in the woods popped into my mind. Too much bad television, I chided myself.

I checked on Tinkie and Marjorie. They were sound asleep. I had to get a grip on my thoughts and emotions and rest as well. I'd be worse than useless in the morning if I didn't.

Just as I was about to step out of my khakis, I heard something outside the door. I froze, listening. I couldn't be certain, but it sounded like someone tiptoeing up and down the hall. Someone creeping. Was it Brandy, spying on us? Or another guest? This might be a great opportunity to "chat."

Moving stealthily like a cat, I cracked the door enough to peer out. My range was limited, but I didn't want to open the door wider. So I listened.

Footsteps.

Slipping out the door, I stood a moment in the darkened hallway and let my eyes adjust to the interior darkness. The hallway was empty in both directions. Yet I'd definitely heard a noise. At the landing, I checked the floor below me. Again, I found only emptiness.

"Oh, my goodness, another body in Cabot Cove."

The voice behind me was cultured and musical—enough so that I didn't jump out of my skin. I spun to find Jitty, pushing a bicycle and wearing pearls, right behind me.

"You are a menace! Dammit! You could have scared me so badly, I fell down the stairs and broke my neck. And then where would you be with no Delaney heir?" It's hard to be emphatic in a whisper, but I managed.

"Even as a child you were prone to exaggeration." She fingered the pearls.

"What are you doing here pretending to be Angela Lansbury acting like Jessica Fletcher?" First Nancy Drew, now the sleuth of Cabot Cove! I could see nothing but trouble in my future. Jitty, when lurking on the grounds of Dahlia House, gave me plenty of grief. Now she was on the loose and in the guise of female detectives—this could only bode ill.

"We need a good television show like *Murder, She Wrote*. All of that *CSI* stuff—" She waved a hand in dismissal and I wondered how long she'd practiced that move in front of a mirror. She had Lansbury's mannerisms down to a T, even the swanlike arch of her neck. I was impressed despite myself.

"What are you doing here?"

"I thought you might need a bit of help."

Jitty never helped me with cases. My instant response was wariness. "Help, how?"

"Don't you want to know about the spirits hanging out at Heart's Desire?"

"Yes." I couldn't believe it. Jitty meant to be helpful. Normally, she harangued me about personal matters. "Are there spirits? What did I see tonight in the session? Was it . . . spirits? Can Sherry really communicate with the dead?" I wanted just a moment of time with my mother or father.

Jitty leaned against the staircase railing. "You know you're sensitive to the spirit world, don't you?"

The question was so matter-of-fact that I straightened my shoulders and faced her squarely. "That isn't true. I see you, but you're a family haint. You're part of Dahlia House." I didn't want to commune with other ghosts. No, sir. Absolutely not. Seeing dead people was *not* a talent I cared to develop.

"Rejecting a gift can bring consequences." Jitty's eyebrows rose, and I thought of the amateur sleuth she impersonated.

"I'm not rejecting it, I'm studying on it."

She laughed, and it was pure Jitty. "How many times did your aunt Loulane say she was 'studyin'' on' an issue? She generally meant no."

I couldn't argue Jitty's point. "I don't think I'm sensitive and I don't think Sherry is a medium."

"Automatic writing is easy to emulate," Jitty said. "Lots of tricks of the trade for spiritualists who aren't on the up-and-up."

I slapped my forehead. "I need to check out that séance room."

"Wait until tomorrow. Then find a good excuse to be down there. Brandy Westin isn't keen on having you in the house, and if you traipse off snoopin' tonight, you might set off an alarm."

Brandy wanted a reason to jettison me and Tinkie, and I had no intention of pushing her hot buttons. "Jitty, are you positive Mariam didn't communicate with Sherry? That the whole thing was pretend?"

She took a step closer to me. "What is real, Sarah Booth? Am I real? Reality is perception, and each person's world is real to them."

She had me there, and on that note she started to dissipate. "You came a long way just to hand me another riddle." I was aggravated by the way she'd pop in and out and leave me more confused.

"Riddles are seldom about the answer." Her voice faded to a whisper and she was gone with a tiny snap and crackle.

The day broke with a golden sunrise and temperatures in the eighties. The humidity was almost tangible. It was going to be a scorcher. Which exactly matched my temper. Sleeping on the sofa with Tinkie wasn't necessarily a hardship—if I'd been able to catch some shut-eye. Instead, I'd spent the entire night running through riddles and scenarios and ending up nowhere.

"You look like hell," Tinkie said as she yawned and stretched.

"Fine for you to say. You were so busy sawing logs, you missed the fact I was up all night."

"Guilty conscience?" she teased.

"Overactive brain." I discovered Marjorie was awake and ready for coffee.

Tinkie hurried from the suite in her pajamas before I could stop her. Palk would have a major heart attack when he viewed her purple Barney slippers scuffling across the parquet floor. Apoplectic would be his next condition. Tinkie could handle him, though.

Marjorie seemed better today. Doc's visit and whatever he gave her to calm her blood pressure had been effective. She caught the hem of my shirt as I walked by. "Sarah Booth, we really must talk. I know you don't want to, but I insist."

Marjorie threw back the blanket and sat up. "Do you think that was my daughter last night?"

I'd hoped to avoid this conversation, but it was inevitable. I sat down beside her. "I don't know. Automatic writing is easy to fake."

"But how would Sherry know I blamed myself for Mariam's death?" Her smile was so damn wistful, a lump rose in my throat. I knew what it was to miss someone who would never return. And Marjorie's loss was coupled with a terrible guilt. Justified or not, she felt it.

She stood up. For all of the fact she'd begun to act

like an eighty-year-old woman on the brink of death, she was in great shape. Petite, agile, she walked easily across the room, and from behind, she could pass for forty or younger.

After she'd brushed her teeth, she returned to the chaise and sat beside me. "I'm not a fool and I'm not a sentimentalist. I want the truth about Chasley. I've pretended for a long time my life was worth living. Inside, though, there is this terrible pain." A hand went to her heart. "The weight of guilt is too heavy. If I can't resolve this, I don't want to live."

"You aren't a fool, but you are acting out of pain. You're vulnerable to unscrupulous people."

When she smiled, her light brown eyes filled with an inner spark. "I don't believe any of this foolishness about being part of an elite mind bank gathering at Heart's Desire to lead the world. All I have to do is invest a lot of money. Don't worry. I've sat in on their planning sessions, because it's expected. But I have no intention of squandering money. I don't want to control the globe. I can't even manage my own life."

"I'm relieved." And I wasn't fibbing. The appeal to ego is difficult to resist. Great leaders had been brought to the brink of ruin by yes-men. Only the truly strongest personalities could resist the insidious delight of ego-stroking.

"Sherry and Brandy are very special women."

Here was a chance. "You know they ran a brothel in New Orleans."

"I do." She didn't flinch. "Brandy and Sherry had a lot of pull in New Orleans in their day. I knew them in the '90s. When I was married to the arms dealer. I often sent clients to them for entertainment. Men who enjoy big and powerful guns often enjoy pliant women."

Marjorie was certainly not provincial in her outlook on the flesh trade. My respect for her notched up. "Do you really believe the Westins can help you connect with Mariam? She's been gone over thirty years."

She smoothed the coverlet she'd thrown over the chaise. "I know it sounds ridiculous. At times I realize I'm grasping at straws." She patted my hand. "You're young, Sarah Booth. Each year you live will bring choices, and some of those will lead to disaster. The day I sent Mariam out the door with Chasley—" She turned away to compose herself.

"You had no idea anything bad would happen. You can't blame yourself. No mother can be with a child every moment. A child would suffocate."

When she met my gaze, she was completely calm. "I knew something was wrong with Chasley. I knew it. But my husband needed my help. We were on the brink of pushing his business into a global concern, and it was so important to him, to his ego." Her voice lowered. "I sent Mariam out of the house because I didn't want to be bothered with her for an afternoon. I had to meet with the florist and the caterers. I had to prepare for a *party*." The last word was spoken with such savage fury, I recoiled before I could stop myself.

"You were helping your husband. I'm sure Mariam wanted to go to the docks with Chasley. The whole thing had to be an accident."

Tinkie entered with a tray of coffee, juice, and toast. She had service for three, and I wondered how Palk had reacted to this latest mutiny of his authority, but I didn't interrupt Marjorie to ask.

Marjorie took the cup Tinkie offered. "I've fought every day to believe Mariam's death was unavoidable. An accident. A terrible tragedy. Chasley said she fell off the dock and he tried to save her, but he wasn't even wet. The police brought him home and he said, 'Mother, Mariam fell in the river and drowned.'" She paused, seemingly lost in the memory. "His clothes were dry. He was always such a neat boy. His pants were still creased. He told me and then went up to his room. It was as if he told me he'd lost his raincoat."

The scene as she described it was surely a ticket to her nightly hell. Could Chasley, even as a boy of fifteen, be so totally deadened that he had no reaction to his sister's death—a death he'd likely witnessed? If not more.

"What did the police report say about Mariam's death?" Tinkie asked.

"It was ruled accidental," Marjorie said. "To be honest, I don't think they investigated. Mariam was ten. She fell into the river, and she couldn't get out. Chasley said he ran to the warehouses for help, but he couldn't find anyone. He found a pay phone and called 911."

The story sounded plausible. He was, after all, a boy of fifteen. "But you felt Chasley should have done more?"

"He was on the swim team of his high school. He was an excellent swimmer. Why didn't he jump in and try to save his sister?"

Tinkie's troubled expression reflected my own. It was a good question, but how many fifteen-year-olds would have the presence of mind to jump into the Mississippi River to save another child?

"What did Chasley say?" I asked gently.

"By the time he returned to the docks and thought to try to swim out to help her, he couldn't see her. He called and called, but she never answered. They found her body downriver."

"Could Mariam swim?" Tinkie asked.

Tears fell from Marjorie's eyes, but she didn't bother to wipe them away. "No, she'd never learned. She was terrified of water. I tried three summers in a row to en-roll her in swimming lessons, but she hated it. So I didn't make her learn. Yet I let her go to the docks with her brother because I had a party to plan. A party."

Tinkie put her arms around Marjorie and simply held her. I sat like a bump on a log, unable to say or do anything to alleviate Marjorie's pain.

A knock broke the silence in the room. When I answered it, I found Palk standing at attention.

"Please have the dirty linens to the laundry by nine," he said.

"And the laundry is where?"

"The washing machines are in the basement. Stella comes in at six and washes, dries, and irons the sheets."

"And what about Mrs. Littlefield's personal items?"

His smile was malicious. "Those are your province, Miss Booth. Since you are here eating the food, you will attend to all your mistress's needs."

"Absolutely. And since you didn't ask, she's feeling much better today." I closed the door.

"That man has a broomstick up his behind," Tinkie said.

To my surprise, Marjorie laughed. "He is overbearing," she agreed. "I had a lovely butler when I was married to my third husband. He was gracious to everyone, and managed the household with kindness. After he retired, I made sure he was well taken care of."

The topic had turned away from talk of Mariam, and

I was glad. Marjorie's complexion was pink and rosy, but I worried about her. "I think you should join the others for lunch today," I suggested. "It isn't good to stay here in your room. And later, I hope Madam Tomeeka will show up with Pluto."

"I've missed him!" She opened the closet doors wide, displaying a massive wardrobe. "In that case, let me get dressed. Perhaps we could take a stroll around the gardens. I've been told they're lovely."

Tinkie gave me a knowing wink. We'd accomplished one thing—getting Marjorie to leave her room. Fresh air and exercise would do wonders for her. Pluto's arrival would be another strong tie to this reality.

While Tinkie escorted Marjorie on a walk in the garden, I stripped the sheets and hauled them down to the laundry. Stella, a middle-aged woman from a crossroads community west of Layland, eyed me with open curiosity.

"You the personal maid of Mrs. Littlefield." She snorted. "Right. I'll bet Palk's fit to be tied."

"What makes you say that?" I took a seat on a washing machine—one of four. Stella had a professional ironing board, several steam irons, a pressing machine, and a steamer for delicate fabrics. She worked as she talked.

"Even a blind fool can see you aren't a maid. Now the question is, what, exactly, are you?" From a refrigerator, she brought out starched shirts monogrammed with an *R.A.* Roger Addleson. Using an old Coke bottle with a corked sprinkler, she dampened the frozen shirt and spread it out on the board. She picked up a heavy iron with an arm defined by muscle. The wrinkles flew out of the shirt like magic.

"I'm here to protect Mrs. Littlefield." But I didn't

want to talk about me. "What do you know about the room down the hallway—?"

"I know about it. That's where they hold their spirit sessions. Palk told me never to open the door." She didn't miss a lick with the iron. "I don't cotton to calling up dead things. No tellin' which ones are gonna answer."

I could appreciate her attitude. "So you've never been inside the room?"

"Nope. And that's not gonna change."

"What's the story on Sherry Westin? Can she really communicate with the dead?"

"That's the rumor." She finished the shirt, put it on a hanger, and picked up the next one. I loved the sound of the sprinkled water hitting the cold starched shirt. When I was a child, my mother's friend Carrie would iron in our kitchen. I'd almost forgotten the sounds and smells of a hot iron on starched cloth.

"Do you think the Westins are on the up-and-up?"

She put down the iron. "Marjorie Littlefield didn't get rich by bein' a fool. I wouldn't lose a wink of sleep on her concerns. Rich folks know how to protect their assets. They can do that when they can't do nothin' else."

She'd managed to evade my question, which was aggravating. Interesting but aggravating. I was about to ask another, but the washing machine stopped. Stella signaled me off. I slid to the ground and she transferred the wet sheets to the dryer.

"Are there any other locals working at Heart's Desire?"

"You sure are a nosy girl." She pushed the iron over a white oxford cloth shirt. "You know the old sayin' about curiosity killin' the cat?" She pointed the iron at me.

"Some things are best left alone. Things in this house don't like a ruckus."

"Things? What do you mean?"

She bent over the ironing board, refusing even to acknowledge my question.

"Stella, what things? Like spirits? Or—?"

"I've said all I'm sayin'. Stay out of the spirit room. Folks around here aren't what they seem. Mind your own business and get on the other side of the gate as soon as you can. And don't go draggin' me into trouble I don't need."

"Nice chatting with you," I said as I eased toward the exit.

Stella only mumbled to herself, and I thought I heard "and good-bye to you, too, nosy girl."

The hallway was long and narrow. The basement's configuration defied me. There should be more rooms, but I couldn't find them. As I cogitated on the dimensions, movement at the end of the hallway was like a punch in my gut. A moment before, the hall had been empty. Now, though, a figure shifted in the dense shadows.

My first inclination was to run back into the room and hide behind Stella. She would brook no nonsense from a ghost. But I wasn't at Heart's Desire to be a coward. Taking a deep breath, I eased forward. One pace, two, three. Something moved at the very end of the hall right at the door that led to the séance room.

"Who's there?" My voice came out a whisper.

Inching down the hallway, I longed for the flickering sconces that had lighted the way the night before. I'd failed to find the light switch, and now my heart pounded in the dim gloom. My gut screamed at me to head for the stairs and my partner. Tinkie was diminutive but stalwart.

Instead, I moved toward the shadowy door to the séance room.

The door hung open. I would never have such an opportunity again. I slipped inside and felt for a light switch. Of course, nothing would be so simple. Stumbling over furniture, I made my way around the room, my hands groping for some means of illumination. When I found the candles and a lighter, I couldn't believe my luck.

With the help of the candle, I located the light switch in a recessed panel to the right of the door. The overhead lights showed me a large room with three mirrored walls. No other exit.

Massive pieces of furniture—some large enough to hide a grown man—were in two corners. What I found made me smile. High-tech equipment that could record and filter low-level sound filled one cabinet along with a voice distorter. This would yield some unique and very personalized EVP, or electronic voice phenomena. Oh, Tinkie would flip over this!

The equipment appeared pretty simple, and I turned it on. A low, guttural sound made me jump backwards. I gave a shaky laugh at my own spookiness. The white noise grew louder and then dimmed, and beneath the static was a voice. Even with the lights on, my skin danced along my arms in goose bumps. Yet I couldn't walk away. Something held me transfixed.

The garbled voice gained clarity, and I froze, paralyzed by fear. This was a recording, a past event. I couldn't shake the sensation, though, that it had been left for me to hear. But by whom? Mariam or the Westins? Or someone else?

"Mother!"

The word was distinct and clear. "Mother. Beware!"

A low-register laugh followed, as if it came straight from hell.

I hit the Off button on the machine and slammed the cabinet door. Around me the dimness felt menacing. There were dark hangings, dark shadows, darkness all around.

Stella's warning reverberated back to me. She didn't want to talk to the dead, because she wasn't certain who would answer.

Who, or what, had just spoken to me?

I replaced the candle, snapped off the light, and made it to the door. I'd gained the hallway when footsteps descending the stairs warned me someone was coming. Likely Palk, spying around. I pulled myself together and met him at the foot of the stairs.

"Miss Booth," he said with distaste. "Are you doing the laundry or weaving it?"

"Neither," I said sweetly. "I thought I heard a big rat. Turned out it was only you." I brushed past him as I climbed from the basement into the light-flooded main floor.

I made a beeline for Marjorie's suite and pulled Tinkie from the room. When I told her about the recording, she insisted we go back.

"If it's a warning for Marjorie, we have to tell her," she insisted. "I need to hear it."

A minor disturbance in one of the meeting rooms where Brandy lectured on global opportunities claimed Palk's attention, and Tinkie and I used the servants' stairs and descended into the bowels of Heart's Desire.

Palk and the maid used the back stairs to go to the second floor, and I'd heard someone climbing them to the third floor where Brandy and Sherry's apartments were. Tinkie had explored and discovered a door at the top of the back and main stairs that opened only with a keyed code. Entry to the third floor was a mission for the future. Tinkie was intent on hearing the recording in the spirit room. She literally dragged me to the lower floor and down the corridor.

Once inside, I went straight to the cabinet with the recording equipment. I played back the CD.

"There's nothing but static," Tinkie said after a few minutes.

Feeling foolish, I motioned for her to be patient.

The whispering white noise filled the room. Like an old AM radio station when the dial has slipped. Nothing more. We waited for at least five minutes. No creepy childish voice spoke.

"I heard it," I insisted. "A little girl with a harsh voice said, 'Mother. Beware!' Just like that."

"There's nothing on this CD," Tinkie said.

I couldn't explain it. I knew what I'd heard. No one had had time to get into the room and change out the disk or erase it. "I did hear it, Tinkie."

"I don't doubt you," she said. The furrow between her brows deepened. "The spirit has chosen to communicate with you, Sarah Booth. If that was Mariam, and I think it must have been, she delivered her message to you. We have to protect Marjorie."

8

After her investor meeting, Marjorie lunched with the Addlesons and Amaryllis. Doc's medication appeared to have done the trick. She looked healthier than I'd ever seen her as she chatted and laughed.

Using the downtime to full advantage, Tinkie and I checked out the spa. The facilities were exquisite, including skilled massage therapists, mud baths—spacious tubs literally filled with homeopathic mud—saunas, high-end exercise equipment, hot stone treatments, facials, anything a pampered girl could desire.

Tinkie sighed. "My feet are throbbing. I'd kill for a pedicure and a little arch massage."

"Not today." I couldn't shake the sensation I'd touched something dark and sinister in the spirit room. My only ghostly experiences centered on Jitty, who was a family specter. She cared for me in her own way. The voice I'd heard didn't leave me feeling warm or fuzzy. Had Sherry Westin tapped into a malignant spirit?

"If I borrowed Marjorie's periwinkle head wrap and robe, I could slip into that mud bath, put on her soothing mask, and no one would ever know." Tinkie ignored my melancholy mood.

"Except that she's in the dining room. I think Palk would snap onto the fact that there were two Mrs. Littlefields running around the compound." As if I'd conjured him, his voice came to me, ordering the downstairs maids about their work.

Tinkie pointed to a laundry hamper filled with robes, towels, and hair wraps. "Seriously, what's with all this color coordination? I mean, Amaryllis is yellow, Shimmer and Roger are ginger, Marjorie is periwinkle. The color theme is a little . . . juvenile."

"Palk uses the colors to keep count of the linens. He'll know instantly if anyone steals anything and where it was stolen from."

"Sounds like one of his asinine control tactics." Tinkie punched my arm. "Let's grab some lunch. Otherwise we won't have a chance to eat again until tonight."

"No doubt."

The staff ate in a dining room off the kitchen, where a long table had been set for lunch. I lost my appetite when I realized Palk ruled the table much as he ruled the house—with an iron fist. No talking. No pleasantries. No civility. My impulse was to devil him with constant questions, but I decided against it. I had bigger fish to fry.

Amanda shot me a few smiles, but we finished a

delicious grilled tuna salad in silence, Palk at the head of the table and Yumi at the foot. The meal was served buffet style, and when it was over, we took our dishes to the sink in the kitchen.

Palk clapped his hands. "To work." He left the kitchen.

"Asshole," Amanda said under her breath, and several of the maids twittered and rushed to attend their duties. To my surprise, Yumi sauntered over.

"Amanda, be careful with Palk. Don't push him in a corner by talking back to him." Her musical accent softened the criticism in her words. Was she trying to look out for the young cook?

"Yes, ma'am." Amanda kept her gaze on the floor.

"I don't care what you say about Palk. But if you embarrass him in front of the staff, he'll have to fire you."

"I understand." Amanda bobbed her head and hurried away. Yumi didn't move.

"What brings you to the isolated Mississippi backwoods?" Tinkie asked.

"I need a permanent chef's job. I prefer private service over restaurant work. I was hoping to meet some influential people here who required such services."

Her goal was the same as Amanda's. Maybe they had found some common ground. "Any luck so far?" I asked.

"I haven't been here long." She smiled. "And you? Why are you at Heart's Desire?"

The way she asked the question made me wonder if she was on to us. Tinkie fielded a reply. "We're both housewives. Divorced, boring life. Mrs. Littlefield has a glamorous life. We thought it would be fun to see how the other half lived, and the work is easy."

"And is it fun?"

"No. Not really. But Mrs. Littlefield counts on us."

"Living in her suite can't be easy." Yumi's smile revealed perfect white teeth. Somewhere along the line, she'd had expensive cosmetic dental work. "No privacy. No chance to live your own life."

"It's only for a short time," I said. "Besides, there's nothing to do at Heart's Desire. I don't understand why the service staff stays here. Surely on their days off they could go to Jackson or even Memphis."

"The Westins pay well. And the work isn't hard." She hopped up on the counter with ease. "The requirement is to stay on the premises. The Westins want to limit the local gossip about Heart's Desire. There are worse places to work. Everyone here hopes to meet people of influence who can move our careers forward."

Amanda returned with a stack of dishes from the staff dining room and started loading the dishwasher. Yumi leaned forward. "If you have influence with Amanda, talk to her. She has a terrible attitude. She's an adequate chef, but she doesn't understand her place." She jumped to the floor and left the kitchen.

As soon as Yumi was gone, Amanda signaled us to the sink. "I just heard new guests are coming today. Two women. Country music singers. Maybe they'll be my ticket out of here."

"I hope so, Amanda." I encouraged her with a smile.

The luncheon in the dining hall was also breaking up and the staff went into high gear. Tinkie and I carried Marjorie's dishes to the kitchen—her appetite was greatly improved, notching my concern for her down a little more.

As I picked up the crystal, I heard a familiar voice in the parlor. "Dahling! I'm here to interview the wonderful Westin ladies."

I didn't have to see her to know that Cece Dee Falcon had arrived. God bless Doc, he made a fine messenger.

"I haven't been informed of any newspaper interviews." Palk huffed as if an elephant were stepping on his toes. "The Westins would never consent to speak with you."

"But of course they did, dahling," Cece said, concluding with a confident laugh. "For the *Zinnia Dispatch*. I spoke with Sherry Westin before lunch. She realizes she can either talk with me or I'll dig up what I can from their past." Cece had a way of closing on the nut of the issue.

Cece was the society editor at the local newspaper in Zinnia, but she was so much more. Had she chosen to leave the Delta, she could have been the head honcho at any news agency. She had a nose for dirt, and in the process of getting the facts, she took no prisoners. Her beat was society, but she was a fine investigative reporter with connections all over the Southeast.

She'd been born Cecil, but her inner woman had refused to be held back. Cece gave up her masculinity—and her place as heir to the Falcon fortune—but gained so much more. She was her own person and one of the best friends anyone could have.

Tinkie took Marjorie up to her room for a rest, and I peeked around the corner to find Palk backed against the wall in the foyer. Cece swept past him. She wore a tailored suit in muted teal and strappy Manolos. Perched on her head was a wide-brimmed sun hat that cast a shadow over her eyes but revealed her lips, colored a fantastic peach. She carried a briefcase that matched her shoes. Cece was styling.

Thank god Jitty wasn't around or she would compare

me to the fashion goddess and I would never hear the end of it.

"Today is not a good day. New guests are arriving." Palk sniped at Cece's heels, and she totally ignored him.

She entered the dining room, her gaze sweeping over the busy staff, including me. There wasn't a hint that she recognized me. Dang! She was cool as a cucumber.

"Where are Brandy and Sherry?" she asked.

"They're busy." Palk tried to regain control of the situation, but it was a lost cause.

"Perhaps they should un-busy. Tell them I'm here for the interview."

"Madam, you can't barge in here demanding an interview and think people will give way to you. The Westins are very busy. I'll be happy to make an appointment for you in the future."

Cece pointed to her watch. "I have an appointment. Sherry Westin has agreed to an interview. I drove nearly an hour to get here. I'm not coming back. I'll be happy to go to press with what I find with a little digging." She lifted her chin. "Such as the fact they ran a brothel in New Orleans."

Palk blanched. "Please come with me to the parlor. You can wait there while I find Ms. Brandy."

"Find Sherry. If she's about to communicate with the dead, I have a few questions for my grandfather. He was one of the meanest men to ever walk the face of the earth and I've always wanted to know why he was such a bastard."

"I'll get you some refreshments." Palk was all conciliatory. He led Cece toward the front parlor.

Somehow, I had to eavesdrop on this interview, but if

Palk caught me, I'd be neck-deep in hot water. I hid behind the parlor door as Palk settled Cece into a beautiful Victorian chair. Spying on them through a crack in the door, I had to admit that Cece looked like a queen.

"I'll have a maid bring you some iced tea, and I'll find Mrs. Westin," Palk said. Before he could finish his sentence, the doorbell rang again.

"Oh, dear me." He was actually flustered. He all but wrung his hands as he told Cece to wait while he hurried to the door.

"Well, lookie there, a butler," a female voice said. "Now, this is exactly the high-class place my letter promised. I'm Gretchen Waller and this here is my songwriting partner and a fine singer, Miss Lola Monee. We're here because we have special talents and the world needs our help."

I'd listened to plenty of country accents in my day, but Gretchen Waller was country with a healthy dash of cornpone. I hadn't heard such dialect since *Hee Haw* went off the air.

"Miss Waller, Miss Monee, welcome to Heart's Desire. Please come in. I'll send the help to collect your luggage. The Rose Suite is all ready for you. Let me show you where it is so you can refresh yourselves."

They trudged up the stairs behind Palk, and I sprinted into the room for a word with Cece.

"Lord, that man might break in two if he limbered up a little," Cece said. "I'll bet you and Tinkie are making his life a living hell."

"We're trying!" I hugged her tight.

She pulled a manila envelope from her briefcase. "This is delicious! I don't know what's really going on here at

Heart's Desire, but I'll damn well figure it out. I smell a Pulitzer in my future."

"Did you get anything on the Addlesons and Amaryllis?"

"It's in the report. The Addlesons are very wealthy. Amaryllis is a cipher. Sherry and Brandy have progressed from madams in a brothel to hobnobbing with some of the wealthiest people in the nation. It's a damn dazzling performance."

"Sherry Westin may be dangerous. She has real hypnotic power." I wasn't speaking lightly. "Cece, your friend Bert Steele, is he reliable?"

Cece frowned. "Bert's a good guy and extremely talented, but it's odd how he was on my mind because he'd just called me about the Black and Orange Ball. I didn't think about it at first, but he sent you guys to the neighborhood of the Pleasure Zone, where you stumbled on videos conveniently put out on the curb. On those DVDs was an image that may or may not be Marjorie's drowned daughter. That's a lot of happenstance. I need a face-to-face with Bert."

Hearing the string of coincidences from Cece's lips gave me pause. "You think Bert is involved somehow?" Had Tinkie and I been played from the get-go?

"I won't blacken a good man's name without evidence, but let me say I'm investigating it. Long ago, there was talk Bert had fallen in love with Sherry. I heard he had a prize-winning photo of something at the Pleasure Zone, and he never turned it in. To protect Sherry."

"What kind of photo?"

She shook her head. "Rumors were rampant. Sherry and a presidential candidate, Sherry and a dead man. It could have been anything in between. But while the details changed, the gossip that Bert gave up a major career moment because he had feelings for Sherry never died down."

"Did you get anything on the woman who bought the Pleasure Zone?" She'd seemed so friendly. Maybe a little too friendly to a stranger. I'd bought into it without giving it a thought.

"Her name is Annabelle Ralston, retired banking official. She's married to a mystery writer, John Defrane. From California. They lived for five years in Los Angeles, where he consulted on a TV show, and returned to New Orleans about four years ago. Pretty humdrum on the surface, but I'll keep looking."

"Is there any way to tell if Sherry is a real medium or not?"

Cece hesitated. "What I found was conflicting information. More than a few people honestly believe she helped them by contacting dead friends and relatives. The stories were truly spooky, Sarah Booth."

"Could they have been planted by the Westin women?"

"There's the rub. There's no way to verify any of it. The reports are what people allegedly 'saw,' but there are no photographs, no videos. No proof. Speaking of videos, I asked a guy over at Ole Miss to examine the DVD Tammy showed me. My film expert said the image *could have been* manipulated by someone who knew what he was doing. But he pointed out it could also be real. He simply couldn't tell."

Palk's footsteps descended the stairs. I scooted back to my hiding spot with the manila envelope clutched to my chest.

"I apologize for the interruption. Mrs. Westin will be

with you shortly," Palk said. "Sherry can't join you. She has a migraine and is indisposed."

In other words, she was hiding out in the Westins' third-floor lair. Sherry spent most of her time there while Brandy ran the show.

Within a few moments, Brandy was seated across from Cece. My journalist friend played it soft and casual, chatting here and there, circling and circling in a fashion that lulled Brandy. By the time Cece got to the meat of the interview, I was shifting from foot to foot.

"Tell me about your past, Mrs. Westin," she said. "Let's start with Mr. Westin. Where might he be?"

Brandy's laugh rang with the sound of a good-time woman with no complaints. "I ran that bastard off the minute I found out I was pregnant."

"So Westin is a married name?"

"It is not. It's my name. I grew up in the Jackson area. Don't bother looking for grubs under rocks there. Everyone in my family is dead. Natural causes."

Cece didn't miss a beat. "Who is Brandy's father?"

"That information will die with me. He never knew I was pregnant and he won't ever know. Hell, he never even knew my last name, a deliberate oversight on my part. I don't want him sucking at Sherry for the rest of her life. The man is a parasite. The only good thing he ever did was donate sperm, and that wasn't a conscious act."

I had to admire her forthrightness and unwillingness to give up her future for the illusion of a marriage. Except we couldn't trust anything she said.

"How did you discover Sherry has the ability to contact spirits?"

I perked up at this question.

"I moved to the country outside Jackson as soon as

Sherry was born. It was isolated and she didn't have playmates, so at first I thought she was making up imaginary friends. But I figured out pretty quickly it was more than a lonely little girl with a big imagination. Her 'friends' knew things. Things Sherry couldn't have known. They warned her about impending problems and steered her toward solutions no child should know."

"For example?" Cece said.

"We moved to a subdivision with a school nearby when she started first grade. One day, she told one of her playmates to stay away from the road in front of our house. It was a quiet street and a small neighborhood with no through traffic. I heard this myself. Two weeks later, Katie was struck by a car and killed. She was playing hopscotch in the street, a game the children played all the time."

Chills marched along my arms.

Brandy continued in her matter-of-fact tone that only made her statements more powerful. "We were all upset by the tragedy, but when I tried to talk to Sherry, she was distraught. She blamed herself, saying she should have stopped Katie from being in the street. She said the woman told her to keep all the children out of the street. When I asked her what woman, she described her in great detail. No one like that lived in our neighborhood."

Cece cleared her throat. "I see. And you take this to mean Sherry had a communication from a spirit?"

"What would you call it? Premonition?" Brandy's full-bodied laugh rang out. "What, exactly, is a premonition? The dictionary defines it as the warning of an event to come. So who warns? Would you find it easier to believe Sherry can see into the future? Is she a clairvoyant instead of a medium?"

Madam Tomeeka had dreams that foretold future events, or at least hinted at them if we could interpret the symbolism properly. Some dreams revealed the past. But I'd never thought to question where these dreams came from. Were they communications from departed people?

"How often does Sherry see spirits of the dead?"

"Let's just say she's never alone. It wears on her. Makes her puny. Gives her migraines."

"Has she ever been evaluated by a psychiatrist? Or would that interfere with the income stream?"

"I think this interview is over. I don't mind answering questions, but I won't tolerate insinuations my daughter is mentally ill and I'm using her for monetary gain."

"The little girl who was struck by a car. What was her name?"

"Katie Baggins. Evergreen Street, Clinton, Mississippi."

Brandy knew Cece meant to probe the facts and she was giving her all the pertinent details. Which meant either the story was true or Brandy was smart enough to have verified the little girl's death and woven it into the story of Sherry's gift.

"And how will your daughter's abilities help your clients contribute to the world?"

Brandy seemed to give up on the idea of booting Cece out. Judging from her response, she wanted to answer this question.

"Sherry communicates with the dead. Often, these departed spirits desire to see their loved ones and family do well, move forward, protect themselves from the tragedies looming ahead of us. They are also conscious of events from a unique perspective. If they have information or warnings to reveal, they can do so through Sherry.

She's counseled very wealthy men and women. Her financial advice record is eighty-seven percent. I defy you to beat those odds anywhere. By pooling the resources of the people who come to Heart's Desire, we can have a major impact on the market, and thus on the world."

"And you'd control a considerable amount of money. I've noticed your clientele doesn't include poor geniuses. Only multimillionaires. Poor, smart people don't have anything to offer?"

"Grow up," Brandy spoke sharply. "In this country, wealth is power. Not brains. Not good intentions. Money. You want to see more money spent on education or health care for children? Don't send a smart do-gooder to Congress. Send a man with a bag of money. That's how things get done these days."

Brandy stood up. "I intend to use money for influence. I admit it. If I had to trade in horse turds, I'd be trolling for the biggest horses that produced the biggest turds. I'm a realist, Cece Dee Falcon. And I'm not ashamed of it. Here at Heart's Desire, we will make an impact, and we'll do whatever is necessary to make it happen."

"Have you had any impact on national politics?" Cece asked, totally unmoved by Brandy's speech.

"We are funding campaigns for KinderCare for working mothers, and the Heart's Desire fund is sponsoring a national initiative to improve teaching. In the area of policy, Sherry has helped with important decisions. Some of our clients have direct connections to the people who control world politics."

"Is there a place I can verify those claims?" Cece asked.

"Sure. Call Donald Rumsfeld. Or maybe Steve Wynn. Do you really think the concept for Facebook just occurred to Mark Zuckerberg? He had a little help from some departed geniuses." Smug would be a perfect description of her.

Her claims were not only outrageous, but they also couldn't be disproved. And she knew it.

"The world can be changed for the better with social networking. Revolutions are sparked by people's ability to communicate." Brandy's voice grew quieter but more powerful. "Here at Heart's Desire, we are going to change the landscape of this planet for the better. My *clients* have the money, the power, and the intelligence to reshape the policies destroying this planet."

The inclusion of a social consciousness was unexpected. I would have given a lot to see Cece's face.

Footsteps on the parquet floor warned me trouble approached. I stuffed the manila envelope in my pants, pulled my shirt over it, and left my hiding spot. Once in the open, I raced toward the stairs.

"Miss Booth!" Palk's voice rang out.

Caught like a rat in a trap. I executed an about-face with military perfection. "Sir?"

"Your laundry is finished. Please take it up to Mrs. Littlefield and replenish her sheets and towels. The vacuum cleaners and supplies are in the hall closet three doors down from Mrs. Littlefield's room. I expect you to make use of them."

"Sir, yes, sir." I gave him a crisp salute and went for the sheets.

In the dimness of the basement, I retrieved the envelope and pulled out the contents. Cece had done a remarkable job on a bio of Roger Addleson, a man accused of owning the most destructive coal mining company in the nation. If these were the movers and shakers reshaping international policy, I figured the planet was in dire straits.

Addleson advocated mountaintop removal to access coal. Addleson Coal owned numerous mines, including one where fourteen miners had died in a collapse. That same year Addleson Coal abandoned the mine where the tragedy occurred and opened another to the protests of several environmental groups. The company generated record first-quarter profits. Addleson's business practices, while bad for the miners and environment, were very good for his company. He was listed in *Forbes*'s top twenty wealthiest people.

Shimmer, on the other hand, married well. She was born Birdie Mae Black, the daughter of a Newby, Kentucky, Pentecostal minister. She'd legally changed her name, and for that I couldn't blame her. I could just imagine the schoolchildren cawing and flapping their arms behind her back. But Shimmer? Lord. Out of the frying pan and into the fire, as my aunt Loulane would have said.

Shimmer's story was more straightforward. She was a dancer in Las Vegas, performing under the stage name Shimmer Black. She married Roger and began to fulfill her dream of establishing her own perfume line.

According to the numbers Cece dug up, Shimmer Ltd. was financially sound. At least on paper. Roger had dropped a bundle on perfume consultants, marketers, packagers. If the perfume caught on, Shimmer might well be a wealthy woman in her own right. Shimmer had no previous marriages and no children. She was twenty years younger than Roger.

Amaryllis Dill was a bit more interesting. She was a Washington, D.C., dance teacher. She'd been in the Martha Graham troupe for a time, then retired and moved to D.C. to teach. Her clientele were the daughters of the wealthiest and most powerful men and women in the world. While her Dun & Bradstreet might not be rated as high as others, she certainly had money, and more important, she had the ear of wealthy and powerful men. And if she was here, one of those men had loads of money and power. One thing I could say for Brandy—she drew people of influence to her.

The only other thing in the packet was information on Heart's Desire. The house was constructed by Alexander March, a sculptor thought to be mad. He'd drawn up the blueprint and lived there alone for a decade, creating metal and wood sculptures erected in public spaces all over the world, including the Plaza de Armas in Cuzco, Peru; Rynek Główny in Poland; Plaza Hidalgo in Mexico City; and London's Trafalgar Square.

From all accounts, March lived quietly, until the FBI showed up in 1990 looking for Regan Bland, March's agent who had been missing for two weeks. Bland was tracked to the Jackson, Mississippi, airport, and a car rental counter. She'd told her associates she meant to "have it out" with March, who'd failed to appear at a contract negotiation with New York City officials and lost a million-dollar commission.

Regan was never found. She was last seen at the car rental counter at the Jackson airport terminal. The 1990 BMW she'd leased was abandoned off Highway 55 between Jackson and Greenwood. Her bags were in the trunk, but there was no sign of her and no evidence of foul play. The car keys were in the ignition.

When the police questioned March, he told them she'd probably been abducted by aliens. He said she'd had one past encounter with visitors from another solar system and was sterile because of it, which accounted for her bitchy moods and erratic behavior.

But local rumor was that she and March had a big fight, and he'd killed her. The stories varied, but the most popular involved a knife, because March was also a woodworker. Speculation maintained that no body was found because he cooked her and ate her. It was believed that her ghost haunted him and drove him to suicide. He hanged himself from an apple tree on the west lawn.

Regan's skeletal remains were purportedly buried on the grounds. Before the Westins bought the property, built the wall, and installed the gate and guards, local teens invaded the house for make-out sessions and horror dares. Reports of Regan's and March's spirits abounded. Whether the stories were true or not, the house and property remained empty for nearly twenty years. Sherry and Brandy bought it for a song from the New Orleans bank.

Cece's report captured my attention so completely that I heard a strange ticking in the wall behind me before I actually registered it. Lowering the pages, I realized I was cold. Cold as in suddenly freezing. Only a moment before, I'd been warm and damp. Now, when I exhaled, I could see my breath.

I glanced down the hall, knowing whatever I saw would scar me for life.

The door to the laundry room—and Stella's no-nonsense presence—was only twenty-odd feet away, but staying in the basement wasn't an option. My actions weren't rational. I simply reacted. Up the stairs I flew. The sheets would have to wait until Tinkie was with me.

At the main floor, I heard Gretchen and Lola chattering away.

"This place is something else," Gretchen said. I deduced from their voices that they were in the dining room. "I hope that nosy reporter doesn't mess things up for us." She spoke more softly. The acoustics in the dining room filtered her voice right to me.

"Hush!" Lola warned Gretchen. "We're here to connect with the spirit of Kitty Wells and move our career to the next level. That's all anyone should know about us."

"Right," Gretchen said. "I hope they don't ask us to perform. If they learn my muse has abandoned me—"

"Shut it!" Lola said. "Loose lips sink ships."

Holy cow! A country songwriter who spouted maxims like my aunt Loulane. I didn't know if I could stand it. Even better, the duo had an ulterior motive, not to mention I'd appreciate a séance with Kitty Wells.

I had plenty to reveal to Tinkie and Marjorie, and I rushed toward the Periwinkle Suite. Amaryllis Dill came out of her room as I was passing.

"Miss! Miss!" she said. "I want to schedule a massage and a facial in the spa."

I explained I was a private maid. "But I'll be happy to stop by the spa and book your appointments. Is six o'clock good?"

"Perfect. I can miss the cocktail hour. I just don't have a thing to say to any of these people." She fretted the sleeve of her blouse, and her eyes filled with unshed tears. "Have you seen anyone unusual around Heart's Desire?"

"Unusual how?" I could classify everyone there as unusual.

"Like, um, dangerous." She bit her lip. "I mean someone who doesn't belong."

Amaryllis feared someone meant her harm.

"I haven't seen any strangers. Two country music

songwriters arrived." I frowned. "They didn't seem dangerous."

"Oh, of course not." She laughed, but it was more of an uneasy twitter. "I can be so silly sometimes. You know, overactive imagination. Being here, in this house with spirits walking about. It's made me a nervous Nellie."

"Has someone threatened you?" I asked.

She blinked back her tears. "I wish I knew. This man . . . I fell in love. He's very powerful, and now, I don't know what he's capable of." She sucked in air and straightened her shoulders. "And I'm acting like a fool. This house gets to me."

I didn't find her statements amusing, but I knew better than to press her. "I know what you're saying. I thought I saw a ghost down in the basement. Can you imagine that?"

Amaryllis's face dropped into real concern. "Was it a woman? Maybe five-six, a hundred twenty pounds. Pretty with brown hair and brown eyes?"

"No, that wasn't what I saw."

"I've been here three weeks and I still haven't seen Linda—the ghost I need to communicate with. Sherry says she's put out feelers and one of the spirits will locate her and tell her I need to speak with her."

"No doubt." When Amaryllis talked, it was like an assault. She was either hyperactive or scared to the point of bouncing off the walls. I sensed it was the latter.

"I have to know her wreck was an accident. The police ruled it accidental, but—I have to hear it from her."

"I don't mean to pry," I lied, "but why would you think otherwise? Was there something strange about the accident?"

Oddly, the question calmed her. "I think there was."

"Such as?"

"Linda wasn't the kind of person to be out in a bad neighborhood at three in the morning. She grew up in D.C. She knew that was an awful part of town."

"Oh, my! Did anyone know why she was in the area?" I itched to ask solid, specific questions, but if I did, I'd scare Amaryllis away. I had to give this interview the feel of two friends exploring options.

"No one could explain it." Amaryllis trembled visibly.

"So was Linda a friend of yours? Was she into something that would send her into a bad neighborhood?"

"She was a straight arrow. By all accounts, she got out of bed, went to her car, and drove to the southeast area. Something happened. The police speculated it was an attempted carjacking. She sped away, lost control, and ran into an overpass support." She teared up again. "She died at the accident scene. She was all alone."

"Was Linda married?"

Tears spilled down her cheeks as she nodded, and I patted her on the arm in a clumsy attempt to comfort her. "Where was her husband?"

"Asleep." She swallowed, and her face screwed into misery. "In my bed." Her sob echoed down the hallway. And perhaps I'd found Amaryllis's link to power.

I put an arm around her and assisted her into her room. The pale yellow room radiated luxury and comfort. "What do *you* think happened to Linda?" I asked her.

"That's why I'm here. I have to find out if her husband killed her. Lucas has a vile temper."

"If he was in bed with you, he couldn't have killed his wife," I pointed out.

She looked stunned at my suggestion. "He'd never dirty his hands." Her eyebrows drew together. "He'd hire a hit man to do it. And if he gets tired of me, he might kill me, too!" Fear crept over her features. "If he thinks I suspect him, he might kill me, anyway."

"Why are you with this man?" It was not the question that would yield a useful answer, but it was the first thing that popped out of my mouth.

"Because I love him."

"You think he might kill you, but you still love him?" I didn't comprehend this.

"What if I'm wrong? What if I'm falsely accusing him, even in my own head? I have to speak with his wife. She's the only person who can tell me whether her wreck was truly an accident or if something happened to *make* her wreck."

9

Teatime was upon Marjorie, and when she asked us to get her a tray, it was the perfect opportunity to speak with my partner alone. I steered Tinkie to the alcove near the kitchen, where we had some privacy, and filled her in on everything Cece had gleaned and what Amaryllis told me.

My partner had news of her own. While I'd been subterranean, she'd been in the penthouse suite—talking with Sherry.

"I feel sorry for her," Tinkie said.

Tinkie's compassion was easy to ignite. "Why?"

"She's not happy here. She wants to go back to New Orleans."

"She said so?"

"She did. This whole Heart's Desire scheme is Brandy's,

not hers. She said she'd be happy with a private practice in the French Quarter, giving readings or sessions for individuals."

I relayed what Cece suspected about Bert Steele.

"She did sound like she missed someone." Tinkie was a sucker for love. "She said she couldn't abandon her mother, and without her talents, Heart's Desire would fold. She feels an obligation to Brandy, but I sensed something more. It's as if she's a prisoner here."

"How did you get in to speak with her?"

"I knocked." Tinkie indicated she'd rather walk than sit on a garbage can. The heat index had to be 108, but we crossed the lawn to the edge of the woods, where at least a breeze could find us. "Sherry let me right in. She was eager to talk. I think she's really lonely."

"Why hasn't she been able to contact Mariam?" If Sherry was the real deal, was this a delaying tactic?

"I asked her. There's something not right. It's possible Mariam is afraid to come forth and tell the truth for fear of the consequences. Sherry said a spirit might be reluctant to impart damaging information to a loved one."

"The assumption being that Chasley is guilty of murder."

Tinkie stopped beneath a sweet gum tree. "Yes. As crazy as it sounds, I believe Sherry has Marjorie's best interests at heart."

I was not so generous. "Or else they're keeping her here in the hopes of fleecing more money out of her."

"Brandy maybe, but not Sherry." Tinkie spoke with confidence.

"Sherry convinced you she's a true medium?"

"I can't say for certain, but she made me believe she's not doing this to scam Marjorie."

The same couldn't be said for Brandy, and one thing Tinkie had ascertained was that Brandy held the reins at Heart's Desire.

"Let's prepare Marjorie's tea," Tinkie suggested. "The longer we stay, the more demanding she gets."

Yumi gave us some special tea cakes she'd prepared and said nothing when I placed three cups on the tray. Tea wasn't my personal favorite, but it was as close to coffee as I was going to get.

Marjorie greeted us from the small table. "Come and sit with me," she said. "What have you two been up to this afternoon?"

I told her a little about Amaryllis, cautioning her to keep all information to herself.

"I feel terrible for her," Marjorie said. "The idea that the man you love would kill someone just to be rid of her." Color bloomed on her cheeks. "Of course, that's what Chasley did."

"We don't know that anyone was murdered," Tinkie said, soothing her. "Don't allow yourself to get worked up. Sarah Booth and I will get to the bottom of it."

I sincerely hoped my partner wasn't promising we'd solve a thirty-year-old cold case that had never been viewed as suspicious. There wouldn't be a shred of evidence regarding Mariam's drowning in New Orleans. It hadn't been investigated, and since it was ruled an accident, there would be no detailed police reports. We'd never be able to prove Chasley's guilt or innocence—unless we figured out a way to make him confess.

Our discussion was interrupted by a knock on the door. I opened it to find only emptiness.

A low, commanding meow came from a carrier filled with a huge black cat. Otherwise the hallway was empty.

"Pluto!" Marjorie cried. "It's my precious baby." She rushed to the doorway and pulled the carrier into the room. Startled by the sudden movement, the cat spat and growled. "Pluto, I'm so glad to see you."

Instead of delight at seeing his owner, the cat squatted in a far corner of the little kennel.

"How did he get here?" Marjorie asked as she freed him. "Come on, baby boy. Why are you so upset?" She gently brought him out and cuddled him.

I stepped into the hall. "Tammy! Where are you?"

She came up the stairs. "Sorry. I had to check something out."

The hair on my arms stood at attention. "What did you see?" I whispered the question because I knew the answer.

"Ooooh! Aren't you the spooky one?" She grinned. "I didn't really see anything. I had a sense someone was watching me, so I went to check. Probably a false alarm."

Marjorie was totally preoccupied with the cat. When Tinkie came out to hug Tammy, I closed the door so we could have a moment alone. "Tell me the truth. Was it a ghost?"

Tammy laughed. "Not hardly. More like the reanimated dead. I think it was that awful butler, Palk. When he saw Pluto, I thought he might foam at the mouth. He had to get his mistress before he'd even let me in the house. Made me go around to the back door like a servant."

"To Palk, everyone is either a rich overlord or a serf. If you had any doubts about your station in life, now you know." I led the way back into the suite.

The cat sat on Marjorie's chaise, looking around as if he disapproved of his surroundings. He was black as ink, a perfect contrast to the periwinkle and white of the room. Green eyes shifted to look up at me with an expression so purely calculating, I felt as if I were being examined by royalty—and found wanting.

"Cocky little feline, isn't he?" Tammy bent to stroke him and he arched his back and purred.

"He's like a . . . god." The cat had more presence than a lot of Broadway actors I knew. I wondered if I should curtsy or possibly prostrate myself in his presence.

"His name is appropriate. The god of the under-world," Tammy said.

Pluto gave a mighty meow and bumped Tammy's hand.

"Pluto!" She picked him up and gave him to Marjorie.

"I'm so glad to see you." Marjorie kissed his head and he tucked himself under her arm. Though some people viewed cats as unaffectionate, I knew better. Pluto proved my point of view—he was snuggling with his owner.

"I have missed him so much." Marjorie brushed a tear from her cheek. "It's terrible to love a creature as much as I do Pluto."

"It certainly isn't terrible." Tinkie put her hands on her hips. "I have Chablis, and Sarah Booth has Sweetie Pie, Reveler, Miss Scrapiron, and a new horse named Lucifer."

Hearing Tinkie go down the list, I realized I'd acquired a lot of pets. Not intentionally, but often the best things in life happened haphazardly. At least I'd found a loving home for Roscoe with Harold.

"Marjorie!" Tammy gave the older woman a hug. "How are you holding up?"

"I'm fine." Holding her cat, Marjorie seemed happier than I'd seen her, but Pluto struggled to be free. At last she released him and the cat jumped onto the chaise. "He's so independent." She laughed at the cat's antics.

Tammy sat down by the cat and gently rubbed his head. "Pluto missed you like crazy. He would take your scarf and drag it around the house. He went to the chair you sat in and curled up with the scarf. That's where he slept every night. I don't think you should leave him again. He lacked for nothing at my house, except you. And you're the thing that means the most to him."

"Oh, dear!" Marjorie was on the verge of crying. "I never meant to cause him to suffer."

"He really loves you," Tammy said.

"I've lost everyone who ever truly cared for me. Except him. I'm almost afraid to love him as I do."

"And he needs you," Tinkie threw in.

They were clearly bolstering the case for Marjorie to take care of herself and not give in to depression. Or thoughts of giving up.

"Why don't you leave this place, take Pluto, and go home?" Tammy suggested softly. "There's nothing here to make your life a single bit better. The past is over and done. Step into the future."

If Marjorie would leave Heart's Desire, Tinkie and I could also go home. From what I'd discovered about the Westins, they might be pulling the wool over the eyes of a few wealthy people with their ghostly tales and manipulations, but they were swindling willing victims. I saw no need to try to catch them in scams involving supernatural beings.

"I want to go home," Marjorie said. "I really do. But I can't. I have to speak with Mariam. Then I'll go home."

Tammy took Marjorie's hands and held them firmly. "You have no proof Sherry can communicate with spirits. I believe if Mariam had something she wanted to tell you, she would have found a way before now."

Marjorie smiled. "You're very kind. All of you. But I have to find the truth. I want to settle my affairs."

"You're in excellent health," Tinkie said. "There's no rush on this. You have many years ahead of you."

"You've all made me see that I *do* want to live," she said. "But I want to do something worthwhile with my money. If Chasley is innocent of—of any wrongdoing, I want him to be comfortable and never lack for anything. He is my son, and I know I've failed him in many ways. But if he's guilty, I don't want him to benefit from a penny."

We were back to square one. At least she wasn't talking about dying in the immediate future.

Marjorie paced across the room and faced us. "At lunch today, Sherry told me we're going to try to contact Mariam again. And someone for Shimmer Addleson. Some long-dead relative who liked perfume. Sherry is confident we can make this connection." When she saw the skepticism on Tammy's face, she added, "I'm committed to this. Even if you think I'm a crazy old woman. I have to try."

"And we're committed to helping you," Tinkie said.

I had to agree. There wasn't another option open to me, though I was more than ready to beat it back to Zinnia. As long as Brandy and Sherry didn't threaten Marjorie in any way, if she wanted to stay at Heart's Desire and play with a Ouija board, who was I to tell her no? I had serious work to do on my relationship with Graf, though. I was ready to put Heart's Desire behind me.

"Sarah Booth, do you think you could tell the kitchen to make fresh tea for all of us?" Marjorie asked. "I want Madam Tomeeka to visit for a spell and I'm afraid we've let this pot grow cold."

"Sure thing."

"I'll help," Tinkie said. She was deliberately leaving Tammy and Marjorie alone to chat.

We crossed the empty dining room and went to the kitchen. Just as I pushed the door open a crack, I heard voices raised in anger.

"I'm on to you, you crazy communist bitch. You're helpful and nice as long as people are around, but I know you're up to something. You keep on riding me like you do, I'm going to stomp a mudhole in your ass and walk it dry!"

I peeked around the door and saw Amanda armed with two butcher knives. She was like some gunslinger—wide stance and weapons drawn. Yumi ducked behind the kitchen island, but she was far from vanquished. "You are sushi! I'll serve your pink flesh in sticky rice. You are a crazy girl!"

"I know a thing or two about dealing with crazy people," Amanda said. "Keep pushing me, bitch, and I'll tell Mrs. Westin everything I heard. I have the goods on you now. You'll be on a fast boat to Gitmo."

"I'll serve your tongue with horseradish and dill." Yumi poked her head above the counter and then retreated. "You're disposable. No one cares about you. No one will miss you when you're gone. Third-rate chef, unpopular chubby high-school girl, throwaway. I know exactly who you are."

Tinkie pushed past me into the room. "Stop this instant! Yumi, that was cruel. Amanda, what's gotten into you?"

"She has weapons! Words are all I had." Yumi wiped a tear from the corner of her eye. "She frightened me with her threats."

"You're a terrible person, Yumi." Amanda put the knives on the counter. "Bad things are going to happen to you."

"And you are unemployed. You're fired." Yumi stood, brave now that Tink was in the room. Her smile was victorious.

"You can't fire me." Amanda was almost breathless with anger. "Palk hired me."

"And he gave *me* complete control of the kitchen. You work at my whim. It isn't a good idea to make threats against the person who employs you."

Yumi had collected herself and was cool as a cucumber while Amanda was bright pink with anger. "I don't know what game you're playing, but I intend to find out. I hope a swarm of cockroaches comes out tonight and carries you away." Amanda slammed past us and out of the kitchen.

"You heard her threats." Yumi braced herself against the counter. "She's spoiled and emotional. She needs to learn discipline."

"Sometimes people get tired of being mistreated." I didn't know what the fight was about, but I felt a duty to take up for Amanda. "There's no excuse to bully and belittle people like that."

"You know nothing about mistreatment." Yumi's voice was soft. "Life is hard. Always hard. Now, excuse me, I must see to the shopping." She stopped at the back entrance. "There's leftover salmon in the refrigerator if you think the cat would like some. Cats are good. They're hunters."

While I poured tea, Tinkie, who'd recovered the sheets without incident, made the bed like a professional. I'd never suspected she knew the meaning of hospital corners. When we were all gathered around the white wicker table in a sunny nook of the suite, Tammy dropped her bombshell.

"I don't want to upset you, Marjorie, but Chasley stopped by my house yesterday and demanded that I give him Pluto."

"Oh, dear!" Marjorie's hand went to her throat. "Did he threaten you?"

"Not in so many words, but he made it clear he intended to have the cat in his possession. He said he would be back with a court order. He said I had no right to the cat. He made it clear he would come back with the full artillery of the legal system. That's why I was so desperate to get Pluto to you. I was afraid he'd win custody and . . ." She faded to silence.

"And he might kill Pluto," Marjorie finished. "Chasley is furious because I suspect he did something awful to his own sister. Yet he inspires distrust in strangers. You think him capable of destroying a creature I love? A cat, a child. It's a matter of extremes, isn't it?"

"He might never harm Pluto," Tammy said. "I just didn't want to risk it. He knows the cat is your heir. Whoever controls the cat controls the money. To be honest, Marjorie, I wasn't comfortable in that position. If something had happened to you, I would have been lost."

Marjorie laughed. "I doubt that, Madam Tomeeka. You underestimate yourself. You would have managed the cat and the money, and you would do good with it."

Marjorie had a keen take on my friend. Tammy Odom had no use for riches. She was a woman who made a difference in the lives of people she met. Personal gain wasn't a term she comprehended.

"At any rate, Pluto is safe here with you. I hope you both leave this place soon." Tammy caught my eye above the rim of her teacup and signaled she needed to speak with me alone.

Tinkie caught the motion. "Tammy, could you and Sarah Booth bring up the rest of Pluto's things?"

"Absolutely." I wasn't overly fond of tea to begin with.

We hurried out of the suite. Once we were outside by her car, Tammy pulled me close.

"I don't like this. Chasley let it slip that he knows more about Heart's Desire than the average person. I think there's something between him and the Westins. Something . . . dark."

That made perfect sense. Of all people, Chasley knew the way his mother suffered guilt over Mariam's death. He would also have the ability to feed information to the "medium" about his dead sister, about her dress, her demeanor. Details only a family intimate would know. If Chasley was the bastard Marjorie suspected him to be, this all dovetailed nicely.

"Is he as bad as Marjorie lets on?"

"He's so damaged. He couldn't contain his dislike of Pluto. He's jealous of a cat, because his mother loves it. Such a desperate need for love can push a person to do terrible things. I believe he would harm the cat."

Tammy's expression told me there was more. "Spill it."

"Chasley is incredibly handsome and charismatic, Sarah Booth. And he's coming here to see his mother. He said he wanted a psychiatric evaluation. I believe he intends to have Marjorie committed. Sarah Booth, if she claims to have seen the ghost of her daughter—"

"They'll commit her." The deviousness of the entire plot became crystal clear.

"Also, if Chasley injured or killed Pluto, that would be it for Marjorie. She'd be pushed over the edge."

She spoke the truth. "How can we protect Marjorie? She's determined to do this. The séance is tonight."

"Keep her away from Chasley. He'll attempt to provoke her into doing something she'll regret."

"Do you know what it is?"

"If I knew, I'd have a better idea how to stop him." Tammy opened her trunk and unloaded a litter box, food, toys, plush blankets, and grooming utensils.

"What's that?" I pointed to a spindly rubber toy.

"Laser light kit. It sends little red dots of light flashing around the room. Pluto loves to chase them. He's so damn smart, he's figured out the pattern and anticipates where the light will show up next."

That was one wily cat. And my equally clever friend had avoided my question. "What is it you know and aren't telling?"

"Sarah Booth, I had a dream."

This was not good. Tammy's dreams were symbolic and unclear, but if we could figure out the meaning, we'd be ahead of the game. Otherwise, tragedy might be our next visitor.

"What did you see?"

"At first I saw the gate here at Heart's Desire. I've never been here, so I had no clue about the gate until a little while ago. I recognized it the moment I drove up. Then I was in a hallway here, inside this house. The hallway was dark and narrow. There was a sense of being underground or with something heavy above me. At the end of the hallway was a door to the right."

She was perfectly describing the basement of Heart's

Desire and the hallway to the séance room. "Is that it?"
I prompted.

"You were standing in the hallway, Sarah Booth. You
were afraid. There was a knocking along the walls. I
couldn't see what it was, but it terrified you. You tried to
run, but you fell down." Tammy gazed into the distance.
"I'm sorry, the dream still upsets me."

"It's okay." I put a hand on her shoulder though she
was taller than me. "Tell me."

"The thudding sound grew louder, and you know
how focus shifts in a dream. In a blink, I was at the base
of a staircase and the thudding had gotten much faster."
She inhaled and steadied herself to finish. "Out of nowhere this body came tumbling down the stairs. It was
all covered in the same shade of lavender blue in Marjorie's room. It was like a peignoir, all lace and fluff and
frills. But when it stopped at the foot of the steps, I realized it was a woman. She was dead."

I hitched a hip onto Tammy's car to digest what she'd
told me. "You think she's going to die here, don't you?"

"I don't know," she said.

"Did someone push her down the stairs?"

She held my gaze but didn't answer.

"Can I prevent this?" It wasn't a matter of could; I
had to stop it.

"I don't have any answers, Sarah Booth. That's why
I'm so upset by all of this." She picked up Pluto's neces-
sities. "Be careful. You and Tinkie both. There's danger
in this house. Lots of it. Whether it's supernatural or human, it doesn't matter. At the end of the day, you'd be
just as dead."

We started toward the house.

"Before I forget, Harold asked me to tell you Roscoe is all you said he was. Harold had to retrieve him from the dog pound. He ate all Mrs. Hedgepeth's chrysanthemums she put out two days before. It's still too hot to plant fall flowers, and they would have died anyway, but honest to god, Mrs. Hedgepeth acted like Roscoe devoured her only grandchild."

"I warned Harold the whiskered little imp was rotten."

"Oh, Harold is delighted. He's paying at least a hundred dollars a plant but said it was worth every penny to drive Mrs. Hedgepeth nuts. He hasn't forgiven her for having Sweetie Pie picked up that time."

"I need to speak to Harold." Cece had brought me info on Heart's Desire, but I had a few more questions.

"Oh, something tells me you'll be seeing Harold sooner than you ever anticipated."

Before I could press Tammy for more information, the door of the servant's bunkhouse flew open and Amanda struggled out, dragging what looked like a duffel bag big enough to contain a human body.

"I won't take any more crap off that bitch," she mumbled as she lurched toward us. She was so engrossed in hauling her belongings, she failed to notice us.

"Amanda, are you okay?" I asked.

She almost jumped out of her skin. "No, hell no. I am far from okay. That crazy bitch Yumi threatened to cut off my fingers if I ate a snack. I didn't have time for lunch. I was busy. We're not *allowed* to have food in the servants' quarters. I got some leftovers from the fridge and sat down to eat and she snuck up behind me and told me I was fired for stealing food."

So that was the genesis of the argument I'd heard. A

set-to over a freaking snack. She turned back to her chore, hauling the bag toward the employee parking.

"Hold on a minute." I blocked her path. "We have some tea and cookies in Marjorie's room. Come on up and have a snack." It would fry Palk if he found out Marjorie was feeding the help, or even the fired help. Too bad.

Amanda gave her bag a giant yank. The strap broke and she landed right on her ass in the middle of the back drive. It was the final straw. Her eyes screwed shut and her mouth opened and a loud "wah-h-h" came out. She reminded me of Lucille Ball, caught in some mad scheme by Ricky.

"Honey, don't you cry," Tammy said. She had the milk of human kindness. I had a classic mental reference box of old television shows and movies.

"Hey, come on, Amanda. It's not that bad." I grabbed one arm and Tammy got the other and we lifted her to her feet.

"I wanna go home," Amanda said. "I can't take it anymore. Everyone here is so damn mean."

While we stood in the wilting heat on asphalt, a dark blue Maserati wheeled to the front of the house. We all dropped everything and ran to get a better view of the impeccably dressed man who exited the car. He was movie-star handsome—chiseled jaw, rugged looks, sharp blue eyes. He gave the car keys to Palk. My immediate reaction was to wonder if he was a good kisser. Whoever he was, he radiated sex appeal, even to a gal with a ring on her finger.

"My bags are in the trunk," the man said. "Take them to Mother's room."

Palk was a bit taken aback. "Is Mrs. Littlefield aware of your arrival?" he asked.

"Oh, she will be any minute now. I suspect I'll be a surprise."

Chasley! Chasley had arrived at Heart's Desire.

"I told you he was a handful," Tammy said.

"You didn't say he was a blond god."

"Inside, he's ugly as a wart hog. And you keep that in your mind." Tammy pinched my arm. "You better run upstairs. He intends to stay in his mother's suite of rooms, and Marjorie needs to be ready to hold the line."

"You're right." The back servants' staircase would give me an advantage. "Be careful going home, Tammy. Amanda, get with Cece Dee Falcon at the newspaper. She can help you find another job."

With that, I ran. Chasley could not get into Marjorie's rooms. He would set his mother back in her recovery. And even my most married partner might be vulnerable to his matinee-idol good looks.

10

Winded and sweating like a hard-ridden horse, I slammed the door and turned the lock.

"Dammit! Saint Jude in a chariot!" I wanted to say something more succinct, but Tinkie had been working on me about my cursing.

"Sarah Booth! Whatever is wrong?" Tinkie rose slowly from the table, where she was sitting with Marjorie.

"Chasley!" I uttered the name with such horror, I might as well have said *plague* or *Satan*.

Marjorie stood up, her teacup falling to the table with a crash. "He's here? At Heart's Desire?"

"He told Palk to bring his bags to your room. He intends to stay here."

"I think not." Marjorie recovered her dignity with amazing speed. "He will stay elsewhere on the premises if he dares to remain."

There was a light rap at the door. I froze. Tinkie swung it open to reveal Chasley with Palk at his heels like a trained dog.

"Is that so, Mother? I thought you'd want me here for your *reunion* with Mariam."

The cruelty of his remark was such that I reacted without thought. I slapped him as hard as I could across the handsome face. The shock of the blow traveled through my elbow and into my shoulder. Beside me, Tinkie gasped. Palk dropped Chasley's bags and looked as if he might flee. Chasley held his ground as a red handprint bloomed on his cheek.

"You will not speak to your mother in that way." I was so angry, my fear fled. And common sense, too.

"Well, so Mother has people who defend her." Chasley's voice was soft as silk as he assessed first me and then Tinkie. "Are you paid to be here, or do you truly care what happens to my mother?"

Pluto took that moment to announce his presence. He strolled, or some would say waddled, up to Chasley, looked directly into his gaze, held it for three beats, and then lifted his front paws to Chasley's expensive pants. He hooked in his claws and then pulled back, an action so deliberate, no one could mistake it.

"You terrible little beast!" Chasley reacted with a kick at Pluto, which Tinkie countered with a very unladylike knee to the groin. In less than five seconds, Chasley was on the floor moaning. Tinkie grabbed the cat and slammed the door.

Electric blue sparks crackled in Tinkie's eyes. "If Chasley attempts to come in this room, I will see to it that he'll never be able to procreate."

"Tinkie!" I was scandalized. She was the head of Delta society. She'd been born and bred to make men feel like conquering heroes, not eunuchs. Outside the door, I heard Chasley moaning. Palk murmured encouragement to get him to his feet.

I faced Marjorie. It was one thing for our client to talk bad about her son, but another for my partner to damage his manhood. "We had to do something, Marjorie."

"Oh, fiddle-dee-dee. She didn't hurt him. He meant to kick Pluto. He got what he deserved." She straightened her shoulders. "His intentions are to fight me. I never thought Chasley would come here. I thought I would be safe. Obviously, he means to have a confrontation. I'll happily oblige. I should have done this decades ago."

"We can't go through with the séance tonight." I had to reason with her. "If Chasley gets wind of this, if he has evidence you're trying to talk to the dead, he can have you institutionalized." There. I'd said it. "He'll gain total control of your money."

"I'm not crazy." Marjorie dared us to contradict her.

"I don't think you are. Tammy Odom is a good friend of mine. She has prophetic dreams. She sees the future. I have my own—" Holy cow. I'd almost admitted to Jitty.

Tinkie rounded on me. "You have your own what?" Her blue eyes narrowed. "I've known for a long time you had a secret, Sarah Booth. Now, tell us."

It wasn't that I didn't want to tell Tinkie. There were times when I ached to confide in my friend, but what I shared with Jitty was . . . private. Our bond, our relationship, was not for others to know. If I told, Jitty might disappear. And damn it, I'd come to rely on her. "I have my own set of issues with calling on the dead. You know I'd love to talk to my parents." I hated serving my best friend a half truth.

"Oh, Sarah Booth, I know how much you miss them." Tinkie hugged me, which loaded the guilt even heavier on my shoulders.

"I do, but the point is, most people don't believe in mediums or departed people or spirits hanging around. If it came to a mental competency hearing, with the right judge, the right circumstances, Chasley can use this against Marjorie."

"She's right," Tinkie said. "Marjorie, we can't give him this ammunition."

Marjorie's chin came up right on cue. "I won't pass up a chance to talk with Mariam because Chasley might use it against me. I came here to do this, and I won't be deterred."

Oh, great. Now she decided to show the starch in her backbone, when twenty-four hours earlier she was ready to lie down and die.

A thunderous knock at the door made Tinkie jump.

"Dinner is served in twenty minutes!" Palk boomed without opening it.

"Do I have to go down?" Marjorie asked. Some of her resolve appeared to melt away.

"Yes," Tinkie and I said in unison. "You have to face Chasley."

"Will you come?" she asked.

"Tinkie will. I'll stay here with Pluto." I didn't trust that Chasley couldn't get to the cat, and I never doubted he meant to see that Pluto went to the domain over which his namesake ruled.

"You're better at observing people," Tinkie said. "You go down. I'll stay with the cat."

I didn't agree with her assessment, but I did want to watch Chasley interact with Brandy and Sherry. And I wanted another chance to scope out Sherry. Except for her séance the night before, I hadn't seen hide nor hair of her. Tinkie believed in her sincerity, even if she still had uncertainties about her talent. I was harder. I hoped to discover if she was a charlatan who ripped off grieving people in the worst kind of way. Tonight would be my chance to evaluate her.

"Let me change into a fresh uniform," I said grandly, making Tinkie and Marjorie chuckle. It was a laugh we all needed.

Our belongings were still in the bunkhouse, and while I was in the servants' quarters, where Palk insisted we stash our bags, for the sake of expediency, I took a shower and changed. On impulse, I tapped at Amanda's room. There was no answer, but the door was locked.

I returned to the main house as the guests were being seated. Sherry and Brandy had taken their traditional seats at the head and foot of the table. Chasley was seated beside his mother, which clearly did not please her. Dinner was roasted duck, sweet potato salad, green beans in a vinaigrette, and a pear tart. After serving Marjorie, I stood behind her chair, awaiting her slightest whim. She was the only one with a personal servant, and she played it to the hilt, requesting that I unfurl her napkin, serve her plate, cut up her duck. She had quite the sense of drama.

The two country music singers were more than amused by the show. They watched as I wiped the bottom of Marjorie's water glass before she drank so it wouldn't accidentally sweat on her.

"I gotta ask," Gretchen said. "Do you wipe your own bum?"

Palk snapped to attention as if a cattle prod had zapped him. "I beg your pardon, madam! Such talk is not allowed at table."

"Do you write your help off your taxes, Mrs. Littlefield?" Lola threw in. "I mean, you're so dependent on your girl, I would think you might call her medically necessary."

"Mother was never so helpless before," Chasley said. "I think those two alleged servants are preying on her. They're making her weak and foolish."

"Shut up, Chasley," Marjorie said. "Each word you speak hammers the nail in the coffin of your inheritance."

Her threat was effective. Chasley shut his pie hole.

Dinner progressed, and I watched Chasley and Sherry with great interest. Chasley focused on his plate and therefore missed the looks of interest thrown his way by the country music singers and even Amaryllis. Had he made an iota of effort, he could have swept them off their feet. His only interest was his mother. He pushed the food around his plate and cast furtive glances at her. At one point, I felt sorry for him. He wanted Marjorie's attention. Even negative attention.

Sherry, for her part, seemed preoccupied. Several times I saw her look behind Marjorie and me, and her expression would shift to one of sorrow. It was only a blink of an eye, and I wondered if I imagined it.

"Mother," Chasley spoke softly.

"I will not speak with you. I can't believe you tried to kick Pluto."

"You have more affection for a cat than you do your

own son." The bitterness of his voice spiked with real hurt.

"The cat is more loyal. And kinder. And easier to be with."

"You've never loved me." Chasley swallowed, and I was stunned by his emotion. He was a grown man—a stunningly handsome man with his swept-back blond hair and hazel eyes—yet he sounded like a young boy painfully rejected.

"I tried, Chasley. I tried."

"Was I never a child you found the least bit lovable?"

Marjorie wiped both sides of her mouth with her napkin. "No. I'm sorry. Even as an infant you grasped at your toys, at me. Everything was yours. You reminded me of your father. He left me with two small children because he was greedy and immature. And selfish. He couldn't come off the road. He needed the high of the live audiences and the drugs. He needed to have everything. I saw that in you."

I wanted to intervene, to stop the brutal conversation. Marjorie acted as if the entire table were a pillar of salt, deaf to the cruelty she spoke. While I understood how Chasley affected her, he was still her son. Flesh of her flesh. How could she treat him so callously? Relief came from an unexpected source.

"Tell them about our new contract, Lola." Gretchen punched her partner's arm, knocking over her wineglass in the process. "Oops! Garçon, garçon, another glass, please!" she yelled at Palk, then turned back to Lola. "Tell them! Seven figures. We've hit the big time now. We're gonna be rolling in it. And Lola has started some rap songs that are incredible. If we can corner both markets, we'll be the biggest names in songwriting since Dolly Parton or Kris Kristofferson!"

Gretchen grasped the fresh wineglass Palk brought her and clinked it against Lola's. "To us," she proclaimed.

The girls were more than a tad in their cups. I wondered how this would affect the séance. Sherry scowled at them, but Brandy shot her a warning glance. Sherry's response was to put her napkin calmly beside her plate and stand. She'd been distracted throughout the meal. For some reason, she'd been staring over Chasley's shoulder at a blank spot on the wall. Unless, of course, she was channeling a stray spirit as a warm-up for the séance.

"Are you finished eating?" Brandy asked, clearly disapproving of her daughter.

"Excuse me, please. I need to prepare for tonight's session. Let me remind you all excessive drinking isn't allowed. You're spending money here to connect with the spirit world. People under the influence distract me." She dared her mother to object. "I won't allow it."

She abruptly left the table. A few moments later, Chasley also excused himself.

Marjorie had barely touched her plate, but she signaled she was done, so I offered my arm to assist her to her suite.

When we were out of earshot of the others, Marjorie whispered, "Chasley is a vile man. Do you think he's talking to Sherry? What if he tries to postpone the séance? What if he tells Sherry not to contact Mariam?"

She was in a dither, and I wanted to tell her that Chasley wasn't the only awful person in her family. "Take it easy, Marjorie. You're paying a hefty fee to be here. Chasley—who knows why he's here. Sherry isn't stupid enough to bite off her nose to spite her face. You're the client. Chasley isn't. Still, I think it would be smart if you canceled and waited for Chasley to leave Heart's Desire."

"I won't cancel. Perhaps Chasley being here will encourage Mariam to tell the truth about what happened to her."

Arguing was pointless. The séance was at midnight, and Marjorie meant to be there come hell or high water.

"What does one wear to a séance?" Tinkie asked, as if she had a choice in the matter.

"Your uniform," I answered.

"I refuse to wear khaki another minute. It washes me out."

Tinkie's rebellion wasn't unexpected. She could run in three-inch heels almost as fast as I could in athletic shoes. Her wardrobe covered every occasion known to man—or woman. And she'd been in rubber-soled shoes, khakis, and a polo shirt for two days. Enough was enough.

"What would you like to wear?" Marjorie asked in a reasonable tone. I sensed trouble. The two of them, both clotheshorses, would put us in dutch. "I have the most incredible caftan. Paisley. It would be perfect for you. Maybe with a matching turban, gold sandals, a few rubies— nothing could be more appropriate for a séance."

"Tinkie is a maid, not a guest."

"She's my maid and I order her to dress up."

Marjorie grew more contrary by the minute. I'd seen a side of her I didn't like. "Marjorie, we have to maintain our cover."

"Horsefeathers. If Chasley plans on accusing me of being crazy for trying to talk to Marian, then ordering my maids to dress up for a séance won't make a lick of difference. Both of you, out of those drab work clothes and into something fun. My closet is at your disposal."

Easy for her to say. I was a foot taller than she was. "Thanks, I'm fine the way I am."

She strolled past me. "Suit yourself." She threw open the closet for Tinkie, who squealed in her best sorority pitch as she dived into what had to be fifty thousand dollars' worth of very nice clothes.

I couldn't help but grin at the sounds of pleasure the two women gave as they went from one possibility to another. "While you two are playing dress-up, I'm going exploring." Palk would have dismissed the rest of the staff, and I might have a chance to poke around.

"Be careful," Tinkie said, her voice muffled by a mountain of sequins, cashmere, and lace.

The house had settled into a creaky silence as I stepped into the second-floor hallway. My goal was the telephone in the library. I wanted to check my messages and see if Graf had called. I'd been able to put my romantic dilemma out of my mind for a while, but it had come tramping back, dragging along a load of anxiety, guilt, remorse, and hope.

Cece and Tammy would both report to Oscar that Tinkie and I were fine. Oscar would report to Graf. But I'd left Dahlia House with too much up in the air between me and Graf. I hadn't realized I'd be held incommunicado by Palk and the Westin women.

I slipped down the stairs and to the library. The library door opened without a sound. I entered, closed the door, and went to the desk. The phone was where Palk had left it. I plugged it into the wall jack and dialed home.

"You have three messages."

The first voice mail was from Tammy, saying she was headed to Heart's Desire with Pluto, obviously left earlier in the day. The second recording was from Sheriff Coleman.

"Sarah Booth, what have you gotten yourself into now? Oscar wants an excuse for me to check into Heart's Desire. He's taking good care of Sweetie Pie and Chablis, but he's worried about you two. Call me and let me know you're safe."

Uh-oh. If I didn't call him, he'd be out at the gate, demanding entrance. Soon.

Graf's sexy voice was my third call. "Hold on to the ring, Sarah Booth. We can work this out. Call me back when you get this. I love you. Despite the fact that you're pigheaded and difficult, I love you."

I checked my watch. It would be nine o'clock in Hollywood. There was a chance Graf was home. I dialed.

His voice mail picked up, and I couldn't tell if I was relieved or disappointed. "Graf, I'm in a place where I don't have access to a phone. Tinkie and I should be home in a day or two. Please don't worry. We're fine. It's a . . . well, sort of a spa. Anyway, we'll talk. Good luck with the movie. I miss you. And I love you, too."

I hung up and called Coleman.

"Well, you took your sweet time calling," he said with a hint of anger. "I was about to find a reason to storm the walls of Heart's Desire."

"Sorry, we can't use a phone. I'm sneaking this call in, so don't fuss anymore. I don't have time. Tinkie and I are fine. Marjorie *and* Chasley are here. This is a very strange place, but I haven't seen anything criminal."

"What do you and Tinkie hope to accomplish?" The good humor was restored to Coleman's voice.

"I thought Marjorie might be in danger. Like the Westins might try to force her to sign over her money and then bump her off."

"And do you still worry about that?"

I hesitated. "I don't know, Coleman. I can't tell if they're con artists or worse. But we're working on it. Tammy and Cece have been out here—"

"And both have reported to me and Oscar. Graf was about to have a conniption, but Oscar filled him in."

Great. I'd worried my fiancé again. Not my smartest move. Nothing to be done now, since I'd let Graf know I was fine.

"Sarah Booth, are you okay?"

"Sure. We're having a séance at midnight."

He chuckled, and the sound reminded me that outside the walls of Heart's Desire were vast stretches of cotton fields and the September heat of the Delta. The sterile atmosphere of Heart's Desire had pushed the lushness of the soil and the crops right out of my head, but Coleman's voice brought it all back. I was only five minutes away from the land I knew and loved. The Delta was all around me.

"You watch yourself."

"I will." I hung up and put away the phone. For a moment I lingered in the library. I loved the smell of books. I went to a shelf and picked up a copy of Flannery O'Connor's short stories. Flipping open the book, I found an inscription to Sherry.

"Beware of the lure of the damned." No signature.

I returned it to the shelf and slipped back to the room. It was twenty after eleven, and I wanted to be prepared for the upcoming séance.

At precisely midnight, we left Marjorie's suite and

gathered with the other guests in the foyer. Brandy arrived last, with Chasley in tow. She took one look at Tinkie's caftan, turban, and bejeweled earlobes and gritted her teeth. I'd tried to warn Tinkie and Marjorie, but no, they were determined to be fashionistas.

"I really didn't expect Chasley to attend tonight," Marjorie said. For the first time all evening, she sounded worried.

"This is what he's here for," Tinkie told her. "It'll be okay. There's nothing he can do to stop you from talking to Mariam if she's willing to talk."

Chasley seemed to sense his mother's unease. "I hope after tonight you'll realize how foolish you're being. Mariam isn't going to go *woooo* and finger me for killing her. I didn't do anything, Mother. I'm here to beg you to give me a chance. You dislike me, yet you don't even know who I am."

"What did happen the day Mariam drowned?" I asked gently.

"I don't owe you an answer about anything." Chasley rounded on me. "If you're responsible for getting her to believe this insanity about Mariam, I'll see that you're charged with something. You're sucking money off my mother, providing services she doesn't need. Convincing her of things that aren't true. You're a parasite."

Tinkie moved up to join us so quickly, I didn't have a chance to respond to Chasley. "We're going to find out the truth of what happened to Mariam. About the time I start to think you deserve a chance, you act like a horse's ass. Now let your mother do what she feels she must to clear this matter up."

Chasley leaned close to Tinkie, his lips grazing her cheek as he whispered, "I don't know how two parlor maids gained so much influence over my mother, but when this is over and done, you'll be out on your ear, that cat will be in a shelter, and my mother will be in a home with psychiatric attention. She's trapped in a delusion, and I intend to get her help. Whatever your game is, you won't benefit financially."

Did he really think we were harming Marjorie? "We're trying to protect your mother. She believes contacting Mariam will resolve some serious issues for her. Whether it will or won't isn't up to me. Or you. This is her call."

"If you care so much for my mother, you'll convince her to seek professional counseling. She's been living alone for years now, wandering around a mansion, shunning company. Her life is a misery and this latest obsession of spirits is not in her best interest."

"She has a right to do whatever she pleases. She isn't harming anyone. What are you so afraid of, Chasley?" I asked softly.

His response was cut short as Brandy clapped her hands. "Sherry will join us once we're in place and seated," she said.

Eager to be away from Chasley, Marjorie, Tinkie, and I fell into line behind Brandy. We started down the steps to the basement like ducklings following a hen. Our only light was a candle Brandy carried, and behind us several people stumbled around in the dark.

A strange *thud, thud, thud* came from ahead of us. For some reason, it unsettled me. I'd been in the basement before and hadn't seen anything to make such a noise, unless the air-conditioning was about to go out. Now that would be hellish in ninety-eight-degree heat.

Tinkie's grip on my arm was bruising. "What is it?"

"Probably the AC unit." The whole séance thing was ridiculous.

Someone behind me lurched and pushed into me, nearly knocking me down.

"I swear, if I break my neck here in the dark, I want you to be sure my ghost goes on to my reward," Gretchen said.

"You're headed to the hot place," Lola countered. They burst into giggles and bumped my shoulder. I wondered if they'd be sober enough to participate.

Brandy stopped abruptly at the bottom of the stairs. "Holy shit." She'd barely uttered the words, but her tone made me stop. Something was wrong.

She lifted her candle high, illuminating a scene as eerie as anything Boris Karloff might have imagined. A body lay at the foot of the stairs. The woman's face was in shadows, but I recognized the uniform and her shape. It was Amanda. The thud I'd heard was her falling down the stairs.

"Is she alive?" Tinkie asked. She pressed against me, looking around my side.

Brandy seemed unable to move, so I eased past her and went to Amanda. I felt for a pulse. When I shook my head, I heard several gasps. Marjorie's scream was like an ice pick in my ear. She rocked backwards into Chasley, and thank goodness he caught her before she tripped and fell.

"What was she doing in the basement?" Amaryllis's voice sounded like she was trapped in a dream. "She works in the kitchen. She shouldn't be here."

"Get Palk," Brandy commanded. "The rest of you, out of here. Now."

"We should check the basement." I couldn't see anything in the candlelight. Amanda might have tripped, or she might have been pushed. "Someone could be hiding."

"You will not do a thing except go up those stairs and care for Mrs. Littlefield." Brandy's voice was iron. "Palk will check the basement. The rest of you, go to your rooms and lock your doors. I have no idea what's happening in Heart's Desire, but I intend to find out."

With Tinkie and Marjorie ahead of me on the stairs, I was only too glad to oblige. At the first floor, the guests scattered like leaves in the wind. Tinkie took Marjorie upstairs. I went straight to the library and the phone.

"Coleman, it's Sarah Booth. Come quick. A young woman is dead, and I don't know if it's an accident or a murder."

11

After the crime scene technicians left and the coroner removed the body, Coleman came to talk with us in Marjorie's suite. The awfulness of Amanda's death was like a phantom lurking at the edge of my awareness—and I pushed it away. In a house where acts and intentions were so distorted, I couldn't accept that the young girl was dead. Only hours earlier, she'd been dragging a duffel bag across the employee parking lot. Now she was gone.

Coleman had barely gotten inside the room when Tinkie asked him, "Accident or murder?"

"We'll have to wait for Doc Sawyer's autopsy. I spoke with the butler, who said the basement was empty. I found a hidden exit in a room with mirrors. One of the panels moved and led to a hallway that goes into the garden."

"Dammit! I should have checked. Brandy made us leave the basement." I'd been in that room and never thought to examine the mirrors.

"It's a good thing you did," Coleman said. "If Amanda was pushed, the killer could have been hiding. If you'd cornered him or her . . ." He didn't have to finish.

Still, it galled me. "Watch the butler. Palk will say whatever the Westins tell him," I warned Coleman. "He's a lapdog."

Coleman was worried; I could read him. I was so glad to see him, I could have hugged him, but I didn't. We'd managed to put our past relationship behind us, but like so many things in my life, I didn't trust it to stay dead and buried. Example: Jitty!

I was engaged to my first love, Graf. I'd been truly, madly, deeply in love with him when I went to New York to try my hand at the Broadway stage. I don't think either of us was grown up enough to hold a relationship together under the duress of two acting careers. At any rate, we parted, and when I came home to Zinnia, I fell for Coleman, a married man. And I mean married. He didn't love his wife, but he was committed to the marriage.

Coleman had since divorced crazy Connie, but he was the kind of man who never truly dropped a responsibility once he shouldered it. It was the thing I loved most about him, and the thing that had destroyed our chance at happiness. We were friends now—better than friends. But we were both careful to walk the line.

"Sit down, Sheriff," Marjorie invited.

But Coleman stood while the rest of us took a seat. I could tell he was upset. Coleman took it personally when someone's life was stolen.

"Glad to see you and Tinkie are still in one piece," Coleman said. The September humidity had taken the starch out of the creases of his shirt, but he could still pose for a lawman poster.

"Until Amanda was killed, the only thing dangerous here was the level of boredom." I could be flip with Coleman, and he'd appreciate my spunk.

"Did you know Amanda?" He looked from me to Tinkie to Marjorie. They gave a negative shake of their heads.

"A little," I said. "She was a sweet girl, naïve but ambitious. I thought she left here with Tammy." I couldn't quite understand how Amanda had ended up in the basement—dead. "She wanted to leave Heart's Desire. In fact, she'd packed her things and I thought she left when Tammy did." I tried to organize my thoughts, but the sight of her corpse had completely undone me. "Amanda was kitchen help. I seriously doubt she was in on any of the deep secrets of Brandy and Sherry Westin. So why would someone kill her?"

"This might have nothing to do with Heart's Desire," Coleman pointed out. "We don't know enough and we can't jump to conclusions."

"Something isn't right here," Tinkie said. She spoke with conviction, not emotion.

"Do you know anyone who might have a reason to kill her?" Coleman asked.

"She had a fight with the chef, Yumi, but I don't think Yumi would kill her over a snack. They both made a lot of outrageous threats." I needed to tell Coleman about Tammy's strange dream of a falling body in a blue peignoir. The subconscious images she'd related to me had been realized, and in a way I could never have predicted. Amanda was a bit player on the stage of Heart's Desire. Her brutal death—and I suspected she'd been killed—didn't make sense.

Unless she'd stumbled onto something. What had she threatened to tell Mrs. Westin about Yumi?

"Have you heard anyone talking about Amanda? Other members of the staff?" Coleman asked.

Tinkie and Marjorie could offer nothing, but I had a few tidbits. "Like I said, she butted heads with the top chef. And Palk was horrible to her, but he's awful to everyone. He's only civil to the paying guests."

"And people pay money to be here, amidst all of this meanness?" Coleman directed the question at Marjorie. "Why?"

"I don't mix with the other people here, except at mealtime, when it's required," Marjorie said slowly. "I'm afraid I've been very selfish. I've focused on what I needed, what I wanted. I haven't paid any attention to others. If there's a killer here, Tinkie and Sarah Booth must leave immediately. I won't put them in danger."

Marjorie could come out with some startling statements. She seemed like a vain, self-involved person; then she'd reverse herself and show compassion.

"We aren't leaving without you and Pluto," Tinkie said. She gave Marjorie a quick hug.

"Sarah Booth, you know the most about Amanda. The forensics will tell me a lot, but you're the best source I have at this compound." Coleman focused his blue gaze on me. His eyes were lighter than Tinkie's, and they could be hard as ice shards. Now, though, they reflected his genuine concern. "What kind of read did you get on the young woman?"

"I talked with Amanda for only a few minutes. She was from a little town near Vicksburg. She wanted to be a great chef. This wasn't the job she thought it would be when she took it. She was a glorified dishwasher and Yumi is demanding. To everyone." I struggled for facts. "I didn't have an inkling anyone would hurt Amanda. She wanted to leave Heart's Desire, and she'd been fired. She'd packed her things and was on her way out of here. This doesn't make sense."

Guilt nibbled at me. I should have made sure she left safely. She'd been so upset, and I'd been distracted by Chasley's arrival. "Call Tammy and ask why Amanda didn't follow her out."

Coleman placed the call, and I had a split-second of phone envy. Strange how I'd fought against owning a cell phone and now I felt naked without one. The thin piece of technology could record conversations, take photographs, make movies . . . lots of handy PI tools.

After a brief conversation with Tammy, Coleman was as puzzled as ever. "They were ready to leave, and Amanda said she'd forgotten something," Coleman reported. "Tammy left. She never dreamed Amanda wouldn't follow.

"As far as you know, all of the guests were accounted for on the stairs?" Coleman asked.

"Except for Yumi and the kitchen staff. Palk dismissed the maids at eight. That's the routine," I told him.

"Can't you arrest someone?" Marjorie asked. "How about Chasley? He should be arrested on general principle."

"Can't do it, Mrs. Littlefield." Coleman was a good sheriff because he kept his eye on the bigger picture, and he didn't jump to conclusions. Normally. There was that time he'd accused me of murder, though.

"She implied she knew something or had some evidence against Yumi," I said. "I can't imagine what kind."

"What would Amanda have?" Coleman's question was as much for himself as for us.

"Why was she in the basement?" Tinkie asked.

"To stop the séance." Marjorie's answer was emphatic. "Is Chasley involved in this? He must be."

"That's a long jump to make," I cautioned her. "Marjorie, why do you think Chasley is capable of such awful things?" It was unnatural for a mother to have such dark thoughts about her son.

"A week after Mariam's death, I picked up the telephone to make a call. Chasley was talking with one of his friends. He said that he would be the sole heir now that Mariam was gone. He said it with such . . . coldness. Chasley knew how dangerous the currents there were. He *knew*."

Her voice broke on the last word, and so did her spirit. She turned away and covered her eyes with her hand. "Chasley and I are both to blame for her death."

Money did not buy happiness—Marjorie was walking proof of that.

"Do you have evidence Chasley played an active role in Mariam's death?" Coleman asked.

"I don't think the law demands a brother jump into a dangerous river to save his little sister. You could charge him with cowardice or perhaps corrupt character. That's about it, unless he confesses."

Marjorie was far more devious than I'd thought. "You've

set this all up, this whole séance thing, to see if you can frighten Chasley into confessing!"

"Damn!" Tinkie saw Marjorie's plan, too.

"I'm not certain I approve of the way you've manipulated everyone," Coleman said with some heat. "A young woman is dead, and if I find out this is a result of a scheme—"

"I assure you, I'm as distraught by the young woman's death as you are," Marjorie said. "Chasley's guilt or innocence has nothing to do with the poor young woman. As far as I knew, she wasn't allowed out of the kitchen except to clear dirty dishes from the table."

"It's a mighty strange coincidence that you kick off your plan to get Chasley to confess and a woman dies at Heart's Desire." Coleman's voice had an edge.

"I'm not denying Chasley may be involved, but I don't see how this could have anything to do with me." Marjorie stood up and faced Coleman though she barely came up to his armpits.

"I'll have a talk with Chasley," Coleman said. He pointed at me, then Tinkie. "You two stay put. Don't leave this room until I give you the okay."

"I could help with the interview," I said.

"And give up the ruse of being a maid. No, I can handle this on my own. Stay put. I'll be back in the morning to finish my investigation," he said. "I want to do some research on the Westins and Chasley."

That was good news, because Coleman had law-enforcement resources Tinkie and I didn't. He might actually be able to turn up something.

Coleman motioned me to the doorway and slipped me a cell phone—a nice one with all the features I'd been missing. "Call me if you see anything suspicious. I don't like that you're here, Sarah Booth. Or Tinkie. I worry about both of you."

He was beginning to sound suspiciously like Oscar and Graf. It wouldn't surprise me if they'd all ganged up to herd me and Tinkie into a role where safety came first and career second. Then again, a young woman was dead. He had a right to be worried. Oscar, when he heard, would go through the roof and be on the phone to Graf. Tink's and my time at Heart's Desire might be short if we wanted to salvage our romantic relationships. We had to get busy.

After Coleman left, I convinced Marjorie to try to sleep. She was wound up tighter than a spring. "I can't sleep. My whole plan depends on the séance."

"Do you really believe Mariam will appear and accuse Chasley of pushing her off the dock?" I asked.

"I believe she will tell the truth. I have to know the truth. I've lived too long suspecting him. This has to be finished. For both our sakes."

"Tomorrow we'll speak with Sherry." I tried to calm her. "I'm sure she'll reschedule the séance. This is her business. This is what she does. Other people are counting on her to contact dead relatives."

"Will you see if you can find Sherry downstairs? Just ask her. Pin her down." She hugged her elbows. "I want to make certain the séance will be held tomorrow."

"I'm sure everyone is in bed. It's been a rough night. The Westins must know Amanda's death will bring unwanted scrutiny on Heart's Desire."

"Everything is in jeopardy," Marjorie said.

"Marjorie, I promised Coleman we'd stay in the room. Let's sleep. Tomorrow I'll speak to Sherry first thing."

Before we crawled into bed, I checked the lock and

forced a chair under the doorknob. If someone was determined to enter, the chair wouldn't stop him, but it would make noise and wake us up.

I'd just pulled the sheet up to my chin when a heavy weight moved up my body. Pluto had crept out from under the bed. He walked the entire length of my body and settled down to cuddle with me. I thought I'd have trouble sleeping, but I was out like a light.

I'm not certain what awakened me. Pluto, too, was wide-eyed. Then I heard the sound again. Not the clanking of chains that would have told me Christmas Past was lurking in the darkness. This was even scarier. It was the tap of high heels on the floor.

Tinkie was asleep beside me. Marjorie snored lightly in the bed. Pluto and I remained completely still as we listened to the footsteps come closer and closer.

"Sit up, you faker. I know you're awake."

The voice was high-class and amused.

A shaft of moonlight coming in the window illuminated the figure of a woman in a suit and heels. The hem of her dress came just below the knee, and the shapely silhouette, complete with curls that circled her head beneath a sophisticated hat, told me my visitor didn't have to worry about fashion or weight. Or time period. She was right out of the 1930s.

"What are you doing here?" I asked Jitty.

"One of us has to work the mystery. As far as I can tell, you and your sawed-off partner do handsome work as maids, but you haven't progressed an iota toward helping Mrs. Littlefield."

"Sic her, Pluto." I nudged the cat toward Jitty, but Pluto

was wise enough to resist. He dug his claws into my thigh and refused to budge.

"Tell me what progress you've made." Jitty sat on the edge of a chair. Her stockinged leg swung back and forth. She was the epitome of annoyed sophistication, and I knew the character she was playing. Nora Charles from *The Thin Man*. Obviously Jitty had a lot of time on her hands in the Great Beyond. She could read books and watch old movies, or maybe she time-traveled. Who knew how she dug up her references, but she was spot-on, right down to the pearl necklace glowing softly in the moonlight.

"Why are you here deviling me?" I was exhausted.

"That lawman came and went and you got nothing out of him."

That wasn't true. "He gave me a phone." I indicated the device on the table beside me. "This is important for our safety. I can call for help now."

"A good first step. But a young woman is dead, Sarah Booth. A girl who meant no harm to anyone."

"I know." I'd managed to push back the emotion of Amanda's murder, but Jitty brought it all home. Remorse and grief are hard to swallow. "She was a sweet kid. I really can't think why someone would hurt her. Maybe she did trip and fall."

"You can't find any clues?"

"Her room in the servants' quarters was locked, but Coleman searched it before he left. No clues as far as I know. But she said she had evidence against Yumi for something."

"You're getting warmer." Jitty was irritating in her sarcasm.

"If you know, then tell me. It's three in the morning and I don't want to play guessing games with a haint."

"A haint who knows a thing or two about solving a mystery." She turned so that the moonlight struck her face. Her hair was softly curled around her cheeks and the back of her head. The little hat, a perky Robin Hood kind of thing, suited her perfectly.

"I miss Graf. I think I made a mistake." The sentences popped out of my mouth before I even thought. Too late to retract it.

Jitty inhaled slowly. "So, you're off your detective game because of a man. Sounds like you need to be deprogrammed."

"What?" I couldn't believe what I was hearing. Jitty was all about a man and sperm and a baby. Now she was fussing at me because I was worried about my fiancé. About my future as a wife and mother. "You are as contrary as a seed wart on a pointer finger."

Jitty chuckled, the tone mimicking a black-and-white movie where the woman held all the cards. "Frustration doesn't suit you."

"Well, it should. You've given me plenty of practice wearing it."

"You need a new tailor, then. How about someone who can wrap you in home, family, bliss, and success?"

"Bring it on." I was tired of the banter. A young woman was dead. I was sleeping with a twenty-three-pound black cat instead of my fiancé. And I was conversing with a dead relative.

"In the hours after she quit and before she was murdered, what was Amanda up to?" Jitty asked.

"Coleman is investigating. Every other man in my life

is annoyed with me. I don't want to put Coleman against me."

"Coleman is in Zinnia. You're here to protect a wealthy woman from her past. Now you've got a new purpose. Someone killed a young woman, and the culprit needs to pay."

Jitty rose and paced the bedroom. "A gin martini would be very welcome."

"Gin?" I'd never heard Jitty utter the word. "You're kidding, right? First, you don't drink. Second, if you did drink, it wouldn't be gin."

"It's all the rage." Her look told me I had no fashion sense, not even in liquor. "Gin is the drink of sophisticates."

"And the cure for malaria, if you add tonic water with quinine. I don't want my alcohol to taste like medicine."

She laughed, and the curtains at the window rippled as if a gentle wind teased them. I forced myself out of bed and went to the window. Light silvered the lawn. The air-conditioned interior was cool, but I knew if I opened the window, humidity would descend like an oxygenated swamp.

"Why Nora Charles?" I often understood Jitty's character selections. But Nora Charles, the sophisticate, was a far stretch from Zinnia, Mississippi, and a hot September night. Then again, Jitty didn't sweat. Being dead was looking better and better.

"I thought you'd appreciate a touch of class, a bit of sophistication and wit. Those qualities are in short supply at Dahlia House these days."

"And I thought your big concern was a fertile womb and an active impregnator. Wit, charm, sophistication, class—those things have nothing to do with an active libido."

She chuckled softly. "You're right about that one. But since Graf is in Hollywood—oh!" She held up a hand. "Gotta go. I've been summoned."

"Jitty!" I whispered her name, because I didn't want to wake Tinkie or Marjorie. Even Pluto tried to detain her. He swept out a claw and caught only empty air. She was gone.

As I turned to go back to bed, I saw a figure running across the lawn. My heart thudded, and I pressed my hands to the window and strained to make out the slender dark-clad figure moving with great speed.

I was too far away to make a positive identification. I couldn't even be certain if the runner was female or a slender male. Members of the kitchen staff were young and lean.

The figure headed straight to the servants' quarters and disappeared into the shadows.

As much as I didn't want to do it, I had no choice but to jump into some clothes and go investigate.

12

By the time I calculated how to disarm the alarm system, the mysterious figure was long gone. All around me Heart's Desire slept. With the rigid rules Palk enforced at the compound, it was possible the person I'd glimpsed moving around the grounds was nothing more than part of a romantic tryst, a lonely heart looking for love. The Westins employed very buff guards and an especially attractive female staff. I didn't need a playbook to figure out Palk would oppose any inter-staff romance.

From the aerials I'd studied, I'd learned the guards' bunker was a mile or so through the woods. I couldn't help but wonder if Amanda had found any pleasure in flirting with the men quartered so near her.

The reality of her unnecessary death slammed home.

She'd barely been a grown-up, a young woman with dreams. And now she was dead. Why? Had she discovered information that cost her her life? The only way to find out was to get busy. I had a little experience with lock-picking, and this was the perfect opportunity to search room 14, Amanda's lodgings. Coleman and crime scene techs had combed her quarters, but maybe I'd uncover a clue. Either Amanda had clamped on to a secret or she'd pissed her killer off. It was also possible romance was the motive, even though she'd never mentioned a beau.

Checking to be sure no one else was up and about, I left the protection of the main house and slipped across the parking lot toward the servants' billets, taking the same route as the mysterious figure. At the bunkhouse, I eased into the shadows and listened intently. My mysterious intruder might have gone to his or her own room, or could still be lurking around. I had to be careful—and vigilant.

If Coleman had found evidence in Amanda's room, he hadn't shared it with me, which made me believe he'd ended up empty-handed. It wasn't that I thought I could do a more thorough search than the Sunflower County sheriff, but I might see something he missed. A tiny detail. Men and women valued things differently.

The crime scene tape across the entrance remained undisturbed, but that didn't mean the room was empty. I crouched at the window and tried to peer inside. The curtains were drawn tight. The best I could tell was the interior was dark. Step by careful step, I made it to the door—and froze.

Someone was in the room, rustling around. I pushed the door open a tiny crack and caught sight of a flash-light beam moving around the interior. I drew back into the doorframe of the room next door, praying I wouldn't coax a whine out of a loose board and alert the searcher of my presence. Who was probing Amanda's things? Who and why would be of interest to me, and to Coleman.

There was the sound of an object hitting the floor. Maybe a drawer, or a box. I ducked to the side of the servants' quarters, and just in time. The light inside room 16 jumped to life. In the same moment, the black-clad figure darted out of Amanda's room and took cover in a thick shrub of five-foot-high redtops.

"Is somebody out there?" a male voice asked. One of the security guards stepped onto the porch of room 16 in boxer shorts and nothing else except a gun gripped firmly.

My lungs burned with the breath I was holding. The guard walked farther out so that he was perfectly back-lit. He was a handsome specimen, and the gun told me he meant business. He listened for a moment, then returned inside and flicked off the light.

I remained totally motionless. The dark-clad figure slipped from the shrubs and ran across the parking lot to the back door of the main house. I could tell it was a woman by her shape, but couldn't ascertain more.

I followed her.

The mudroom was empty, and the old house seemed to sigh, almost as if it were contented to retain yet another secret. The thought pissed me off, and I went through the pantry into the kitchen and finally into the dining room. There was no trace of anyone.

From what I'd been able to fathom of the house, the guest rooms, some empty, were all on the second floor, with Brandy and Sherry retaining the top floor for themselves. The kitchen, food services, storage, and various offices constituted the east wing, which fed into the employee parking lot. The north wing, or main portion, included the parlors, dining room, spa, library, and meeting rooms. The west wing was unexplored so far by me or Tinkie.

That's where I headed.

As I slinked down the hall, I tried to visualize which guests correlated to the size of the mysterious woman who'd been in Amanda's room. Amaryllis Dill, or Gretchen, the country music singer came to mind. Both were thin and fit, about five foot five. Amaryllis, though, didn't strike me as much of a night wanderer. I seriously doubted she owned an all-black garment in her wardrobe. The only clothes I'd seen her wear were floral and frilly.

The west wing, interestingly enough, was closed off with solid doors that could be locked. To keep someone in or keep others out? Pushing against the oak panels, I was gratified to gain entry on silent hinges.

I found myself in a carpeted corridor with a half-dozen closed doors, much like the guest rooms upstairs. Very interesting. I was about to continue on when I heard a soft click and creak. I ducked behind a massive cabinet, and just in time. Yumi, wearing a black kimono-type gown, sashayed from a room. She wore black cowboy boots and held something at her side. She went down three doors and knocked softly.

Palk opened the door as if he'd been standing at it. To my shock, he wore a Hannibal Lecter mask, a lacy red teddy, and a garter belt. Something about the mask struck a chord, but I had no time to think it through.

Yumi dropped her robe to reveal a black leather

breast binder and chaps equipped with handcuffs. She also held a riding crop and used the butt of the handle to push at Palk's chin.

"Where is my dinner?" she asked in a threatening voice.

"For your dining pleasure, I have some fava beans and Chianti," Palk said.

"I wouldn't eat your crap on a bet. Kneel, you dog." She brought the whip sharply across Palk's chest. He dropped to his knees. "Crawl."

And he did.

Yumi followed his groveling form into his room and the door closed.

I wouldn't have been more stunned if Frankenstein had appeared. Palk and Yumi? My mind recoiled at the images. Satan dancing on a church steeple! Those two were the worst combination of personality, fetishes, psychological wounds, and authority complexes I could imagine.

I didn't know if their meeting—in the wee hours of the morning—was purely sexual, business, or monkey business. What I did know was that Palk and Yumi created an unholy alliance of power in Heart's Desire. And both enjoyed wielding it. Was this the secret Amanda had stumbled upon? The one she'd threatened to reveal? Palk had been with us when Amanda took a tumble, but Yumi was unaccounted for.

It seemed likely that Yumi was the intruder in Amanda's room, and if I knew what she was after, I'd have a possible motive for murder. Obviously, Amanda had something Yumi wanted. And badly. Another sex video? But was that really enough to warrant murder? Palk and Yumi were certainly careless enough, flaunting their affair in the hall. If it was such a dangerous secret, why were they risking detection?

I couldn't afford to draw the wrong conclusion. I'd been a PI long enough to realize that the obvious wasn't always, well, obvious. The one conclusion I could put in the "proven" column was that Palk and Yumi had a high kink factor in their relationship.

Thinking of Palk and Yumi—my mind rebelled. Holy candlesticks! I couldn't wait to share this with Tinkie.

I tiptoed to the heavy exit out of the west wing. I didn't take a breath until I closed it behind me. Yes! I was out of the worst danger of being discovered. Now I had to make it back to the room without getting caught. At least I knew Palk and Yumi were . . . preoccupied. I cringed involuntarily.

I turned to head back and stopped. A young girl in a pale blue dress wavered at the end of the hallway. The lighting was dim, but I could see her—and see through her.

Water dripped onto the polished floor. "Help her. Help my Mommy." Her voice had an echoey quality, like sound underwater.

"Mariam?" I inched toward her and she disappeared. When I got to the place she'd been standing, there wasn't a trace of water, though I'd clearly witnessed it puddling.

Chill bumps danced over my arms and back as I ran toward the stairs and the safety of Marjorie's room. The ghost girl hadn't threatened me, but nonetheless, she'd unnerved me.

I awoke to sharp claws digging into my chest and a terrible weight pressing the oxygen from my lungs. Gulping for air, I sat bolt upright—to the amusement of Tinkie and Marjorie. They were at the small table near the windows, pouring cups of coffee.

"Good morning, sleepyhead," Tinkie said.

Pluto yawned right in my face. Ah, kitty breath. No joy on earth compares. I pushed him aside and stretched. "Why does Pluto insist on sleeping on top of me?" I asked Marjorie. "He's your cat."

"He likes to spread his love around," Marjorie answered.

"You look like warmed-over hell," Tinkie said, holding out a cup of black coffee. "I went downstairs this morning and ran into Yumi. She looked almost as bad as you do. You two have a tête-à-tête?"

I pulled the covers over my head at the thought. "Satan stick me with a pitchfork!" The duvet muffled my words.

Sleep made Tinkie frisky. "Marjorie and I have nicknamed Yumi 'the Dragon.' I think she might be capable of breathing fire."

I peeked out. "If that's true, I'll bet she scorched Palk's boxers last night."

That got their attention. Before they could question me, I continued. "She was searching Amanda's room last night." I stretched nonchalantly. "I didn't get much sleep last night, because I followed her."

"Did she find anything?" Tinkie asked.

"I don't think so. A guard woke up and cut her search short."

"Thank goodness you weren't caught," Marjorie said.

I forced myself out of bed and poured some coffee. Pluto circled my legs, indicating that he, too, wanted morning refreshment. I poured heavy cream for him in a saucer, which he tucked into as fast as his little sandpaper tongue could slither in and out. No wonder the cat was fat.

"It was close. Something else interesting happened." I toyed with them. I couldn't help it. This gossip was the juiciest yet.

"What?" Tinkie put down her coffee cup and rose to her feet, hands on her hips. "You are a torment, Sarah Booth Delaney. You are holding out, making us beg."

"Yes, I am."

"Then tell us! Please!" Marjorie showed more life than she had since I'd met her.

"Yumi and Palk had a little assignation last night. At three A.M. In Palk's room. She wore cowboy boots and leather chaps and brought a riding crop. He wore a Hannibal Lecter mask, a red teddy, and stockings.

Marjorie's eyes widened. Tinkie burst into laughter, but then her lips turned down at the corners.

"What's wrong?" I asked.

"It's the mask. There's something . . ." She concentrated. "I can't make the connection. I'll think about it."

She'd given me just enough push to make the link. "The sex video! The man in the mask! Palk must have been affiliated with the Westins when they were in New Orleans. He's a longtime . . . servant."

Marjorie's gasp indicated distress. "Palk worked with the Westins in New Orleans?"

"We can't be certain," Tinkie said. "But it would seem so."

"And Palk and Yumi have aligned themselves?" she continued.

"I just don't see those two together romantically," Tinkie said. "When I do, I feel sick."

"Do you think they killed Amanda?" Marjorie asked.

"I don't know." I tried never to jump to a conclusion by putting blame on a suspect without solid evidence. What I had was suppositional, at best.

"What if Chasley was responsible for Amanda's fall?" Marjorie stirred her coffee without looking up.

"Why would Chasley kill an assistant chef who was leaving the compound, anyway?"

Marjorie rubbed her eyes with her hand. "That was wrong of me. I have to stop it. I can't accuse him without proof." She looked genuinely contrite. "One thing I hope is that whatever Mariam tells me, it clears Chasley. I don't want to die having lost my daughter and my son."

"A good point for all of us to keep in mind," I said. I needed to tell Tinkie about the ghost I'd seen in the hall-way, but I wasn't about to bring the subject up in front of Marjorie. It would send her into a tizzy.

"I'll have breakfast with the others." Marjorie made her announcement and pulled a summer capri set from her closet. "I can help you. I'll cause a scene. Something that will send Brandy and Sherry over the edge. You two should check Amanda's room and see if you can find anything."

Surprise must have registered on my face, because Tinkie laughed out loud. "Marjorie reads a lot of mysteries." She pointed at a stack of paperbacks. "Carolyn Hart is as big a cat lover as Marjorie. And you should have heard Marjorie going on and on about Dorothy L. and Agatha, these two cat characters."

"Pluto adores it when I read aloud to him about those cats," Marjorie said. "Now, you two scat. I'm going to give a diva performance that will turn the whole household upside down."

The first thing Tinkie and I had to accomplish was pilfering the key to Amanda's room. After Coleman's search, Palk had ordered the room locked—which hadn't deterred the midnight stranger. That one fact convinced me Yumi was indeed the intruder. She'd obtained a key from Palk. By hook or by crook. Another cringe overtook me at the thought. I had to stop picturing the two of them in flagrante delicto. It was driving me nuts and giving me a twitch. Even Marjorie's mind was more on the case than mine.

And the case was where my mind needed to be.

Palk took his breakfast in the staff dining room. I went there while Tinkie went out the front door with the intention of walking around the grounds. Amanda's car had to be on the premises and might yield pertinent information.

Palk was seated at the table with a crisp linen cloth. A pot of tea steeped at one side of a plate of unbuttered, blackened toast. What a pretender he was. All proper and starched, except in his sexual preferences. He probably wore steel-wool drawers.

He'd removed his jacket and draped it over the back of a chair. No doubt to keep it free of crumbs. I'd seen him pocket the household keys. With any luck, they'd be in his coat. Now all I had to do was wait for Marjorie to cruise into the dining room and create her promised distraction. And I didn't have long to wait.

"Where is Palk?" Marjorie demanded in a strident tone. There was the clatter of cutlery as people dropped their forks.

"What's wrong?" Brandy asked. "Mrs. Littlefield, whatever is wrong? You look like you're about to faint."

"I demand to see Palk. Last night, I caught him in the hallway, lurking around my door. Had it not been for my loyal servants, he might have raped me!"

I had the benefit of catching Palk's reaction. He paled and slowly rose. For a moment he remained motionless.

"There must be some mistake," Brandy said. "Palk doesn't fraternize with my guests. He knows better. That's a strict violation of the rules."

"It isn't your damn rules he wanted to violate!" Marjorie put her whole heart into the performance. "I demand he be brought before me. Now."

Visibly shaken, Palk dashed toward the dining room. The staff and I remained totally silent so we could eavesdrop. I had to hand it to Marjorie. She'd come up with a plot guaranteed to get results.

"I beg your pardon, madam," Palk said. "I was nowhere near your room last evening or at any time, other than to bring your son up or to announce a meal."

"Prove it."

Good for Marjorie! She knew he was with Yumi and would never own up to sexual peccadilloes in front of Brandy Westin and the other staff. She had him over a barrel, and judging from her voice, she barely contained her glee.

"I don't have to prove anything." Palk stumbled over his words.

As he searched for plausible excuses, I searched his coat, found the keys, and hauled ass out the back servants' door. Palk was on his own at the inquisition. I'd worry about returning the keys after I did my search.

Tinkie wasn't visible in the parking lot, so I ducked under the crime scene tape and unlocked the door.

The draperies were pulled tight, leaving the room with the dimmest of light. I hadn't thought to bring a flashlight, but I did have gloves. Not the thin latex used at crime scenes but the thick rubber ones used for cleaning. They'd work fine, though.

The room was Spartan. The double bed, a table beside it, a dresser, and a desk. Old grocery receipts and tissues, along with socks, shoes, blouses, and slacks—the Heart's Desire uniform—were scattered around the floor. Had Yumi had time to do all of this? Or had Amanda abandoned everything that tied her to Heart's Desire and scattered her belongings about the room, telling anyone who saw it she was leaving angry?

Or scared.

I studied the chaos to see if I could tell which emotion.

A drawer was pulled out and dumped on the floor. A tube of toothpaste, almost empty, old hair curlers, crumbling eye makeup—nothing Amanda valued enough to pack. But this was likely the thing I'd heard hit the floor when Yumi was searching the room.

So what was she seeking? An item that could be tucked in a shallow drawer. So it was smaller than a bread box. I stopped. To my knowledge, I'd never seen a bread box. Not even a photo of one. My aunt Loulane had often repeated that saying, and I'd never stopped to think what it really meant.

A click distracted me.

I whirled around. A white-haired old lady sporting the strangest hat sat on the foot of the bed, knitting needles chattering like two possessed imps.

"Oh, dear," the woman said, "this doesn't look good. It reminds me of the time the milkman's granddaughter disappeared from the McWhorters' country house. Her room was a mess and everyone thought she'd had a disagreement with young Charlotte McWhorter. But that wasn't the case. No, it was much more dire."

The voice was thin and reedy, and the woman never lifted her eyes from her knitting. She was familiar, though. I'd seen her before. Who was Jitty pretending to be this time? I refused to give her the satisfaction of asking. Then it hit me.

"Miss Jane Marple!" I had it. The Agatha Christie spinster who solved mysteries in the English village of St. Mary Mead. Miss Marple was a staple of the mystery crowd, and her prowess as a sleuth spanned decades.

"Your powers of deduction are impressive," she said, putting her knitting needles away. She took in the disarray. "Poor, poor child. Take a gander at this mess. Makes one wonder why she was in such a hurry. Do you think they were on to her?"

"They?" I jumped on it. Jitty never told me how far her powers reached, and I'd frequently wondered if she knew the answers to my cases but wouldn't—or couldn't—tell me. The rules of the Great Beyond were often enigmatic and incomprehensible to me, yet I knew there were guidelines governing Jitty's interaction with the living. Hell, there was policy for everything; I'd come to accept the fact.

"Certainly there's more than one culprit at Heart's Desire and more than one crime," Jitty said in her softest elderly British gentlewoman tone. She picked up her needles and yarn and clicked away. She appeared to be knitting a sweater for a Cyclops. She might be able to imitate certain characters, but that didn't mean she could knit. "The dark corners of the human heart are capable of producing all kinds of mayhem."

Okay, so Jitty was *not* being helpful. No big surprise. "Why *are* you here? Surely you can latch on to something more interesting to do in the Great Beyond."

"I came to check up on you." She rose in a fluid movement that belied her supposed age. "Heart's Desire is similar to a village, Sarah Booth. What's happening here is a bit like a locked-door mystery, wouldn't you say?"

"Well, the killer has to be on the grounds. *If* Amanda was killed. Was she?" Could Jitty communicate with Amanda's spirit? I had another important spirit question. "I think I saw Mariam's ghost last night. For real, Jitty. She told me to protect her mother. Was it really Mariam?"

She ignored my questions and asked a couple of her own. "Was Amanda seeing anyone? Maybe one of the guards?" I should have known she'd give me no feedback on the Great Beyond. I'd tried before.

The thought had occurred to me. "Maybe she was dating someone here." I didn't know for certain what the young chef had been up to.

"Crime of passion. Tsk. Tsk."

I cut a sideways glance at Jitty. She was deep in the character of Miss Marple to tsk at the thought of passion. She was always after me to do the wild thang with Graf—or any suitable male—and get myself with child.

"What if it wasn't passion? What if Amanda discovered a secret?"

"Then if she has a fellow, he might know about it. Use your noggin, Sarah Booth."

I couldn't believe it. Jitty had provided a lead. "I like this incarnation of a famous detective," I told her. "It works for me."

The shift in her face was subtle. The wrinkles pulled tight and the lips filled, rounding into Jitty's full face with a hint of mischief. "You came to that conclusion on your own, missy. You needed a kick to jump-start those ole brain cells clackin'." She tossed the yarn onto the bed. "Lucky for both of us, I won't ever be no old lady knittin' on an ugly-ass sweater no one will ever want to wear."

"Yeah. Lucky for me," I agreed wholeheartedly. She was already starting to fade, and a good thing. I needed to conclude my search and escape Dodge before Coleman—or even worse, Palk—caught me. Time, when I was dealing with Jitty, seemed to stretch and compress. I checked my watch. Less than two minutes had passed. Still, as my aunt Loulane would say, only a fool tarried in a cuckold's bed. I stopped. Had Aunt Loulane really said such a thing to a twelve-year-old? More likely I'd over-heard a conversation I shouldn't have listened to. None-theless, it was enough to jolt my butt into high gear.

I searched the room and discovered a crumpled movie ticket stub in the bathroom trash can, a romance novel with a pressed flower between the pages, and a handwrit-ten note saying, "You deserve the best in romance. I hope Kyle is the man for you. Happy Birthday, Pammy." The copyright on the book was very recent. Which led me to believe that Kyle was someone she'd met at Heart's Desire.

An excellent morning's take, if I did say so myself.

I cleared out of the room, making sure Palk's keys were in my hand before I slammed the door.

"Pssst!"

I edged around the building to find Tinkie hiding be-hind a giant trash can. Lucky she was wearing her maid outfit or she would have ruined her expensive clothes.

"Amanda's car is parked in a building back there." She waved to a warehouse-type structure. "It's locked, dammit."

"Did you see the duffel bag she'd packed?"

"No. It's probably in the trunk."

I told her about the lead I'd discovered. "Now we need to find Kyle."

"Leave it to me," she said. "This will require a wardrobe change."

The smile spread wide on my face. Tinkie, when she set her mind to it, could be devastating to the male species. While there were rules governing the ethical conduct of a born-and-bred Daddy's Girl, when it came to the art of male manipulation, Tinkie didn't always follow "accepted procedure." With Tinkie going rogue, even the strongest man was at risk.

"I need a distraction to return Palk's keys," I told her as we scurried back to the main house.

"Your wish is my command." Tinkie went inside first. The kitchen and dining area were quiet. The furor Marjorie created by accusing Palk of lurking around her door had died down. Order had been restored. The feel of the house was like the quiet after a terrible storm. Everyone was hiding.

"Mr. Palk!" Tinkie yelled his name so suddenly, I jumped.

She waved me toward the employee dining area. "Get rid of those keys," she commanded.

She went straight to the dining room and on through to the parlor. "Mr. Palk, someone has been tampering with the things in my room. I need to know who and why."

Palk appeared, tie and jacket in place. "Lower your voice, madam," he said severely.

"Who went through my belongings?" Tinkie buttonholed him in a corner of the hall and I hustled into the employee dining area and tossed the keys in a corner behind the puddled draperies. He would find them eventually and wonder how they'd fallen from his coat pocket.

"Well, I never heard of a place where an employee's suitcase would be violated. Someone at Heart's Desire is a crook." Tinkie turned abruptly on her heel and headed up the stairs to Marjorie's room.

I followed, taking the back staircase meant for the hired help. The less Palk saw of me, the better. The less I saw of him and Yumi, the better for my sex life.

13

While Tinkie reassessed her wardrobe for the task of finding Kyle, I ran the vacuum and cleaned the bathroom. It wasn't a difficult job, but it was one Tinkie had likely never done in her life. She was accustomed to maids and servants. It never crossed her mind that dirt had to be assisted out of a house. Still, when she spun in front of the mirror, I had to admit the end result of all her primping was definitely worth it.

Marjorie had loaned her a long, red silk top with a handkerchief hem. Tinkie turned it into a minidress. With some flash and dazzle high heels—and a diamond necklace that had to weigh a pound—she was primed to take on the guards. All I had to do was walk with her and keep my lips zipped. And keep an eye out for Palk, Yumi, or other trouble.

We made it to the front gate without incident, and Tinkie stopped to chat up the four guards. Holding their semiautomatic assault weapons, they were gruff and resistant—at first. Tinkie dropped an earring and bent over to get it. To great advantage. Then she moved in for the kill with big baby-doll eyes and her lip-popping thing that shattered all resistance in the male species. I could do the same maneuver and it would be laughable. With Tinkie, it unleashed the male's most vivid lust.

"I heard the man to know is named Kyle," Tinkie said, stroking the barrel of one guard's gun. He literally trembled.

"Kyle? He's nothin' special," the guard said. He had to clear his throat. "I'm free tonight."

"A fine catch like you, runnin' wild tonight?" Tinkie pressed her hand against his chest. "I might have to reconsider my game plan. But I have to at least check this Kyle out. I heard from some of the kitchen help he has special . . . talents."

Oh, Lord, she was piling on the crap.

"He don't do nothin' any one of us can't," the man said. "In my case, with more . . . attention to detail." He'd regained his bravado. The backs of his fingers grazed Tinkie's cheek and she trilled up at him in a sort of combination giggle and sigh.

I was fascinated, and doing my best to make like a statue. I had no talent for this kind of flirting. Tinkie could turn a man inside out with minimal effort. It was her posture, her voice, her direct gaze, the way she trilled and simpered. She was a mirror, giving back to the man the image of himself he most desperately wanted to view.

And almost every man I knew was mesmerized by that reflection.

This manipulation was taught in the cradle by mothers who followed the Daddy's Girl tradition. For a long while, I'd disdained this behavior, but as I'd grown to know Tinkie and watched her, I'd changed my position. This was a skill, like Cece's great ability to interview a subject and draw out secrets. It was not unlike the trained ability of an investigator—a person who listened and watched and put together the puzzle pieces.

Tinkie wasn't dishonest. She reflected what a man wanted to be. The dishonesty came in his own failed ability to recognize himself.

"Now, where might I find this Kyle, so if he doesn't work out, I can come right back here and continue this fascinating encounter."

The guard sighed. "He's at the barracks." He pointed down a narrow trail that led through the woods. Outside the eight-foot wall were cotton fields—flat, wide-open rows of money crop stretching to the horizon. The land within the compound remained densely wooded. "It's about a mile. You'll break your neck in those heels. I could arrange a ride in one of the Jeeps."

Tinkie only laughed up at him. "I've run a marathon in these heels, honey. I was born in a pair of stilettos. My mama wore hers in the delivery room. She meant to style even while in labor."

The men laughed with approval, and Tinkie signaled me to follow her as she sauntered down the trail, making sure the hitch in her get-along held the attention of all.

Out of earshot, she moaned and removed the shoes. "I'm exhausted."

"How do you do that?" I'd seen it more than once,

but I was always amazed. "You could have stripped them down and shaved a barber pole around their bodies. Not a single one would have protested."

The sly smile faded and she was all business. "It takes hard work. You have no idea how my sorority sisters and I used to practice back at Ole Miss." She checked over her shoulder to be sure we weren't followed. "You were doing the same thing, only on a stage and pretending to be Kate the shrew or the older sister in *Crimes of the Heart*."

"You saw my plays." I was dumbstruck. In college, I'd viewed Tinkie about as useful as navel lint. Yet she'd come to watch me onstage in college productions. And I'd never known. "Why?"

"Folks said you were a great actress. And you were from my hometown. I always went to see you. Even though you were a real weirdo and a social outcast, you were a talented actress."

Shamed by this revelation, I walked on beside Tinkie. I'd written her off as silly and a waste of time, yet she'd viewed me as talented. An actress. I had seriously, and sadly, far too many times, underestimated the woman who traveled beside me.

"Do you ever regret being trained as a DG?" I asked her.

"My heavens, no." A smile moved across her face. "This is a powerful tool, Sarah Booth. Your aunt Loulane tried hard to help you learn some DG skills. She arrived on the job too late. Your mother had already turned you into an independent woman." She laughed. "But I clearly remember Aunt Loulane telling you things like 'You can catch more flies with sugar than vinegar.'"

"That's a DG saying?" I had no idea my aunt was

versed in the rules of DGdom. She was a genteel woman with proper upbringing, and she'd given six years of her life to care for me until I was old enough to go to college. I appreciated all she did, all she tried to do, even though she was nothing like my mother.

"Not a rule but a well-stated principle. Men will give you what you want a lot easier if you convince them *they want* to give it—if they think it's their idea. Sarah Booth, you just state what you want and expect them to do it because it's the right thing or fair or some such malarkey. You make it six times harder than necessary. A little giggle, a sigh in a man's ear, a touch on his big, strong muscles—he's happy to make you happy. But it has to be his idea, not yours."

I understood the theory. And god knew I couldn't deny the results. "But it's . . . dishonest."

Tinkie threw up her hands. "*You* want to convince a man's brain. *I* work on other parts of the anatomy. My method is more direct, and also more effective. The man enjoys it more. So how is it dishonest?"

As I tried to formulate an answer to her question, we rounded a turn and came upon the barracks where the security guards lived. It was bigger than I expected and half a dozen off-duty men, all rugged and buff, turned to watch us draw closer. Or I should say watch Tinkie. She slung those heels over her shoulder and headed straight for them.

"Which one of you is Kyle?" she asked with body language that promised a wonderful reward for the right answer.

One of the men pointed to a young man seated alone on a bench beneath a poplar tree. Kyle slumped with his head hanging, dark hair falling over his face, visibly upset.

It wasn't hard to deduce he'd heard about Amanda and was deeply disturbed.

"He's about as low as a snake's belly," I said.

"I wonder why he's still here, at work, and not with—" She inhaled sharply. "Do you think they won't let him off this compound to go to the funeral home?"

Anything was possible at Heart's Desire. "Let's see what he has to say."

He saw Tinkie headed his way, but he didn't react. He was either deeply depressed or dead. "Kyle, we're friends of Amanda's," I said as we approached. "We'd like to ask you some questions."

"I don't have any answers," he said glumly. Then fire sparked in his eyes. "What the hell happened? Who killed her? She was just a kid."

He was hurting, and I didn't know what to do to comfort him. Tinkie didn't hesitate, though. She sat beside him on the bench and took his hand. "I'm so sorry. This is a terrible thing. Sarah Booth and I want to figure out what happened to your friend. The person who hurt her deserves to be punished."

He blinked back tears, and my heart ached with a dull pain. "All I know is that she called me, hysterical, saying she had to get out of Heart's Desire before they hurt her," he said.

"They?"

"That's what she said. She was so upset, she wasn't making a lot of sense. She talked to me while she packed. From the sounds I heard, she went through her room like a tornado. I told her to find me before she left. The terms of my employment dictate that I can't leave the compound. Screw the rules! I should have gone with her. I should have quit!"

He waved a hand at the barracks and men. "This is a ridiculous crock of shit. All these guns and guards—for what? A bunch of rich people who wouldn't cause a ripple if they all disappeared. Amanda hated her job. I should have seen to it she quit Heart's Desire."

He was tense with fury and pain, but Tinkie hung on to his arm. "It's not your fault, Kyle. We would have helped Amanda if we'd had any idea she was in danger. Disliking a job normally doesn't lead to murder. You can't blame yourself."

"She was freaking out when she called. She was afraid." He flayed away at himself.

"Did she say why?" I asked.

"She only said they meant to hurt her and she had to escape. We made arrangements to meet by our tree. It grows close to the wall, and even though we never did it, you could climb the tree and drop over the wall. We found the tree together and talked about how we'd see each other if one of us quit, using the tree. She was so unhappy with that Korean chef in the kitchen." His anger burned away his tears. "I planned to climb out tonight and meet her. But she never made it off the compound. They killed her."

"It's possible it was an accident," Tinkie said, tightening her grip on his hand. And a good thing, too. Her words were like gas on a fire.

"Amanda didn't fall down those basement steps. What was she doing in the basement? Was she meeting someone? She had no reason to be down there. She was afraid of the place where they hold the séances. She said there were ghosts down there and she wasn't kidding."

Fury and frustration contorted his features. "We had plans! Once we were done here, we were moving to

Austin, Texas. I wanted to work on a ranch, and she could find work as a chef."

He was breaking my heart, but it was Tinkie who put her arms around him and hugged. "I'm so sorry," she said. "Sarah Booth and I want to find the truth. We want to punish the people who did this, but you have to help us."

I gave him a moment to compose himself. "I saw her in the parking lot, and she had her things and was dragging them to her car. She was supposed to follow a friend of mine out of the compound, but for some reason she turned around and went back. Do you know why?"

"Hold on," Tinkie said, tipping her head toward a trio of men drawing close. Two watched Tinkie, but the third one focused on Kyle. "You two go someplace quiet," Tinkie said. "I'll handle the troops."

Tinkie did have her ways. I left her to it, and Kyle and I walked to a screened-in recreational area and took a seat in a corner. Tinkie charged the men in full-tilt flirting mode. Within two minutes, she had their complete attention.

"I can't believe this," he said. "Amanda was a child, really. She never did a bad thing to anyone."

"You said Amanda was afraid. You don't have any idea why?"

He struggled to find an answer. "She said there were spirits in the house. Unhappy spirits." He closed his eyes briefly. "I thought it was her imagination. Amanda hated Yumi and the butler. She despised her job. I thought her imagination trumped her common sense. I should have listened closer, believed in her more."

His hands clenched and I had a split-second fantasy of Kyle landing a fist on Palk's arrogant chin. The butler brought out the violence in me. "Did she tell you what happened to make her quit?"

"No. We didn't have time. It's against the rules for employees to date, so we had to sneak around late at night. This came up all of a sudden." He looked at Tinkie making googly-eyes at the other guards only fifty yards away, and hardness settled into his features.

"You can't blame yourself." He would. My words offered no healing balm.

He put both hands on his knees, as if he meant to steady himself. "She called me when she was almost at the gate. She was crying hard. She said she had to tell someone at Heart's Desire something—she couldn't leave until she spoke with one of the guests or maybe a staffer. She thought someone was in danger." He frowned. "She left her cell phone at the base of the tree where we used to meet."

"She had a cell phone?" Good news at last.

"I got it for her after they took hers. She kept it hidden. We used it to make dates, you know, text each other. She was afraid to try to sneak it past the guards. In case they searched her on the way out. They'd be able to see we'd been communicating. She was afraid she'd get me in trouble, so she left it. I retrieved it after I heard she was . . . dead."

"Could I see it?" I asked.

He looked around, but no one was paying any attention to us. Tinkie had the other guards gamboling about her like puppies. From inside his shirt, Kyle brought out the cell phone. "When she didn't ever leave, I thought she'd changed her mind. It wasn't until I heard . . . You can keep the phone. I don't need it anymore."

"I'll bring it back," I promised. He seemed so dismal that I added, "I'm sorry, Kyle. I liked Amanda, too. If someone did push her down the stairs, we'll find out who. Do you have any ideas?"

"No. Palk's an ass, but not a murderer. When you find the bastard who did this, I want ten minutes alone with him."

I couldn't promise that. Coleman would never allow it. I rose slowly. "We'll be in touch."

"Don't come back here," he said. "They know everything that goes on. Once is happenstance. Twice is a reason for them to investigate. I don't want to be fired—or worse—until I find out who killed Amanda."

"Thanks." I took his words to heart as I joined Tinkie. She bade her admirers farewell, and we headed back to the big house. I was eager to check out the phone, but I didn't even want to try until we were somewhere no one could see us.

Halfway down the wooded trail, I stopped to examine Amanda's phone. The only calls on it were to Kyle. Those kids stayed up all night messaging each other. Young love.

"That's just heartbreaking," Tinkie said. She had lost a lot of her sass as we read the sweet notes between Kyle and Amanda. "He texted her twenty times the night before she died." She shook her head as if to dislodge the pain. "Man, that's just too hard."

The texts yielded nothing new. The phone had a camera, so we plowed through the photos. Most were of Amanda, dressed up for a rendezvous with her lover. A few sneaky shots of Yumi showed her working in the kitchen—or fussing at someone. Several were photos of the interior of Heart's Desire.

"There's nothing of any use," Tinkie said. I'd told her

what Kyle had related to me, and we'd both gotten our hopes up the phone might reveal something.

At last I came across what looked like a blurry picture of Yumi. I pulled it up. To my surprise, it was a video. Yumi was in the kitchen, and judging by the light, it was nighttime. I couldn't tell what she was doing—cradling her ear? I clicked the video into action.

"I will take care of this matter," Yumi said into a cell phone, and there was iron in her voice. "I always finish my mission. No one cracks the whip at me. I crack the whip."

I had no doubts about that statement.

Yumi continued her rant. "I will handle this gnat, do not worry. Your political career is safe as long as you leave me to my job."

The sound of a dish rattling caused Yumi to whirl around. The picture went crazy, then black, and I realized Amanda had slipped the phone into her pocket.

"What are you doing here?" Yumi demanded. "Why are you in my kitchen, little piggy? Here for a midnight treat?"

"I want baking soda and a lemon," Amanda said. "I have heartburn, and those Nazis on the gate won't let me go off the grounds to get some Prevacid. My granny used to make a lemon whiz when she had heartburn and I thought I'd give it a try."

"You're here to spy on me, aren't you?" Yumi was furious.

"Why would I care what you do?" Amanda's voice quivered.

"Who sent you?"

"Nobody sent me. I came for baking soda."

"Get it and get out."

There were rustling noises, then footsteps as Amanda retreated. The phone went dead. She'd turned it off.

"No wonder she hated it here," Tinkie said.

"No wonder she didn't want to try to smuggle this phone past the gate."

"Do you think Yumi killed her?" Tinkie asked. "What could her mission be? She's a chef."

"She's the best suspect we have right now." I had a grand thought. "There are a couple of photos of Yumi in the kitchen. Let's e-mail one to Coleman. Maybe he can do a background check on this crazy chef and see who she really is."

Tinkie gave me a hug. "Some days you surprise even me with your mastery of technology."

Without further ado, I zapped the best photo of Yumi to the sheriff's office with a note and a question. "What have you found?" It was good to be in communication with the rest of the world again.

Tinkie and I returned to the big house to find Marjorie nearing a hissy fit. Clothes had been torn from hangers and thrown about the floor. "There's a séance tonight," she said. "Thank goodness. I was afraid we wouldn't have another."

My conscience pinged—I'd failed to tell her of the "visit" I received from a young girl who greatly resembled her daughter, the eerie concern the young girl had expressed. The ghost of Mariam—if it was Mariam at all—bothered me. Why was this spirit presenting itself to me instead of to Marjorie? If Marjorie was in danger, why didn't Mariam talk to her?

In my dealings with the spirit world I'd learned a few things. One of the most important: Jitty might devil me, but she was always on my side. Mariam appeared to me, a stranger. Water dripped from her, as if she were forever caught between the Mississippi River and the present. If Mariam was in Heart's Desire, why not communicate directly with her mother?

And another thing bothered me about the ghostly presence I'd seen. Jitty's spectacular wardrobe spiked envy in me. Not so with the dripping ghost of my vision or on the DVD. Why was the ghostly little girl still wearing the dress she'd drowned in?

Was it because Mariam died suddenly and unexpectedly, and somehow was trapped in that moment? Was it because she was pissed off? Jitty had embraced death— and her role as resident haint of Dahlia House. Was it possible a spirit's ultimate end was determined by attitude? That hardly seemed appropriate.

The point was, I had questions and no answers. And time to kill, until Coleman showed up or the séance began.

"I need a walk," I announced.

"You just returned from a walk," Marjorie pointed out.

For a moment I was speechless. It sounded like she thought I was really her maid. "Tinkie is here and I need to check something."

"She is the more loyal of you two," Marjorie said, annoyed.

Saint Francis on a trapeze! She was miffed because I wasn't babysitting her. "I'll be back." I did my best interpretation of the Terminator.

"Watch out for ghosts," Tinkie said, unable to suppress a smile.

I didn't bother with a response but went out the door and along the hallway. At the first floor, I squeezed behind a decorative screen as Palk, with a half-dozen maids parading behind like chicklets, zipped past.

I ducked into the spa, where Amaryllis Dill—or so I assumed by the yellow towel wrapped around her head and the yellow eye mask—lounged in a mud bath. Okay, not my cup of tea. I could manage dirty on my own.

The two country singers were working out on elliptical trainers. I took a moment to appreciate their athletic abilities. They were no slouches. Maybe they needed the level of fitness to perform onstage. Dancing and singing could be pretty taxing, as I remembered from my days in musicals.

The Addlesons were nowhere to be seen, but there were several attendees working in the spa I'd never met. The staff at Heart's Desire must cost the Westins a pretty penny.

I backed out and headed for the servants' stairs to the basement. I wanted a word with the laundress. Stella had worked in the basement for a number of years. I didn't believe she was ignorant of all of Heart's Desire's secrets.

The laundry was empty. No Stella. Even the washers and dryers were quiet. The basement, in fact, ached with silence. Or maybe my nerves were stretched to the point of hypersensitivity. I couldn't help but think of Amanda.

When something in my pocket buzzed, I jumped so high, I struck my head on the doorframe. It took a moment for me to realize it was the cell phone Coleman had brought me. I'd wisely put it on vibrate.

Stifling the curses that wanted to leap from my lips, I answered.

"Hello, dah-link," Cece said. "Harold and I have been busy little beavers on your behalf. We have news!"

14

Cece's voice, low and well modulated, gave me a wealth of details about the property of Heart's Desire. Her original report contained the sordid gossip. The financial history of Heart's Desire, acquired thanks to Harold, was equally interesting.

"The house changed hands a number of times," Cece related. "Three owners defaulted and walked away. The property is rumored to be cursed. Many Layland residents simply won't go near the place. This has worked to the Westins' advantage. Most people had forgotten about the old place—until Brandy and Sherry showed up. They've kept talk quiet and limited gossip by keeping all of the employees shut up inside. The death of the young chef has changed all that. The old talk of curses has re-surfaced."

"Cursed?" That was a new one. "Not haunted?"

"Both, actually." Her enthusiasm was hard to miss. Cece was pumped at the prospect of a haunted house that was also cursed. A death—most likely a murder—was the perfect hook to hang the story on. Now, this was good copy. In fact, the whole Heart's Desire episode was an embarrassment of riches from a journalist's point of view.

I did believe in ghosts, but I didn't believe in curses. People were superstitious. They often made their lives much harder than necessary by believing in crazy notions.

"Thanks, Cece. I don't understand how this fits to-gether, but this is a significant piece of the puzzle. What about the country music singers?"

"Lola Monee and Gretchen Waller—they're legit. At least they have top hits in the country market. They should be well off, based on the big names who've cut their songs."

Good to know. "And our chef, the mysterious Yumi Kato?"

"She worked in D.C. before coming to Mississippi. She was in the White House in 2003. There's not much of a trail to follow before that. She defected in the early 2000s. Harold and I don't have international contacts. At least not in North Korea."

"North Korea?" Amanda had called her a communist bitch. What had Amanda discovered about the chef?

"Right. Her birth country. Because her life prior to arriving in the U.S. is such a blank, we figure she has a political connection. Maybe granted asylum. She left the White House under a cloud. Seems she chased the presi-dent's dog with a meat cleaver."

"There couldn't be two chefs with a fondness for meat cleavers. This has to be her."

"Seems the dog slipped into the kitchen and stole a roast off the counter. Yumi took it personally and chased the dog, making threats. The First Lady nearly had a heart attack and Yumi was dismissed."

I had to laugh. Yumi's heart softened not a whit for man or beast. "Thanks, Cece. Have you talked to Coleman?"

"He's a hard man to track down. He's been chewing on some bone he won't drop long enough to answer a phone call from me."

There was something in her voice. I couldn't put my finger on it, but some little something gave me pause. "Are you up to something?"

"Not me. See ya, Sarah Booth. My other line is ringing."

I put away the cell phone. I'd been away from the second floor too long. Even though I was doing most of the housework, Tinkie had performed the bulk of the baby-sitting and likely needed rescue from Marjorie, who was a tricky cardsharp.

Marjorie sometimes acted dotty and played the sympathy card, but when she was into rummy, she was cold-blooded and ruthless. She'd already taken Tinkie for close to two hundred bucks.

Marjorie insisted on a nap, but at eight o'clock, she was ready for the séance. Sherry had changed the séance time to nine o'clock, and she'd relocated to the front parlor.

When we arrived, Palk and his minions had brought the round table from the basement. Sherry took her place at the head, Brandy at the foot. The others selected seats, and once again, Tinkie and I stood against a wall behind Marjorie's chair. Palk would never consider allowing us to sit.

My curiosity was aroused when Chasley was not in attendance. I wondered if he was still in the house. Marjorie, too, searched around the room. Before she could ask a question about her son, Sherry spoke up.

"I know last night we were all dealt a terrible shock. Amanda's death is an awful, awful loss. I want you to know I won't contact Amanda. Often a spirit who has just crossed is disoriented and upset. To bring her back here, to Heart's Desire, after what happened, would be unwise."

Tinkie and I exchanged a glance. Was Sherry worried about what Amanda might reveal?

The participants at the table held hands. Palk dimmed the lights, and Tinkie and I edged closer together. Earlier, as Marjorie napped, I'd had a moment on the balcony to share Cece's findings with Tink. Now she was determined to dig up more information. Tinkie, who seemed to be the epitome of a ditzy blonde, had a real head for figures. She could tally up a column of digits in a heartbeat. And she understood how money worked—a body of knowledge I'd never managed to get a grip on.

While I was woolgathering, I failed to listen to what was happening at the table. I figured some new disaster would strike to prevent a séance. I'd come to conclude Sherry was about as much a medium as I was. She could hypnotize with the best of them, but she wasn't dishing up any dead people.

Against my will, I caught the cadence of Sherry's voice. She spoke softly but with passion. She called upon the spirits to cooperate, to breach the veil separating the world of mortal and immortal. I was drawn into a state of relaxation despite my resolve not to be tranced by Sherry again. Fight as I did, I saw the scene she described—the golden light, a wooden door, the handle gripped in my hand, the portal opening into bright white light—

Tinkie's sudden grip on my fingers almost made me cry out. The toe of her shoe in my instep stopped me. Lucky she was wearing her maid brogans with the soft leather toe. She indicated the curtains by the window.

The sheers moved slowly, as if stirred by a gentle wind. No one else seemed to notice. They all sat with their eyes squinched tight, concentrating on the chant Sherry muttered.

But it wasn't at the window the entity appeared. It was across the room, in the doorway. She wore a brocade gown, and her bearing was regal.

"Who summons me to this plane?" the woman asked in English heavily tinged with a French accent.

I thought the people at the table would stand up and run in all directions.

"Remain seated!" Sherry commanded them. And they obeyed. Amaryllis cowered slightly but didn't bolt and run.

"With whom do I have the pleasure of speaking?" Sherry asked.

"You are so common, you don't recognize your empress?" was the reply.

"It's Joséphine! It's Joséphine Bonaparte!" Shimmer Addleson tried to shake free of her husband's and Sherry's hands, but they clung harder and kept her in her chair.

"If you break the circle, she will leave!" Brandy whispered savagely. "You'll never hear the answer to your questions."

That was as effective as a bolt in the head. Shimmer dropped into her chair.

"Why do you bother me?" the spirit asked again. "The journey here is tiring, and I find the . . . atmosphere unpleasant." She glided around the opulent room with a scowl of distaste.

I studied the entity as carefully as I could with Tinkie climbing on me like I was a tree. She was quiet in her panic, but she was about to melt into my skin, she was so close.

"A distant relative is here," Sherry said softly. "She needs your counsel, Queen . . . uh, Empress Bonaparte."

The spirit seemed mollified by Sherry's obsequious tone. "Does she need to know how to charm her lover? That is my specialty. Napoléon was a man amongst men, but I tamed him. I made him beg for me. Ask me any questions about the art of love, and I will answer."

Shimmer laughed nervously, but a warning glare from Sherry quelled her. "No, Your Highness. It isn't advice on love I seek. I want to create a fragrance worthy of your name. I need help with my cosmetic line. I want to call the perfume Joséphine's Potion . . . if you don't mind."

Rich laughter filled the room, and the entity drew closer. I could see the creaminess of her shoulders and chest, the shine of her hair. Was it really Joséphine Bonaparte, famous wife of an emperor? Or was this a trick? Because I was forbidden to move—by the Westins and because Tinkie was clinging to my waist and shoulders—I couldn't explore the entity.

Yikes! I didn't have to. She walked toward me. There was a sense of occlusion, as if she were solid but not. When she glided, light shone through her.

"You want to use my name to sell your perfume, is that right, little strumpet?"

Shimmer almost swallowed her tongue. "Yes."

Joséphine laughed. "You are a woman I admire. You have a dream and you're willing to risk extreme measures to see it to fruition. You are like me."

"Oh, madam!" Shimmer almost collapsed in a puddle of pleasure at the compliment. "I've studied you and tried to pattern myself after you. I—"

"Did you have a question for Empress Bonaparte?" Brandy interrupted. For a brief second, boredom seemed to touch her features.

"I, uh, I wanted to know—" Shimmer looked around the table as if a guest would prompt her. "I wanted to know your favorite scent!" She was triumphant.

"The delicate perfume of the narcissus, the flower you call the paperwhite, is perfect for morning. But for the evening, it must be heavier, more sensual. The gardenia is like a white stain in the night. Now I must be off. And if you call the perfume Joséphine's Potion, it should be Joséphine's Potion of Amour."

"Oh, yes! Yes, that's perfect." Shimmer was all atwitter.

Joséphine was worse than Jitty. She was there and then she was gone. No chance for more questions. No chance for anyone to discern if the whole thing had been rigged.

Shimmer took a moment to regain her senses, and then she sprang from the chair. "Thank you! Thank you, Sherry. You did it! I have permission to use Joséphine's name and I know which scent to use. This is everything I need. By this time next year, my cosmetic line will be in every major department store in the United States. Then the world!"

She broke free of the circle. "Come, Roger, we have to budget for *two* perfumes. One for morning and one for the night!"

Roger Addleson sat stunned, as if he couldn't process what had happened. Slowly he rose to his feet. "Thank you," he said to the room in general before he went after his wife.

"Well, I never!" Marjorie's face clouded. "What about the rest of us? Perhaps we'd like a chance to hear from the spirit world. But no, Shimmer has what she needs, and now she's gone."

Sherry swayed in her chair. She planted her hands on the table and steadied herself. "I'm sorry. I'm exhausted. Let us adjourn until tomorrow evening."

"I need help," Amaryllis spoke up first. It was one of the few times I'd heard her open her mouth. "I can't stay here much longer, and I have to speak with . . . a departed person. I must. Before I make a fatal mistake." She appealed to everyone at the table.

"And my daughter. What about Mariam?" Marjorie said, indignant. "I must contact her. You can't stop now. I've been here days and you haven't brought Mariam to me."

"I'm sorry," Sherry said. "Connecting with the spirits drains me. If I don't have enough energy, I can't help them come through."

"I've paid a pretty penny to be here to speak with Mariam." There was iron in Marjorie's tone.

"And you will speak with your daughter," Brandy intervened in a soft, conciliatory voice. "Of course you'll speak with her. But not tonight. Sherry is exhausted. This takes a toll on her. You have no idea how it pulls the life force from her to bridge the gap between the worlds. You must allow her to recuperate."

I thought Marjorie would resist, but she settled against the back of her chair. "Where is my son, Chasley?" Marjorie asked. "Why wasn't he invited?"

"I asked him to join us. He said he wouldn't participate," Sherry answered. "He said you were crazy to do this and he refused to get involved."

Uh-oh. He was probably watching, putting together information for his case against his mother. I didn't doubt, given the least opportunity, he would question her sanity in court if he thought he could get control of her billions.

"Please! Try to see if Mariam will visit with us," Marjorie said. The starch had gone out of her. She was a woman in her sixties who looked it. "I implore you. Try."

Brandy whispered to Sherry, who finally spoke. "I will make one more attempt to contact a spirit. I don't know who will come through. As weak as I am, I can only cast out a plea and see who responds." Sherry held out her hands as she talked. She indicated Tinkie and me. "Come and join us. Complete the circle."

Tinkie jumped at the chance. She was at the table in a flash and reaching for Brandy's hand on one side and mine on the other. Everyone looked at me. I didn't really want to do this. I liked my position standing against the wall.

"Miss Booth?" Brandy would have snapped her fingers if Tinkie hadn't been holding her hand.

I slid into a chair and allowed my hands to be captured.

"Close your eyes and concentrate your energy," Sherry said. She did sound tired. I disobeyed and watched the expressions of everyone. They all looked sincerely focused on the task at hand. At last I yielded to Sherry's hypnotic voice and my eyelids drifted shut.

Sherry took me to the wooden door again. I pushed it open and stepped through. A numbing cold crept over my body. I knew without looking an entity was behind me, and it wasn't the bossy Joséphine or the super-bossy Jitty.

I opened my eyes to find everyone else at the table completely unaware of the spirit's presence. I shifted to check behind me and Tinkie pinched my hand hard. One day I was going to whop her upside the head for doing that. I was contemplating the satisfying sound a whack would make when I saw movement in the far corner of the room. When I saw the female, I lost all thoughts of punishing Tinkie.

The spirit stood in the shadows, a woman a bit shorter than me with thick black hair styled as if she cut it herself. She was fit, and the black dress she wore hugged her curves. She stepped away from the wall and moved—sort of floated—toward Tinkie. I didn't have a clue who she was or what she wanted.

Sherry had dragged in a stray spirit and this one had a big interest in my partner.

Even stranger was that no one else sensed her. Sherry continued with her calm, mesmerizing tone, lulling everyone at the table into a trancelike state. Only I watched the approach of the entity. I let out a breath and the air crystallized with frost. Holy cow, this was the real deal.

I tried to communicate with her mentally, but she had no interest in me at all. She studied Tinkie as if she were a rare art object. At one point, I thought she might touch my partner, but she stopped, her hand hovering over Tink's shoulder, and she floated over to Marjorie Littlefield, who sat with her eyes closed and her face upturned as if in prayer. What was everyone at the table doing that they didn't feel the cold in the room or sense the spirit inches from them?

My first thought was to intervene, but the ghost couldn't hurt a human. Spirits might scare a person into a coronary, but physically they had no power. At least Jitty didn't. But enough was enough. As I pushed back my chair, the ghost spoke.

"We share some things in common, Sarah Booth."

"Who are you?" I asked mentally. Better yet, why did she know my name?

"A colleague."

"What do you want? Why can't they see you? Or hear you?" I stared hard. I knew this woman, but she wasn't a ghost; she was a character in a series of mystery novels. Smart, tough Kinsey Millhone and clad in the world-famous, indestructible black dress. "You're PI Millhone."

"You've got me pegged." She was pleased. "You're smarter than you seem."

"Thanks. But you're not a ghost. You're a fictional character."

"A technicality. I'm here for you. I've got my own cases to work, but I heard in the Great Beyond you were headed for real trouble."

That sounded ominous. And it also sounded like— "Jitty!"

She stepped closer to the candles on the table and I saw the curve of her cheek and the beautiful mocha skin. "You're a little slow on the uptake, Sarah Booth."

All around the table, eyes were closed as Sherry continued her hypnotic spiel. "Did you really hear I was headed for trouble?"

She tilted her head, thinking. "Details are not available. You believe me, though, don't you?"

"I do."

"I have certain . . . advantages in this case."

Jitty wasn't one to breach the confidentiality of the Great Beyond, but I had to try for some answers. "You can talk to Mariam, can't you?"

She hesitated. "You know the answer in your heart. Even if I could, I can't relay information to you." She walked around the table to stand beside me. "You're smart, Sarah Booth. And observant. You're a good private dick. Everything you need to know is right in front of you."

With that, she was gone.

Sherry was still speaking, entreating Mariam to connect with her mother. Tinkie's eyes were closed, and there was a frown of concentration on her face. Amaryllis Dill was biting her bottom lip, and the two country music songwriters opened their eyes and surveyed the room. I realized that Brandy, too, had opened her peepers. She was about to speak when a bloodcurdling scream echoed from upstairs.

"What the hell?" Brandy broke the circle and knocked over her chair.

"My goodness." Marjorie slumped, leaning on the table for support. "What was that?"

The scream came again, this time followed by a curse. "You black son of Satan. I will squeeze the life out of you!"

"Chasley!" Marjorie lurched up from the table.

Tinkie and I were already running toward the staircase. We made it to the second-floor landing, and it took only one glance to ascertain the source of his pain and suffering.

Pluto sat at the top of the stairs. The door to Marjorie's room was wide open. Chasley was on his stomach, and a long red streak of blood slashed across the whiteness of the back of his shirt.

"Call the pound. That beast jumped from the transom onto my back and injured me," Chasley said. "I told Mother he was dangerous."

Pluto calmly turned and walked toward Chasley, who scrabbled backwards on his stomach as if the hound of the Baskervilles was after him. I couldn't help it; I laughed. Chasley reminded me of a really awful Harold Lloyd slapstick comedy. "If this were a silent film, you'd be ingenious. Now you're just sort of . . . pathetic."

Chasley's expression was indignant. "The cat is rabid. I assure you, he will be impounded and his head cut off and sent to the state lab for a rabies test."

"You suffer from a real fondness for the visceral," I noted with a heap of sarcasm.

"You won't touch a hair on Pluto's head." Tinkie scooped the big kitty up in her arms. She started to give him to Marjorie, but the cat hissed and jumped free. For a fat black puss, he ran like greased lightning. In three seconds, he ducked under the bed, his little nails scrabbling a moment as his gut hung.

Tinkie radiated fury. "You've terrorized the cat." She rounded on Marjorie's son. "You're a bully and an ass." She went into the suite and slammed the door.

"The cat is crow bait." Chasley sought majesty but fell short and landed in lame-threat territory.

"Pluto isn't going anywhere, but I can't say the same for

you," I told him quietly. "What were you doing in Marjorie's room? The cat was shut inside. Had you not attempted to enter the suite uninvited, you wouldn't be hurt. Any accusations filed against Pluto will result in charges of trespassing and breaking and entering against you." How could someone so damn handsome be so mean?

"Heed her, Chasley," Marjorie said. She looked flushed, as if her blood pressure had skyrocketed out of control. "Can't you simply leave me alone? I only want to speak with Mariam. I want to settle things with her. Then I can die in peace. Why can't you let me have that cold comfort?"

"Drama queen," Chasley hurled. "If you aren't the star of your own melodrama, you aren't happy. Your cat attacked me and I'm sure I'll require plastic surgery. Perhaps you'll refer me to the man who does all your work."

"I know we've never been close, but why do you hate me so much?" Marjorie asked.

"You never loved me, Mother. And you rubbed my nose in the fact. Even when Mariam was alive, you never had a moment for me. After she died, you couldn't bear to be in the same room with me. I was only fifteen. I was a child."

"You were much more than a child, Chasley. You were a—"

Brandy planted herself between them. "Chasley, take yourself down to the kitchen and let me put some antibiotic salve on those scratches." She offered Chasley a hand, and as she did, her foot dislodged a digital recorder from beneath him. It landed at my feet, and I picked it up.

"That's mine!" Chasley sprang to his feet, not wounded nearly so much as he'd pretended. "Give it back to me."

"After I hear what you were recording." I whipped it behind my back.

"Mother!" He implored Marjorie. "Make her give it to me. I need it." He gritted his teeth. "I really need it."

To my confusion, Marjorie reached out her hand for the recorder. "I'll take that. I'm too upset for this kind of argument."

I hesitated. At last, though, I gave it to her. We'd listen to it in the privacy of her room, which might be a better plan.

Chasley leaned into my face. "This is not the end of this. I will have that creature destroyed. Mark my words. Tomorrow, animal control will be here and that abomination will be taken and put down."

"You will do no such thing." Marjorie's voice was carefully controlled. "I can't take any more emotional strife. This has been an exhausting day. I'm not feeling well. I want to lie down."

Brandy offered her arm and assisted Marjorie into the room. The other guests departed. I was left alone in the hallway with Chasley.

"I'm on to you," I told him. "Before this is over, it's highly probable you'll be investigated for the death of your sister. For Marjorie's sake, I hope there's no proof you played a role in Mariam's drowning, but if there is one iota of evidence, I will find it, and you'll be sorry of the day you were born."

"There is no proof, because I didn't do a damn thing. I've lived with the rumors and innuendos my entire life." He was angry, but there was another emotion present. Hurt. "I hope Mariam shows up. She'll tell Mother I'm innocent of any wrongdoing. I turned my back on my

sister for five minutes while I went behind a cargo con-
tainer to smoke a cigarette. That's my sin. Neglect. I was
a child, not a murderer."

For the first time, I felt what it might be like to have
spent thirty years with the taint of a crime everywhere I
turned. If Chasley was innocent of his sister's death, his
life had been more hellish than Marjorie's.

"You should tell Marjorie this, not me."

"Don't you think I've tried? I even came here, to this
house of insane schemes and undead spirits, to try one
last time. Mother won't meet with me."

"It doesn't help that you keep threatening her cat."

"She loves him more than she ever loved me. I'm bitter.
I can be an ass." He turned so that I saw only his handsome profile. "I would give anything for my mother to
call my name one time and smile. I've watched her. When
you or the other maid enters a room, she's glad you're
there. I step in and she has only contempt."

"Tinkie and I are only here to help Marjorie."

"She prefers the company of two maids to that of her
own son. How do you think that makes me feel?"

"This isn't completely her fault. You—"

"Act like a cruel bastard?"

"Yes." It was fish or cut bait as far as I was concerned.
I could sympathize with Chasley, up to a point. He was
responsible for a lot of his own woes.

"I do lash out. I know it doesn't help my cause, but
I'm frustrated."

"Talk to your mother." I had no helpful advice. "Before this goes any further."

"I've tried, Miss Booth. Oh, I've tried. I feel my only
recourse will be in the courts."

"We'll see about that." I entered Marjorie's suite and witnessed a scene from a Vincent Price movie. Pluto was on the chaise, arched like a Halloween cat. The sound he made would have sent zombies shambling in the opposite direction. He was seriously disturbed.

"What's wrong with the cat?"

"Marjorie tried to pick him up and he went bonkers." Tinkie warily approached the feline, who glared and growled.

"Chasley must have done something to Pluto," Marjorie said. "He's never behaved like this to me. Pluto loves me. What if he's hurt? What if Chasley abused him?"

Tinkie's slow approach worked. Pluto calmed down, and she gently stroked his fur. In a moment she had him on her lap. As she petted him and whispered endearments, she checked for any sore places or injuries.

"I think he's okay," she said at last.

Instead of relief, Marjorie's face showed alarm. "Then why is he acting like he's lost his mind?"

"He's confused and upset," I offered. "Cats are territorial. They bond with their environment, often more than people. Think about it. Pluto has been living at home, then at Madam Tomeeka's, and now here. I'm sure he's feeling insecure. It's possible Chasley did god knows what to him, but Pluto will settle down."

Long ago I'd worked a case involving Zinnia's literary genius, Lawrence Ambrose. A great cat lover, Lawrence had shared basic tips in taming the savage feline beast.

Marjorie pressed a tissue to her nose. "Maybe it's a sign I should give up." She sort of melted into a chair. "I can't go on. I want you both to leave tonight. I'm done here. Mariam won't come to me, my cat hates me. It's time to abandon this vale of tears."

"Nonsense." Tinkie eased toward her with the cat in her arms. I saw what she meant to do and couldn't react in time to stop it. She put Pluto in Marjorie's lap. The cat perched for a moment and then hissed and hopped down.

Marjorie's waterworks came on full blast. "What kind of person am I? Everyone I ever loved hates me."

"Pluto is simply unsettled." Tinkie sought support from me, but I had nothing. Marjorie did have a tad of drama queen. Chasley had pegged her on that one. "All of this emotion, Marjorie. Cats are sensitive to this. If you'll compose yourself, Pluto will settle down."

Marjorie looked like she'd been betrayed by her best friend. A change of subject was in order. While I might not be great with sympathy and consoling, I had my eye on the case at hand. "Let's hear the recording Chasley had. It must be something really good. He wanted it back badly." Despite what I viewed as his heartfelt sentiments toward his mother, I didn't trust him.

Marjorie handed me the recorder. It was tiny enough to fit into a pocket, and I wondered how long and how much ole Chasley had been snooping and recording. I clicked the machine on. Static roared for a moment, and then Tinkie was talking about Pluto. It was the conversation we'd just had.

"What is this?"

Marjorie paled. "I had it in my pocket."

Tinkie took the device and examined it. "Marjorie, I think you recorded over what Chasley had."

Disappointment didn't begin to describe my feelings. "Maybe there's something farther along."

Tinkie pressed fast-forward, but there was nothing. Just our conversation about Pluto and then emptiness.

"I sound like such a sad sack," Marjorie said. "How do you two stand putting up with me? I'm filled with self-pity. I promise you I'll snap out of it."

"That's wonderful." I tried to sound as if I meant it. While Marjorie had taken a step of self-discovery, she'd possibly erased a valuable clue into Chasley's plans and motivations.

15

It was well after midnight before Pluto relaxed—along with his mistress. The cat had blood in his eyes, and he had prowled the room, yowling and looking for someone to attack. He tolerated Tinkie's petting and cuddling, but he hissed at Marjorie and ignored me.

Another episode of high blood pressure warned me that Marjorie was on the verge of serious trouble. Common sense—which was in short supply at Heart's Desire—indicated the need for a medical professional, but Tinkie's soothing ministrations gained a lot more ground in destressing Marjorie than my nagging about Doc Sawyer. My partner had more than a touch of the Nightingale in her, whereas I obviously had the personality traits of a Lyme tick.

"Do you think I'll ever manage to speak with Mariam?" Marjorie asked in a voice that sounded halfway to the grave. I had no faith Sherry Westin could pull off a rendezvous with a departed spirit. Jitty came to me because she chose to. And some would say Jitty was a figment of my imagination, a manifestation of my subconscious.

"We have to be realistic—" I started before Tinkie cut me off.

"Of course you will." Tinkie gently removed the pill bottle Marjorie had retrieved from the bathroom. Our client had a host of herbal remedies and prescription drugs for relaxing and sleeping. "You've already taken a sedative. Lie down and try to rest. Tomorrow is another day, Marjorie. Sherry called up Joséphine. I'm sure Mariam will be next."

My worry about Marjorie's emotional stability had increased. Her moods were erratic. She was down, then hopeful, then down. Her stash of prescriptions troubled me. If I'd been quick to think, I would have shown them to Doc and asked which were safe and if any presented a risk. Yet Marjorie was a client, not my patient. Where did my responsibility end?

I paced back and forth by the windows. The night outside was black and dense. A few stars blinked through the overcast sky, but the grounds were inky.

Tinkie didn't need to encourage the séance angle. I had no reason to believe Sherry had any talents as a medium. In fact, I had evidence to the contrary. But I needed physical proof if I hoped to convince Marjorie to leave Heart's Desire. And with each passing moment, I knew that was the only solution.

"I feel dizzy." Marjorie clutched Tinkie's hand. "I think

I'm dying. I'm going to die without ever speaking to my daughter."

"You're fine," Tinkie assured her, though worry threaded her voice. "I gave you one of the pills Doc Sawyer left for you, to help you relax. That's probably why you're dizzy." Tinkie put a cool cloth on Marjorie's forehead. "Now take some deep breaths and remember a time when you were happy."

After a moment, Marjorie spoke. "I've had moments of happiness with a man, but nothing as deep or satisfying as the spring before Mariam drowned. The winter hadn't been too cold or wet. New Orleans was alive with exciting people. Artists, actors, folks drawn to Mardi Gras and my husband's import/export business were frequent guests in our home. Mariam had conquered her shyness around strangers, and she could charm the most sophisticated of my husband's clientele. I was so proud of her. You should have seen her. She played the piano and could carry on a conversation in Spanish or French. She was amazing."

I was tempted to ask her what Chasley did that spring—his exclusion was almost painful to me. I didn't ask the question because I feared upsetting Marjorie, and to what effect? The past was done and gone. Chasley was who he was, and making Marjorie feel responsible would serve no good for either of them.

"I'm sleepy," Marjorie whispered, and she inhaled once deeply and her eyelids fluttered closed.

"Thank goodness," Tinkie said softly. "Judging from the dizziness and red face, her blood pressure must have been nearly two hundred. I gave her the medication but it scared me when she got dizzy. That shouldn't have happened."

"Come out onto the balcony," I urged her.

"Why?"

"I need to tell you something." What did she think, that I wanted to practice the lines of *Romeo and Juliet* for amateur talent night?

When at last we stood beneath the star-spangled sky, I told her of the ghost I'd seen during the séance. A ghost that Sherry wasn't aware had entered Heart's Desire. Though I knew it was Jitty, I didn't share that. I wanted Tinkie to understand Sherry Westin was a fraud.

"I didn't see a ghost," Tinkie said. She examined me with a certain amount of awe. "No one else did, either."

"Perhaps that's a clue." I couldn't completely stop the sarcasm. "Sherry claims to be a medium. She's supposed to be sensitive to entities. I find it troubling she wasn't even aware a spirit was in the room."

Tinkie didn't smile. "Why do you see the spirits and I don't?"

"You had your eyes closed."

"And you didn't!"

"No, I didn't. I wanted to watch Sherry, to see if anyone entered the room. I thought maybe Palk was manipulating events. The Westins keep the place so dark, Palk or someone else could have tricked everyone."

Tinkie's face dropped into stubborn lines. "I don't think Joséphine was a trick."

The problem was I couldn't be certain. It *appeared* to be the first real manifestation of an entity, and she looked and behaved a lot like Jitty. Some things troubled me, though. "Would the mistress and wife of Napoléon Bonaparte speak English?"

"Wouldn't a spirit be able to converse in any language?

I mean, spirits aren't bound by the rules we live by. Maybe all spirits are multilingual."

I'd ask Jitty, but who knew if she'd tell me the truth. Jitty revealed only what she chose to and at the exact moment she felt like it.

"Don't you think it was a little convenient—the spirit Shimmer Addleson wanted to hear from appeared? Seriously, that's pretty amazing. And keep in mind, Joséphine is long dead. How can we check to see if her mannerisms are accurate? We don't have the means to verify if this apparition mimicked Joséphine accurately or not."

Tinkie's mulish expression softened. "True. I've looked up historical figures before, and the pictures are often very different. Painters didn't capture the real person. They created a flattering likeness."

She caught my point perfectly. "And Mariam hasn't made an appearance. Mariam is an entity Marjorie would know instantly. It would be harder to fake Mariam than it would Joséphine."

Comprehension lit Tinkie's expression. "I understand what you're saying. There aren't any videos of the real Joséphine, and certainly no one alive today can describe her. I looked at several paintings of her when Oscar and I honeymooned in Paris. She looked so different in each one."

"Exactly. And consider Marjorie has been waiting a while for a visitation from Mariam, which hasn't occurred. I think the Westins are doing their research to try to create an apparition as near to Mariam as they can. But it's taking them time to compile the images. Hence the arrival of Chasley. He could feed them accurate details. Tinkie, I think Chasley and the Westins have gone to great lengths to conjure up the ghost of Marjorie's daughter. This is all aimed toward manipulating Marjorie."

"If this setup is a sham, the Westins could get the ghostly Mariam to suggest or demand anything from Marjorie. If the Westins and Chasley are working together, they'll use Mariam's image to gain his bidding."

Tinkie was nobody's fool. "Exactly my fear."

"Marjorie has to leave Heart's Desire," Tinkie said. "Chasley had pawed all through her things. What's he looking for?"

"I don't know. Maybe her will?"

"Do you really think he'll call animal control?"

I wondered myself if he would follow through. "He's capable. If he does, though, I'll call Coleman and have him arrested."

"That won't help Pluto. He clawed Chasley's back pretty badly."

"And Chasley was trespassing. Pluto is a trained guard cat. He didn't do anything a security dog wouldn't have done." I had figured this all out. Sweetie Pie and Roscoe had given me plenty of practice in creative ways around the law for criminally intentioned critters.

Relief swept the furrows away from Tinkie's brow. "So how can we forestall this?"

"The video we found of Mariam . . . it had to be staged. Either the Westins have the most phenomenal luck in the world, or they have confederates in this scheme. Think how we got the DVD. Bert Steele."

"He's an old friend of Cece's." Tinkie was appalled that I would suggest one of Cece's buddies.

"He also knew a lot about the Westins and pointed us to the person who gave us the video. He had to be behind that video. But why?"

Tinkie concurred. "Of all the lingerie shops in New Orleans, Bert directed me to that out-of-the-way little shop. It was completely lovely, and I found exactly what I needed to turn Oscar's thoughts away from controlling me to pleasuring me, but he sent us to the neighborhood where the Pleasure Zone used to be."

"I thought he sent us there *because* of the Pleasure Zone. Because he knew we might want to see it. But now . . . it was mighty convenient that we got our hands on the video. And Cece thinks Bert may be in love with Sherry." I went over each point.

"Love will make a fool out of a man."

"I want to go down and explore the small parlor where we had the séance and the basement."

Tinkie showed her doubt. "You need sleep, Sarah Booth. Tomorrow, I promise, I'll come up with something that runs Palk and everyone else out of the house."

I was exhausted. I felt so tired, I didn't even argue with her. As I crawled under the sheets, I was smiling. Whatever Tinkie came up with, it was bound to be a doozy.

Pluto traversed my legs on his pile-driver kitty paws and traveled up my abdomen to flop on top of my chest with a deep purr. His weight was somehow comforting. Listening to the deep rumble of his purr, I relaxed as sleep chased me into the darkness.

A downstairs maid brought up a carafe of coffee and three fine china cups, plates, and croissants with homemade scuppernong jelly. I wondered if Palk was aware the other household help had decided to treat Tinkie and me as human beings rather than furniture.

Now that I thought about it, I hadn't had a real meal

since arriving at Heart's Desire. We'd managed a few sandwiches and things from the kitchen, but no one had made the smallest effort to be sure Tinkie and I had food. One more reason to book it out of Heart's Desire as soon as possible.

"Marjorie, what are your plans for today?" Tinkie asked.

"Palk must bring a phone. I'm calling my solicitor to visit me here. I'm revoking my prior will and completely redoing it."

"You're disinheriting Pluto?" Her moods were like the wind.

"Of course not. I'm appointing Tinkie as my administrator.

"And Chasley?" I asked.

"I don't trust him." She popped the last bite of buttered croissant into her mouth. "If he calls animal control, I won't leave him so much as a penny. As it is, I may institute a payout formula. If he does this, he'll get that amount, et cetera, et cetera."

I wasn't shocked. Marjorie had grown up in an environment where money was used as both the carrot and the stick. Behavior modification with incremental payments. If she wrote it in the will properly, it would keep Chasley on a leash for the rest of his life.

A noise outside caught my attention, and I went to the balcony and leaned out far enough to gain a glimpse of the front. An elegant Rolls pulled up in the circular drive. A spit-and-polish driver walked around the car to assist a passenger. There was something familiar about the driver. I tiptoed and stretched for a better view.

A tall blond man with broad shoulders and a tailor-made suit stepped out of the backseat into the sunshine.

Sunlight glistened on his oiled hair. Very European. Another victim for the Westins. And a damned handsome one to boot.

"Who is it?" Tinkie asked.

"I have no idea, but he's a fine example of man flesh." Jitty would be circling like a vulture.

Tinkie joined me on the balcony. "He is indeed. And the chauffeur isn't bad, either."

"I'll say one thing for Heart's Desire, they have a host of handsome men on the premises."

"The compound is filling up. Hard to believe so many people fall victim to their egos. Want to examine the new residents?" Tinkie asked.

"Nothing would please me more."

I had no doubts Marjorie would gain access to a phone and call a lawyer, but before she did anything else, she had a financial meeting with the Westins and the other guests. With any luck at all, they'd be busy until lunchtime.

I snatched up the breakfast remains and Tinkie and I marched toward the kitchen. As soon as we'd deposited the dishes, we shot out the back and angled to the front of the house.

Palk was unloading several expensive leather bags from the Rolls as the handsome blond looked on. There was something about him. . . .

"Who is that?" Tinkie whispered.

"A singer?" I couldn't place him, but I knew I'd seen him.

"No, not a singer. Maybe a writer."

I could almost put my finger on who he was. The chauffeur moved around the car to help Palk with the bags. I couldn't believe it. "Those are Harold's riding boots. And that's . . . Graf!"

"And Oscar!" Tinkie was in awe.

Indeed. My fiancé had arrived at Heart's Desire and I could see he was putting his acting talents to great use. He'd come as a wealthy patron of the Westin women. And Oscar had come as his chauffeur and manservant.

I controlled the laughter that welled up and wanted to spill out. Of all things. Graf had decided to show me he accepted my detective work by joining me on a case. He was a man who understood the power of action over words. If I could have levitated, I would have flown across the yard and into his arms.

"Get over there right now and at least let him see you! You can't talk to him, but let him know you want to. What are you waiting for?" Tinkie asked.

"What about Oscar?"

"Deal with Graf. Oscar and I'll have plenty of time."

I didn't wait for her to change her mind. I had to fight the urge to run, but I walked to Graf like a heat-seeking missile. My fiancé had come home to Mississippi to show his love for me. He hadn't called or written; he'd boarded a jet and flown. And he was at Heart's Desire. For me. No girl could ask for more support. All the things I wanted to tell him ran through my head as I made sure he saw me before I entered the foyer as if I had business to attend to.

The front door burst open behind me, and Oscar, resplendent in his chauffeur uniform, preceded Graf into the foyer. "Mr. Desmond Graf has arrived," Oscar announced as he clicked his booted heels together in the best demonstration of obsequiousness I'd ever seen. He bowed so low, I could see that Tinkie had really limbered up his spine in the last few weeks.

When Graf entered, I was smitten anew by his incredible good looks and presence. The bleached-blond hair complemented his California tan. He gave me a quick wink and then let his gaze sweep past me as Palk loomed up beside me.

"Mr. Graf, your room is ready. Have your man put your bags in the Lotus Suite, and then I'll show him his room in the servants' quarters." Palk turned to me. "Miss Booth, what are you doing in the foyer? Your place is with your mistress. Servants are not allowed to wander the house."

Graf's fists clenched, and I saw the fire spark in his eyes. Good! Before this adventure was over, Palk would be knocked off his high horse.

"Sorry, Mr. Palk. Mrs. Littlefield sent me to book a spa session." I desperately wanted to touch Graf, to hug him and kiss him and do the little things he loved. Now was not the time. If I lip-locked a guest, Palk would stroke out. Then again, there was an upside to that scenario. I had to remind myself to hold back. Graf now resided in the Lotus Suite. Tonight, I would join him there, and my single ambition was to set the sheets on fire.

Palk snapped his fingers in my face. "Wake up, Miss Booth. Perhaps you should tend to your duties and quit gawking at our guests. Mr. Graf is not a dessert."

"Oh, I beg to differ." My gaze met Graf's and he winked again. Oscar, who stood at attention, rolled his eyes.

"You are a cheeky thing. I shall report this incident to Mrs. Littlefield." Palk aimed a finger at Graf's luggage. "You might help Mr. Graf's man take the bags up to his suite. I gather Mrs. Littlefield's employment is rather . . . sedentary. A little exercise would be good for your waistline."

"Sir, yes, sir." I stopped myself from saluting. It was particularly hard to swallow Palk's domineering attitude in front of the man I loved, but as my aunt Loulane would say, "In for a penny, in for a pound." My job description read *maid* and I had to fulfill the role. It didn't escape my notice Oscar was about to bust a gut laughing, either. Oh, he would pay. I bent to pick up a suitcase. A loud, shrill scream echoed down the hall from the spa.

"What on earth!" Palk set out toward the commotion. Someone was in line for a reprimand. He pivoted and spoke to my fiancé. "I assure you, Mr. Graf, Heart's Desire isn't normally so filled with bedlam and sassy maids. I'll handle this and return to be sure you're settled in your room. Miss Booth, the Lotus Suite. Chop, chop!"

Forgetting my vow to create new curses, I mouthed the F word followed by a big *you,* but I hefted two bags as another brain-jolting scream erupted.

"Heads will roll!" Palk hurried away, and I was left alone in the foyer with my fiancé and Tinkie's husband.

"What are you doing here?" I whispered.

Graf took the luggage from my hands and dropped them. "That's not the greeting I was hoping for."

"Seriously, how did you get in here?" I couldn't believe it.

"Oscar and Harold concocted an invitation for me. I'm a gambler and a big investor. Sir Desmond Graf." His smile was filled with mischief. "They gave me quite a cover."

"This is crazy." In a good way. I clutched his hand tightly.

"I was hoping for a little more . . . enthusiastic greeting," he said.

I needed no further invitation. I hurled myself at him. My hands moved over his chest and up to his face. "I am so glad to see you." I closed my eyes and traced the contours.

"I'm not Braille," he whispered against my ear, sending chills along my spine.

"I've missed you." My kiss told him of my loneliness and fear, and of my desire. I hungered for him. For the past days, I'd held my feelings at bay, afraid the love we shared was over. Now, with my arms circling his neck and his hair twined in my fingers, I allowed myself to feel the full measure of my love for him. The physical need for his touch was crippling, but even stronger was the tide of emotions.

Graf's lips moved along my cheek and down my throat.

A clearing throat brought me back to the present. "Where's Tinkie?" Oscar asked softly.

I waved a hand toward the stairs. "Periwinkle Room, second floor, to the left at the landing. Hurry! She saw you arrive." I was relatively certain she'd used the back servants' staircase to return to Marjorie's room.

Oscar needed no second invitation. He sprinted up the stairs.

I pushed against Graf's chest, putting distance between us. We were completely exposed. Anyone could walk into the foyer and see us. "We can't do this here," I said.

"Oh, yes, we can." He kissed me again, long and demanding.

There were things I had to tell him, to make it right between us, to let him know I never stopped considering his feelings, even when I worked on a case. "Graf, I'm so sorry. I—"

He put a finger on my lips. "No. No apologies. I was wrong." He swept me into his arms and carried me to a more secluded place beneath the stairs. He pressed me against the wall, where we were hidden by a huge cabinet. "I love you, Sarah Booth. I love you just the way you are. Hardheaded, smart, determined to find the truth, protecting the underdog. I love you."

"You do?" His words were a heady mixture.

"I owe a lot to a Sunflower County lawman and an old, contrary country doctor."

"Coleman and Doc."

"Them's the varmints. They double-teamed me. Doc warned me you were entrenched in a way of life your parents taught you and that I'd better not try to tamper with it. Coleman made me see I was trying to control you. My actions were wrong, even if my intentions were good."

"Hush up and kiss me."

And he did. Long and deep, a kiss that spanned time and place, from our apartment in New York City to the beach of Costa Rica and the bedroom of Dahlia House. Graf, too, was part of my life. We'd grown apart and back together, and beneath the surface of any argument was this tidal pull of passion. I allowed myself a long, blissful moment; then I strong-armed some space between us.

The foyer of Heart's Desire was not appropriate for our reunion. We deserved privacy and time.

A terrible commotion echoed down the long hallway from the spa. Even with Graf in my arms, wanting me as much as I wanted him, I listened to another shrill scream and the sound of sobbing from the spa.

"Go," he said. "To quote Coleman, you're drawn to a dead body like a fly to a turd."

I kissed him again, joy bubbling inside me. "That sounds a lot like Coleman."

"He'll never get over losing you," Graf said. "He knows that. But he loves you enough to want you to be happy."

I smiled up at him, but a tiny little piece of my heart broke loose. I loved Graf. No doubt about it. But Coleman owned a portion of my heart as well. My job also claimed a part of me. "I have to—"

"I know." He stepped away. "I'll see you later. In the Lotus Suite. I'm going to make you forget everything except my touch."

I could hardly wait.

I had gone no farther than the foyer when a young woman burst through. Her hands and body were covered in red, and she was screaming like she was dying. Palk was on her heels like a bloodhound.

"Block her!" Palk ordered me. "Misty! Misty!" Palk grabbed her shoulders and gave her a hard shake. He frog-marched her out of the foyer and back toward the spa. "Snap out of it! You have to tell me what happened."

Chasing after them, I blew Graf a kiss. Before Palk could close and lock the spa doors, I pushed through. Palk was green around the gills, and once I looked past him, I understood why. Amaryllis Dill, yellow turban covering her hair and a yellow facial mask on her face, floated in a bathtub of bloody mud. A red arterial spray covered the wall beside the tub.

"Cromwell on a broomstick," I said softly. "Her throat's been cut from ear to ear." I'd heard the expression all my life but never visualized it. Someone really wanted Amaryllis dead. She'd been right to be worried about her safety.

"Get out of here," Palk said to me. "Now." He held Misty in one cruel hand and pointed the other at the door. "Go!"

"We have to call Sheriff Peters." I had no intention of leaving Palk alone with a crime scene.

"You aren't calling anyone." Palk reached for my shoulder but reconsidered, and a good thing. I might be a maid, but nobody manhandled me.

"I quit," Misty sobbed. She repeated it louder. Then she glared at Palk and screamed it. "I quit! I'm not putting up with your shit another minute. I am out of here!"

"Stop that nonsense." Palk assisted her, with some force, to a chair, where he planted her. "Calm down and tell me what happened. Stop sniveling and shrieking and speak clearly!"

By sheer force of intimidation, Palk pressured Misty to gather her emotions. She grasped the seat of the chair with both hands. "She came in the spa and wanted the mud bath. I told her she couldn't use Ms. Dill's bath items, but she said she wasn't walking all the way back upstairs. She said Ms. Dill wouldn't care. She entered the tub, and I went to the supply room to collect the oils for her hands and feet. I was gone five minutes. No more. When I came back, she was . . . dead."

Palk looked from Misty to the dead woman in the tub. "That isn't Amaryllis Dill?"

Misty lowered her head into her hands. "I told her she had to use the bath towels and wraps provided for her, but she told me to leave her alone, that she'd paid to be here and she meant to get every benefit."

I sidestepped Palk and pushed up the head wrap on the body. Instead of blond, the hair beneath the wrap was brunette. I lifted the eye mask and stared into the wide-open gray eyes of Lola Monee, country music songwriter.

Sitting in a corner of the spa, I waited for Coleman to arrive, an ironic twist since my intention had been to keep the crime scene safe from Palk. Now he refused to let *me* leave. He was a master at embargoing gossip—and keeping me from the delight of *amore*. Graf was upstairs, waiting for me. I would have spent the time with him while I waited for Coleman to arrive, had Palk not decided I might call in the tabloid press.

I wasn't cold to Lola's death, far from it, but Coleman wouldn't appreciate my mucking around in his crime scene. There was absolutely nothing I could do until Coleman and his techs did their jobs.

And I had missed Graf. I'd failed to acknowledge, even to myself, how intensely I'd felt his absence.

A hubbub outside the spa proved to be Gretchen Waller attempting to gain access. Palk fended her off with a mixture of firmness and kindness I'd never seem him display.

"What happened to Lola?" Gretchen demanded. "She should have been out of there twenty minutes ago."

"Please go back to your room. Please. For your own sake." Palk refused to let her in, undoubtedly for the best. It was a gruesome murder scene.

Gretchen was scared and angry. "Listen, you pompous ass, I'm going to call in the feds! Our songs are very popular with the director of the FBI. If you don't open this door, I'll call him right now. I want to know my partner is okay. Let me talk to her."

The FBI had no authority here. Gretchen's threats

were toothless. The homicide fell squarely in the jurisdiction of Sunflower County Sheriff Coleman Peters.

I thought his name and he appeared in the doorway with Deputy DeWayne Dattilo at his side. DeWayne had put on about twenty pounds since he'd started eating three squares a day at Millie's Café, and it dawned on me he was there for more than biscuits and coffee. He was sweet on one of Millie's waitresses.

Behind DeWayne were two forensic technicians.

"Sarah Booth," Coleman said, nodding as he surveyed the scene. "Everyone else clear out and let the crime scene technicians do their job."

"Surely you don't mean to have that maid in here and everyone else must leave?" Palk looked flummoxed.

"That's exactly what I mean," Coleman said.

Palk left in a huff, the spa employees in tow. Misty was crying again. Her wild moment of independence was gone. Coleman slowed her with a gentle hand on her wrist. "There's fresh coffee in the kitchen," he said kindly. "Wait for me there. I'll need to ask a few questions."

"Not the kitchen!" She looked terrified. "Yumi hates it when we hang around the kitchen."

"Then in your room. I'll be there shortly." He closed the door after she was gone and went to examine the body. He didn't touch anything, just looked for a good three minutes. He sat down on a stool across from the massage table where I perched. "Are you okay?"

"Two deaths in two days. Not the type of statistics I like racking up."

"Two murders. Amanda's death wasn't accidental. Doc Sawyer says she was struck in the head."

I'd suspected as much, but it was still hard to hear. I told him what I'd learned and handed over Amanda's cell phone with the strange recording of the chef. "She did have a boyfriend here. Have you talked with Kyle?"

"Yeah, I know his family. He showed up voluntarily this morning and made a statement. He didn't have a lot of nice things to say about the work situation at Heart's Desire. Bottom line, though, he doesn't have a clue what happened to Amanda, which is probably a good thing. If he finds out who's responsible, he says he'll hurt them."

"And I wouldn't blame him." Coleman had to uphold the law, but I wasn't a sworn law officer, and I understood the desire—and temptation—for physical retribution. Sometimes revenge was the sweetest nectar. "Do you think it's a coincidence the murders started as soon as Chasley was on the premises?"

"I don't know." Coleman walked over to Lola's lifeless body as the techs snapped photographs. "I'll know more when I run a full background check on her."

"Cece confirmed she's a country music songwriter. Big time." Another tidbit came to mind. "She's wearing the spa towel and mask for Amaryllis Dill. The killer might have thought it was Amaryllis." I told him about her fear that someone meant to harm her. "And Cece couldn't find a thing on Amaryllis Dill, except she's a dance teacher in D.C."

"Heart's Desire seems to be a pit of deception and danger." Coleman rolled his shoulders to relax the tension. "I think you and Tinkie and Mrs. Littlefield should leave."

"Graf and Oscar just arrived. And thank you." I wanted to say a lot more, but now wasn't the time.

"If only Marjorie would consent to pack up, I'd be happy to call it quits."

"You're too hardheaded to abandon her."

It was a statement, not a question. "I'm afraid if we leave her alone, she'll do something tragic. One foot is always mired in a big pit of depression."

"Like your aunt Loulane used to say, 'Money can't buy happiness.'"

"Does everyone quote my aunt?" I asked.

"Every chance we get. Now, let's see what the techs can tell us."

16

It was a long day, and I chafed at the thought of Graf waiting for me in the Lotus Suite. I visualized him, reclined on the bed, pining. It helped me block out the horror of what was happening around me.

It wasn't hard to eavesdrop on Coleman, DeWayne, and the techs. Their findings were preliminary, but they felt Lola had not struggled. Someone had slipped behind her, grasped her chin, and sliced across her throat with a sure stroke. The inference was the killer had been hiding in the spa area and had acted without hesitation. Whoever had claimed Lola's life had entered the spa, murdered her, and departed in under five minutes, based on Misty's insistence that she'd been solo in the spa.

The consensus of opinion pointed to blood loss, a result

of the wound, as the cause of death. Based on the angle of the cut, Coleman believed the killer was right-handed, not a lot of help since the majority of people were. And all unverified until the forensic evidence had been gathered and examined.

Lola's body was removed and taken to Sunflower County Hospital, where Doc would perform an autopsy. Forensics were always a lawman's best ally, but I wasn't certain what else, if anything, Lola's body could tell us. She'd gone to the spa to relax, and now she was dead.

While DeWayne questioned the staff and guests, Coleman allowed me to tag along for the interview with Misty.

She'd pulled herself together, tendered her resignation, and was eager to pack her things as soon as Coleman gave permission. She would stay with a cousin in Zinnia, she said. Her story remained consistent. She didn't see or hear anyone enter the spa; she didn't know of anyone who might want to harm Lola or anyone else on the premises of Heart's Desire.

DeWayne's interviews indicated solid alibis for the guests, who were all gathered in the parlor for the financial summit seminar led by Brandy. Sherry had taken migraine medication and was comatose for all practical purposes. The waiters, maids, and chefs had been busy with daily chores. No one was unaccounted for, yet any number of people could have slipped away long enough to slice Lola's throat.

The guards reported no entry through the front gate. It was as if a ghost had materialized to murder at Heart's Desire.

"Someone is lying," Coleman said to me as we waited for Gretchen Waller to pull herself together for an interview.

"Probably more than one person." For the life of me, I couldn't figure out who at Heart's Desire might want to kill the songwriter. She was annoying when she was in her cups, but that wasn't a reason to cut her throat. Or at least not a good one.

I left Coleman to speak with Gretchen alone and went with DeWayne to examine the songwriters' suite. The layout was much the same as Marjorie's room, except there were two queen-sized beds instead of one. The songwriters wouldn't win any awards for orderliness—their clothes were thrown on every available flat surface. Two guitars were propped against furniture. Clutter and mess, but nothing to indicate an argument or trouble of any kind.

The laundry hamper in the bathroom overflowed with towels, wraps, and robes.

I clearly saw why Lola had swiped a few of Amaryllis's linens. There wasn't a dry towel in the bathroom. Everything was damp and wadded into the hamper.

Tinkie had the computer expertise in Delaney Detective Agency, but I knew enough to open the files on the laptop. Song lyrics, a calendar with appointments—nothing obvious that might lead to murder. DeWayne took the computer for a more comprehensive examination.

Coleman had finished with Gretchen when I returned. "What did you find out from her?" I asked.

He shook his head. "Nothing that makes any sense. She doesn't know who would hurt Lola. Or Amaryllis. Or Amanda."

Before we could get into it any deeper, Amaryllis appeared for her interview. I'd filled Coleman in on what she'd said to me, but she refused to admit any of it to him. Not even in front of me.

"I have no idea where you came up with that wild

story," she said, and I had to admire her chutzpah even as I noted her trembling. She was terrified.

"You told me you feared for your life. You think your lover may have offed his wife and intends to kill you."

"I didn't tell you a damn thing. I don't socialize with maids." She wouldn't budge. She said only that Lola must have taken her spa supplies when they were left outside her door. "Lola and Gretchen hogged the spa all the time. You'd think they'd never stayed in a luxury accommodation before. They couldn't get enough of the facials or saunas or massages. They must have booked appointments at least four times a day. Lola mentioned earlier that they'd used up the spa supplies in their room and asked to borrow some of mine. I didn't care. I'm not interested in the spa."

"Why are you here?" Coleman asked. "Are you investing with the Westins?"

She started to answer angrily but thought better of it. "My reason for being here has nothing to do with money." She pressed her lips together. "It doesn't matter. I'm leaving today. I'm returning to D.C. I booked a flight out of Memphis for tonight."

"I'm sorry, Ms. Dill, you can't leave Sunflower County until I've completed the investigation." Coleman's tone made it clear he meant business.

"Surely you don't think I hurt the songwriter? I didn't know her. I have no reason to harm her."

"Someone did, and I believe it was someone living in the main house."

"You can't make me stay here." She looked as if she might throw up.

"I'm sorry. I'll wrap this up as fast as possible," Coleman said.

She appealed to me, but there was nothing I could do. "Tell the sheriff the truth. That's the quickest ticket out of here," I counseled her.

Anger flared for a moment. "I've told him everything I can." She stormed away from the interview. I started to stop her, but Coleman caught my arm.

"Let her go. We can get her any time we want her."

DeWayne and the techs began loading their equipment into the patrol cars, leaving me alone with Coleman. "Gretchen believes a hit was taken out on Amaryllis Dill and the wrong woman was killed."

"It's possible. Amaryllis was sleeping with a married man, and she's hinted that he's a powerful man. His wife died in a car wreck. Amaryllis fears Linda was murdered, and she's afraid she'll be next."

"I'll run some checks. Be careful, Sarah Booth." His finger brushed a stray curl from the side of my face. "I'd never forgive myself if I talked Graf out of taking you to Hollywood and you got yourself hurt."

"I'll keep clear of danger." His concern touched me. Coleman had no right to order me, but he did have plenty of right to caution me. We shared too much.

"I'll believe that when the sun freezes." He tugged my hair gently the way he'd done in school.

"I promise to be cautious." I wanted to hug him, but the line we walked was too fine. "Let me know what you find out."

"Roger that," he said, and followed DeWayne.

Finally cut loose, I made a beeline for the Lotus Suite and one handsome actor. Graf was surely pacing the room, anxious for us to celebrate our reunion. I imagined him languishing on a chaise, one leg on the floor. One naked leg, giving me a tantalizing preview of what awaited—a throw covering part of his torso, but enough of his manly chest peeking out. I knew his body so well.

"Feets, don't fail me now," I whispered as I sped on my rubber-soled shoes toward the Lotus Suite. In less than a minute I'd be in Graf's arms. In his bed. In the throes of pleasure. It had been way too long. I cleared the spa hallway and hooked right toward the foyer and stairs.

I didn't make it that far. When I passed the dining room, I heard loud laughter and Graf's voice. He wasn't in his room yearning for me; he was holding court in the dining room. I stopped to listen as he regaled the Addlesons, Mrs. Littlefield, and Brandy Westin with tales of diamond mining in Africa. I could not believe my ears. According to the anecdotes Graf was telling, he'd traveled extensively around the world, been everything from a diamond mine owner to a sunken treasure finder. He had a line of bullshit ten miles long, and everyone in the dining room was eating it up.

"Idle hands are the devil's workshop." Palk came up behind me. I was too worn down to spar with him.

"Back off, Palk. I've had a rough day."

"You're not paid to have good days. And you're not paid to lurk outside rooms and snoop."

My fists clenched, but I gathered my temper. "Care to see how bad I can make your day?"

"Threats don't work with me."

"Maybe a good spanking . . . I have this very interesting hockey mask I could wear." I was rewarded with a profound blush that swept across his face.

"You eavesdropping little—"

"Careful. I have your number, Palk. Either back off or I'll make sure the entire staff knows."

He didn't have time to respond. The doorbell chimed. He had indeed been saved by the bell.

Curious, I followed Palk to the front.

"Who might you be?" Palk asked. "And what is that creature on a leash? In all my days I've never seen a more demented animal."

"I'm Harold Erkwell, and I have urgent papers for Mr. Desmond Graf to sign immediately. The guards delayed me for over an hour. Now I need to see Desmond and obtain his signature before he loses money."

"Wait here and I'll be happy to take them to him." Palk had reached his limit—not another single person or pet would breach the walls of Heart's Desire.

Harold jammed a foot in the door. "I must speak with Mr. Graf. Immediately. And I must take care of this matter personally."

"No dogs allowed in the house."

"I beg to differ. This is not just a dog, this is Mr. Graf's financial prognosticator. The dog has psychic abilities. If Mr. Graf loses money because you've delayed me with your foolishness, I'll make certain the Westins are sued for the loss. Out of my way, man, or suffer the consequences."

Right on cue, Roscoe loosed an evil growl followed by a high-pitched whine that made my teeth grind.

Harold pressed his advantage, entering with Roscoe at his side, actually *heeling* on a leash. Palk pointed toward the dining room, and the duo swept past him.

I followed right behind, amazed at Harold's role.

"I beg your pardon, Mr. Graf, but if you're to sell

that stock before . . ." Harold cleared his throat. "I do apologize. I need only his signature and then I'll be gone."

Graf accepted the sheaf of papers and signed with a flourish. He motioned Palk over. "Prepare refreshments for Mr. Erkwell, my banker. He's made a long drive and I'm sure he'd like something cool to drink. And a bone from the kitchen for the noble Roscoe. The last million-dollar investment I made, Roscoe picked it."

"The dog?" Roger Addleson was instantly intrigued. "The dog picked a stock?"

"He's divinely inspired," Graf went on. "The dog is a genius."

"How does he pick a stock?" Roger asked.

"We write the names of potential buys on pieces of paper and scatter them on the floor. Roscoe then sniffs them all and pees on the one that's going up. He is one hundred percent accurate. I've made millions relying on his instincts."

Harold leaned close to Roger and stage-whispered, "Graf believes Roscoe is Warren Buffet's doppelgänger. Can't you detect a tad of Warren in his face?"

"We need paper," Roger said. "I want to see how this works."

"No dog will be allowed to pee in this dining room." Palk was appalled at such an idea. "I have never heard of such antics."

"I want to know if this is real," Roger demanded. "Mrs. Westin, could we get paper."

Brandy considered Harold and Roscoe. "I think we'll hold off on this."

"Great idea," Harold agreed. "I could do with a bite to eat, if it's no trouble. Maybe later we could relocate on the lawn. Roscoe loves to show off his abilities, and I wouldn't mind one free session. Right-o, Desmond?"

"If you insist." Graf wasn't pleased.

Palk remained frozen, but Brandy Westin hopped into action. "Mr. Palk, have Yumi prepare refreshments for our new guest."

Palk did the sharpest pivot I'd ever seen.

"What about the dog?" Shimmer Adleson asked. "He isn't staying in the dining room, is he? I'm allergic."

"Roscoe is a snaz-a-pooty," Harold said with aplomb. "He has hair, not fur. You simply can't be allergic to him."

Shimmer's mouth snapped shut. Contrary to everything I'd witnessed regarding Roscoe, he settled under the table without any fuss. Harold had either sedated the damn dog or lobotomized him.

At the first opportunity, I'd ask Harold about snaz-a-pooty. I was positive he'd invented the term. Then again, there were DNA tests available at local vet clinics to determine the different breeds mixed in a mutt. Had I guessed Roscoe's lineage, though, I would have said imp-a-demon. It would not surprise me to learn Roscoe didn't have a single fiber of canine DNA. I couldn't wait to see how Harold would escape Heart's Desire without Roscoe peeing on some paper.

I busied myself setting the table for Harold's snack while he and Graf talked with great gusto about the stock market and what investments were doing well. Roger Addleson was nobody's fool, and when he joined in, I saw Brandy was surreptitiously making investments notes on a small pad in her lap. Graf would never be questioned now. He was accepted as a high roller.

"Mr. Graf, what brings you to Heart's Desire?" Marjorie asked.

"The same thing as everyone else," Graf said. "I want to participate in developing a strategy to rule the world. We must stop the wars and the strife. One world, one rule. Greed for oil resources has defined the last forty years of global history." He refilled his wineglass. "I have it on good authority that in the next decade, we'll be fighting a foe far more advanced than the Middle East or each other."

I held my breath.

"What foe?" Brandy asked.

"The extraterrestrials." Graf didn't blink. "They're out there. Watching for the opportune moment. After we've depleted the water supply on this planet, we'll be ripe for the plucking. They'll make us their slaves."

A profound silence settled over the room.

"You believe in aliens and a dog that picks stocks by peeing on them?" Roger Addleson shifted his seat away from Graf. Five minutes before, he'd hung on Graf's every word. Now he questioned Graf's sanity. It was a bravo performance by the man I loved.

"Indeed, I do. I received Sherry's letter outlining the whole plan for building a consensus of wealth and intelligence to forge better governing power. That's why I'm here." He smiled at Brandy. "These two ladies who founded Heart's Desire, with their connections to the plane of the departed, have insights to benefit the rest of us. Am I right, ladies?"

"Absolutely." Brandy was monotone.

Graf ignored her lack of enthusiasm. "I do believe Mr. Erkwell needs to return to the bank and make these transfers. It takes time moving large amounts of money around. I want a substantial sum available for the work we're engaged in here," Graf said. "Tomorrow, I'll invite

Mr. Erkwell to return with Roscoe for a demonstration of his talents. Of course, there will be a fee involved. But right now, I require a nap and utter privacy. I don't want to hear so much as a footfall outside my doorway, is that understood?"

At last, Graf had cleared the deck for our reunion.

"You've lost weight, Sarah Booth." Graf's hands grasped my waist. "I like a woman with a little meat on her bones." We embraced at the foot of a king-sized bed in a room painted in shades of mocha and cream. Where the other rooms I'd visited were soft and feminine, this was a masculine room. Instead of sheers, the windows were covered with heavy damask, a paisley print that incorporated shades of espresso, latte, and café au lait.

"I don't think I've had a decent meal since I've been here. Palk hates for the staff to eat, and the head chef doesn't approve of snacks. Why is this called the Lotus Suite when the color scheme has to do with coffee? I could use a good strong cup of coffee." I was babbling. Nerves. Imagine, I was nervous with my own fiancé.

"I can call for a tray of something."

I captured his wrist and quickly spun his arm behind his back. "Not unless you want me to hurt you." I couldn't turn into some simpering, virginal girl. Graf loved me because I was tough and daring.

He laughed as he twisted free and scooped me up in his arms. In a moment, I was bouncing on the bed and he was on top of me. "We should talk," he said. His expression was so serious, I did a double-take. Then I saw the devilment in his eyes.

"Talk, my foot. I don't want to talk. I want to make

love. For the rest of the day. I don't want food or drink or anything except you." My words came straight from my heart. "I want to wallow in our love."

"Not exactly the sentiments for a sonnet." Graf uttered a *tsk, tsk*. "I can see you need your rough edges smoothed out."

"A nice metaphor for getting—"

He put a finger to my lips. "Sarah Booth, you shock me! Remember, men like to pursue a woman. The chase gets our blood up."

"Seems to me you don't have any trouble in the circulatory department right now. Unless you're carrying a gun in your boxers."

"Why, Sarah Booth! You make me blush."

"Graf Milieu, I never dreamed of you as a coy tease. After your performance today as a mega-macho millionaire, I think you should do a Dos Equis commercial." I adopted a sultry, Latin accent. "You are the most fascinating man in the world. You enter a room, other men wilt. Ah, but women, their panties spontaneously combust."

Graf laughed, and I loved that he could find humor when I teased him about himself.

"Don't pretend to be a shy, retiring John-Boy Walton–type. *I* make you blush? I daresay the scenes you filmed for your new movie will make me jealous."

He tugged the waistband of my khakis and unbuckled my belt. Very carefully, with great attention to the art of seductive disrobing, he began to remove my clothes. "I hope so, Sarah Booth. I want you to be so jealous, you won't let me out of your sight."

The truth was, I didn't want to see Graf in bed with another woman. It was only a movie and I trusted him completely. Still, I was only human, and I'd compare my-self to the actress Natasha Crowley, a brunette nuclear reactor who was a decade younger than me. What a time to hear the loud ticking of my biological clock! Jitty would be impressed with the way she'd trained me. "How in-tense was the scene with Natasha?"

Graf's answer was a crooked smile and a sliding gaze.

"How intense?" I tried to keep it light but failed mis-erably.

"You're jealous." Graf pulled off my slacks and set to work on the placket of my polo shirt.

His hands slid beneath the shirt and moved over my rib cage and then higher. The warmth of his palms against my bare skin made my breath grow faster. "Maybe a little." I hated to admit it, but I refused to lie.

"I am thrilled." He pulled the shirt over my head and kissed me hard. He gathered me into his arms and re-minded me that nothing on earth compared to these inti-mate moments with him. "Knowing you're jealous makes me love you more."

Men. What a crazy species.

Graf's kiss softened, and he gently eased me, a panting mess, onto the pillows. "Does she kiss better than I do?" I asked, hating my weakness. Where had this sudden jeal-ousy come from? Up until this moment I hadn't thought of Graf filming scenes with Natasha Crowley, and now I was letting some movie business make me unhappy and worried. As my aunt Loulane would say, "What's good for the goose is good for the gander." I was feeling Graf's career-induced pain. He was worried I'd be injured, and I was worried he'd found too much pleasure in the arms of an actress.

"Nobody kisses better than you, Sarah Booth. I

think there should probably be a warning label on your kisses. 'Sample this and lose your mind.' I can't think about anything but how much I want you. I've never known another woman who makes me feel what you do. You're my drug of choice."

Maybe being a little jealous wasn't a bad thing. I was determined to please my man and let him know how much I'd missed him. My arms circled his neck and I caressed him with my lips and tongue. "I know how to bring you to your knees, Graf Milieu."

"You're playing a dangerous game," he whispered as he nuzzled my ear, sending shivers all over me. "I know your weakness, Sarah Booth Delaney."

His fingers found the ticklish spot on the inside of my hip bone and I squealed. "You are a devil man!" I tried to wriggle away from him, but he had me pinned. Struggle as I might, I couldn't battle his superior strength. Truth be told, I didn't struggle too hard. My body against his body—what was to struggle away from?

He caught my arms and pinned them above my head while he used his leg to hold my body on the bed. "Will you behave?" he asked.

"Behave?" I laughed out loud. "What 1950s male-dominance tract have you been reading? Women don't *be-have* in this century."

Graf's lips trailed from my ear down my neck, inch by inch down to my collarbone, and farther south. He was driving me insane, and enjoying every second of it.

"I've been reading up on my Southern menfolk, and I believe Rhett should have used a firmer hand on Scarlett." His breath teased my breast.

I had to fight to concentrate on the conversation.

"Do I remind you of Scarlett?" No Southern girl in her right mind wouldn't preen at a comparison to Scarlett O'Hara.

"Oh, you do. Headstrong, willful, uncompromising, incapable of recognizing the right choice even when it's in front of her nose—"

Nobody was dissing my Scarlett! Not even a man who was driving me to distraction with his choreographed seduction. "Beautiful, strong, independent, brave—"

Graf countered with "Misguided—"

"Maligned—"

"Selfish." Graf gave me another goose. I squealed and squirmed, but he wasn't going to get the last word.

"Determined to save her heritage."

"My god, Sarah Booth, you are magnificent! I've missed—" He ended his sentence with a strangled sound, bucking and jumping like Satan had possessed him. I hadn't seen anything like it since I slipped into the back of a Holy Roller church service when I was in the fifth grade. Graf flailed as if in the throes of either conversion or exorcism.

"Graf?" What the hell happened? Was he having a heart attack? What was wrong?

"Knock it off me!" He flopped over onto his side on the bed, and then I saw the cat, clinging to Graf's back with all four claws.

"Pluto!" I lurched for the feline, but he was having none of it. He jumped to the headboard of the four-poster and struck a Halloween pose. He was damn good with the frizzed-out tail and arched back. Maybe he could find gainful employment as a model for fright-night posters when I booted his ass out the window.

"What's wrong with that cat?" Graf twisted to determine the damage to his back. Good thing he couldn't see it. Pluto had left his mark. Instead of a Z for Zorro, there were eight long, bloody claw marks from eight little kitty toes. So far, Pluto was two-for-two with Chasley and Graf.

"I have no idea why Pluto attacked you, or how he got into the room." The bedroom door was shut and locked. I went to retrieve soap and hot water from the bathroom and noticed the grille for the air-conditioning vent hanging by one screw. The cat was using the duct system to navigate the house.

I soaked a washcloth in cool water and tended to Graf's back with tenderness—and a bit of victory. "I hope you don't have any more bedroom shots with Natasha. These claw marks would look . . ." Like they'd enjoyed hot, wild sex.

"Ouch!" Graf flinched as I applied a bit more pressure than I meant to.

"Sorry."

He shifted so he could eye Pluto. "Is Chasley right? Is the cat a danger? I mean, why shouldn't animals be psychotic if people can be?"

Still sitting on the headboard, Pluto licked a front paw and purred. "I don't think he's dangerous. He's only displayed aggression when Chasley tried to break into Marjorie's suite and now. Maybe he suffers from multiple personalities."

Another thought occurred to me. "Or maybe he thought you were hurting me. When you tickled me and I screamed. He had to be hiding in the AC vent." I pointed it out to Graf. "He heard me yell, and he jumped right on your back. From his perspective, he might have thought you were brutalizing me."

An expression crossed Graf's face, and in it I saw trouble.

"Oh, no, we are not testing that theory!" I tried to grasp his wrist.

He grinned. "Just a tiny test."

"How?"

I should never have asked. He grabbed me and I let out a startled whoop. Pluto cleared the space between the headboard and Graf in under a second. He sprang between us, arched his back, and growled.

"He's your protector, Sarah Booth." Graf gave the cat an appreciative nod. "He attacked me because he perceived me as a danger to you."

"But he's Marjorie's cat."

I wasn't screaming, and Graf risked offering his hand to Pluto, who seemed to accept Graf meant me no harm. He rubbed his whiskers on Graf's fingers. "He's one smart kitty."

"I never considered you might be a cat person, Graf." My fiancé had taken to my horses and he loved Sweetie Pie as much as I did. My mother had adored cats, and we always had half a dozen at Dahlia House. By the time I went to college, they'd died of old age. Knowing I was moving to New York, I hadn't gotten any more. Since I'd been home, I always figured a cat would find me when it was the right time. "We can adopt a cat if you'd like one. Dahlia House is a great place for felines to romp and roam."

"I would. Growing up, I had a gray tabby. Stripes. He slept with me every night. I broke my leg tagging out a runner at home base when I was fourteen. I was the star catcher, and I had to sit out the last of the season. I was upset because I couldn't participate in the play-offs. Stripes spent every day for the whole six weeks I was in a cast lounging across my lap, purring and making sure I stayed calm. He lived to be twenty-two."

Graf had charmed me yet again. Christmas would be a snap this year. One gray tabby straight from the animal shelter. Maybe it also meant that Graf planned to spend more time in Sunflower County with his soon-to-be bride. We'd made it past the engagement, but we hadn't started planning our wedding. My future as Mrs. Graf Milieu Delaney had hung by a thread days ago. Now, I couldn't imagine any future that didn't include Graf. And I meant to show him.

This time I put the moves on Graf. I tended his wounds and softly sang the lyrics of a 1970s David Allan Coe song, "Would you lay with me in a field of stone if my needs were great, would you lay with me?" Graf didn't seem to mind that I didn't have perfect pitch.

One thing led to another, and finally tired of being pushed and shoved around the sheets, Pluto abandoned the bed and curled up on a chair beside the window to sleep while Graf and I made love. I couldn't have told you if two hours passed or two days. For that measure of time, I immersed myself in Graf and the emotional and physical sensations that alerted me to the depth of my love.

17

A knock at the door woke me out of the soundest sleep I'd had in weeks. Light from the bedroom window told me dusk had settled over Heart's Desire.

Graf slipped into his pants and opened the door to a sheepish Oscar. "Sorry, but Brandy Westin wants to speak with you. I told her you were resting, but she wouldn't take no for an answer."

It didn't take a private investigator to detect that Tinkie had tied Oscar in a knot and then shook him loose. Satisfaction oozed from every pore.

"I'll get dressed and go down," Graf said with only a hint of reluctance.

Oscar looked past Graf and grinned at me. "How's it going?"

Oscar was about as subtle as a keg of C4. "Real good. And you?"

"Best afternoon I've had in a while. Maid work seems to be good for Tinkie. I'm thinking I might hire her out at least twice a week."

Bold talk for a man who'd been turned inside out. "I'd like to be around when you suggest it."

"Suggest what?" Tinkie popped around the doorframe and pushed Oscar inside so she could shut the door.

Oscar begged me with a look and I let compassion win out. "Oscar was just saying what a fine afternoon he'd had."

Tinkie slid an arm around his waist. "That would make two of us. You both look like you got the kinks snatched out."

I had to laugh. Tinkie seldom fell into the use of common expressions, but I did feel exactly as she described. In fact, I would be willing to bet I was at least two inches taller.

"Oscar was telling us about your afternoon activities." Graf had the very devil in him. "In explicit detail."

"Yeah, beats the hell out of banking, doesn't it?" I had to gig Oscar a little because he'd given Tinkie such a hard time lately.

"Oscar, a gentleman never kisses and tells!" Tinkie's face burned pink. "Did you tell them about—?"

"They're goading you," Oscar said. He silenced Tinkie with a kiss.

There was nothing Graf and I could do but applaud his decisive action.

"I'll see you downstairs," Oscar said to Graf. "Be careful and get out of here," he said to me. "Palk is pacing around all over the house. He knows something is up, he just hasn't figured out what."

"Marjorie is asleep right now, Sarah Booth, but she's down in the dumps in the worst kind of way. I removed her prescriptions. I don't trust her not to take a rash action." Tinkie patted her pockets. "She has way too much medication. I'm afraid all of the ground we gained has been undone by Chasley."

"Have you seen Chasley?" I asked.

Oscar shook his head. "Not hide nor hair. Tinkie and I were rather busy for a while. Since then, I've been out in the servants' quarters and wandering around the grounds. Chasley hasn't put in an appearance. Palk doesn't take kindly to service staff in the 'big house.' He actually told me to leave."

"Palk loves class distinctions." At least he was consistent in his awfulness.

"The Zinnia bank has dealt with Chasley on some investments. Do you think Chasley will recognize you?" Graf asked Oscar.

"He dealt with Harold. They knew each other as children, a brief period between Marjorie's marriages when she was back in Mississippi. I never knew him." Palk's voice carried to us as he snapped an order on the first floor. "Palk alert. I've got to go." He grabbed Tinkie and split. Graf and I were alone for another few moments.

My body told me to pull the covers over my head and refuse to leave Graf's bed. My heart agreed. My conscience forced me up and into my clothes. I had work to do.

"What are your plans?" I asked Graf.

"I have a session with Sherry. I'm hoping to use my

considerable charms to find out whatever you want to know."

I turned slowly and appraised my fiancé. "You're undercover in disguise, and now you're *snooping*."

"It's research for the movie we'll film in November. Remember, I sent you the script for *Delta Blues*."

Oh, I remembered. I hadn't read the script, and I didn't want to admit it, because things were so good between us. "You're really helping me with the case?"

"Of course, Sarah Booth. Oscar and I both are here to assist. Because you and Tinkie are of the lower class here at Heart's Desire, I can find out different kinds of information. Oscar can hobnob with the guards and such, and I will charm any information you want out of the other guests and the Westins. Two new avenues of fact-gathering. So brief me quickly. What are you thinking about the murders of Amanda and Lola?"

"They don't seem to be related, but they must be. Amanda was little more than a kid with a dream. She was dating a guard, Kyle McAty. She really just wanted to be done with Heart's Desire and find a job as a chef."

"Are the Westins involved in the deaths?"

He was asking all the right questions, but I had no answers. "What could they possibly benefit from killing Amanda and one of their guests?"

"Nothing, unless Amanda and Lola discovered something. Something secret that had to be kept quiet at all costs."

It was the scent I'd been pursuing, but now I *had* to run it to ground. Something dark and sinister was happening at Heart's Desire, and it was my job to find out what. "When you talk to Sherry, see if you can ascertain if she has any abilities as a medium. So far, I'm not impressed. This is all hocus-pocus stuff anyone could set up. As a client, she should give you some evidence. You have a right to challenge her."

"I'm on it." Graf pulled me into his arms for a long, passionate kiss. "Let's solve this case and hie ourselves back to Zinnia. I want to go horseback riding at daybreak, and I want to make coffee and cook French toast for breakfast. I need some time with you, Sarah Booth."

"I love you, Graf."

"Then get busy." He slapped my behind and pushed me toward the door.

I slipped through the door of the Periwinkle Suite to the rhythm of Marjorie's soft snores. I listened for a moment and then left again. Tinkie's fears ate at me. Our job at Heart's Desire was to help Marjorie. So far, I'd discovered zip about her drowned daughter. Two women were dead, and I didn't have a clue if Sherry Westin was a true medium or a con.

The only thing I could say for certain about Chasley was that he was handsome, arrogant, and rightfully upset with his mother. None of it made him a sister-killer or schemer. I'd wasted several days and ended up empty-handed. This was not the reputation the Delaney Detective Agency was built on. I had to engage my investigative talents. I'd spent the whole time at Heart's Desire tracking down ghosts. In essence, I'd been sniffing the wrong trail. Amanda and Lola hadn't been killed by ghosts. A flesh-and-blood killer stalked the halls of Heart's Desire and it was time for me to figure out who that was. Answers were not to be found in the Periwinkle Suite.

Two doors down, I tapped lightly on Amaryllis Dill's

door. I wanted to talk to her. Privately. The door swung wide on silent hinges.

The room was a buttery yellow, the walls soft and soothing. Pale sheers floated at the open windows. In ninety-eight degree heat? Before I moved, I listened intently. While I didn't think Amaryllis was in the room, someone else might be. I thought of Yumi slipping across the lawn to break into Amanda's digs. What was happening at Heart's Desire?

I was uncomfortable, but I couldn't weasel out the door like some kind of coward. What if Amaryllis was hurt, unconscious in the bathroom or beside the bed? I took a deep breath and tiptoed into the room.

Restraining the impulse to call out to Amaryllis, I checked the off side of the bed, in the dining area, and finally in the bathroom. There was no sign of her—or anyone else.

Since she wasn't there, I made the best of the circumstances and began a thorough search of her personal possessions. I hit pay dirt in her underwear drawer. Folded into a neat square was a newspaper clipping. I scanned the article. Linda Faver, wife of Congressman Lucas Faver, was killed in a one-car accident. Police ruled the death an accident. Mrs. Faver lost control of her car and struck an overpass abutment at a high rate of speed. So this was Amaryllis's secret lover. She'd called him Lucas. Her ticket at Heart's Desire wasn't wealth but access to power. What had really happened to Linda Faver?

Perhaps a more in-depth investigation was covered in a later newspaper article, but judging from what I held in my hand and what Amaryllis had told me, I believed I could guess why she wanted to talk with the dead Linda Faver.

Coleman had to know about this. He could check with the D.C. police for additional details. If my suspicions were correct, Amaryllis was the third party in a very messy affair with a powerful congressman. Even worse, Amaryllis suspected the wife's accidental death was no accident at all. Hence her desire to speak with Linda's spirit.

And very possibly the reason someone tried to murder her in the spa. It was a hit. But who at Heart's Desire would be a paid assassin?

And where in the hell was Amaryllis?

I went to close the windows and discovered sheets knotted together and dropped halfway to the ground. Amaryllis had pulled a teenager's stunt of scrambling out the window. She could be anywhere on the grounds. And she had no protection. I took off like a scalded cat. Turning into the hallway, I smacked into Chasley.

"Whoa. Where's the fire?" he asked as he caught my arm, partly to balance me and partly to hold me.

"Let me go." I schooled patience into my voice.

"Looking for someone?"

"I am. Amaryllis. Have you seen her?

"She's gone?"

"Gone. It's a four-letter word. *G-o-n-e*. As in bye-bye."

"I'm not surprised," he said. "The way she was acting, I figured she'd blow out of here like she had fire in her pants. I presume she's headed to Memphis. She mentioned earlier she had a plane ticket waiting."

I didn't believe him for a minute. All her things were still in her room. She wouldn't leave everything, even her jewelry. She was probably still on the grounds, and likely terrified. I tried to jerk my arm free but he held on.

"Chasley, take your hands off me."

He dropped my arm instantly. "Sorry. I have to speak with you."

"About what?"

"Mother. I'm genuinely concerned."

"Why? Did something happen?" He truly sounded worried.

He shifted from foot to foot. "I finally spoke with her this afternoon while everyone was busy. I think she listened."

If it was about their screwed-up relationship, I didn't have time. "Chasley, could we do this later?"

"No. Mother said she'd consider what I told her. But it was like she . . . shrank. She said the strangest thing about wasting her life. I have a bad feeling."

"Let me find Amaryllis and then I'll do what I can for Marjorie."

"Please, do it now." He grasped my elbow a little too hard and I gasped.

Out of the corner of my eye I caught movement. Not Graf or Oscar. Not Palk. The handsome devil who came to my rescue weighed only twenty-three pounds, but he had claws and an attitude.

"Watch out!"

Confusion touched Chasley's handsome face for a moment. Awareness dawned a second too late as Pluto launched himself at the back of Chasley's head. Two black paws dug into Chasley's face just below his eyes. It was like something out of *The Texas Chain Saw Massacre*. Blood spurted and Chasley screamed like a woman and dropped to his knees.

I shooed Pluto away and knelt beside Chasley to check the damage. The delicate skin above his cheekbones was bleeding, but it wasn't a serious injury. "He thought you were hurting me."

"The cat is a danger."

"I'm sorry, Chasley. You aren't seriously injured, and I promise, I'll have a conversation with your mother. Soon." I pushed Pluto into Marjorie's room and set off after Amaryllis. I had to find her. I didn't trust anything Chasley said.

Crime scene tape covered the door to the spa, which led me to believe Amaryllis wasn't there. I'd searched the first and second floors. Tinkie took the servants' quarters and other outbuildings, and Oscar volunteered to speak with the guards at the gate.

Not a trace of Amaryllis could be found. I couldn't believe she'd left Heart's Desire, but I was beginning to hope she'd somehow made good her escape. Otherwise it didn't bode well for her safety.

I passed the front windows and realized night had fallen. Dinner would be served, and then, if patterns could be trusted, Sherry would attempt another séance. Speaking of Sherry, I wondered how Graf's session with her was shaping up. They were locked in the library; I'd ascertained that much when I was poking around.

The underground rooms of the basement unnerved me, but that was the only place left to search. In Mississippi, normal people didn't have basements. Too much humidity and sandy soil. I headed down the stairs.

"Sarah Booth." A male voice called my name and I stopped.

"Oscar?"

He joined me and we descended. At the bottom of the steps, he touched my back. "Amaryllis never made it out the gate. The guards said they had orders from the sheriff not to allow anyone to leave."

"Coleman did tell her she couldn't take off."

"If she's gone, she didn't drive out."

"Did anyone leave?"

"The guards said no one." He thought for a moment. "How reliable are the guards?"

"A pertinent question." One I couldn't answer, but Coleman might sweat the truth out of them.

"If ever a spook decided to show itself, it would be down here," Oscar said.

"Let's check it out and split. This place is creepy." I didn't mention Amanda, but I felt a great sadness for the young woman. "If Amaryllis is down here, she'll be scared to death. Let's find the lights."

"Good idea."

I would never admit it out loud, but I was glad Oscar was with me. I flipped the light switch. For a moment, illumination filled the darkness; then the lights stuttered and went dark. In the brief flare of light, I saw a figure at the end of the hall near the séance room.

"Saint Paul in a nun's habit," I whispered.

"Have you lost it, Sarah Booth?" Oscar asked.

"I'm trying not to curse. I'm creating vivid and provocative images." I spoke in a whisper.

"Why are you whispering?"

"Because I don't want the person at the end of the hall to hear me."

Oscar's hand gave me support. "Who's there?" Now he whispered, too.

"I couldn't identify him, but he's tall, dark, and dark."

Oscar stepped in front of me. Just what I always wanted. My best friend's husband as a human shield.

I tried to pull him back, but he shook me off. So it was okay for him to put himself in danger, but I couldn't. I'd have to deal with the machismo later.

My total focus zeroed in on the end of the hall. Moving slowing and quietly, Oscar and I crept forward.

We passed another light switch and I flipped it. Nothing. Either a fuse had blown or someone deliberately cut the power to the lights in the basement. I voted for the second scenario.

A soft moaning emanated from the end of the hallway. My mind leaped instantly to the classics of horror written by Edgar Allan Poe. This was a moment the melancholy master would employ to great effect. Corpse in the wall, living person in a coffin, pendulum. Black cat! Had Pluto made his way to the basement? If so, who was he tormenting?

"No, help." The words were distinct, echoing from the black void. "Please, help."

I leaned toward where I assumed Oscar's back would be. The hall was pitch black and I was disoriented, but I recognized the voice. "It's Palk."

"You're sure?" Oscar asked.

"I'm positive. Even when he's begging for help, he still sounds like a dick."

The moan came again. "Get me down, now. Someone help me."

"He sounds hurt," Oscar said.

"Good things happen to bad people." We inched closer to the end of the hallway.

"We need a flashlight."

"There are candles in the séance room." Dozens of

them. Feeling down the wall, I found the knob, twisted it, and stepped inside, trying to remember the placement of the furniture. I stumbled a few times, but I found the candles and the lighter, left just where I'd last placed them.

The flint clacked as I spun the Zippo, and the flame gave me some relief from the darkness. I lit four candles. Doing my best to avoid dripping hot wax, I took them to the hall.

Holding up the candles in front of us, we cast wavering illumination into the inky hall.

Oscar gasped and backed into me. I almost set his hair on fire with my candles, but I managed only to drip hot wax down the collar of his shirt.

"What the hell?" Oscar said as he stepped forward again, candles extended.

Palk stood on tiptoe on a stool in the middle of the hall, a noose around his neck, wearing black fishnet stockings, a garter belt, and the Hannibal Lecter mask over his face. Every other part of him was naked as the day he was born.

"Help me. If I move, I'll strangle."

"If you move and expose anything else, I may throw up." Wrong though it was, I enjoyed the sight of Palk brought to such a humiliating pass.

"You're in a predicament, my man," Oscar said. "I hate to say it, Palk, but this is a cliché. Uptight butler, kinky sex fetishes."

"Get me down this instant." Palk reached for authority but fell short.

"How about a *please*?" I asked.

"I refuse to beg you, a maid, for help."

"Fine by me. Let's head upstairs, Oscar. I'm sure Mrs. Littlefield and Mr. Graf need our services."

We turned around and walked. I stopped. "By the way, Palk, who put you up on your stool? Was it an insurrection of the household help, sort of a symbolic hanging of your overbearing authority complex?"

"I don't want to talk about it."

Oh, so it was a personal matter. "How did Yumi talk you onto a three-legged stool when your . . . vital statistics are dangling precariously? She must be very persuasive."

"Could be he's a perv," Oscar offered. "Judging by the height of the stool and—"

"Stop!" I knew where he was going.

"Autoerotic asphyxiation gone wrong." Oscar was proud of himself.

"I was not alone," Palk blurted.

"I'll send Mrs. Westin down here to cut you loose."

"Don't do this, Miss Booth."

Even though it was a command, it was the nicest he'd spoken to me since my arrival. "Why did Yumi run off and leave you like this?"

He sighed. "I don't know. We enjoy role-playing. I know it's hard to believe, but being a head butler is a wearisome burden. I need a little relief. Yumi is a woman who knows how to . . . persuade a man to do things he might not otherwise do. She heard something. Some noise. She said she'd be right back. I'm afraid something awful has happened to her." Even though she'd gussied him up like a pimp's Halloween delight, he longed for her. Amazing. The human animal could always surprise me.

"You've found your fashion niche, Palk. A garter

belt, stockings, and a Hannibal Lecter mask. Sort of *Rocky Horror Picture Show* meets *Pretty Baby*. Have you considered the possibilities of a reality TV show? *Born to Boogie . . . Man*."

I wasn't about to let Palk off the hook easily, and I had Oscar holding his sides, he was laughing so hard.

"*Please* get me down," Palk snapped.

He'd finally used the magic word. "Your wish is my command."

My first impulse was to kick the stool, but Oscar wouldn't approve. I hurried forward to find the rope pulled through a sconce and tied off. The knot was professionally done, easy to untie. Maybe Yumi meant to release him, but why had she left him? I tugged the rope and Palk was free.

When the rope fell around his feet, Palk removed the mask and stepped to the floor. For a man who spent his days with a broomstick up his . . . he was certainly nimble.

"Where are my clothes?" He was clearly panicked.

The area around him was bare—just like his . . . I shut that train of thought down before it reached a destination. "Tough luck, Palk. You'll have to hoof it to your suite à la pervert."

"My keys." He didn't attempt to hide his worry. "She took my pants and jacket."

"Yumi?" Call it instinct or contagious panic, but my heart squeezed. If she had Palk's master keys, Yumi had access to every locked door in the house.

"She constructed this entire scenario. She called me down to the basement for a game, but she took my clothes. I have to find her. On top of everything else, Mrs. Westin will be furious. I should have been in the dining room checking the dinner setup ten minutes ago. I told Yumi we didn't have time, but nothing would dissuade her." He started to brush past me, but I blocked him.

"Where's Yumi?"

"Check the kitchen or her room. You know where it is, you little snoop. Tell her taking my clothes wasn't amusing. Nor was leaving me tied up like a Christmas goose."

"What did Yumi hear?" My brain drilled out a *red alert! Red alert!*

"I don't know. My mind was elsewhere." His forehead furrowed. "Actually, I think it was a woman's voice."

"Can you be more specific?"

"One of the guests, calling for Stella. Strange." The furrow grew deeper. "Why would Amaryllis wish to speak with a laundress?"

Lazarus on a trapeze! "And that's when Yumi left you?"

"She said she'd be right back. Something must have happened to her." His mouth thinned. "But why did she take my clothes? And why didn't she come back? I've been down here for ages. Do you think she's injured?"

He was actually worried about her. She'd left him in a situation where he might have hanged himself, yet he would ultimately forgive her. He had it bad for the chef. The faces of love were myriad and, in his case, terrifying.

"Did you hear anything else?" I asked, keeping my cool.

"Nothing. What should I have heard?"

I might fault Palk for being slow on the uptake, but I had to tar myself with the same brush. "We have to find

Yumi and Amaryllis," I said. The puzzle had clicked into place. Yumi had worked in Washington, D.C. She was handy with knives, and I'd seen her impressive physicality. I believed I'd found the assassin hired to kill Amaryllis.

18

Oscar, admirably silent about the whole sordid scene, kept watch on the first floor so Palk could run to his apartment and find suitable clothes. While I'd have given a hundred dollars to witness Brandy's reaction to his choice in lingerie, I was more concerned for Amaryllis. For the moment, her safety was my priority.

If my deductions were correct, Yumi had been sent by Lucas Faver to eliminate Amaryllis. Sleeping with political figures could be righteously dangerous in the climate of intolerance that had brewed up in America. For a politician with a super-conservative base, killing a troublesome mistress might prove more appealing than owning up to her. Especially if he'd killed his wife and was about to be exposed.

If Congressman Faver thought Amaryllis suspected him of murder, she could be in serious danger. If he figured she'd rat him out to the police, she could be a dead woman walking. Normally, I didn't pay a lot of attention to the political scene, but I knew Faver's story. He was a media darling, a poor boy risen from a hardscrabble background to rule key committees. His supporters bought into his devout religious hyperbole. Based on his press, all he needed was a civil war and a top hat to rise to the level of Lincoln. He wouldn't give up power without a struggle, and like many elected officials, he'd begun to believe he was above the laws he was paid to write.

This development required Internet access and a willingness to spend hours sifting through Web sites and newspaper articles.

Damn the Westins and their obsession with isolation; I needed help. I pulled out the cell phone Coleman had given me and dialed the sheriff's office. The dispatcher told me Coleman and DeWayne were working a shooting in a rural river community, but she would radio them and Coleman would be in touch. I hung up and called Cece.

I told her what I thought was happening. She went dead silent.

"Are you there?" I feared my connection had been disrupted.

"I'm here. I'm on the Internet, checking into the congressman and his wife. Oh, I've found the car accident where she died. Photos of him nearly crumpling to the ground at her funeral. Whatever else the man is, he's a genius at playing the political moment. He's feasting on public sympathy. If he killed his wife to accommodate his mistress, this is the sickest thing I've seen."

Oh, I could match that and up the ante with Palk's

lovefest. "Any evidence he killed the wife? Any hint of a scandal?" I waited—impatiently.

"There're no news reports about infidelity, no rumors. Which could mean he's either innocent or a very careful man. I'll keep researching."

"Thanks, Cece. I'll be in touch."

"Oh, you will indeed. I should head out to Heart's Desire. I'm worried. Half of Zinnia is there, and if something gruesome occurs, you may need my muscle."

I didn't want to involve Cece in dangerous situations. "Take care of Sweetie and Chablis. That's the best help of all. I think we'll resolve this soon, and I'll call you the minute we do."

I hung up and darted up the stairs to Marjorie's room. And stopped. Roger Addleson slithered out of Amaryllis's room. He held something in his hands, but I couldn't see clearly what it was. He saw me and almost jumped out of his skin.

"Where's Amaryllis?" I asked.

"I have no idea. She's not in her room."

I waited silently, an invitation for him to continue. When he didn't, I asked, "What did you take from her room?"

He tried to hide it behind his back. "Step aside. Don't make me call Palk. I've never heard of a personal maid who dared question a guest. I'll have you dismissed."

"Give it your best shot." I was tired of being treated like a second-class citizen. I had a new respect for the arrogance of the wealthy and the awful way they treated those they labeled inferior.

I made a grab for the object wrapped in a shirt. Too late, I realized he meant to fight. Like a linebacker, he stiff-armed me. My foot slipped on the edge of the top step, and I fell. For a few seconds it was like flying, but then I hit the treads and my world went black.

"Sarah Booth! Wake up!"

Tinkie's face slowly came into focus. Behind her, Oscar wore an expression of concern. "She's coming to."

Indeed I was. And I was gunning for Roger Addleson. I pushed up on an elbow with a groan. "Where is the bastard?"

"Who?" Tinkie asked. "What happened to you?"

"Roger Addleson pushed me down the stairs."

"You could have broken your neck," Oscar said. "I'll get Graf."

"No!" Tinkie and I spoke in unison.

"There's no point dragging Graf into this. He's with Sherry." I tried to get up, but my body protested. Nothing was broken, but I'd sure as hell been banged around.

Oscar offered a hand, and I let him pull me to my feet. "I'm okay." I wanted to curse and weep—and kick the daylights out of Roger Addleson—but I maintained a stiff upper lip.

"One day, Sarah Booth—"

Oscar was cut short. "Don't even say it." Tinkie rounded on him. "Don't you say something bad is going to happen to Sarah Booth. She was pushed down a flight of stairs by a coal company CEO. That's not something anyone would expect and has nothing to do with our case." She turned back to me. "Why did Addleson push you?"

I tried to piece the chain of events together. "He had something in his hand he'd taken from Amaryllis's room. I tried to grab it and he pushed past me." I had to be honest, though the temptation to paint him guilty was strong. "I don't know that he meant to knock me down."

"But he sure as hell didn't hang around to make certain you weren't dead." Tinkie was unforgiving when it came to her friends.

Footsteps in the hallway stopped our conversation. Graf and Sherry Westin rounded the corner. Sherry broke away and ran past us up the stairs. The look she threw at me was almost an accusation, and I wondered what had transpired with my fiancé. Graf stood befuddled for a moment before he joined us.

"Is Sherry the real deal or a fraud?" I asked, giving Tinkie and Oscar warning scowls to keep their lips zipped about my tumble.

Graf didn't seem to understand my question. He stared at me, but he didn't seem to see me.

"Hey!" I put a hand on his chest. "Graf, are you okay?"

"Do you remember Granger Reed?" he asked. He was positively dreamy. Had she drugged him?

"Of course. We studied theater under him in New York."

I'd adored the old codger. He was a veteran of musicals and dramas, and he'd taught me technique, improving my acting by 80 percent. I explained to Oscar and Tinkie who he was. "He died my second year in New York. He was like a father to Graf, though. They worked together a number of times. He used his influence to help Graf."

"Now isn't the time for a trip down memory lane," Tinkie said. She frowned and whispered in my ear, "What's wrong with Graf?"

I couldn't answer her, but something was definitely up. "Graf, why are we talking about Granger Reed?"

"I spoke with him. Just now," Graf said. The bemused expression deepened. "It was . . . incredible. He stood right there in the room, and he told me things. Sarah Booth, you should have been there. He said he was proud of me, that I'd made the transition to film and he thought I was brilliant."

I reached up to touch Graf's forehead. He acted like he was running a fever. "We need some blood work done on you." Judging from his numbed behavior and the flush on his face, my assumption that he might be drugged could prove correct. We had to document it. So that was how Sherry convinced people she was a medium. She got them one-on-one, drugged them, likely hypnotized them, and made them see whatever in the hell she wanted them to see.

"I'm not drugged," Graf said rather pointedly. "I'm not that stupid. I didn't eat or drink anything. She really brought Granger back to speak with me. He knew things about my career only he would know. And Sarah Booth, he says the script I sent you is the right career move for you. And me! He was thrilled we're together. He said he always knew we had chemistry. He said you never appreciated your abilities, that you had more talent than anyone he'd ever taught, but you didn't believe in yourself."

Tinkie's mouth formed into a tiny O of dismay. Oscar put his arm around her and shot me a look of sympathy.

"Did Granger's ghost blow my cover?" I asked as gently as I could.

The glaze slowly left Graf's eyes. "What?"

"Did your ghost tell Sherry that you and I are a couple?"

Graf's Adam's apple rose and fell as he swallowed. "I'm so sorry. I don't know how this happened. I didn't ask to speak with Granger. He showed up, and he started talking, and then he was so excited that we were to be married. I can't believe I did this, Sarah Booth. I came here to help you, not sabotage your case."

"Sherry either drugged you or hypnotized you." It wasn't Graf's fault, but I had to fight back my annoyance. "The cat is out of the bag now, for sure."

"Good." Oscar took control. "We can all quit pretending. Graf and I will pay whatever is required to be a part of this Heart's Desire. Tinkie and you will join us in our suites, as it should be. We'll attend the séances and find out what the Westins are really up to. Enough of this maid and valet silliness."

In a way, Oscar was right. Tinkie and I had accomplished all we could in our disguise as maids. We could simply investigate for Mrs. Littlefield, maybe prevent her from ruining the rest of her life. That was what we were hired to do, not deceive the Westins. It was time to put aside our covert operations, move Mrs. Littlefield and Pluto home, and help Coleman find out who had killed two young women.

"If Sherry could hypnotize Graf and get him to spill his guts about you and everything else, she's a very dangerous woman," Tinkie said. "She's had private sessions with all of the clients at one time or another. We can assume she knows their innermost secrets."

"Then she'd likely know who killed Amanda and Lola," Oscar said. Leave it to the moneyman to apply logic. "Why hasn't she told Coleman?"

"Two possibilities. Either she has something to gain, or the killer is someone she's never consulted with. Someone like Yumi Kato." While Oscar had dibs on logic, I knew human nature. "We need to work fast. Amaryllis is missing, and Yumi stole Palk's keys. She can go anywhere on the compound."

"I'll speak with Roger Addleson," Oscar said. "He knows something about Amaryllis, and he won't push me—"

Tinkie took his arm and steered him away.

"Who did Roger push?" Graf asked.

"Talk to the Westins. Find out what they know about their chef. Please."

It was the "please" that did the trick. "Will do."

"Tink and I will see how our client is doing," I said.

"She's gotten used to having us to order around," Tinkie said. "This is going to be hard on her."

We trudged back up the steps I'd so recently bounced down. Graf must have noticed my stiffness, but he didn't ask. At the second-story landing, Tinkie and I turned to Marjorie's room.

She'd been asleep earlier, and I suspected she might still be. She slept a lot. Probably due to the bottles of medication for anxiety and nerves. We weren't especially quiet when we entered the suite. The bedroom was empty.

"Where's Marjorie?" Tinkie asked.

Pluto frantically dug at the closed door of the bathroom. "Stop it," I told him. He'd already managed to claw off several layers of paint. Marjorie would have a major repair bill tacked onto her visit. "Ease off." I picked him up, but he jumped from my arms and clawed at the door again, his fat little black paws moving like he was churning butter.

"Marjorie?" I tapped on the bathroom door. "Marjorie?" I heard water running. "Marjorie?" I smacked the door a little harder. To my horror, when I looked down at my feet, a growing puddle of bloody water seeped around my shoes.

Pluto let out a gut-wrenching yowl and attacked the door again.

Jiggling the handle, I discovered the door was locked.

"Get the men!" I used my shoulder as a battering ram while Tinkie ran to get Oscar, Graf, and Palk.

Within minutes, Palk, dressed in his tuxedo, was there. He forced the door open but allowed Tinkie and me to enter first.

"Call 911!" Tinkie ordered. Marjorie's slender body, terribly childlike, floated in an overflowing bathtub stained pink with her blood. One wrist hung over the side, dripping bright red onto the flooded floor.

Her eyes rolled open and she smiled groggily.

Marjorie's pulse was weak but steady after we lifted her out of the water, wrapped her in a blanket, and settled her on the bed. Tinkie applied pressure bandages to her wrists while we waited for Doc Sawyer to arrive.

Chasley paced the room, one wary eye on Pluto, who'd assumed a sphinxlike pose on top of my best white shirt. "She should be taken to the hospital," Chasley said. "She's a danger to herself. Clearly you can comprehend that? It's not about the money. I don't want her to die. Can't you understand? She's my mother and I don't want her to die."

Tinkie and I had our share of worries about Marjorie, but we resisted Chasley's pleas. He seemed sincere in his worry, but I couldn't forget that a hospital record of attempted suicide—and there could be no doubt what

Marjorie's actions implied—could become a real problem for her. Once she was in a hospital, it would be one more tiny step to send her to a mental ward. I feared that was Chasley's ultimate goal, no matter what he said. And Tinkie had assured me the cuts on her wrists were not life-threatening.

"I don't want to be hospitalized." Marjorie turned her head away from Chasley. "You want to declare me insane. I'm not crazy, I'm just so alone."

"You attempted suicide, Mother. That isn't the action of a sane person."

Instead of responding with anger, she sighed. "I've had enough of all this. I want to go home. I thought this would bring me happiness, but it's only generated misery. I want to live quietly for the time I have left. Enough séances and investment strategies. My life has become a series of chores that mean nothing to me. I've clung to a foolish dream. I believed something magical would happen to show me what to do with the rest of my time on this plane. Life doesn't work that way. I'm done. I simply want to go home."

Excellent news! If we could put Marjorie on the road home, then we could fully focus on finding Amaryllis, capturing Yumi and proving her guilt or innocence, and picking up our lives in Zinnia. I rushed to the closet to bring out her bags and pack.

"I want you to stay here, Mother." Chasley pushed off the far wall. "You came here to talk to Mariam. You shouldn't leave until you do."

I wanted to beat him with a stick.

"What is your problem?" Tinkie asked, obviously sharing my annoyance at Chasley's stupidity.

He took a deep breath. "I've come to a few conclusions myself. Mother will never believe I'm innocent unless Mariam tells her. I never harmed my sister. I may be guilty of neglect, but I was a fifteen-year-old boy. When I realized Mariam was missing, I panicked. I knew I didn't pay enough attention to her. When she fell into the river, I thought at first she was hiding from me, paying me back for ignoring her. When I realized she was truly gone, I searched for her. Had I seen her in the water, I would have tried to save her, even if I drowned myself."

"But you didn't call for help until much later," Tinkie said softly. "That's what troubles your mother. And you showed no grief."

Chasley paced as he gathered his composure. "I'd taken Mariam to show her how much Ramón trusted me, but the offices were locked. When she disappeared, I'd been trying to break in through a window. I was frustrated, so I smoked a cigarette. I wanted Mariam to see me as grown-up and sophisticated, someone Ramón trusted. Finally, I realized she was gone and what had likely happened. I couldn't get into the office to use the phone. I tried some of the other buildings, but they were locked, too. By the time I found a pay phone . . ."

Sorrow touched his handsome features, and I felt real pity for him. As much as Marjorie had blamed him, he heaped more guilt on himself. He had been, after all, only fifteen.

"You never spoke about what happened," Marjorie said.

"I didn't know what to do. I tried, but it was like being in a nightmare. At first, I didn't want to believe anything had really happened to her. I thought if I could pretend that it wasn't a big deal, maybe she'd be okay. Maybe she'd show up. Maybe she'd come home."

"Chasley." Marjorie spoke so softly. "All these years, you've carried the burden of guilt. I always thought you didn't care, that it didn't matter to you. You were so . . . blasé about her death."

"Inside I was dying, but you were so angry at me. Callousness was the only defense I could manufacture." He dropped to a knee beside Marjorie. "I didn't harm her, Mother. Believe what you have to, but I want you to understand I never laid a finger on her. If I could bring her back, I would."

He reached for Marjorie's hand but stopped when Pluto rose up and stalked toward him. The cat walked like a line backer, and his green gaze locked on to Chasley. Pity the fool who took on that cat.

For a moment we froze in the tableau. Marjorie began to sob. Hard, rending noises that sounded as if her guts were being shredded. "I'm so sorry, Chasley," she said. "I'm so sorry."

I could see her blood pressure spiking by the flush in her face. "Chasley, let Marjorie rest. When the doctor gets here, I'm sure he'll speak with you. We need to keep her quiet."

Brandy Westin tapped lightly at the door, and when we'd relieved her worry—Marjorie was not in danger of dying—she put her arm through Chasley's and gently urged him toward the door. She whispered to him. Whatever she said did the trick. He left without further protest.

I cleared everyone else from the room. I needed a word with my client. Tinkie went downstairs to brew tea, an excuse to give me time alone with Marjorie.

I sat on the side of the bed. A spot of blood had seeped through the pressure bandages Tinkie had wrapped on Marjorie's wrists, but the cuts were shallow and Tinkie's nursing more than up to the task. The worst of Marjorie's physical wounds was over, for the moment.

"Do you believe him?" I asked.

"Part of me wants to, more than anything," she said. "What I do know is that it doesn't matter. I'm tired of all this. What if I do talk to Mariam? What if she tells me Chasley is innocent? Or guilty? It won't make any difference. She's still dead and I'm still alone. I've focused so long on protecting my money and using it as a means to punish Chasley. I've been a rotten mother to him. I don't deserve better."

Even though I agreed with her, the defeat she expressed was hard to accept. "Maybe you can make it up to Chasley. The two of you can start fresh. It isn't too late."

"Call my lawyer, Sarah Booth. No, I want a new lawyer. Donald Allen has wielded too much influence in my life. Call a Zinnia lawyer. A young person who isn't jaded by life. I want to change my will. I'm leaving all of my possessions—everything—to Chasley. It won't make up for the years I've cheated him out of having a mother, but he can stop fighting me for the crumbs. Let him have it all. I'm done with this. I just want to go home."

"Are you sure? This is so sudden. Give it until tomorrow at least, Marjorie. Acting rashly is never smart."

"I've never been more sure of anything in my life. Call an attorney you know and trust, or give me the phone and I'll call the first lawyer I can find."

I used the cell phone Coleman gave me to contact a bright young lawyer I knew in Zinnia. Lacey Polaterri said she'd be at Heart's Desire in two hours. I figured that would give Doc time to check Marjorie over. Soon I would be packing her bags and taking her home. I felt as if I'd been at Heart's Desire half my life. The only thing left to do was find Amaryllis and safely remove her from the compound.

Coleman would find Amanda's and Lola's killer or killers. If it was Yumi, she'd experience the hospitality of the Sunflower County jail. Tinkie and I could go back to Zinnia with Oscar and Graf. I had a script to read and a man to play house with.

Doc Sawyer signaled me outside the front door of Heart's Desire. It was time for dinner, and Marjorie had insisted she would dress and go downstairs. Graf was in her room, waiting to escort her.

"Tinkie was right in her diagnosis. The cuts were mostly superficial. She's determined to go home." Doc rubbed the corner of his mouth. He was clearly dubious.

"Should I stop her?"

His hesitation said a lot, but his answer was firm. "No. I think she'll be happier in her own place. Her blood pressure is fine, her pulse steady. I'm concerned about these spikes in blood pressure. The medication I gave her should control this better. She says she's not taking other medications, but something isn't right here."

"She had a bagful of medicine, but Tinkie removed it. You're worrying me, though. People with money can get whatever they want."

"Marjorie has changed so much. The woman I knew was indomitable. She'd never harm herself. Time has extracted a harsh price."

"Do you think she should be put in a hospital or clinic?"

Doc sighed. "She seems to have come to a decision about her life, and that will have a positive impact on her health. She needs a total workup—physically, mentally, and emotionally—but she won't hear of it right now. We can't stop her from leaving, and right now, I think that's the best plan for her. Marjorie has to come to terms with her emotions, and she has to want to live a happy and productive life. Maybe she's turned that corner."

"I'm a worrywart."

"She's releasing the idea that Mariam is lurking around in the nether regions, waiting for a chance to talk to her. She told me she'd given Mariam's spirit multiple chances, and that if she truly wanted to communicate, she would have done so. I think Marjorie is ready to live, because she's finally accepted that Mariam no longer needs her, and she doesn't have to punish herself."

19

Tinkie and I helped Marjorie pack her mountain of belongings. I was eager for her to be clear of Heart's Desire and the murders. With Marjorie on the way out, Tinkie and I could concentrate on stalking a killer. Even though Marjorie was leaving, I had no intention of abandoning the search for Amanda's killer with so many other things left up in the air. Palk had conducted another search for Amaryllis and Yumi. The guards were insistent no one had left the premises, yet both women remained missing.

Graf and Oscar questioned the staff and guests about Amaryllis, but they'd turned up nothing. She'd vanished without a trace, or at least a trace we could find. Her belongings were in her room. Her rental car was in the client garage. If she'd left, she was on foot. Not exactly the mode of transportation that came to mind when I thought of the well-turned-out blonde. I feared the worst.

Humping luggage to the front of the house, I ran into Brandy and a strangely apathetic Sherry. The Westins, mother and daughter, assumed no responsibility for anything that had happened. "You brought this mess into our house," Brandy accused. "I had no role in this."

Tinkie, hauling two more bags, joined us in the foyer. "We'd like a copy of Yumi's résumé," she said. "Now."

"I'm not obligated to give you anything," Brandy said.

"You might want to rethink that." Tinkie drew herself up to her full five feet two inches.

"The buck stops with you, Brandy. When you called Yumi's references, did they give her a good report?" I asked.

"I didn't bother to call. Her résumé was excellent. I was lucky to hire her."

"You didn't do a background check on the head chef?" Tinkie was incredulous. "You could have hired Velma Barfield."

"Who?" I nudged Tinkie.

"Executed for poisoning." Tinkie wasn't in a mood to hand out facts.

Brandy's chin tilted up. "Yumi worked at the White House. She has all of her papers. She's a superb cook and knew how to run a kitchen. What more could I want?"

"A reference who could say she wasn't a killer," Tinkie snapped. "You people! I run a garden club luncheon with more professionalism."

Brandy bristled. "I knew you weren't a maid. Too sassy. And you!" She drilled into me. "You aren't a maid, but you aren't society, either."

"Correct on both counts. I'm a private investigator, and you have a huge problem on your hands. Finding Yumi and your missing guest should be your top priority, not bickering with me and Tinkie."

"Mother, I don't feel well." Sherry's eyes were glazed, and it struck me that she was honestly sick. If she was truly a medium, and Graf believed she'd channeled Granger's spirit, she might need pharmaceuticals to find peace. I knew from dealing with Jitty that haints could be very demanding.

"Go to the penthouse," Brandy said.

Sherry started to obey like a willing child, when I touched her arm. "Do you know who killed Amanda and Lola?" It was worth at least asking.

Her shoulders rounded even more. "They won't come to me. They're afraid. I'm sorry, I'm exhausted." She stumbled away, and I thought I heard a sob.

"Palk! Palk!" Brandy called the butler. "Dinner is canceled. Have the kitchen staff prepare trays. Serve everyone in the private suites. Tonight's séance is canceled. My daughter is unwell. Heart's Desire will resume normal operations only after the riffraff has been pushed off the premises."

For all intents and purposes, Heart's Desire was in shutdown.

Graf and Oscar showed up as the gathering disbanded. Graf pulled me aside. "Shimmer Addleson is sitting in the middle of the floor surrounded by crushed perfume boxes. She's out of control. She believes Roger helped Amaryllis escape Heart's Desire and she's furious. Oscar and I calmed her down, but she's still threatening to kill Roger when she finds him."

My fiancé and Tinkie's husband were a great addition to the detective agency.

My head was still spinning when Lacey Polaterri, the

Zinnia lawyer I'd called, arrived. Marjorie reclined on the chaise and dictated the contents of her new will as Lacey typed on her laptop. Upon Marjorie's death or permanent impairment of mental faculties, Chasley would inherit everything. Stocks, bonds, real estate, bank accounts, property, a yacht anchored in Miami, a villa in Spain—the list went on and on. Marjorie, who had a bachelor of science degree in home economics, had displayed amazing abilities to invest. Her other talent was marrying well, an art honed on the campus of Ole Miss.

"She could feed and care for a small country," Tinkie whispered to me.

"Don't hold your breath." Feeding third-world countries was not on Marjorie's agenda. Her entire focus had shifted to patching the rift with Chasley, and she was throwing every penny she had at it.

Through the long listing of goods, Chasley was propped against a wall of the suite. He showed no emotion, and I wondered if he'd known what all his mother had accrued in her lifetime.

Lacey printed the document in Brandy's office and presented it for signatures. Marjorie signed with a flourish. Tinkie and I had no choice but to serve as witnesses, and lo and behold, Brandy appeared with her notary seal. The talents of the Westins went on and on.

Marjorie was adamant that not another minute should pass without the new will created, signed, and prepared. Spoiled and used to having her own way, Marjorie let us all know that instant gratification was not fast enough for her.

Luckily Marjorie had no life-threatening illnesses. Given enough time, she might change her mind about the dispossession of her wealth. Or perhaps she would come to terms with Chasley and they would undo the past and become a loving family.

I'd seen glimmers of a hurt and unhappy man behind Chasley's perpetual sneer. Being excluded can make a person mean and spiteful. This rapprochement might lead to a kinder, gentler Chasley. Hell, if I stood to gain billions, I could work hard to be loving and tender.

Five minutes after Lacey left, my cell phone rang. Coleman's warm baritone, filled with concern, asked if I was okay.

"We're all fine," I assured him, then told him our covers were blown, Amaryllis was missing, Roger was hiding out from his irate wife and a pissed-off me, and Yumi Kato might be a hit woman.

"I'll be heading your way as soon as I wrap up this murder. Peckerhead-on-peckerhead crime spree. One man is dead and two gut-shot. They argued over the best battery for an ATV."

"Say that again?" Surely I'd heard him wrong.

"Baxter Ray shot his cousin Earl Ray and killed him, and then shot two other drinking buddies in the gut because they disagreed with Baxter that Polaris was a better battery than Yuasa."

"He killed a man over which battery is best?"

"Like I said, peckerhead-on-peckerhead crime."

I bit back a remark about Darwin and evolution. Coleman took all crime seriously, and I respected that. "When do you think you'll get here?"

"Couple of hours. Let me round up Baxter Ray. He took off through the woods vowing to kill Earl Ray's wife and kids. I don't think he'd really do it, but he was pretty drunk."

"Make it as quick as you can."

"I'll put out an APB for Ms. Dill. If we find her, that's one less worry. We still have to find Amanda's and Lola's killer. Watch your back, Sarah Booth." Coleman's words mimicked my thoughts and I was aware once again of the bond we shared.

"Will do."

Marjorie, will in hand, wanted to hit the road. Dwarfed by all her possessions, she tossed orders left and right. "Call Palk to move the remainder of my things downstairs. You, pack my shoes." She gave the order as if Tinkie and I really were hired servants. The path of least resistance dictated I do what she asked.

I got Palk and two of the guards to haul the rest of the bags to the hired car that waited in front of the house. Marjorie had not wasted a moment. When everything was loaded, Marjorie kissed both Tinkie and me on the cheek. The driver handed her into the backseat. She let the window down. "I'll put a check in the mail to you. Thank you for all you've done."

"No rush," Tinkie said, and this time I kicked her on the back of her calf. She might not need the money, but I did.

"You've both been wonderful to an old woman." She took a deep breath. "I believe Chasley and I will work this out. We have to."

"We didn't really resolve the issue of Mariam," I reminded her. I couldn't shake the feeling of unease. I was ready to tell her about the ghostly presence I'd seen, the young girl asking me to protect her mother. I worried for Marjorie and consoled myself that now she looked better than I'd seen her. Strong and determined. Hopeful, even. Perhaps it was time to put Mariam to rest and focus on the living.

Marjorie grasped my fingers lightly. "You made me understand resolution isn't important. What matters is Chasley, my living child. Because of you and Tinkie, we have time to repair those years of damage."

Chasley exited the house, his bags in hand. He continued past me and Tinkie and kissed Marjorie tenderly on the cheek. "I'll be right behind you, Mother." Her car began to pull away.

"Wait a minute!" Tinkie ran alongside the window. "You forgot Pluto!"

Holy bejesus, in all the excitement, the cat had been overlooked. If Pluto realized how severely he'd been snubbed, he would definitely make someone pay for the oversight. Marjorie had a lot of shredded furniture in her future. "I'll get him."

"Wait!" Marjorie's voice was strong. She motioned both me and Tinkie to the car window. "Would you find Pluto a new home? I can't take him."

I couldn't believe this. Pluto was once the heir apparent of her fortune. Now he was dumped? "You aren't going to abandon Pluto, are you?" I couldn't understand how someone could simply walk away from a living creature that was part of a family.

"I have to, Sarah Booth." Her eyes filled with tears. "Chasley needs for me to do this. For once in his life, he has to come first. Pluto attacked him. Justified or not, Chasley has not forgiven the cat. He's asked me to get rid of him. In this instance, I have to make my son believe I choose him over anyone or anything else."

I started to say something harsh, but Tinkie grabbed

my arm and squeezed. "It isn't fair of Chasley to ask you to pick him between two things you love," she said softly.

"Perhaps it isn't, but what I've done to Chasley isn't right, either. As much as it distresses me, I need to find Pluto a new home."

"If you leave him here, the Westins will take him to the pound." What in the hell was she thinking—just to walk off like he was an unwanted shoe?

"You and Tinkie won't leave him here. I know you that well." Her smile was sad. "I have no choice."

"You have a huge home. Surely you could put Pluto in a part of the house where he wouldn't interfere with Chasley." I couldn't accept this. "The cat is attached to you. Think how he'll feel when he realizes he's been thrown away."

"Maybe, after some time, I can reclaim him. Right now, though, I have to make it clear to Chasley that nothing stands between us. Not even a cat. I'll include a handsome amount in my check to cover his future vet bills and food." She reached out the window and caught hold of my wrist. "I know you'll find someone to take good care of him. Thank you."

She disengaged and leaned back into the seat. "I'm ready to go."

The limo pulled away, followed by Chasley's car. Marjorie had taken a huge step in her life. I hoped it would bring her happiness and peace, but it was my personal opinion such things couldn't be bought by shirking responsibility.

"I can't believe she just left Pluto," Tinkie said. "Maybe she never really cared for him. Maybe she left everything to him to piss off Chasley."

"Maybe." Tinkie was angry, but my anger had given way to confusion. I didn't understand her action. I'd worry about that another day, though. I was bone weary. Every muscle I had throbbed from my tumble down the stairs, but the night was far from done.

Graf, Tinkie, and I gathered in the drawing room. Palk had been sent by the Westins to give the perimeter guards their orders, but I was growing concerned. He should have been back, and I wondered if he'd tricked me. Were he and Yumi working together?

Oscar joined us. He'd been called to the Westins' inner sanctum. "Brandy has informed me we're not wanted here," Oscar said. "She's ordered us all to leave. Immediately."

"There may be a killer on the loose," I protested. Brandy's actions made no sense. "We can't leave. At least not until Coleman gets here. The other guests could be in danger."

"Brandy and Sherry are locked on the third floor with all sorts of electronic security." Oscar ticked off the reasons. "The other guests are supposed to be locked in their rooms. The help has been ordered to their rooms in the bunkhouse, with the exception of the guards, who are all on alert. She claims they're perfectly safe and we are the only danger."

"Yumi could be anywhere on the premises. If she is the killer, what's to stop her from striking again?"

"Motive," Tinkie said. "She killed Amanda because Amanda found out what Yumi was. Remember the video on Amanda's phone. She had evidence of Yumi talking to Lucas Faver, only we didn't put it together at the time.

Yumi had been paid to kill Amaryllis. And she killed Lola, thinking she was her designated target, Amaryllis. If Amaryllis has skipped out, there's no reason for Yumi to stay. She's probably on the dance teacher's tail. Yumi didn't strike me as someone who gave up easily."

Justice had not been served in my book. Two women were dead and the killer was still in the wind.

"We have no authority to stay here," Oscar said. "I hate to leave like this, but we don't have a choice. Your work with Marjorie is finished. She's safely gone and reuniting with her son."

Oscar's sensible approach left me uneasy. "We'll leave when Coleman gets here. Shouldn't we warn Gretchen and Shimmer? We can't just waltz out of here."

"Graf and Oscar alerted them both and offered to take them with us. They refused. Let's pack our things," Tinkie said. "It won't take long. Maybe Coleman will arrive before we're loaded."

Graf's warm embrace took away some of the sting, but I'd never left a case half solved. Sure, finding a killer wasn't what I'd been hired to do, but we were in the middle of it. It felt wrong not to finish.

"I'll get our clothes from the bunkhouse," Tinkie offered. "Oscar will go with me to protect me." She batted her lashes while her hands circled his arm. "He'll make sure no one bothers me."

Clever girl. I wished I could emulate her, but it wasn't who I was. "I'll check upstairs. Graf, would you bring the cars around front so we can load?"

"Anything for my fiancée." He kissed my forehead.

So it was done. We dispersed and went about our separate chores. Except I couldn't give up that easily. Before I left, I had to search the rooms where Palk and Yumi stayed. I didn't expect to find the Korean chef, but I might find evidence. It wasn't in me to quit without trying.

While padding softly down the carpeted hallway, I heard steps behind me. I caught the scent of rain, even though I was indoors and the weather outside was hot, humid, and rain-free. I turned to see a shapely silhouette in a trench coat. Beautiful waves of light brown hair fell below the brim of a hat that shadowed her face.

I was on to Jitty now. I knew exactly who she was. She'd abducted the character created by Sara Paretsky, V. I. Warshawski. "Sometimes the shit comes down so hard, you have to wear a hat," I said wittily, quoting a line from one of her movies.

"Don't ever go on *Jeopardy!*, Sarah Booth. Right actress, wrong movie. That was *Body Heat.*" Jitty glided forward, her hands tucked in the pockets of her coat. "A dame has to be careful in these halls. Chicago's a tough town, but Heart's Desire has more murders per capita," she said. "No telling who, or what, you might run up against in this dump."

Despite Jitty's penchant for provoking, she worked on me like quinine on malaria. One mention of the possibility of danger, and I spun in all directions, positive I would come face-to-face with a killer.

The hallway was empty.

"What are you doing creeping around the staff's quarters?" she asked. "This place smells like sex."

The remark threw me completely off my investigative stride. I took a deep breath and several short sniffs. "What do you mean, it smells like sex?"

She gave me a glare from under the brim of the hat.

"You know, funky, sweaty sex. Somebody's been having a marathon down here."

"How can you tell? I can't smell anything except carpet cleaner and wood wax."

"You've been working as a maid too long. Snatch the dust mop out of your nostrils and take a whiff. Or better yet, climb those stairs to Hollywood Handsome's bedroom and practice exchanging bodily fluids with that man before your eggs rot and crack open."

"That image really makes me want to get carnal with Graf." Just when I thought she'd given up on haranguing me about my ticking biological clock, she body-slammed me again. "I still don't smell anything."

She waved aside my objections. "I asked you what you're doing down here."

"Investigating."

"I would have said snooping."

"Have it your way. I'm snooping. I want to search Palk's and Yumi's digs. Palk's marshaling the guards, but he's been gone a long time. I consider him MIA. Yumi may have eaten him, or he may have hooked up with her. What are you doing here?"

"The same."

My eyebrows shot up in surprise. "You've come to help?"

"Don't act so shocked. I'm worried about the home-wrecker. And where the heck is Roger Addleson?"

That couldn't be good. Did Jitty have inside info? "Is Amaryllis alive?"

Jitty shrugged. "I don't always get the full details."

Great. A half-informed ghost who was wasting my time sniffing in empty corridors. "I have to get busy." I continued down the hall to Palk's door. His cracked door. Curiosity got the better of me, and I pushed it wider with my toe. What would Palk's lair contain? Leather masks, chains, manacles?

"Don't leave any fingerprints, Sarah Booth. If it's a crime scene, you don't want to implicate yourself."

"Palk's perversions may be creepy, but they aren't a crime." I inched inside. "But I might find evidence that is."

"Listen."

Jitty's whisper brushed like a spiderweb against my face. An erratic thumping came to me. "What's that?"

I turned for her response, but Jitty was gone. Damn it. She wasn't any kind of crime-solving partner. One minute she was helping; the next she'd flown the coop. I was on my own in Palk's apartment. His *dark* apartment. His apartment that *did* smell of sex.

"Eeeewwww." I pushed those images out of my brain and got busy.

The thumping came again from an interior room. I had two options. I could use the flashlight, which might give away my position, or I could turn on some lights. That, too, would reveal my presence, but it would also allow me to see the landscape.

I found a light switch, pushed it up, and dived against the wall. Light flooded the tastefully decorated apartment. Antiques, leather-bound books, a stereo system that was on but silent, several well-tended plants, lovely ceramics on the mantel, and Victorian prints hanging on the walls. The décor spoke of an established home and a person who selected his possessions with great care.

Not a single trace of a hockey mask–wearing crossdresser who liked stockings and women with whips.

The thumping resumed, this time with more urgency. It was almost like a code. Was it an SOS? Was it Amaryllis?

I turned down a narrow hallway and silently made my way to a closed door. I wasn't an idiot—it crossed my mind I'd stumbled into a setup. I hesitated. The bumping thudded again, combined with someone trying to yell. Someone gagged.

I kicked the door and rolled into the room, gaining my feet with the flashlight swinging. The narrow beam captured Palk, trussed like Tom Turkey awaiting the axe and chopping block. "Saint Sebastian jumping hurdles!"

Palk's face was so red, I thought his head might pop like a zit. He thudded his feet and tried to scream at me, but a ball gag stifled him. His hands and legs were bound with bungee cords.

I removed the gag and gave him a minute to catch his breath. I didn't doubt that Yumi had once again horn-swoggled the butler, and she could still be in his apartment. I remained alert, but I couldn't resist tormenting him. "Another case of sex gone bad? Forgot your safe word, did you?"

"That bitch! She knocked me out. I decided to search her rooms. I thought she'd taken a runner, escaped. I didn't hear her. She's only been gone ten minutes. Untie me, quick."

Palk's words galvanized me to action. I managed to unhook the bungee cords, and he scrambled to his feet. "Let's find Yumi before she harms anyone else." My fiancé and friends could be her next victims.

"She's like some martial arts expert. She kicked me in the back of the knees and then clobbered me with a statue.

I've never seen anything like her except in a movie. She's been skillfully trained." He picked up a bronze statue from the floor.

A rendering of Venus, goddess of love. A bit of irony.

Palk grasped my arm. "She's going to dice Amaryllis like an onion if we don't find her fast."

Palk and I tore out of his apartment and searched the remaining rooms. Yumi's bedroom was enough to make anyone suspicious. Her closet contained only generic black slacks and black tops. In four shoeboxes we found an arsenal of handguns and knives. A crossbow was propped against the back wall of her closet.

"What? She thinks she's Robin Hood?"

"She thinks she's going to kill Amaryllis and then flee the country. She already has a passport in another name and citizenship papers for Argentina. I found them, too."

Palk yanked empty drawers from her dresser. It was evident she viewed her stay at Heart's Desire as temporary.

"She took the keys to my car. I suspect she's managed to get out of Heart's Desire, but I'll question the guards at the gate to be sure. Yumi destroyed the radio transmitter we used to speak with the main gate, and the telephone line. I'll have to walk there. Working here, spending time with me, she learned how everything functions at Heart's Desire. I betrayed the Westins, and she betrayed me."

I couldn't believe it, but I felt sorry for Palk. Even ogres suffered when betrayed.

I called Coleman and got his voice mail. All I could do was leave a message, but I made it urgent. We needed the firm hand of the law to help us find and contain Yumi.

Yumi's apartment yielded nothing else. I returned to the foyer, where the others waited.

"Palk is fairly certain Yumi has gone after Amaryllis, but we have to tell the Westins she may still be in the house," I said. "I've called Coleman and left a message."

"We have news, too," Tinkie said. "We found Roger Addleson hiding out in our room. He's upstairs with Shimmer right now. I hope he survives the encounter. She is furious. He admitted to paying Stella, the laundress, ten grand to drive Amaryllis out in her trunk. That's how she got past the guards."

"I hope she has a fighting chance to get away from Yumi." I didn't like the odds.

Tinkie crossed her arms. "We don't know that Yumi has left Heart's Desire, and we can't leave with a chance the killer is hiding in the compound."

"It wouldn't matter if we told the Westins that Jack the Ripper was walking the parapets, they aren't going to do anything but barricade their rooms." Oscar was adamant. "We should get out of here before we get hurt."

"If Sherry were any kind of medium, she'd know where to find Yumi *and* Amaryllis," Tinkie said.

"She's a medium, not a psychic." It really wasn't worth pointing out the difference.

"Sarah Booth and I will make one last attempt to try to talk to them," Graf said as he linked arms with me. "Then we're out of here. No second thoughts, no looking back."

My stomach dropped to my feet. "Pluto!" I'd forgotten all about the cat.

"What about Palk?" Oscar asked unhappily. "Shouldn't we be sure he's safe?"

Graf hesitated, and I made a decision. "Graf, you talk with the Westins. They like you, anyway, and they hate me. I'll find Pluto and put him in his carrier. Oscar, you and Tinkie stay together and check for Palk at the gate. Graf and I can each drive a car and meet you there."

"Sounds like a plan." Graf put action to words as he passed me, fingers trailing through one of my curls. "Grab the cat. We'll be on the road to Zinnia in five minutes. I think we'll hit Millie's for some late-night breakfast, and then I have plans for you that require a bed, privacy, and my imagination."

I'd shared more than a few of Graf's imaginative encounters. "Will it involve warmed oil, the ceiling fan cooling my skin, and your hands touching my body?"

"That and so much more."

I sprinted to Marjorie's old suite. I couldn't help but feel bad for Pluto. I wondered if he'd realize he'd been cast aside. I'd do my best to make him feel loved until Tinkie and I could find a new home for him. Right now, though, I wanted to put him in the carrier and haul him down to the front door.

"Kitty, kitty," I called softly. Pluto was rather slippery for such a large kitty. If he got the chance to dart out the door, it might take hours to catch him.

There was no sign of Pluto in the room. Normally he was stretched across my clothes, but every flat surface in the room was bare. I poked in the closet, empty now without Marjorie's abundant wardrobe. Nothing.

I checked under the bed and chaise and other furniture, and finally in the bathroom. Not even a wisp of kitty hair. The damn cat had vanished.

"Pluto." I used my flashlight to check all of the corners. He had to be there. When I got down on my hands and knees to probe under the vanity, I saw the open vent. Somehow, Pluto had gotten the ornate screen off—again— and was now loose in the vent works. Ernest Angley with a hula hoop. I'd screwed that vent in myself. It had been tight!

"Dammit, Pluto." I had no clue where the cat might end up. He could get lost wandering through the internal structure of the house. If his luck didn't hold, he might jump out where Yumi could get him.

The last time he'd gotten in the vent, he came out in the Lotus Suite. I would work my way down the suites. Chasley's old room was next door, and I started there. Since he'd left with his mother, the room was empty. I scurried inside. I reached for the light switch and felt something hot strike my arm. "Shit." No time for inventive cursing when my arm was on fire.

I flipped on the light and instantly saw the blood. A large slice had been cut in my arm, and the person who'd done it was standing only four feet away.

Yumi Kato whipped a skinning knife through the air, missing my face by only an inch.

20

"Meddling bitch." The blade whipped at me again. I ducked, but not fast enough. The tip caught the side of my head and sliced my ear. Blood gushed down my neck and shirt. I tried to console myself with words I'd heard Doc Sawyer speak in the emergency room—nothing bleeds like a head wound. Even nonserious ones.

"You won't get out of here," I bluffed as I stumbled over an ottoman and went down. It seemed my coordination had abandoned me. I was left with empty verbal threats. Yumi didn't strike me as someone who would give a rat's ass about my predictions of her future.

"Don't worry about me." Her smile never touched her eyes. *Psychopath* was the word that came to mind. Hired killer. Cold-blooded.

Anger gave me courage. "Let me just point out what a slipshod assassin you are. Congressman Faver will be extremely agitated with the news stories resulting from this. He'll be mocked in the media for hiring an incompetent."

My arrow struck the mark. Her face tightened and she advanced toward me. "You will beg for death."

"No. I won't." I pushed up into a squat. I wasn't about to lie on the floor and let her stab me or cut my throat. "You won't get out of Sunflower County. What a joke, at your expense. World-class assassin imprisoned in rural Mississippi jail. You're a laughingstock."

"My escape route is already planned."

The longer she talked, the longer I lived. I'd searched around the apartment and didn't see a single thing I could use as a weapon. A lamp on a bedside table held promise, but I'd never get there before she gutted me. She was quick and deadly.

"My friends are downstairs. You'll never make it out of the house."

She laughed softly. "I never thought you'd be so desperate."

Another tack was called for. "You haven't harmed Pluto, have you?"

"The cat." She advanced toward me. "He will be next. I'll put his head on the stump of your neck."

"You are one sick bitch."

The chitchat was over. She raised the knife. She meant to plunge it into my heart. I pushed off the floor and hurled myself straight into her. My action caught her by surprise, but the knife blade grazed my ribs. Blinding pain wrapped around my body. I struggled to gain control of her wrist and the knife. She was stronger, quicker, and trained in martial arts. But I had thirty pounds on her and I used it to my advantage.

For one moment I thought I had a chance to overpower her, but she got a leg loose and kicked the back of my knee. I went down like a house of sticks huffed by a wolf. She gathered herself for the attack and rushed me.

A lethal black blur hurtled from the shadows and smacked her right in the face, claws extended. Pluto took no quarter, raking his hooked digits into her eyes. Thank god Marjorie had never done the barbaric declawing.

Yumi gave a strangled gasp. She drew back the knife. She couldn't see—blood covered her face—but still, she meant to kill Pluto. I tackled her around her knees and sent her flying backwards. Her head struck the edge of the bedside table.

Yumi Kato sank to the floor, unconscious.

Bleeding from numerous injuries, I crawled to the door and yelled for help. Much to my joy, I heard feet pounding on the stairs. Graf, Oscar, and Tinkie burst into the room.

A great weariness overtook me. I couldn't faint. I only wanted to close my eyes for a moment. Just a moment. The last thing I remembered was Pluto walking up Yumi's body. He sat on her chest and hissed right into her face. It was a thing of beauty to behold.

"You need stitches in your ear," Graf said as he handed me a fresh, icy cloth to hold against the side of my face.

"Maybe a few in her scalp," Tinkie threw in.

"Where's Pluto?" I asked.

"Right at your feet." Tinkie reached down to pet the cat. My friends had lifted me to the bed. Yumi, her head swathed in bandages, sat on the floor, tied to the bedpost. She'd regained consciousness and refused to say a word. I feared her vision might be permanently damaged, but medical help was on the way. And Coleman.

Pluto sauntered over and walked up my body to settle onto my chest. His purr was loud enough to hear across the room. "My hero," I whispered before I gave him a kiss on the top of his head. "Pluto saved my life."

"I don't think Pluto has to worry about a permanent home," Tinkie said.

"Never again. Graf?"

"I told you I wanted a cat." Graf scratched Pluto's head. "This one may be smarter than both of us, Sarah Booth. He'll be a handful." His hand drifted to gently cup my cheek. "Our handful."

Doc came with the ambulance. I think it was morbid curiosity to see how I'd been injured this time, but he tended to Yumi and sent her, handcuffed to the stretcher, to the hospital and an ophthalmologist. "I don't think the cat blinded her, but best to let the specialists deal with it," he said. "Now, let me see that ear."

Ten minutes later, he'd glued my ear back together. "Hard as hell to stitch cartilage," he offered. "Glue ought to hold it."

"Will it grow back?" I asked. I didn't want a Spock ear, nor one that was notched like I'd been spayed by a feral cat society.

"Can't promise anything," Doc said. "The skin should grow back, but the cartilage may never. Just wear your hair down."

Vanity was so simple for Doc, who looked like a dandelion with his nimbus of white hair. But I wasn't seriously hurt, not even enough for stitches. I'd been very lucky. And I'd nabbed a paid killer. Not bad for a day's work.

"Where's Amaryllis?" For a moment, I'd forgotten about the missing woman.

Tinkie's eyes brightened. "Coleman's deputies found her at Stella's house. Actually, it was a pretty good hiding place. I don't think Yumi would ever have thought to look there."

"Brilliant." I squirmed, trying to wiggle to the edge of the bed. Doc relented and helped me.

"We've wrapped the case," Tinkie said with well-deserved smugness. "But we still have a big problem."

"What?" I didn't know if I could handle another problem.

She pulled back the collar of her shirt to reveal at least two hundred grand in diamonds. "I forgot to give Marjorie her necklace she loaned me. If you're up to it, let's take it back to her. I don't want to be responsible for it a minute longer than necessary."

Though I longed to go home to Dahlia House with Graf, Tinkie's decision to return the jewelry was probably the smartest move. With our luck, someone would break in and steal the necklace before we could even put it in a vault. I looked at Doc to see if he'd veto the idea.

"You're too tough to kill and too ornery for me to try to make behave. Be off with you." Doc packed his gear in his old-timey black bag.

"Call Marjorie before you two go running off to her house," Oscar suggested.

I did just that. To no avail. "She isn't picking up."

"How far is her place?" Tinkie asked.

"Across the county. They should be home by now," Oscar said.

"Maybe they're asleep. I know I'm exhausted," Graf threw in.

"Graf, will you and Oscar give your statements at the sheriff's office while Tinkie and I run over to Marjorie's?"

"She could send her driver to fetch the necklace," Graf reminded me.

"I know. But still—" I indicated Yumi. "Coleman is going to be a little busy. And Marjorie is our client. I want to be sure she's settled in at home. And I want to give her one more chance to keep Pluto."

He kissed my forehead. "Hurry home to Dahlia House. We have plans."

Tinkie drove the compact we'd brought to Heart's Desire. The guards waved us out of the compound without so much as a blink. The gates opened and Tinkie, with Pluto in a carrier in the backseat, revved up the car and drove for freedom. A heavy weight lifted from my shoulders as Heart's Desire disappeared in the rearview mirror.

It took forty minutes to drive to Marjorie's home. Tucked down a long lane of old magnolia trees, the place would be beautiful in the daylight. In the spring when the trees produced blossoms, the scent would be like heaven. Marjorie also had plenty of privacy. The house was hidden from the road.

"Have you ever been to Marjorie's?" I asked Tinkie.

"Honey, I didn't even know she'd returned to Mississippi until Tammy asked us to help her. She's lived in

New Orleans, New York, and Europe most of her life, and she's changed her name half a dozen times."

"We should call Tammy."

Tinkie stopped halfway down the drive. "Yeah, we should."

The first pink herald of dawn appeared in the east. "You think she's up?"

Tinkie shot me a disbelieving look. "Call her."

I did, and Tammy answered on the first ring. "Sarah Booth, are you hurt?"

I hated it when Tammy asked questions like that. "Just a few scrapes, but Marjorie is out of Heart's Desire and at home. She and Chasley have made up. She's leaving everything to him." It was too complicated to go into Pluto's story. "In fact, Tinkie and I are pulling up at Marjorie's house."

"Don't go inside!"

Her tone was so emphatic that I paused. "Why not?"

"Don't go in there, Sarah Booth. I have a bad feeling about this."

Tammy's feelings were nothing to sneeze at. "A dream, what?"

"Call Cece. She was pretty upset."

"Why?" I was more puzzled than worried.

"Something to do with that photographer. Speak to her before you do anything else."

"I'll call her," I promised.

"Good. Now turn around and hightail it for home. Nothing for you to gain at Marjorie Littlefield's."

"Are you going to tell me your dream?" I asked. I never wanted to hear Tammy's visions. They often came true. But forewarned was forearmed.

"It involved blood and a large knife. You were cut. I

can't bear the thought of you being injured because I asked you to look out for Marjorie."

My relief unclenched muscles I didn't know were tight. "I was attacked with a knife, but I'm fine. It didn't have a thing to do with Marjorie." Yumi was another story too long for a dawn phone conversation.

"Thank goodness."

"Hey, I'll give Cece a call." The eastern sky had brightened up nicely. Dawn was giving way to morning. "And I'll call you when I get back to Zinnia."

I did call my journalist friend, but the phone went to voice mail, and I decided to let her sleep. Cece was Miss Cranky Pants if she didn't get her eight hours of z's.

Tinkie drove down the lovely driveway toward a Grecian-inspired home that rose like a fairy-tale vision. Once we delivered the necklace and checked on Marjorie and her true wishes for Pluto, we could go home. Like Dorothy, it was the only place I wanted to be.

The house was dark and shuttered as we pulled up to the front door. "Do you think they went somewhere else?" Tinkie asked.

"They said they were heading here. Hey, leave the windows down so Pluto can breathe. It's not hot right now, but if the sun lifts above the trees . . ."

"Good thinking. What does Marjorie drive?" Tinkie asked.

I didn't have an answer. The limo had been hired. "Okay, we'll knock."

Tinkie didn't wait for an invitation; she went to the door, pressed the doorbell a dozen times, and finally knocked. When that yielded no results, she took her tiny little fists and beat.

At last, a bleary-eyed Chasley answered the door. He

didn't bother to hide his displeasure. "What the fuck do you two want?" His stiff upper lip and polished manners had been left behind.

"I need to return something of your mother's." Tinkie didn't waste her time on people she didn't like.

"Are you kidding me? This couldn't wait until another day?"

"No, it couldn't wait. Let us in."

He started to slam the door, but Tinkie caught it. "Not so fast, Snidely," she said.

"Chasley," he corrected her, obviously deprived of Saturday-morning cartoons, as well as the milk of human kindness.

She wedged half into the house. "I want to talk to Marjorie."

"But she doesn't want to talk to you. She said she'd mail a check."

"It's not about the money."

"Too damn bad. She's asleep, and I won't wake her."

I wanted to give her one last chance to claim Pluto. I'd keep the cat, but he loved her. Maybe she'd change her mind if she knew he was right outside. "I want to speak with her now." I added my bulk to Tinkie's.

He hesitated and I took the advantage, pushing hard enough that Tinkie could slip in, and then I followed. "Where's her room?"

"She's asleep." Instead of angry, Chasley looked panicked. "She's sleeping and I won't let you bother her."

"We're not leaving until we speak with her," Tinkie said. "Until we're paid, we're still on the case."

"Who are you people?" he asked. "She said she'd pay you. Why don't you go home? Leave us alone."

"We will talk to Marjorie. Now." Tinkie had dug in her heels.

My cell phone rang. Cece was calling. It had to be urgent for her to be up at dawn. She wasn't the farm-girl type. I turned aside and answered.

"Where are you?" she asked.

"Marjorie's."

"Get out now. Coleman is on the way there."

I was taken aback. "What's wrong?"

"Bert Steele called me, Sarah Booth. He was upset. He said he'd involved himself in something seriously wrong, and it had to do with the DVD you got in New Orleans. He rigged it. He sent you to the Pleasure Zone and made sure it was left for you to find. He and Annabelle Ralston are friends. Bert's been in love with Sherry Westin for years, and he believes her mother is drugging her and holding her prisoner. This thing has been a setup from the very beginning. He didn't do it for money. He thought you might be able to save Sherry from her mother."

"Who hired him?"

"Chasley. Bert was led to believe he was helping Marjorie."

"Holy relic of Saint John Kemble's hand!" I didn't dare say anything else, so I hung up. I felt Chasley staring at me. The slow smile told me he might not be psychic, but my thoughts were clearly showing on my face.

"What?" Tinkie asked.

"Where's Marjorie? I want to see her right now." My heart was pounding. Surely Chasley would wait until the new will was filed before he did anything to harm his mother. My brain was in high gear as the different clues we'd uncovered took on their true meaning. The DVD, the efforts to manipulate Marjorie with guilt over Mariam's death. And ultimately, the real ghost of Mariam, who asked me to help her mother.

"I don't think Mommy wants to see you." Chasley knew he had us.

"You put something in Marjorie's herbal supplements, didn't you? You made her blood pressure unstable, and you gave her depressants. You've been working with Brandy Westin to manipulate all of this." Chasley had taken matters into his own hands. I had no doubt he'd had plenty of help from Brandy Westin. And it had worked. He'd managed to win his mother's affections. At least long enough to be named heir.

"It doesn't matter what you two suspect." He reeked of smugness. "You can't prove anything, and now Mother doesn't care. She has her son back, and that's all that matters to her."

"I want to see her."

"She's asleep. Now, if you ladies would take your leave. I was preparing for bed myself. It's been an exhausting twenty-four hours."

"We aren't going anywhere until we speak with Marjorie." Tinkie pulled the necklace from her purse. The diamonds flashed rainbow brilliance. "I believe she'll want this back and I certainly am not leaving it in your possession." Tinkie kept looking at me to see if she could figure out where my thoughts had gone. Even without knowing, she backed me up.

"If I have to call the sheriff to remove you, I'll do so." Chasley signaled toward the door. "Out." He made a grab for the necklace, but Tinkie snatched it from his grasp.

"The sheriff is on his way," I said, smug myself.

A split second of unease crossed his face. "I'll get Mother. Then you have to leave."

"We're waiting." I went to the parlor and took a seat with Tinkie right beside me.

Chasley climbed the stairs three at a time. He was suddenly in a rush to produce Marjorie. As long as she was okay, there was little I could do to stop what I assumed was happening.

"What did Cece say?" Tinkie asked as soon as we were alone.

I told her about the connection between the video and Bert Steele.

"What a skunk," she said. "He used us."

"Sarah Booth, Tinkie, what are you doing here?" Marjorie walked toward us in a flowing silk caftan. Except for obvious signs of fatigue, she appeared fine. "Chasley said you insisted on speaking with me. I hope you don't intend to make this a habit."

Her last sentence forced me to my feet. "We went into Heart's Desire as maids to help you. You hired us, through Madam Tomeeka. We've put ourselves in danger, because we were there to protect you. We aren't a habit, we're private investigators. We're here because we're concerned about you and to return your property."

"Of course you are, dear. But I'm fine, as you can clearly see. I've released you from any concerns. Chasley and I will have time to repair our relationship. I have a chance to undo the damage I've done." She went to Tinkie and held out her hand. "Now, I don't mean to be rude, but give me the necklace and then you have to leave. I must rest. Your friend, Doc Sawyer, warned me how dangerous it was to exhaust myself."

My friend. Doc had been her friend, too. Once upon a time.

The front door creaked, and we all turned to look as Pluto sauntered into the house.

"That beastly cat!" Chasley lunged toward Pluto, who ran through the foyer and up the stairs. "Stop him!"

"I'll get him," I said, snatching Chasley's jacket hard enough to knock him off stride. I raced past him. "Give me a minute and I'll put him back in the carrier. He must have gotten hot in the car."

Before Chasley could stop me, I ran up the stairs after the cat. Chasley was hot on my heels as I followed Pluto down the second-floor hallway to a closed door, where he stood on his back legs and used his front paws to turn the doorknob.

Chasley screamed at him to stop, but Pluto darted into the room. I went after him.

Inside the door, I stopped short. A woman who looked a lot like Marjorie Littlefield lay on the bed. Her chest barely rose and fell, and she appeared starved and dehydrated. I turned around to face Chasley—and a gun.

"You simply couldn't mind your own business, could you?" he said. "Another day or two, once the will had been filed, and she would be gone."

I saw it all then. The genius of it. Tinkie and I were hired so that if anyone questioned Marjorie's death, we would say she'd been depressed, that she'd tried to do herself in at Heart's Desire. It would be tragic, but nothing to cause suspicion. The real Marjorie would be murdered and buried in the woods, while the impostor would be handsomely paid to leave town. Chasley would have it all.

"How much are you paying Brandy and Sherry?" I asked.

He gave a lopsided smile. "Brandy drives a hard bargain, but I'll have plenty to spread around."

"It's a perfect plan." I could admire the strategy even as I despised it. "This is your mother, Chasley. Look at her. Have you fed her in the last few days?"

"She's so drugged, she won't miss a few meals."

"Where did you dig up the other Marjorie?" If he was like most insane criminals, he'd take the opportunity to talk about his own brilliance.

"Out-of-work actresses willing to undergo a bit of plastic surgery are a dime a dozen. I just had to find the one who could pull it off and wouldn't get upset over the untimely death of her double."

He was cold, and I wondered if he really had killed his sister. I wouldn't put it past him. "You've been planning this for years."

"Good things come to those who wait." He laughed at my reaction. "If you lived longer, you'd have to develop a sense of the absurd. As it is, you won't have time to use it."

He aimed the gun at me. "I'd better get this done before the law arrives. I can't have you creating trouble. I wouldn't want to have the murder of a law officer on my record."

I closed my eyes. Some people could look death in the face, but I preferred to put my mind somewhere else. After I tried to warn Tinkie. "Run, Tinkie!" I yelled as loud as I could. "Run!"

From downstairs, there was the sound of furniture crashing.

The next thing I heard was a cry of pain. When I opened my eyes, Pluto hung off Chasley's back, all four paws dug in. Chasley spun like a top, the gun whipping around. He tried to aim at me and fired once, but the shot went wide and I ducked to the floor.

"Chasley!" the fake Marjorie screamed.

"Smack her! She's an impostor!" I yelled down to Tinkie.

Chasley angled his body toward the wall, intending to crush Pluto. I couldn't let that happen. I looped a lamp cord around one foot and pulled with all my might. Chasley went down like a big timber and Pluto jumped free. Before Chasley could scramble up or aim the gun, Pluto leaped on him with his signature move—front claws across the eyes. The scream that erupted from Chasley let me know the cat hit pay dirt.

Without a qualm, I picked up the heaviest thing I could find in the room, an art nouveau bronze nude, and whacked him as hard as I could on the head. He didn't even groan.

Downstairs, dishes were breaking and furniture crashing. Pluto jumped on the bed with his mistress, licked her cheek once, then took the lead down the stairs.

Tinkie and the fake Marjorie were locked together and rolling across the floor. I still held the nude and made toward the tussling couple, but Pluto beat me there. He flew halfway across the room and landed on top of the woman's head. From her shriek, I knew every claw connected.

She let loose of Tinkie and tried to use her hands to clutch the cat. Pluto was too quick for her. He bit through a finger, and that took the fight out of her. For good measure, I whacked her on the head, too.

I helped Tinkie from the floor, hearing sirens. Coleman had arrived. He could handle Chasley and the woman on the floor. Tinkie and I had to get the real Marjorie to the hospital. We needed a helicopter, and Coleman was just the man to fetch it for us.

Graf held me in his arms, the sun setting outside the bedroom window.

"Thank goodness for Pluto," he said as his fingers combed my hair in a way that relaxed me like nothing else. "He saved your life, Sarah Booth."

"And Marjorie's. Doc says she'll be fine once they clear the drugs out of her system and pump in some nourishment. She was severely dehydrated. Do you think she'll want Pluto back?"

"I hope not. But we'll roll with whatever is best for our champion." Trouble settled into the lines around his mouth. "How could Chasley do that to his own mother?" he asked. "I suppose it was greed. Money, the root of all evil."

My man was channeling Aunt Loulane. That was one of her favorite maxims. "He was going to kill his own mother. And Coleman said he confessed to killing his sister." I understood greed and revenge and jealousy and all of the sins that caused folks to murder and destroy, but I did not understand killing family.

"I can't explain it. I'm just glad it's over."

The bed shook as Pluto jumped up with us. Sweetie Pie lifted her head from the floor and gave a mournful howl. She was adjusting to the cat, who'd entered Dahlia House as if he owned the place and the rest of us were his servants. Typical cat attitude.

Graf pulled Pluto up to his chest and let him settle there. "He's a big boy, isn't he?"

"Once Dr. Lynne examines him, she'll put him on a diet."

Graf picked up his paws and pretended to make him box. "Oh, no! A kitty diet. Ka-pow. Take that, you calorie restriction!"

Pluto responded by biting his nose, to my complete amusement. "Pluto is not a cat to make fun of."

Pushing Pluto over to me, Graf got out of bed, the morning sun highlighting the perfection of his lean body. He was a joy to behold. A joy to touch. Even though my ribs were sore and my ear funky with glue, I was in a state of bliss. Graf was home with me at Dahlia House.

"I'm cooking French toast," Graf said. He'd taken my family recipe and improvised, making it his own.

"And coffee?"

"Whatever my darling desires."

"Would you pass me the script, please?" I was ready to think about another acting gig. I would never be a Hollywood star, but if the director of the movie could work around that fact, extra acting cash would be welcome. The whole episode at Heart's Desire would have to be counted as life experience. Since the real Marjorie Littlefield hadn't hired us, she wasn't obligated to pay us. I wasn't the first PI stiffed for a case, though Tammy assured me the real Marjorie Littlefield would generously compensate us for saving her and capturing Chasley.

Graf handed me the script, kissed my forehead, and went to cook our long-delayed breakfast. It had been such a long time since I'd eaten a real meal that I was no longer hungry.

I'd just readjusted my pillows when the phone rang. I

answered and felt a rush of excitement at Coleman's hello. "Heart's Desire is shut down?" I asked.

"Sure thing. And Lucas Faver has been charged with the murder of his wife. He confessed after Yumi sold him down the river."

"Were you able to find out anything about Sherry's circumstances?"

"She's in New Orleans. Brandy is threatening to sue the sheriff's office, but I removed Sherry, and once Doc took a look at her, he was able to counteract the sedatives she'd been given."

"Is she with Bert Steele?" I asked.

"Check with Cece. She's in charge of that aspect now. She had to head down to Sin City to take care of some details for the Black and Orange Ball. She told me to remind you that you will attend, even if she has to dress you in an orange jail jumpsuit."

I owed Cece that much. "Thanks, Coleman."

"You okay?" he asked.

"I am."

"Let Graf take care of you," he said. "A man has to feel needed."

I caught the hint of sadness in his voice, but we both knew not to go there. "I will. And thank you, Coleman."

"Anything for my favorite girl detective."

I hung up and picked up the script. I'd begun to read when I caught the odor of cigarette smoke. Instantly I craved one. No matter how many years passed, the craving was on me at the first whiff of smoke. I peeked over the top of the script and felt my heart squeeze. A thin man in a pin-striped suit and fedora stood at my window, smoking a cigarette.

The hair on Pluto's back stood on end.

It wasn't until Jitty turned her profile that I realized who she was. I hated to say it, but she was stunning in a man's suit and hat.

"I can stand a certain amount of trouble," she said in a gruff tone, then added in her own voice, "but you've given me more than my share."

"Oh, please. You thrive on trouble. You were all over Heart's Desire. Just think, if I never took a case, you'd never have reason to leave Dahlia House."

"Take my advice, sugar, keep that fancy butt in your comfy bed and please our man."

I frowned. She was speaking a weird combination of Sam Spade and herself. "I don't plan to move a muscle for the foreseeable future."

Jitty threw off the hat and shook her hair free. "You are sittin' in the catbird seat, aren't you? Got your man in the kitchen cookin' for you, got your hound asleep on the floor, and your cat on the pillow."

"And my ghost aggravating the snot out of me." But I grinned to take away the sting. I was glad to see Jitty. Glad to be home. Glad that Graf and I had patched things up and the road ahead was dotted only with joyous events like marriage, children, picnics at Dahlia House, and ultimately, the family cemetery where all my loved ones waited. Life could never be long enough, but mine was certainly sweet.

"How long will Graf be home?" Jitty asked.

I'd failed to ask. "Until he has to go back to Hollywood. I don't want to know."

"And your next case?" she pressed.

I shrugged, which made Pluto put a warning paw on my thigh. He did not like to be disturbed when he was snoozing.

"Maybe the criminals will take a sabbatical," she said.

"Maybe." I couldn't help but devil her. "Unlikely but maybe. Too many secrets in the world for crime to vacation."

She pulled on her hat. "I know that, sweet thing. Everybody has something to conceal."